Praise for Erick Setiawan and *Of Bees and Mist*

"This curious novel has dug its way under my skin in a way I can tell will last for quite a while."

—Maggie Stiefvater, author of *Shiver*

"[M]emorable, identifiable characters and an enjoyable story rooted in human emotion. Love, longing and the pain of compromise are indeed recognizable to all, no matter our culture or geography."

—*San Francisco Chronicle*

"This is a debut that is a looping joy to read, a journey in a world that is jointly anchored in the fantastic and earthy humanity."

—*Denver Post*

"[Setiawan's] stately, elegant writing freely mixes fantasy with reality in a way that doesn't alienate those of us who haven't yet run across a mystical tale that we truly enjoy."

—*Arkansas Democrat Gazette*

"[A] heartfelt magical-realist story of two rival families living in a mystical world that transcends both time and place. . . . While filled with fortune-tellers, ghosts and unexplained phenomena, the relationships between the various characters are true to life so that fans of fantasy and fiction lovers alike are sure to enjoy this magical tale."

—*Publishers Weekly*

"A fascinating domestic drama."

—Carolyn See, *The Washington Post*

of

BEES

and

MIST

ERICK
SETIAWAN

SIMON & SCHUSTER PAPERBACKS
New York   London   Toronto   Sydney

Simon & Schuster Paperbacks
A Division of Simon & Schuster, Inc.
1230 Avenue of the Americas
New York, NY 10020

First Simon & Schuster trade paperback edition July 2010

SIMON & SCHUSTER PAPERBACKS and colophon are registered
trademarks of Simon & Schuster, Inc.

For information about special discounts for bulk purchases,
please contact Simon & Schuster Special Sales at
1-866-509-1949 or business@simonandschuster.com.

The Simon & Schuster Speakers Bureau can bring authors
to your live event. For more information or to book an event,
contact the Simon & Schuster Speakers Bureau at
1-866-248-3049 or visit our website at www.simonspeakers.com.

Designed by Jaime Putorti

Manufactured in the United States of America

10 9 8 7 6 5 4 3 2 1

The Library of Congress has cataloged the hardcover edition as follows:

Setiawan, Erick.
Of bees and mist : a novel / Erick Setiawan.
p. cm.
1. Young women—Fiction. 2. Family—Fiction. 3. Family secrets—Fiction.
4. Psychological fiction. I. Title.
PS3619.E8404 2009
813'.6—dc22   2009000155

ISBN 978-1-4165-9624-0
ISBN 978-1-4165-9625-7 (pbk)
ISBN 978-1-4165-9848-0 (ebook)

For my mother,
whose stories continue to delight and inspire me

of

BEES

and

MIST

ONE

Few in town agreed on when the battle began. The matchmaker believed it started the morning after the wedding, when Eva took all of Meridia's gold and left her with thirteen meters of silk. The fortune-teller, backed by his crystal globe, swore that Eva's eyes did not turn pitiless until Meridia drenched them in goose blood three months later. The midwife championed another theory: The feud started the day Meridia held her newborn son with such pride that Eva felt the need to humble her. But no matter how loudly the townspeople debated, the answer remained a mystery— and the two women themselves were to blame. Meridia said little, and Eva offered conflicting explanations, which confirmed the town's suspicion that neither one of them could actually remember.

THE TOWN FIRST TOOK notice of Meridia at the hour of her birth. That evening, following what would be remembered as twenty-seven hours of labor, she was extracted blue and wrinkled from Ravenna's womb. Her lungs, despite the ten slaps administered to her rump, refused to take even one breath. The midwife was about to bundle her away when Ravenna scolded: "What are you doing, woman? Give her to me!"

In her calm, ordinary voice, Ravenna told the baby that after putting her through eight months of discomfort and twenty-seven hours of unadulterated pain, after ruining her figure and swelling her breasts and wreaking havoc on her appetite, the least *she* could do was give her mother a farewell cry. "The tiniest squeak would do," said Ravenna. "A yowl would be even better." Ravenna went on for some minutes, rocking her daughter gently, and by the time she recited the intimate details surrounding the baby's conception—"if you could only see the ungodly contortions your father had me do"—Meridia spluttered a cough and inhaled her first breath.

"Stubborn little creature," chuckled Ravenna. "Do you think you're too good for this world?"

The midwife waited in vain for the baby to cry. Meridia gasped and grimaced, but one thing she did not do was cry. An hour later, shaking and scratching her head, the midwife departed. To every person she saw she confided, "One hundred babies delivered, and I've never seen one like her. Whether she is an angel or a demon only time will tell."

A few months shy of Meridia's first birthday, a blinding flash of light traveled at great speed in the dark of night and awakened her. There was a crash and a tumble, followed by a terrible scream, and suddenly she was snatched up from her bassinet and crushed against Ravenna's bosom. At the age of three, after Meridia learned enough words to speak, she tried to articulate to Ravenna what she had witnessed. All her mother did was sigh and mutter, "Some things are better left as dreams, child." Was it a dream then? Meridia wanted to ask, but Ravenna had turned to her vegetables and forgotten her. Her mother's back was straight and sturdy—capable, Meridia suspected, of holding unknowable secrets.

The house at 24 Monarch Street was made of glass and steel. Perched on a high hill, it boasted a mansard roof, large latticed windows, and a veranda banked by daffodils. Stone steps climbed the sloping garden to the front door, over which an ivory mist hovered regardless of weather. The mist was a bane to peddlers and visitors alike, for it often held them suspended in midair, stole their hats, or chased them away with terrifying noises. Inside, the house obeyed a law of its own. The wood floors echoed no sound of footsteps, and people simply appeared in doorways without warning. The spiral staircase shortened and lengthened at random, and it could take toddling Meridia two seconds to two hours to go from one floor to the other. Mirrors were especially treacherous: In them Meridia could glimpse unfamiliar landscapes and all shapes of apparitions. Despite the large open windows, dusk never quite left the rooms; the sun could be blazing yet inside, the brightest objects looked dim and unappealing.

It was always cold in the house. Even at the height of summer with the fire going, Meridia was unable to keep warm. In the mornings, the nurse dressed her in heavy winter clothes as though a storm was brewing. At bedtime, the good woman wrapped her in two or three blankets and still her bones chattered. The cold emanated from one room, where at all hours a frosty wind fluttered curtains and rattled lamps. Meridia did not know how Ravenna could sleep in that room; her father, Gabriel, certainly never did. Meridia was four when she noticed that no words had ever passed between her parents. Five when she realized that the three of them were never in the same room at the same time.

Gabriel spent his days in the study at the front of the house. Exactly what it was he studied, no one could say. In hushed tones, the nurse and the maids referred to him as a man of science, a celebrated scholar, an astute investor who had doubled his inheritance and was now living for the sake of knowledge. They were all terrified of him. No sooner did they sight his shadow than they trembled like leaves. Gabriel seldom spoke to them. A gesture or a look was all he needed to convey his command, which everyone but Ravenna followed like a mandate from heaven.

Meridia regarded her father with both fear and respect. A tall and elegant man, Gabriel was direct in manner, limited in patience, scrupulous in appearance. He had a firm chin and a grim mouth, and his dark eyes were severe and without warmth. He walked with a slight stoop, which gave him the appearance of a swooping raptor. Not once had Meridia heard him laugh. That he resented her—for reasons that would not become clear until years later—was the first thing she noticed about him. If he were to ever take her in his arms or speak a kind word to her, she would not have the slightest idea of what to do.

One day, despite the nurse's warnings, Meridia stole into the study when no one was looking. She had simply meant to peek around the door, but when she saw that Gabriel was out, she braved herself to enter. Though she had no previous recollection of being there, the room looked welcoming and familiar. She grinned at the towers of books that made up the walls, at the hanging maps and graphs full of numbers. Cabinet after cabinet was jammed with flasks, beakers, burners. Meridia skipped toward the massive desk by the window. Jars of growing seeds populated the surface, and they were all winking at her. She was reaching to touch them when a shadow fell across the desk.

"Who gave you permission to enter?"

Meridia turned and shrank. Her grin instantly melted from her face.

"Speak up! Don't just stand there drooling like an ape."

"I—I—"

Gabriel had not raised his voice, yet Meridia felt the whole world was screaming at her. Confronted with his immaculate suit and shiny oxford shoes, she felt dirty, small, purposeless. As she beseeched the maps and books for a way out, every object in the room darkened like an artifact of hate. Meridia dropped her eyes and did not dare lift them.

"You are five years old and quite capable of forming a sentence. Do you mean to stand there and insult me with your silence?"

"Papa—I—"

She was saved from further agony by her nurse, who ran into the study trembling with fright.

"It's my fault, Master. I didn't think—"

Gabriel did not deign to look at her. "It is immaterial what you think or don't think. If I ever find her in here again . . ."

Quick for her considerable bulk, the nurse yanked Meridia out of the study. Once upstairs, she berated her charge soundly, but soon took pity and enfolded the child in her arms.

"You darling girl," she said with infinite tenderness. "Don't you mind your father too much. Some men can't help themselves when they're battered."

Her eyes pale and small, Meridia stood without moving. What had she done wrong? Why did Gabriel despise her like an enemy? Failing to stop the chill where his shadow had touched her, she wondered if all fathers were cruel and all mothers forgetful.

IF THE STUDY WAS Gabriel's shrine, then the kitchen was Ravenna's sanctuary. In this large, bright room where the ceiling soared two stories high and the tiles were scrubbed four times a day, the lady of the house poured her venom into the endless meals she cooked. As she chopped, grilled, and boiled, Ravenna addressed the vegetables in a dark and private language, telling them of sorrow and despair. The fury of her pots and pans kept visitors away, while her air of absentmindedness spun a web of solitude about her. These endless meals, much more than her family could eat, were invariably donated to the poor. Apart from the kitchen, Ravenna entrusted the house to the care of the nurse and the two maids. This included the rearing of Meridia, whose existence she seemed able to recollect only with difficulty.

Ravenna's attire was limited to a plain black dress, which she kept protected with a white apron while she cooked. Long-sleeved and high-necked, the dress hid her pale arms and pointed shoulder blades, but did little to soften her appearance. Her face was so sharply angular it was saved from gauntness simply by her generous nose. Perfumed with verbena, her black hair was swept up into an implacable knot, so tight and bonelike it seemed a natural projection of her skull. Ravenna moved in a stiff and sudden manner, as though the aim of her action was decided at the tail end of a moment.

Due to her mother's forgetfulness, Meridia did not correctly estimate her date of birth until she was six. For years, using her own approximation, the nurse had always given her a present—her one and only—on July 2. However, on the morning of July 19 in her sixth year, Ravenna made a great clatter in the kitchen and summoned her. "Child!" she said breathlessly. "Why do you wear such a long face on your birthday? Look, I've made you a caramel cake. Go up to your room and put on a nice dress. I hope you don't mind that our party will be smaller this year." Meridia did not care for caramel and Ravenna never once held a party for her, but she did not trouble to correct her mother.

On the few occasions when they sat together in the living room, Ravenna would often drop her knitting and regard Meridia as if she had no idea who she was. Recognition, if it did occur, was swiftly followed by a tremor of shame. "Are you unhappy, child?" she would ask anxiously, sinking her chin to her bosom. Before Meridia could reply, Ravenna would snatch back her knitting and let fall a torrent of words: "Keep your spine stiff at all times. Never show anyone your tears. Never be at anybody's mercy. Nod if you're listening, child!"

Owing to her fear of infectious diseases, the nurse seldom allowed Meridia out of the house. Twice a month at most, when the sky was clear and the sun gentle, the good woman would take her to Cinema Garden for a brisk stroll. These outings were far from pleasurable for Meridia. Boiling inside a contraption of scarves and underclothes, knee socks and unyielding rubber boots, Meridia attracted as much jeering as pity as she staggered from one street to the next. The nurse, oblivious to her condition, would embarrass her further by remarking loudly, "Mind that dirty boy—from the looks of him he hasn't seen soap in weeks . . . See that wart-ridden woman over there? You'll end up like her if you don't do as I say . . . You're sweating an awful lot, dear. Tell me if you feel an attack is coming on . . ." Ten minutes after they arrived at Cinema Garden, before Meridia had time to inspect the blossoms or feed the golden swans in the fountain, the nurse would insist that they return home immediately before a contamination could occur. All of Meridia's objections would be met as follows: "You're irritable. Are you sure you haven't touched anything? Let's leave before it gets worse."

One afternoon in Meridia's ninth year, after she had been housebound for three weeks, Ravenna suddenly switched off the stove, untied her apron, and declared that she would take her to the market. Curious to know what a market was, Meridia hurried to put on her shoes. The nurse attempted to fortify her with the usual garments, but Ravenna stopped her with a bellow. "Have you lost your mind, woman? It's hot enough outside to brand a cow!" Amid the nurse's scandalized look, they set off, Ravenna severe in her black dress, Meridia torn between a smile and a sense of disloyalty to the nurse. She soon forgot the latter, however, when Ravenna took her hand and led her across the street. To her amazement, no one laughed at her. Several onlookers even complimented Ravenna on her pretty daughter.

"I can't and won't argue with you," Ravenna answered solemnly. "Any woman would be lucky to have a darling like her."

Meridia blushed all the way down to her shoulders. It was the first time her mother had ever praised her.

That day, Ravenna took her to a hot and crowded square. Meridia's eyes flew wide at the sight of people jostling and arguing, stalls crammed with fruit and vegetables, sacks of rice and flour, spices sold in egg-shaped jars. There were fowls dead and alive, fish heaped on beds of ice, crabs in bamboo crates, meat suspended from iron hooks. A woman grew herbs out of her body—thyme on her arms and rosemary on her chest—which customers plucked fresh with their own hands. A tattooed man swallowed whole radishes and spat them out chopped, seasoned, and pickled. The air was thick with aromas—both pleasant and odious—and the ground was wet and dirty. Had it not been for Ravenna's hand, which she clutched tighter as they made their round, Meridia would have felt overwhelmed. The nurse would never have taken her to this place.

Somewhere along the butchers' aisle, Meridia lost her mother. A current of people swept her back; she was pushed and prodded, stepped on, then driven against her will up and down the square. Ravenna was nowhere in sight. Without her, Meridia went unnoticed, glared at by shoppers only when they found her in the way. The butchers' cleavers frightened her beyond measure, the ruthless thwack of blade against bone and meat chucked hastily onto grainy papers. Along the ground, blood formed a fly-spotted river. The louder Meridia shouted, the more the crowd roared to drown her.

Perhaps she cried for hours. Her throat was certainly hoarse when a hand brushed against her cheek.

"Why are you crying, little girl?"

Meridia looked up to find a well-dressed woman in a sea green hat. Choking back tears, she labored to explain, but the woman interrupted her.

"Don't worry. Your mother is only playing hide-and-seek. Come, we'll find her soon enough."

The nurse's warning about the ghastly things that happened to children who followed strangers went off in Meridia's brain. However, not knowing what else to do, she took the woman's hand and followed.

They searched the square twice without finding Ravenna. On their third try, just as the last ray of hope was fading in Meridia's breast, the scent of verbena came strongly to her nose. She froze in her tracks, then quick as lightning dropped the woman's hand and charged against the crowd. She had spotted Ravenna's implacable knot. So great, so complete was her relief that her heart felt like bursting.

Standing before a flower stall, Ravenna was carrying packages in her hand. She turned abruptly when she felt the urgent tug on her dress.

"What is it, child?"

Ravenna's face was calm and untroubled. Meridia could not speak, for tears had once again sprung to her throat.

"What is it? Why are you crying?"

"What do you mean?" rebuffed the woman in the sea green hat. "She's been looking everywhere for you!"

Ravenna shot her a puzzled look. "What on earth for? I've been right here all along."

Unable to contain herself, Meridia broke out sobbing. Ravenna bent down and wiped her tears with her sleeve.

"Tilt your chin up, child. Keep your back straight. Why are you letting the whole world see you cry?"

Meridia sobbed all the more. Tossing her head, the woman in the sea green hat snorted, then gave Ravenna a sharp look before leaving. This look, unnoticed by the mother, sliced deep into the daughter's heart.

Though Ravenna held her hand all the way home, Meridia took no pleasure in it. The stranger's look burned in her vision, and along with shame and sadness, it stirred a reckless dark feeling inside her. More than once she wished she had a cleaver to hurl, not at the woman in the sea green hat, but at the forgetfulness that imprisoned Ravenna in a different world. She wanted to strike until her arm was tired, scream until her voice was gone, and hound down whatever demon had erected this wall between them.

T W O

One morning in the spring of her twelfth year, Meridia was arranging her school books in the hall when she glanced up into the mirror and beheld the face of a ghost.

It was old, ravaged, and female. Skin creased, chin hollowed, eyes dulled to a dirty yellow. Accustomed to seeing strange things in the mirror, Meridia did not become alarmed until the ghost grimaced like an old friend. She sprang back with a scream when the yellow eyes spun.

"What is it? Is there a ghost in there?"

The nurse, puffing into a coat a few feet away, was instantly at her side.

Shaking, Meridia pointed to the mirror. The nurse inched closer, rolled up her sleeves, and throttled the frame with both hands. She saw only her own reflection.

"What did you see?" she teased, her generous bosom rocking with laughter. "A pink dolphin or a three-headed horse? How many times must I tell you, if you think brightly, you'll see only bright things around you."

The nurse fixed her silvering hair in the mirror and pinched her robust cheeks to give them color. Still shaking, Meridia wanted to ask her, Did other houses have mirrors like theirs, full of tricks and surprises, incapable of reflecting the plainest truth?

The nurse opened the front door and stepped into the mist. Meridia followed with her books. On her lips wavered another question. Why did the mist never leave their door, harassing the mailman and the paperboy like a jealous presence?

After countless pleas on Meridia's part and a bemused intercession on Ravenna's, the nurse finally agreed to let her go to school dressed like other students. In place of scratchy knee socks and woolen underclothes, Meridia now wore light cotton shirts and green pleated skirts, a pretty bow for her hair and shoes that did not pinch her calves. This small victory, however, did not come without costs. For one, the nurse kept a tighter watch on their walk to and from school, sticking to the same route, disallowing detours, forbidding Meridia to go off by herself. Not one to conceal her pride, the nurse let every mother in the schoolyard know that Meridia was the best student in her class. Once, she read Meridia's composition out loud, her ample figure brimming with maternal fire while Meridia flushed bright red. The other students she held under the greatest scrutiny, convinced they were carrying lice in their hair and bacteria under their nails. As for Meridia's teachers—she patronized these gentlemen with pursed lips and pointed brows, skeptical of their skills and qualifications.

"If only your father would undertake your education at home," the nurse often grumbled to Meridia, who shuddered at the thought of Gabriel and her shut up in the study. "Schools expose children to unsavory influences."

That morning, the nurse talked even more than usual as they walked. She chatted about the arrival of spring, praised Meridia on her recent examination score, and told her she was lucky to have an extraordinarily good head for numbers. "It gives me a cramp to see you sweep through a long column of figures without gagging. You must've gotten it from your father. I'm glad all my calculations can be performed on two hands." Pale and nervous, Meridia did not reply. In fact, she had not spoken a word since they left the house. They were a block away from school when the nurse realized this.

"You're quiet this morning. Still thinking about the mirror?"

Meridia chewed her bottom lip until the nurse's silence compelled her to respond.

"I had that dream again last night," she said with uncertainty. "The bright flash in the middle of the night."

The nurse slowed down and faced her. "Did you tell your mother?"

Meridia nodded. "This morning, while you were upstairs."

"And what did she say?"

"What she always says. 'Some things are better left as dreams.'"

The nurse frowned, stopping completely, and then dispelled this with a shake of the head. "Your mother *does* say that a lot."

Meridia grimaced. "What does she mean by it?"

The nurse picked up her pace. "How many times have you had this dream?"

Meridia thought carefully. "Twice this past week. It's been like this for years. It will turn up night after night for some time, and then nothing for months."

"And you see—"

"The bright flash. Something fell and someone screamed. Mama snatched me up and a hot, wet thing dripped down my face. Tears, I think. But it could be blood."

The nurse said nothing. Meridia, seized with conviction, suddenly swung in front.

"It was no dream," she insisted. "I was small but I was there in that room when it happened and I saw it all. What was it, Nurse? What was I seeing? And why does the dream come and go every few months like this?"

The nurse swallowed, opened her mouth, and closed it again. She tried to look into Meridia's eyes but managed only another shake of the head.

"It isn't my place to answer these questions," she said. "If your mother said it was a dream, then you must take her word for it. She knows what's best for you."

Meridia found this as maddening as Ravenna's answer. But before she could object, the nurse had resumed walking. At the gate, the good woman smoothed Meridia's long black hair with both hands and hugged her more firmly than usual.

"Go on, don't be late for class. I'll meet you here at three."

Meridia nodded reluctantly and joined the stream of students. Sighing, the nurse waited until her charge went inside the building before turning home.

In the corridor, a damp hand appeared out of nowhere and fell on Meridia's nape. In a panic she turned, books flying in every direction, but there was no one nearby. It was then she remembered where she had seen the ghost in the mirror. The dirty yellow eyes had glared at her before, wide and burning, in the dream.

ONE OF THE UNWRITTEN rules of the house declared that Gabriel must have a proper breakfast before work. He ate lunch in his study and dinner elsewhere, but every morning, he sat down at the dining table and waited for Ravenna to serve him. During this time, husband and wife never spoke to each other, and no one, including Meridia, was allowed to enter. After breakfast, Gabriel took his coffee and paper to the front hall and smoked there for a half hour. This half hour was the most excruciating time of the day for Meridia. Ravenna, who seldom made demands, was adamant that she greet her father before school.

On the best of days, Gabriel ignored her. On good days, he examined her coldly through a cloud of cigar smoke. On the worst, he spoke to her. Gabriel rarely raised his voice, but his words always managed to cut her. It could be as simple as a command to fetch things, open the window, relay a message to Ravenna, but the end result was the same: Meridia would go about the rest of her day shattered and distracted. She would feel as if she had been given a test and failed. Had she only performed better, pleased more, been smarter and prettier, he might not look at her with such contempt. If she never learned to resent him, it was because she never felt worthy of his love. In the nights when her tears came, they flowed silent and strangled. Often, Gabriel's hatred prevented her from breathing.

Over the years, she managed to assemble an unflappable front before him. Though her heart might rumble like thunder, her lips no longer quivered when he scolded, and she became skilled in employing Ravenna's advice to her defense. Hold your shoulders up. Do not blush. Do not even think about crying. In the back of her mind, Meridia was aware that her calm could only increase Gabriel's hostility, but her pride did not allow her to act otherwise. As time passed, she endured his torment bravely. Her night tears, though they never completely stopped, fell less and less. But one day, something irreparable happened. Gabriel cut deep enough to sever the thread that joined them.

It was a hot Sunday morning in June. The house, despite the scorching sun, was colder than usual. Meridia entered the front hall shivering and distressed. The dream had come again in the night, and the yellow-eyed ghost had this time turned up in her bedroom mirror. Again she had tried to question the nurse, and again the nurse had refused to answer. Frustrated, Meridia was halfway through the hall when she realized her father was not alone.

"Come closer," ordered Gabriel. "Give these gentlemen a better look."

Two men were sitting with him, smoking and drinking coffee. One was bald and whiskered, the other wore spectacles that kept slipping down his nose. Meridia greeted them formally as the nurse had taught her. They continued to talk but did not take their gazes off her. After some time Gabriel said, "Turn to the right and open your eyes wide."

Meridia did as she was told.

"She's quite pretty," said the one with the whiskers. "She'll go far with that nose."

"The eyes leave much to be desired," said the other. "Too wide and too far apart. And if you don't correct her posture, people will think she's consumptive."

Gabriel smiled. "Go on. What else do you see?"

The two scholars went on arguing. Meridia was instructed to lift her arms, bend her elbows, raise her skirt, stick out her bottom, and stand with one arm akimbo.

Square your shoulders, she reminded herself, feeling like a specimen in one of Gabriel's jars. Plant your feet so your knees won't buckle.

The men finished their cigars. Standing as still as she could, Meridia waited for her dismissal. But Gabriel, perhaps sensing her eagerness to be off, had another idea.

"You are far too generous, gentlemen." He folded his arms neatly and reclined against the chair. "I have a dull and plain daughter. Anyone with half a wit can see she has neither charm nor talent."

"Oh, come on!" said the whiskered gentleman. "Why are you being cruel to her?"

Gabriel grew solemn. "Have you known me to speak unfairly? That little girl has no grace or beauty. She is awkward, unattractive, and silly. Her mind, if you could call it that, is idle and easily distracted. I expect nothing from her. She will bungle through life and slip out of it without leaving the faintest mark . . ."

Meridia stood as if every part of her had become stone. On and on the shells exploded, but the more Gabriel raged, the harder and emptier she became. Her young mind understood what he wanted: a sign of defeat. All she had to do was show him a tear and he would stop. But for the life of her she could not summon the thing within her he most wanted to ridicule. So she set her jaw and denied him. There was no telling how long she would have gone on denying him had he not dragged Ravenna into the mud.

"But what can I expect?" His voice was even now, scalpel-like in its precision. "*Her* blood is in the child's; her madness, too. They are both fickle, illogical creatures. They crave to be touched and admired, and then without reason they shut you out cold in the dark. And when your heart no longer has a place for them, they blame you for the hell and the ruin that is their own making!"

The blow hit. All at once Meridia's stomach jolted, her insides squeezing out from between her thighs. She looked down and saw blood on her dress. While the two scholars sat dumbstruck, Gabriel sprang to his feet.

"You animal!"

He yanked her arm as if he might tear it off and shoved her into the hallway. Just before she smashed into the wall, Meridia caught herself. Behind her the door slammed. Another jolt assaulted her stomach.

She dashed for the staircase, hoping it would not play its usual trick. Yet the second her hand touched the banister, the treacherous thing lengthened interminably. She ran and ran, panting and wincing, but it seemed she would never reach the top. A trail of blood marked her steps, scattered petals on smooth, shiny marble. Through the hall door Gabriel's voice was booming, apologizing to the scholars for his daughter's barbarity. Meridia clamped her hands over her ears and kept on running.

When she reached her room, the nurse screamed in horror, letting fall the blanket she was folding.

"My dear! Why is there blood on your dress?"

The good woman rushed toward Meridia. Another glance told her there was no reason to panic.

"You silly girl." The nurse smiled with indulgence. "Or perhaps I'd better call you a little woman now. Why did you frighten me like that? I told you this would happen. Come, let's get you changed before your mother sees you."

Meridia wrenched free and regarded her with angry eyes.

"Why does he do this to me?"

"What are you talking about?"

"Papa! Why does he take pleasure in tormenting me?"

The nurse gave a start. "What—what did he do?"

Meridia told her. The nurse clenched her lips until they drained of color.

"Why does he hate me, Nurse? Why did he say those ugly things about Mama? Tell me why they never speak to each other."

The nurse turned to the window. Meridia stole up and yanked her arm, as forcibly as Gabriel had yanked hers.

"Look at me!" She jerked at her bloodstained dress. "How much more do I have to take before you tell me?"

Tears began to cloud the nurse's eyes, but still she clenched her lips. Shaking like a ribbon, Meridia shouted, "I will hate him if you don't tell me. I will hate him with all my heart!"

There was a terrible appeal in her voice, more forceful than if she had been crying. The nurse drew back, shocked to see the small, pale girl grow hard and savage. The air was filled with things Meridia could not yet phrase, things dark and unspeakable, heavy like clouds on an ominous day. It was the threat of them bursting and drenching Meridia whole that finally parted the nurse's lips.

"All right. I'll tell you. But let's get you out of that dress first."

TEN MINUTES LATER, SITTING in bed facing Meridia, the nurse began her story.

"You must understand that your parents did not always live like this. There was a time before the mist when the house came alive every night to the sound of music. Everywhere you looked there were flowers and candles, drinks served in tall glasses, lanterns twined over the garden. Men in evening jackets and women in silky dresses piled into the dining room and flooded it with laughter.

"I was a maid then, and no one in those days entertained like your parents. The best food. The best wine. The smartest conversations. Clever and handsome, your father sat on one end of the table while your mother ruled the other end with her grace and beauty. Even a stranger could tell how much they loved each other. It was said that an electric current jolted the room every time their glances met.

"When you were born two years into the marriage, your father threw a banquet that lasted three days. He covered your mother in jewels, took enormous pride in your survival, and proclaimed to the town that he was the happiest man alive. 'My daughter, who has defied death, is the loveliest creature in all the lands,' he said. It was not long before a handful of people took offense.

"'What arrogance!' they fumed behind his back. 'His child is barely alive, and already he's trumpeting his good luck to the winds!' Your father dismissed this as idle talk, but the more he ignored it, the louder the rumbling became. Soon everyone in town was whispering, 'Pull up a chair and watch. Heaven is bringing Gabriel down.' Oh, those ingrates! How easily they forgot his dinners! I don't believe in curses, but to this day I wonder if all their ill wishes contributed to what happened. By the time your father took notice, it was too late. The cold wind was already tearing the house upside down.

"It happened one night while the house was asleep. A gentle wind clattered the bedroom window, loud enough to wake your mother but not your father. Thinking the latch was unfastened, your mother got up to fix it. The instant she touched the window, the wind gathered force and flung her back against the bed. It howled like a beast of prey, ruffling the books on the desk, fluttering curtains, sliding your bassinet across the room. Your mother tried to wrestle it out the window, but the wind proved too quick and strong for her. She was on the brink of waking your father when the tumult died of its own accord. Shaking her head, your mother returned to bed. You and your father remained asleep.

"By then I had been promoted to look after you, and I was the first to notice the changes. The drop in temperature, starting in the master bedroom. The ineffectiveness of blankets and fire. The dusk inside the house, even at the height of noon. Every morning the maids set about their duties grumbling and shuddering. Bathing was a torment. Boiling water grew cold in a matter of seconds. By the time I discovered ice on your lips, I decided I could no longer keep silent.

"To my surprise, your mother told me she had noticed some of the same things. She was a different woman then, gentle and confiding. She told me about the incident with the wind, and confessed that she was troubled by it. 'A fluke in the weather, madam,' I tried to assure her. 'There must be a logical explanation for all this strangeness.' She did not believe me. As I turned to leave, she said something that made my heart lurch. 'No matter what happens, promise me you'll take care of my child. Think of me as you do today, even if I become a stranger to myself.' Stunned, I stood staring as if she had struck me. A part of me wanted to weep for I didn't know what.

"A few days later, your father complained about the chill in his bed. All night long a slab of ice was rubbing against him, making him so stiff he could hardly stand in the morning. The next night your mother kept the fire up until dawn, but it only made your father shiver all the more. A building inspector was summoned on Monday morning. After a week of combing floors and knocking on walls, the man sent an enormous bill and reported that the structure of the house was as sound as the day it was built.

"The cold seemed to affect your father the most. The rest of us—including you—could sleep with a few extra blankets, but not your father. He tried sleeping in different rooms at different times of day, but the chill followed him wherever he went. The occasional rest he managed to get was short and fitful. He became extremely irritable, critical of everything, and before long, he stopped inviting guests to the house.

"Your mother responded differently to the cold. She grew agitated and withdrawn, lost her appetite, and frequently complained of headaches. Keeping a relentless watch over you, she seldom left her room, and I often found her crying for no reason. She had trouble making up her mind, and in her frustration often harmed herself physically. Alarmed, I persuaded your father to send for a doctor.

"The doctor said she was suffering from an ancient feminine malady, 'unpleasant but not at all uncommon.' For remedy, he prescribed a combination of soft diet and pampering. 'Horseshit!' yelled your father before the doctor was out of the house. He stormed into his study, cold and weary, and ignored my petition for a second opinion.

"In a matter of days, the house bore witness to a series of unprecedented events. A plate traveled at breakneck speed and shattered over your father's head. Doors slammed. Tables stamped against the floor. Arguments spilled from hot mouths and sullied the air. The dusk was by then a veritable presence, draping over the rooms like a funeral shroud. Your mother lost her gentle voice, your father his cool head. They bumped and pushed against each other, two creatures in splints and stitches. As time passed, they spoke less and less. When their glances crossed, the room thickened with frost. Finding no warmth in the house, your father went wherever he was invited, alone, and stayed out longer and longer.

"One day, three months after your mother wrestled with the wind, I sensed that things had turned for the worse. Your father did not come home until the cocks crowed. That morning, the mist appeared at the door and has stayed there ever since. That same morning, your mother, who had worn her hair long and unbraided since childhood, twisted it into that implacable knot. To this day she has yet to let it down.

"After the mist appeared, your father spent all his nights away from the house. While the temperature dropped, the arguments rose to a fever pitch. Your mother wept around the clock. More plates met their demise. More doors were banged and bolted. The staircase began its stretching and condensing, the mirrors their mischief-making. A string of terrified maids came and went, feeding the town with news of downfall. Then one day, your mother dried her tears and ordered dinner from the cook. At eight that night, she came down the stairs in red heels and a low-cut gown, sat down to a meal of pressed duck, and pleaded with your father to stay the night. Thrown off guard by her downcast eyes, your father agreed. They ate in silence and stole glances at each other.

"Oh, your mother was a clever one! She had me so convinced that that dinner would be the end of our trials. Once again she was the calm and graceful lady of the house, incapable of a harsh or reckless thought in her head. Looking at the two of them then, I did not doubt for a second that they had found a way to defeat the wind. I remember telling the cook that the townspeople could just kiss their ill wishes good-bye. 'We'll show them what we're made of,' I crowed before dessert was served. 'This house will be warm again, and those bastards will fight for a seat at the table.'

"After dinner, your mother gave your father a meaningful glance before taking you into the bedroom. Your father followed. Armed to the teeth with excuses, I installed myself in the hallway. My conviction that a reconciliation was under way grew stronger when I heard you laughing from behind the door. At ten o'clock, I left my post and retired to bed. For the first time in months, I slept soundly without need for a blanket.

"A few hours later, I was awakened by a scream. I jumped up, thinking of your safety, and ran out of my room. The house was dark and cold. I rushed up the staircase as fast as I could and made my way to your mother's door. I hesitated a second, but then you started crying as if you were hurt and I burst in without knocking. Your mother was holding you next to the crib, sobbing without sound. Your father was leaning against the wall, shouting words I couldn't make out. The window was open, and a powerful gust was blasting about the room. The moon gave the only light, and in the dark I could make out a broken lamp and an upturned chair. I remember thinking the house would never again be warm. Those damn fools had won after all . . ."

"WHAT HAPPENED THEN?" PURSUED Meridia, wide-eyed at the edge of the bed.

Carefully, the nurse chose her next words. "That night your parents had their last argument. When morning came, they stopped speaking to each other. Your mother moved you to this room, and your father has never spent another night in this house."

"But the bright flash—what was it that I saw?"

The nurse dropped her eyes and took a hard swallow. "It was the moon, dear. A silver light was shining from the window right onto your crib."

Meridia shook her head with vigor. "It was no moon. You said it yourself that the night was dark and the moon was not bright enough for you to see. You're hiding something from me. What was it, Nurse? Tell me what you saw!"

The nurse expelled a long breath. "You were so little then, not even a year old. How can you be so sure there was a flash, or anything for that matter?"

"I'm sure," said Meridia firmly. "You've told me this much. Don't stop now."

Slowly the nurse took Meridia's hand. Her gaze was sad and heavy, her grip urgent as it was unsteady. Again the air rang with that terrible appeal, the hard, savage cry for which Meridia's trembling figure seemed the most improbable source.

"Heaven forgive me," said the nurse. "Promise me you won't think any less of your mother. She was distressed and hardly knew her own mind. Had she been well, she wouldn't have done what she did. She made me swear I would never tell, but there is one thing you must understand—"

The nurse suddenly seized up with terror. Dropping Meridia's hand, she leapt from the bed as if she had been scalded.

"What is it? What's the matter?"

The nurse had turned paper white. A vein on her forehead stood out and twitched with panic. She shook her head, muttered some chore she had forgotten, and walked quickly to the door. Before

Meridia could follow, the nurse stopped her with a whisper. "Stay where you are. I'll tell you another time." The next second the door swung open and she was gone.

"But you *will* tell me?" Meridia called after her.

The door shut with a dull echo. Meridia leaned back against the bed and searched the ceiling for clues. Then almost at once she sat back up again, pointing her chin toward the door. Two short sniffs confirmed why the nurse had left so abruptly. It was faint yet unmistakable. The scent of verbena was pervading the room.

THE NURSE DID NOT appear at lunchtime. Sitting at the table opposite Ravenna, Meridia pretended not to notice her absence. Ravenna was her usual self. She lunched with her apron on, held grave conversations with invisible persons, gave Meridia a startled look when she noticed her, then hurriedly returned to her cooking before the meal was over. She made no mention of the nurse, the earlier incident with Gabriel, or the blood on the stairs, which the maids must have cleaned and reported to her.

As soon as Ravenna disappeared into the kitchen, Meridia went to look for the nurse. Without a noise, she crept past the kitchen to the narrow corridor behind. Located here were storage closets, the room shared by the two maids, a linen cabinet, and a bathroom. At the end of the corridor, across from the door leading to the garden, was the nurse's room. Meridia opened the door and entered.

The room stood empty. The bed was stripped and all personal articles were gone from the dressing table. Despite Meridia's frantic search, the drawers yielded not a thread of clothing. Grasping the situation, she flew at once out of the room. In the corridor she ran into one of the maids.

"Where is Nurse?" she asked breathlessly. "Have you seen her recently?"

"Not since breakfast, miss," said the maid. "She's probably upstairs in your room."

Meridia ran straight into the kitchen. Ravenna was cutting up a fish, her implacable knot aimed toward the door. Without turning or slowing the knife, she greeted her daughter.

"I forgot to tell you, child. The nurse received news an hour ago. Her father is ill. She left for the train as fast as she could. I doubt she'll be coming back soon . . ."

THREE

The days of Meridia's invisibility began with the nurse's departure. Ravenna, retreating deeper into solitude, remembered her less and less. Meridia was now thirteen, old enough to take care of herself, and therefore did not need another nurse. Instead, as a token of confidence, Ravenna assigned her a generous weekly allowance. "Buy anything you like," she said. "I'll never ask you to account for a cent of it." Ravenna continued to prepare Meridia's meals with exquisite care, saw to it that she had a lunchbox to take to school every morning, but asked no questions regarding her study, her friends, or how she occupied her time. Once a month Ravenna ventured into her daughter's room with a most severe expression, but only to inspect if anything needed mending or cleaning. The nurse had become a buried matter. When one of the maids mentioned that the good woman had left her raincoat behind, Ravenna betrayed no recollection of who she was.

After the incident with the two scholars, Gabriel's persecution abated to a degree. Though Meridia still dreaded their encounters, for the most part he now allowed her to pass without a remark. Every so often, the ancient hatred returned and he would glare at her with scorn. "Go away." He would spit the words with an effort. "Go before you grow as hateful as your mother."

How did love die between her parents, Meridia frequently wondered. If the nurse was to be believed, how did two people who could not stand the sight of each other ever kiss, lie in bed, make love, beget a child? *An electric current jolted the room every time their glances met.* Did the nurse lie? Why did Ravenna dismiss her? One morning, dizzy from the questions in her head, Meridia ran into the kitchen and lifted her fist to pound on the table. Once and for all she would have it out with her mother. She would demand answers and explanations. But before her hand could strike, her heart failed her. What if the truth was so monstrous, so scarred and riddled with meanness she had neither the strength nor the courage to bear it? Slowly Meridia dropped her fist and left the kitchen. All morning long she sat in her room, alone and forgotten, and the questions clamored.

Between Ravenna's forgetfulness and Gabriel's disdain, Meridia found herself transformed into a phantom. Bereft of the nurse's love, she was not heard, seen, registered, questioned, or attended to. Little by little her fingers ceased to leave marks on the surfaces they touched. Her skin no longer smelled of the powder she used. If she sat still enough in a room, she would blend in with the furniture and no one would notice her for hours. Though initially distressing, her condition also came with advantages. She was accountable to no one, and could act as her curiosity demanded. In this way, Meridia became determined to find the ending to the nurse's story.

She began by studying the ivory mist that guarded the front door. She watched it from her bedroom window, from the living room, from the garden, far away from across the street. She watched it at dawn and at dusk, in sun and in rain, and followed its movement as the wind shifted. After a few days of observation, Meridia made the following conclusion: Although the ivory mist never left the front door, two other mists frequented the house at different hours. Every evening, shortly after Meridia finished dinner, a yellow mist swirled up the stone steps and rubbed its nose against the study window. A few minutes later, dressed in a long coat and top hat, Gabriel slipped out of the house and hid himself inside the vapor. The yellow mist then traveled west along Monarch Street and gradually became thinner until it vanished with Gabriel. In the morning, it was a blue mist that appeared at the end of the street, traveling in the reverse direction and growing denser as it approached the house. At the porch it merged with the ivory mist, and out of the union came Gabriel, still clad in the previous night's clothes. Quiet as dew, he would hang his hat and coat in the closet, brush off his suit, and take his place at the head of the table before Ravenna came in with breakfast.

How did Gabriel spend his nights? Meridia imagined places—silver hill, velvet river, warm meadow—where Gabriel could go to escape the cold of Monarch Street. For despite his cruelty, her heart never turned against him. On the contrary, the nurse's story had awakened Meridia's tender sympathy. She pictured Gabriel as a man fleeing from a broken dream, a father and husband cast out of his own house to seek happiness elsewhere. She watched him intently whereas he did not see her, and although she was not old enough to call it by name, it was desolation she glimpsed beneath his hardness.

In those days of invisibility, Meridia also tasked herself to observe Ravenna. Her mission: to unravel the dark and private language her mother used to vent her grief. Thus, before and after school Meridia planted herself inside the kitchen, crouching between two cupboards as she absorbed the furious deluge of Ravenna's words. Whether steaming snow peas or chopping red peppers, Ravenna spoke rapidly in an odd, guttural voice. Meridia wrote down everything she heard phonetically and later went over her notes in her room. With a red pen she drew arrows and circles, and in an attempt to impose patterns, she liberally excised vowels and transposed consonants. Some words were repeated over and over, some phrases uttered before others. Beyond this, there was no meaning she could extract. A fundamental element was missing, a key to unlock the code. After a time, Meridia stopped going into the kitchen and buried her notes in a drawer. And there they rested, bleeding with questions, an undecipherable tongue from an unknown land.

ONE AFTERNOON IN EARLY October, Meridia overheard the maids whispering in the garden. The two were but lately hired, the previous pair having lasted six weeks before Gabriel's terror drove them away. Meridia was doing schoolwork on the sun-warmed veranda when a breeze brought the whispering to her ear. The maids, pruning daffodils not ten paces away, were unaware of her presence.

"It was a beast. All night long I heard it stamping on the front lawn."

"What beast is capable of swearing? No, it was a ghost all right, and it was doing something awful to this house. I checked the ground this morning. Damp, but no footprints. It was a ghost, I tell you. And not a friendly one at that."

"We should have looked. If only you hadn't been so terrified."

"I wasn't the one ducking under the blankets!"

"It's true then. No maids could bear to stay here more than a few months. The house is always freezing, Master is a terror, Madam has all but lost her mind, and there's pitiful Young Miss, who skulks around and never says a word to anybody. Now we have a ghost added to the bargain. Do you think the other maids left because they saw it?"

"I wouldn't be surprised. Why else would Madam pay more than other mistresses? Better stick to our business. Save money and quit before we wear out our welcome."

Meridia sat petrified, her schoolwork forgotten on the table. This was the first she had heard of the swearing, stamping ghost. The night before she had slept soundly, though her windows were opened to the front lawn. Was this the first time the ghost had appeared, or had it frightened other maids before? The nurse had never mentioned it. And during her observation of the mists a few months earlier, she had not crossed paths with a single apparition.

Meridia resolved to stay awake that night. She sat up pinching her arms, solving mathematical puzzles at her desk, and drinking untold cups of water so as to use the bathroom every half hour. Still, she fell into a dream not long after midnight. It was the same dream she had been having for years. The bright flash of light traveling at great speed, followed by a thump and a dreadful scream. Then came Ravenna's arms, squeezing her while a burning liquid fell over her cheeks. This time, she managed to peer into the darkness and catch her mother's face. To her shock, it was not Ravenna who stared back at her. It was the ghost she had first encountered in the mirror more than a year ago. The dirty yellow eyes spun and exploded out of their sockets.

Meridia woke up in an instant. For a minute she lay still, afraid to open her eyes for long, but when no ghostly hand alighted, she pulled herself up and adjusted to her surroundings. A faint ivory light was illuminating the window, but the room was otherwise dark and cold. Meridia ran a hand over her face and her fingers came away moist with sweat. She tried to remember what she had been doing before she fell asleep, and suddenly a fresh wave of fear broke over her. She had been sitting at her desk, working on a particularly difficult puzzle, but now she was lying in bed. The light had been on then, and now the room was dark. Someone had entered, carried her to bed, spread blankets over her, and turned off the light. Was it one of the maids? But they had retired hours ago. Ravenna? Her mother only entered her room on inspection days. Someone else—something else—had been present in the room and come into contact with her. Meridia had no time to think further, for a hissing, stamping noise began sounding in the dark. It was coming from the stone steps below her window.

Fear strapped her from head to toe, but a power outside and beyond her was steadying her legs and pulling her toward the window. In a dizzy roar, blood rushed to her ears, so loud it almost

drowned the snorting, stamping noise. Meridia drew back the illuminated curtain by an inch. Trembling violently, she thrust an eye
into the gap and looked down on the ground below.

The moon was hiding behind a veil of clouds. The ivory mist
obscured the light from the street lamp. Yet in spite of the dimness,
one look was sufficient to confirm Meridia's fear. It was indeed the
ghost in the mirror, stumping up the stone steps as if her legs were
made of metal. Her yellow eyes were no longer dull, but glistened
like gold. The rest of her face remained in shadow. What at first
sounded like hissing was in fact a chanting, directed at the glass and
steel of the house like a malediction. The ghost was cloaked in black
from head to toe, with a long train dragging heavily behind her. Even
if she was human, the train would sweep away her footprints from
the damp earth.

Pressing her head against the window, Meridia struggled to
think clearly. Her breath came short and stifled, her bladder
screamed to be relieved, and the cold of the house had mingled with
fear to rattle her bones. She was sure that at any second the ghost
would turn those yellow eyes on her, enter the house, storm up the
staircase, and break down her door. What could she do? Where must
she hide? As the thoughts clanged in her brain, a curious thing was
happening on the ground below. The ghost, having reached the topmost step, was glaring at the mist. Her yellow eyes were sharp and
burning.

Then the ghost charged. Like a hawk on the wing, she tore at the
vapor, her fingers beaked like talons, her arms slashing, quartering
the air. Her chant leapt into a battle cry, while snakelike, her train
jerked and slithered along the ground with each blow. The harder
she hit, the thicker the mist grew. The vapor appeared to have
become solid, more robust than a wall of steel. Losing her ground,
the ghost backed down the stone steps and fell to the grass in a heap.
The ivory mist swirled around her, claiming victory, then retreated to
its post. The ghost unhooked her cloak and muttered a curse.
Meridia gasped and yanked the curtain open.

A strong breeze blew from the east and shifted the mist from her view. The moon emerged from behind the clouds, and for a brief second poured its light unobstructed upon the ghost. First there was the face, severe and angular; then the nose, long and generous. The yellow eyes had faded to gray, restive with fatigue and anguish. A cry broke from Meridia when she glimpsed a bonelike structure projecting from behind the head.

In a second she was out of the room. Night shadows roved the hallway, but Meridia pushed past them without stopping. Reaching the whimsical staircase, she struck her fist against the banister and in two steps made it downstairs. The front door opened with a grunt and let her out into the mist.

"Mama!"

She could not see a thing. The ivory mist roared at her, a thick powdering of flakes that stung and blinded. Meridia shielded her face with her arms and advanced as best as she could. It was deathly cold inside the mist. The hard hand of the vapor spun and tossed her, muddling her sense of direction, closing every path of escape. Then all of a sudden the commotion died. Meridia opened her eyes to an aching white silence. She had fallen into a place where time was suspended. Everything—her movement, the swirl of the mist, even her heartbeat—slowed to a deathlike pace. From inside this vacuum she could see Ravenna clearly. Foiled like a mad prophetess whose desires were lost in their own labyrinth, her mother sat on a stump of grass, less than three feet away, but worlds and worlds apart. The ghost was, and had always been, Ravenna. That night in her infancy, after the bright light flashed and the crash followed, it was this ghost who had snatched her and held her. Ravenna had worn the same expression then as she did now, one of absolute terror and hopelessness, bleeding out life from every crevice in her soul.

The shout Meridia gave was a forceful one, but not enough to penetrate the mist. Trapped in that vacuum without being heard or seen, she was suddenly seized with a painful affection for her mother. She longed to run to her and bury her face in her neck. She longed to feel, even for only a moment, warmth and guidance, acceptance, comfort, and, above all, forgiveness for the tumult that raged in her heart. But cold and impregnable, the mist stood between them and would not let her go. Sinking her teeth into her hand, Meridia wept quietly. She told herself that any other daughter would have found a way to drive back the mist.

The words that finally pierced through the vacuum were the same ones that lay in the bottom of her drawer. A dark and private language, expelled in a deluge from Ravenna's mouth with a furious passion. The mist carried the words without distorting them, forcing Meridia for the first time to hear them in their purest rudiments. Long after Ravenna rose from the ground and went back inside the house, Meridia stayed still. She was now free to move, but something kept her paralyzed. She had located the missing key, the fundamental element to unlock her mother's words. There inside the mist, she at last understood that for almost as long as she had been alive, Gabriel had been keeping a mistress.

FOUR

For weeks Meridia puzzled over her notes in the company of the mists. Each at first resisted in its own way but, worn down by her persistence, gradually surrendered a different part of the story. First to concede was the ivory mist. Following their fateful scuffle in the night, it now made space for her as she approached, a warm, dry space that sheltered her from wind and even rain. In turn, Meridia did her best to delay answering the door, thereby exposing the milkman and the paperboy to a longer period of bullying. In order to appease her guilt, she gave the victims chocolates and whatever treats she could smuggle out of the kitchen.

The yellow mist was not so accommodating. Not only did it make off with Gabriel faster than she could run, but it spat dirt on her face, flipped her skirt over her head, and scattered her notes peevishly up and down the street. Hiding behind a tree or a neighbor's fence, Meridia learned to ambush it, racing in hot pursuit while reciting as much of the notes before her lungs gave out. This was torture, and yet she preferred the sulkiness of the yellow to the duplicity of the blue. When the latter appeared in the morning, it never hurried or harassed her, but injected so much noise into her notes that they became incomprehensible. In this way, she wasted a lot of time disclaiming false information, chasing after erroneous clues, and going over grounds already examined. Nonetheless she persisted, and after many weeks succeeded in translating her notes. She found Ravenna's dark and private language to be this:

Gabriel's mistress has a face that resembles a baboon's and a behind that puts any goat's to shame. In fact, so vast is the terrain of her flesh that the woman needs a map to identify her parts. She has been known to blind people with the paleness of her skin, for she does nothing all day but hibernate in her room while half a dozen maids feed her raw meat. The length of her armpit hair alone has inspired legends. Gabriel, a tyrant elsewhere, is putty in her hands; all the she-demon has to do is crook a finger and he will come panting on his knees. He puts her up in a mansion on a hill, showers her with gifts, and wipes her very drool with his hand. Heaven knows what acts of perversion that woman is willing to perform for him. Bestial acrobatics surely, even immersions in blood and excrement. A tart like her never stops from putting all her apertures to use. Oh, curse her blasted face! Curse any bastards she might have borne Gabriel! Her predatory arts might have locked him in her embrace these twelve years, but one of these days, that nasty lecher will see her for who she is and beg for forgiveness. And when that day arrives, his home will be barred to him, his wife and daughter will spit in his face and turn their backs and chuck his repentance to the dogs . . .

Shocked by the intensity of Ravenna's hatred, Meridia returned her notes to the drawer and stopped interrogating the mists. Ravenna was absentminded, yes, but Meridia had never known her to speak cruelly. Had she misunderstood the notes? Or had the mists deceived her from the start? Meridia's loyalty naturally lay with Ravenna, but she found it impossible to despise a woman whose existence was confined to a few pages in her drawer. There was one thing left to do. By hook or by crook, she must trick the yellow mist to take her to the mansion on the hill.

So Meridia began to plead, bribe, and bully, but the yellow mist continued to vanish without a trace. In vain, she scoured the sky for clues, and went as far as dusting the street with starch in hope of trapping Gabriel's footprints. In the morning, the blue mist similarly swooped down out of nowhere, invisible one second and impregnable the next. Stymied, Meridia had no idea how to proceed.

If Gabriel was aware of what his daughter was up to, he did not let on. It was possible that the mists sheltered him so completely that he never saw her run after him with her skirt aflutter. It was also possible that he never noticed the looks she gave him—piercing and melancholy, as though she was both hoping and dreading to surprise a confession. Every morning, she placed herself in his way, pecking his proud stoop with her eyes as he emerged out of the mist. She followed him as he marched into the dining room and faithfully stood guard outside the door even after Ravenna bolted it. Later, she examined the food he did not finish, the cutlery he used and the cigar stubs he left in the front hall, but found no trace of the woman in the notes. Gabriel betrayed nothing, keeping his face as blank as a rock. It occurred to Meridia that the mistress, despite the names Ravenna called her, was no more visible than she was. They both came into view only when Gabriel and Ravenna invoked them from the bitterness of their memory.

MERIDIA BECAME SO ATTUNED to the sound of Ravenna's grievance that she would snap awake if she heard it in her sleep. Because of this, she knew every time her mother stumped up the stone steps and attacked the ivory mist below her window. It was Ravenna's habit to storm for a few nights, then, finding no victory, retreat into a silence that lasted months. Meridia noticed another thing: her dream of the bright light always preceded these attacks, and it came and went with the same frequency. In addition, the yellow-eyed ghost was more likely to appear during this time, haunting mirrors around the house with her grimace. After a few recurrences, Meridia concluded that the dream and the ghost were a direct reflection of her mother's emotions.

The discovery deepened Meridia's devotion to Ravenna. Often, propelled by an overwhelming feeling, she would run home from school and stand outside the kitchen just so she could rest her eyes on her mother's back. She felt as if she could speak to her then, could promise and assure her that no ghost or mist would ever again come between them. Yet when the feeling inevitably passed, Meridia was left with the impression that a greater distance had in fact opened up between them. There were many things about Ravenna she still did not know, perhaps would never know. For one, she was no closer to learning what the bright light was or why it traveled at great speed in the dark of night.

TO MERIDIA'S DISMAY, HER invisible state did not persist inside the school gate. The second she walked past the handsome plaque that commemorated the founding of the school, she became painfully and awkwardly conspicuous. It was not her look or dress that set her apart—it was her inability to blend in with the rites of the schoolyard. At recess, as she ate or walked alone along the dappled row of almond trees, she radiated Ravenna's air of solitude without being conscious of it. Her teachers, who applauded her accomplishments in class, called this a case of shyness—"something she'll grow out of in time." A number of boys found her attractive, but she unnerved them by responding stiffly to their advances. The girls were a different story. One camp was awed by her intelligence and respected her from a distance. Another dismissed her as odd and dull, and wanted nothing to do with her. The third and largest was the most critical. Since she seemed to project no need for them, they retaliated by talking viciously, always out of earshot, for in actuality they feared her. They said that if she would only tame that wilderness of a jungle on her head and learn how to match colors, she would look less like the wrath of God. They took a keen interest in the contents of her lunchbox, both appalled by and envious of the strange delicacies their mothers never prepared for them. The fact that Meridia appeared not to notice them only increased their resentment. "Proud and scornful," they called her. "Are we no better than dirt to Her Majesty?"

Contrary to their belief, Meridia was aware of everything that was said of her. But among those girls whose mothers attended the school fairs and whose fathers rubbed elbows with the teachers over coffee and tea, she felt her presence was unwanted and immaterial. As much as she wanted to, she did not know how to make friends; Ravenna never taught her the necessary skills, and the nurse had been too protective to let her spend much time with other children. The small talk that sprang readily to their lips came to hers only with a tremendous effort. After an opportunity had come and gone, she often scolded herself for not saying this or doing that, for laughing too loud or smiling too little. Whenever she tried to re-create the moment of contact, she was easily rebuffed by the slightest gesture, withdrawing all too quickly if she thought she was in the way. The old stone-and-brick schoolhouse, with its four gabled roofs and round little windows, was the only thing that seemed steadfast to her, while the beings that populated its rooms and thundered down its corridors were unreal and unpredictable. It gripped her like a monstrous truth that she was condemned to lead life without belonging or feeling close to anyone.

Meridia was fourteen when she had her first taste of friendship. One warm October day, when the term was already half over, a new girl walked into class and took the seat next to hers. During History and Geography, the girl looked several times in her direction, but looked away again before Meridia could meet her eye. When the recess bell rang, Meridia ran as usual with her lunchbox to the farthest bench in the yard. The new girl followed, sitting down next to her without invitation.

"You might as well tell me your name," she said with a smile. "We're going to be the dearest of friends."

Meridia could do nothing more than oblige. Listening to the girl talk on, she felt a curious tremor invading her heart.

Hannah was the daughter of a traveling merchant. A little older and shorter than Meridia, she was expressive and high-spirited, with agile feet and flowing reddish hair. Although she was not beautiful, Hannah carried herself with a self-assurance that made her striking. She had been in town only a week, and due to the nature of her father's work, she did not expect to stay more than a few months. She took it upon herself that Meridia should be the one to show her the town.

"But I don't know anyplace to go," said Meridia. "I walk between school and home and nowhere else."

"Then we'll explore together," decided Hannah. "Imagine living in a town and not knowing what it's got to offer!"

Thus began their after-school and weekend adventures. Strolling east along Majestic Avenue took them to Independence Plaza, where an endless parade of entertainers performed on rough cobblestones around the statue of the town founder. There Meridia saw her first jugglers and magicians, sword eaters and fire dancers. An ageless man whose beauty once launched a thousand ships sold love letters guaranteed to end in marriage. A seven-year-old girl turned into a pillar of salt whenever she faced the sun, and a jigging elephant made Meridia laugh so hard she doubled over in pain.

Four blocks east of the schoolhouse was Cinema Garden, that serene paradise of golden swans and jasmine blossoms where the nurse used to take her for brisk strolls. Now, accompanied by her new friend, Meridia could spend as much time there as she liked, sitting idly on the grass, eating hard-boiled eggs and strawberry sandwiches while Hannah poured syrup into tin cups. Every Friday night, when the weather permitted, a big white screen was put up in the middle of the Garden. On it were projected the most incredible moving images she had ever seen: birds of the sea and fish of the air, sparkling stars and a radiant moon, shadow puppets singing and dancing, titanic beasts waging battles over the universe. The two girls laughed and screamed along with the crowd, snuggling under their coats and coiling their arms around each other. At such times, they had no thought in the world and were as glad as they could be.

Traveling west on Majestic Avenue one Saturday, they ended up at a loud and dirty square. As soon as Meridia saw the crowded stalls and smelled the thousand different odors, she stopped cold in her tracks. The memory of being pushed and stepped on, of cleaver hacking against bones and flies feasting on rivers of blood, rose up and horrified her. It was here that she had lost Ravenna, crying her throat hoarse until the woman in the sea green hat came to her rescue. Overwhelmed by the memory, Meridia hung back, but Hannah would have none of it.

"Come on!" said the redhead. "I bet we can get anything we want here."

At the touch of her friend's hand, Meridia sent her doubts to the firing squad.

Up until that day, Meridia had saved the money Ravenna had given her in a pewter box under her bed, not knowing how or where she would use it. But that afternoon, she bought Hannah and herself sweet flour omelets and deep-fried potato cakes from the tattooed man who swallowed radishes whole. On their next trips, she purchased ribbons and hairpins, cinnamon pastries, milk candies, preserved mango slices, and perfume from a woman who bottled her own exquisite-smelling sweat. Next to the courthouse was a bookshop, and here Meridia wandered happily from shelf to shelf while Hannah gobbled up the fashionable magazines that told her which hats and shoes were in for the season. One day they stumbled across a beauty parlor, and at Hannah's insistence, Meridia agreed to have her hair trimmed. Forty-five minutes later, the girl Meridia saw in the mirror was a complete stranger, her hair so short it barely grazed her shoulders. "What do you think?" asked Hannah anxiously. Meridia turned her head to the right and left and right again and finally said, "I think I like it." Hannah whooped and the two girls clasped each other. It was then that Meridia realized, looking once more into the mirror, that she could not see her friend's reflection. Inside the mirror the hairdresser was frowning and Meridia was embracing nothing but air.

As November slipped into December, Meridia could think of no one but Hannah. Nothing got her down—not Ravenna's absent-mindedness or Gabriel's rage; not the dampening weather, the un-predictable mists, or even the vicious girls in the schoolyard who took relish in the misfortunes of others. When she woke up, it was Hannah she thought of. It was as if with this one person, this one person alone out of the multitudes, she had been granted ease of movement, eloquence of speech, and the exquisite privilege of laughter. At night, exhausted from their adventures, she would recall fondly their mad dash across Independence Plaza in the rain, or their animated talk over biscuits and grape soda at the bookshop café. In the moments before sleep came, she would imagine Hannah lying next to her, so near she had only to reach out a hand to touch her.

Meridia did not think it odd that she never mentioned Ravenna or Gabriel to her friend. In the same way, she exercised silence over the antics of 24 Monarch Street. Hannah herself talked little about her family. What information she disclosed amounted to the exis-tence of a father, the traveling merchant, and a brother. Her mother had passed away when she was little, and soon after her death, her father had made it his goal not to stay too long at any one place. Hannah had lived in a lot of cities and found it difficult to tell them apart. On one occasion she admitted, "I know it's time for me to pack again when I start remembering the names of people."

On the last day of school before the New Year's holidays, Meridia walked into class and found Hannah was not in her seat. History came and went and still there was no Hannah. Halfway through Geography, a boy entered with a note from the principal and handed it to the teacher. The teacher did not read it aloud, but Meridia could hear the announcement in her head: Hannah's father, having been summoned by work to another town, had left early that morning with his family. Meridia did not blink when she realized this, and for the rest of the day she sat up as rigid as a tomb. When the afternoon bell rang, she was the first to slip out of the gate, walking quietly, furiously, yet allowing no expression to escape. When she got home, there was a letter waiting for her on the hall table. She tore it open and the first line hit her like a fist. "You must forgive me, but I have said too many good-byes in my life." Meridia read no further. She tossed the letter into the wastebasket and went up to her room.

That day she went back to saving her allowance in the pewter box under her bed. In the following months, she revisited all the places Hannah had shown her, kept her hair the same length as Hannah's, and even forced herself to applaud the performances in Independence Plaza. Nothing held her interest. After a while, though she retained no bitterness toward Hannah, she tried her best to forget her. Only in the coldest hours did the feeling sneak up, creeping over her like a dream of heat, and for a moment she would know what it was like to be warm.

FIVE

After the initial rush of assurances, Hannah's letters arrived with declining regularity. In them she bemoaned her fate as the daughter of a traveling merchant, declared how dearly she missed Meridia, and swore that neither time nor distance would diminish the strength of her affection. In terms equally impassioned, Meridia replied as promptly as she could, but it was difficult to keep up with Hannah's change of addresses. Before many months passed, their letters crossed each other, got lost or misdirected, and finally stopped altogether. Meridia took it for granted that Hannah had found another friend and was even discovering a new town with a new girl. The realization hurt less than she had anticipated, for by that time she had embraced the belief that people would pass from her life in the manner of shadows sliding over a room. The nurse was one, Hannah another.

Loneliness had a way of marking her. In the middle of her sixteenth year, a melancholy expression settled permanently in her fine-boned face. Her dark and earnest eyes became more searching, the quick leap of intelligence tempered by a studious discernment. The strain of Gabriel's scorn and Ravenna's forgetfulness showed most clearly on her cheeks, which hung tense and lean without their previous bloom. At school she continued to inhabit her role as the girl who could not belong. She had grown as tall as Ravenna, but instead of reinforcing her presence, her height only pronounced the solitude she carried within her. A few of her teachers likened her to a creature without ties or anchors, capable of being swept up into the sky by the slightest gust. And then one day, just when she thought her life would know no other manner of existing, a song summoned her into the Cave of Enchantment.

It was in this year that the town celebrated the inaugural Festival of the Spirits. For two days in January, Independence Plaza packed up its performers and entertainers and played host to one hundred spiritual counselors from the world over. They were teachers of mysticism, faith healers, doctors of the occult, prophets, exorcists, flagellants, and fortune-tellers. Standing on boxes or in booths decked with colorful banners, they distributed pamphlets and bulletins, offered guidance, and for the price of a few coins gave their blessings before the statue of the town founder. They administered healing by fire and ice, performed surgery without scalpels, and removed tumors by the laying of hands. A giant sheepdog barked away sins from afflicted souls. A one-eyed woman transmitted messages to the dead with the help of a lyre. For sale were crosses and prayer beads, relics of holy beings, antidotes to common poisons, and talismans against sickness and heartbreak. Those who had not done so were encouraged to secure the happiness of their loved ones by entering their names in the Book of Spirits.

On the first day of the festival, Meridia wandered through the plaza like a dazed soul. The air was ripe with salvation, clamoring to be plucked if she only knew which speaker to heed. In her pocket was the allowance Ravenna had given her that morning, and after studying the different banners, she decided to approach the table where a monk stood guard over the Book of Spirits. Producing two silver coins, Meridia asked him to append the names of her father and mother. "Anyone else?" said the monk gruffly. "It's better to register everyone at once so you don't confuse the spirits." Meridia hesitated before taking out two more coins. The nurse and Hannah. The monk wrote down the four names and placed a golden seal next to each. Meridia was turning to leave when the monk spoke again. "What about yourself? You don't want to be left out, do you?" Suddenly embarrassed, Meridia gave him one more coin and whispered her own name. She was beating a hasty retreat when her foot stomped on someone's toes.

"I'm so sorry!" she cried out.

"Please don't be. I'd rather maim my own foot than give that cheat another cent."

The voice was light and full of grin. Due to the bright sun, Meridia saw only a pair of hazel eyes, so pale and luminous they seemed to float without a face. The young man smiled—she could discern the outline of his mouth now—as if waiting for her to say something. Meridia shifted nervously, wishing a single word, any word at all, would come to her lips. In an instant it was over. The sun dimmed. The young man disappeared. Meridia craned her neck and searched for him in the crowd. Had he not singed her with his touch, she would have thought him a mere spirit, conjured from a nameless region by the prayers surrounding her. Yet his grasp had steadied her elbow; the spot of flesh now burned with a thirst that brought sweat to her face.

The next day she sat in class without allowing herself the hope of seeing him again. When the last bell rang, she made her way to the festival, calm to all appearances, though not for a second could her heart stop from skipping. Above her the sky stretched blue and benevolent. The chrysanthemums bordering the plaza on four sides had never looked lovelier. The same monk was guarding the Book of Spirits, his face as stern as the grimmest of relics. Anxious to avoid him, Meridia mingled with the rowdy mob of prophets and exorcists. A great many people were purchasing crosses and love brew that day, though no one showed interest in obtaining insurance for the afterlife. It was at this deserted table that Meridia sought refuge, hoping to recover her breath away from the crowd. A saleswoman in a white turban immediately chimed in.

"Care to insure your afterlife, dear?"

Meridia said she was not sure and accepted a brochure. She was pretending to examine the prices of various plans when a storm of fever broke over her. Gripping the brochure, she turned sharply to the right. The young man was standing not three booths away, his pale hazel eyes regarding her with an expression both tender and mocking. He had a strong jaw and longish black hair, and his trim, dark suit showed to advantage his lean and long-boned figure. He smiled slowly, lazily, shifting his weight to one foot as though it was the most natural thing in the world. Feeling a sudden dryness in her throat, Meridia parted her lips and quivered.

"What do you say?" prodded the woman. "You can start with the least expensive plan. As you age and commit more offenses, you can upgrade by writing to us."

Meridia wheeled around in confusion, having completely forgotten about her afterlife. "I—I will think about it," she stammered. She found it impossible to concentrate, and when she turned again, the young man was gone. In his place was a maroon-haired matron, threatening a psychic with the tip of her umbrella to lower the price of a tarot deck. Unable to suppress her disappointment, Meridia braved herself to approach. She was about to ask them where the young man had gone when suddenly she blushed. A band of fire had snaked up from the ground and latched onto her thighs. Stifling a cry, she instantly realized that she had brushed the spot where the young man had stood. Her flesh was soaking up the heat he had left behind.

Meridia spent the next hour searching for him in every booth. In the process she weathered a reading from a palmist, who badgered her to purchase two prayer beads and an amulet against heartbreak. Though no one had seen the young man, she saw traces of him everywhere, shimmering in the air like a wistful promise. Nonetheless, she knew her options were exhausted after circling the festival six times, especially when the woman in the white turban began to glare at her with suspicion. Defeated, Meridia withdrew to a bench on the far edge of the plaza. For the first time she considered the possibility that the young man might be nothing more than a lonely product of her imagination.

The song started low and desultory, scarcely audible above the crowd's din, but by the time the notes reached Meridia, they had become part of a lush and vibrant melody. Meridia sat up and looked around her. On the bench opposite were three university students, arguing loudly about the properties of the soul. On her left, two boys were pinning flowers in their mother's hair. A group of shop assistants a distance away were twirling silk gloves and flashing their teeth at passing young men. Meridia began to tremble. No one seemed aware that a most splendid song was playing. She waited a few seconds and then followed it.

She edged along the neat row of chrysanthemums to the southeast corner of the plaza. This was the section reserved for the fiercest flagellants, yet their rapturous screams, instead of drowning out the song, only increased its beauty and lushness. Meridia did her best to duck the scourging steel whips and pine branches, and after a few close calls, she escaped with a few errant drops of blood on her dress. The song, meanwhile, was leading her to a dove blue tent beyond the last cluster of the flagellants. She felt sure she had searched this area before, but she did not see the tent then. The banner flapping from its triangular top read THE CAVE OF ENCHANTMENT. The song was coming from inside.

Meridia pushed aside the curtain that served as a door and went in. All at once the song stopped, as though someone had abruptly shut off a record player. A deep silence fell all around her, so thick she could no longer hear the screams of the fanatics. It was night inside the tent. The dark purple panels were lit up by a constellation of stars. Amazed that this vast, jeweled universe could exist in so

meager a space, Meridia was searching for an explanation behind
the illusion when out of the darkness boomed an ancient-sounding
voice:

"The spirits have requested your presence. Sit down."

A crystal orb blazed in front of her, flooding the round table on
which it spun with a silver light. Behind the table sat a hoary-bearded
seer in a magnificent blue robe. His eyes were narrow and greenish,
his mouth skewed to the left, but Meridia did not fear him. She took
the nearest chair and stared at the man openly.

"Why did you bring me here?"

"The spirits have chosen you. Picked your name out of the thousands in the Book. But hush a minute more. They have not informed
me of their final decision."

The seer shut his eyes in concentration. The crystal orb continued to spin, spraying jets of light over the constellation on the walls.
Meridia sat as still as she could, torn between awe and an inclination
to tap her foot against the base of the table.

Some minutes later the curtain behind her blew with a force and
brought the orb to a standstill. The seer opened his eyes, which had
turned from green to milky white, and pointed his right hand at
her.

"The spirits have spoken. See for yourself."

Meridia swung around. The curtain, fluttering fiercely, went up
in a flame of smoke. Sunlight flooded the tent, and with it, rapidly
swirling motes of debris. A tall, upright figure emerged from the explosion, coughing noisily. Meridia's heart leapt to her throat. Even
before those pale eyes turned their gaze on her, she already recognized the figure as belonging to the young man.

"I demand an explanation for this! Whoever thinks this cheap
ploy is amusing—"

Meridia's glance skated across the air and arrested him.

"Well, hello there." He advanced toward her and smiled. "I have
been dying to meet you, miss."

Meridia moved to rise but the seer stopped her.

"Don't hasten your fate before it's ready!"

The young man stopped as well. His brows arched as he took in the seer's long beard and magnificent blue robe. Before he could get a word out, the seer spoke again:

"The spirits have entwined your paths. Out of all the names in the Book, it is the two of you they have summoned together. I assure you—"

"My name is not in the Book," interrupted the young man.

The seer turned on him with a wilting glare. "The spirits do not make mistakes. It is no small matter for them to select—"

"My name is not in the Book," the young man repeated. "I never registered and have no intention of doing so."

The seer gasped at this sacrilege. "No intention of registering! Have you no care for your future and the happiness of your loved ones? Don't say another word or the spirits will forsake you!" The young man took this stoically, although a quiver in his lower lip alerted Meridia of a buried smile.

"Consider the possibility," continued the seer in a stinging tone. "You may be indifferent to your own well-being, but someone close to you might care enough to enter your name in the Book. Think! Have you a special friend? A family member who knows what's good for you? Believe me, the spirits have too much on their hands to be drawing names out of thin air!"

The young man thought for a moment, then conceded with another quiver of the lip. "I suppose my mother could have done it. She's a great believer of the spirits."

"Bless her heart! At least someone is looking out for you!"

The young man bared his gleaming white teeth, unsettling Meridia to the edge of her seat. "Please continue."

"As I was saying," said the seer with redoubled gravity, "those whom the spirits have joined will not be parted. Yes, you have been marked. Yes, you now have a claim to all the wonders the spirits have to offer, but unless you take immediate action, you will forfeit everything you have gained. At present, your future is suspended inside this orb, balanced equally between joy and sorrow, wealth and penury. If you do nothing, chance alone will determine its direction. This is a great risk, and a terribly foolish one, considering that the spirits have already favored you. What you need is an intercessor, someone who can tip the scale positively in your favor. You need someone like *me*. I have the gift to delve inside this orb and reserve a glorious future for you. All I need is a gesture of goodwill, and my service will be at your disposal. A tiny sacrifice on your part will go a long way."

Meridia was much too dazzled by the young man to grasp the subtlety of the proposal. With difficulty she managed to suppress a smile as he put on an exaggeratedly solemn look.

"A *tiny* sacrifice? Please allow me to ask, what would such a sacrifice entail?"

"Twenty silver coins," said the seer without missing a beat. "But the more you give, the more I can do to safeguard your future."

The young man threw his hands up in the air. "Twenty silver coins? I'm sorry, sir, but has my appearance misled you to think that I am a man of means? I'm lucky to have two coppers in my pocket! But perhaps this lovely young lady has enough to save us. What say you, miss? Do you have twenty silver coins to secure our happiness?"

He swung on Meridia with such suddenness that she nearly fell off her chair. Rallying her mind on the spot, she noticed that his eyes were secretly beaming at her.

"I have one," she said, although she still had two left from her purchases. "I'm sorry but I can't afford it either."

"Can't afford it either!" the young man cried, and wrung his hands in despair. "Oh, what are we to do now? The spirits must be disappointed in their choice! I suppose we'd better resign ourselves to misery and poverty."

Meridia hastily bent her head, feeling again the ripple of a smile on her lips. The seer propped both arms against the table as if readying himself for a battle.

"That's all you have? Not a coin more? You are testing the spirits' patience! Very well, I have been known to work smaller miracles. I can't promise you a golden future—that's out of the question—but with what you have, I can guarantee you'll always find comfort in each other. Give me the coin and we'll start the procedure at once."

"You're simply too generous," said the young man in a heartfelt voice, which prompted Meridia to bend her head lower still. "What do you think, miss? Would you like to find comfort in me for the rest of your life?"

Meridia looked up and found herself consumed by something she had never felt before. Not only were the young man's eyes shining on her, but his entire figure, it seemed, was regarding her with a flame that had singed her earlier. In an instant he made his intention clear. Under his bright gaze she gave the only possible answer.

"Yes, I would."

"The spirits applaud you!" cried the seer. "Now place the coin on the table."

Meridia got up, keeping an eye on the young man, and made to search her pocket. Then suddenly, at a sign from him, they both bolted toward the door and shot out of the tent. They ran full speed past the screaming flagellants, upsetting a table of cilices, and had it not been for Meridia's last-second warning, the young man would have had his eye gouged out by a steel-tipped whip. Behind them the seer shouted angrily, speeding them faster on their flight.

"You fools! Do you think you can horse around with the spirits? You'll both pay for this! Mark my words!"

They ran from Independence Plaza to Majestic Avenue, wove in and out of half a dozen alleys, and did not stop until they reached the market square. Catching their breath under a pepper tree, they laughed and panted and broke out laughing all over again.

"I didn't think you'd do it!" exclaimed the young man, winded and incredulous. "I didn't think you'd follow my lead!"

"Oh, what have we done?" Meridia laughed and struggled for breath at the same time. "Do you think we've angered the spirits?"

"What spirits? That man is a swindler if I ever saw one! That smoke-and-flame trick he pulled when I walked in is the oldest stunt in the book."

"You don't believe in the spirits then?"

"Not the ones who put themselves up for sale." He smiled. "But don't tell my mother. She'll have me hanged by the thumb for it."

Meridia shyly returned his smile. Before she could stop herself, the question slipped from her mouth. "Were you following the song, too?"

Amused, the young man clacked his lips. Then slowly, without taking his eyes from her, he shrugged off his dark linen jacket and slung it over his shoulder. Beneath this he wore a vest and a rumpled white shirt, whose sleeves he proceeded to roll unevenly to the elbows.

"It was your scent I was following," he said. "I knew you were looking for me."

Meridia blushed, thrown off guard by the faint black hairs on his arms. In spite of herself, she followed his long, slender hand as it rose from his thigh, scratched his elbow, and flicked idly at his nose. The movement drew her to his eyes, which blazed and winked at her without warning. Meridia looked away quickly.

"I wasn't looking for you," she managed to stammer. "I was following the crowd around the plaza."

"For two days? Even my mother couldn't last that long at the festival. I was watching you the whole time. One place you never looked was behind you."

Feeling her color rise, Meridia seized on his words but carefully avoided his stare. In the gravest voice she asked him:

"And what were you doing watching me for two days?"

The young man threw his head back and burst into a laugh. "To see if you would find me. May the spirits forgive you, but yesterday when you stepped on my toes, you not only hobbled me but also stole my heart."

He continued laughing, which made it impossible for her to tell if he was serious. She stood about confusedly, not knowing where to rest her hands or her eyes, until his laughter died and he made her promise that she would meet him again the next day.

SIX

Daniel was the oldest child of a jeweler. Eighteen and handsome, he was carefree by nature and, rarely distressed, considered himself immune to temper. He was loyal and generous. He saw no faults in those he loved, and despite his share of skepticisms, he believed the world a just and harmonious place. Many in town noted that he moved with a kind of languor, one derived not from idle habits, but from the certainty that in due time, every problem would solve itself. Years later, Meridia would recall that it was this ease that had first attracted her to him, self-possessed and indestructible, as if his waking hours had never been troubled by ghosts or mists.

On the couple's first afternoon together, they revisited the plaza abandoned by the spirits. The street performers had reclaimed their spots, dismantling so thoroughly every booth and banner from the festival. Too nervous for words, Meridia occupied herself with the pineapple soda Daniel bought her. A magician was holding the crowd captive that day. He locked a young woman in a box, hacked her into twenty-four pieces, and opened the box to reveal her intact, but with one catch: her head stood upside down on her shoulders! The crowd gasped in horror. Assuring them that all was not lost, the magician passed around his upturned hat, which the crowd eagerly filled to the brim. Meridia held her breath as the magician once again locked the woman inside the box, waved his arms about, and produced her with head corrected. The crowd broke into a raucous applause. Clapping along, Meridia let go of the soda and began to relax. Next up was the blind violinist, whose performance had been known to invoke rain from the sky and move dictators to tears. Pushing against the crowd, Daniel led Meridia to the front. Without giving her time to settle, he said the three words that at once sounded so simple and horrifying.

"Dance with me."

Meridia stared at his open palm and attempted a laugh. "I already maimed your foot two days ago. Don't you remember?"

"Give me some credit. My bones are far from delicate."

"You can't be serious. I hardly know—"

Before she could utter another word, he guided her hands to his shoulders. A second rush of panic rooted her to the spot. She became aware of the crowd around them, laughing and staring, whether at them or at each other she could not tell. A drum pounded in her ears, and the sun flashed directly into her eyes. When Daniel began to move, she thought she would collapse like a pile of stone. They had not taken more than three steps when she stomped on his toes. Meridia's clumsiness made her wince, but Daniel feigned such an anguished look that she roared into laughter. He smiled a second later, broadly, and her embarrassment dissipated with the breeze. As the violin soared into a finale, she forgot the crowd and rested her cheek against his. In those seconds, Meridia wondered how she could have lived for sixteen years and seven months without the touch of Daniel's hand.

For the next three months they met whenever they could. Meridia played truant from school. Daniel made excuses to his father and abandoned his work at the jewelry shop. Together they scoured the flower market, tossed coins at dancing snakes, viewed the evening projections at Cinema Garden, and tested the limits of their appetites with snacks made from goat testicles. In the bohemians' quarters, Daniel showed her a former actress who gulped down baby mice to preserve her youth, and a hirsute man who annually gave birth to a burning bush. In a secluded corner where the poets starved, they saw a merchant hawk blood, breath, and bones for the ailing. When spring came, they sat for hours in little garden cafés, sharing, to the exasperation of the waiters, a cup of rice pudding. Sunset often found them in Independence Plaza, for at that deserted hour the town founder raised his marble fist and the rough cobblestones thundered with the march of an invisible army. If Meridia was aware that she was retracing some of her adventures with Hannah, she kept the thought to herself. She felt she owed it to Daniel to capture every sight afresh, unmarked and untainted by a previous memory.

Daniel taught her how to interpret the stars. One night they scaled a secluded promontory and spied upon the lady in the moon. Another afternoon, they dipped their feet in a spring of immortality while archaic turtles nibbled at their toes. He took her to golden fields of lilies, and, on a broad plain of grass, they listened to bald nuns ululate with the wolves. From these jaunts, Meridia learned that they lived in the only part of the world where snow fell but never chilled, where the sun blazed with tropical intensity but never scorched. Viewed from the same secluded promontory, the town with its neat streets and ordered houses appeared bathed in an otherworldly light. The brightness of this light was matched only by Daniel's eyes, shining with life and vitality as he initiated her into the mysteries of the earth.

One day, he was explaining to her the paths of summering birds when she asked him, "How do you know all this?"

"My father," he answered. "He thinks the secrets of the universe are far easier to understand than a woman's heart."

Daniel said this with such a straight face that Meridia laughed. Little did she know that many times in the years to come the words would return to haunt her.

In a short time, Meridia fell into devastating love. Without hesitation she forged Ravenna's signature and excused her absences from the school with imaginary illnesses. At the bookshop next to the courthouse, she studied the fashionable magazines that Hannah had found so indispensable, and for the first time in her life took their advice to heart. She used up her allowance on shoes and dresses, on velvet hats and gloves and lotions, all of which lost their appeal the second she unwrapped them at home. She fought tooth and nail against the apparitions for a space in the mirror, and stoically ignored their catcalls when they allowed her reflection to appear. One morning, it was Gabriel who caught her while she examined herself in the hall mirror before school. He frowned at her lace dress and glossy pink lips, but before he could say a word, she bowed and swept to the door with the arrogance of love shimmering in her breast.

Every night she feasted on her memory of Daniel. Neglecting her studies, she summoned him through sighs and whispers, rendering in her mind his deep eyes and chiseled jaw and full lips parted on the verge of a kiss. At the stroke of midnight, the smell of his skin magically filled the room, a heady scent of sun and sea that braced her unlike anything she had ever known. Meridia smiled with pleasure at the remembered touch of his hand. Reliving a single, fugitive glance down the side of his throat drove her mad with longing. In the infernal hours, the bed creaked under her delirium, and sleep, if it came, offered no refuge from the tempest in her blood.

After they had spent twenty-seven afternoons together, Daniel took her to a beach of pure white sand. Sprawled on a blanket under a palm tree, they were taking turns reading from a book when a dozen seagulls ripped the sky open with their wings. The birds were falling, plummeting fast out of the clouds as if they had been shot. Daniel dropped the book and jumped up. The seagulls landed on the sand not far from them, hopping and squawking like mad with their beaks pointed toward the sea. A minute later a wooden chest rode the surface of the waves and bobbed to shore. The birds crowded around it; at Daniel's approach they flapped their wings and took to the sky. Meridia got up from the blanket and followed him.

"What is it?" she asked anxiously.

"A coffin. A child's, from the size of it. How in the world did it ever get to sea?"

Meridia felt something crawl in her belly. Tilting the chest to one side, Daniel pried it open and drew back after a brief struggle. Meridia looked over his shoulder and immediately wished she had not.

Curled in the chest's center was the carcass of a newborn fawn. Frothy and bluish of skin, its stomach was pecked to pieces, the innards splattered over the ribs like cords of ribbon. There was a deep welt around the fawn's neck, and tiny brown worms were spilling out of its eyes. Meridia had just enough time to cover her nose when a rodent pushed its way out of the gaping mouth. Her scream was followed by Daniel slamming the lid back in place.

"I hope it didn't suffer much," he said. "At least someone was kind enough to give it shelter."

"How could it not suffer with those wounds?" she challenged him at once. "Whoever stuffed that poor thing in that box is probably the same person who killed it."

Meridia surprised even herself with her sharpness. Turning abruptly, Daniel regarded her with concern. His stare was exceedingly tender, yet for some reason she found it more unbearable than Gabriel's disdain.

"Are you all right?" he asked, lifting a thumb to her cheek. "You look as pale as a ghost."

Before she could answer, the sand slipped from beneath her feet. She fell flat on her back, screaming because a thousand birds were suddenly pecking at her womb.

"What is it?" cried Daniel, dropping to his knees and pulling her to his lap.

Blinded by tears, Meridia rolled away in agony. As she struggled to rise, a wracking heave seized her and she began to retch. The next thing she knew, she was sitting back on her heels and blinking in bewilderment. Aside from the remnants of her lunch, the sand stretched pure and white. The sea was a dancing, swaying mass of gold. It took her a moment to realize that the birds were no longer pecking at her womb.

"What is it?" repeated Daniel as he helped her stand. "Tell me where it hurts."

"It doesn't hurt anymore," she said, absently throwing sand over the vomit. "I suppose the stench was too much for me to handle."

"Ah, women and their nerves," he said in obvious relief, pressing her shoulders gently. "Are you sure you're all right?"

Meridia nodded with a smile, more out of politeness than conviction. Seeing Daniel's bright gaze, she decided not to tell him that even then fear was clawing its way into her heart. She was certain that the fawn was an omen for a calamity to come. They had angered the spirits. The seer had cursed them for making a fool out of him. In her agitation, she became convinced that the future held only doom and misfortune.

"What are you thinking of?" asked Daniel. "Right this second, what is going through your mind? Tell me."

Meridia snapped out of her musing, sweeping clean the merest hint of it.

"Nothing," she said. "I'm not thinking of anything."

Daniel lowered his voice playfully. "You're full of clever little secrets, aren't you? Don't you ever let anyone know what's brewing in your head?"

He leaned close. In that second, just when she felt the heat of his glance subduing her knees, she became aware of the acidity in her breath. The thought that she had retched before him, groveled like an animal in pain or labor without the slightest dignity, mortified her beyond reason. Quickly she raised a hand to her mouth, not realizing until too late that it was smeared with sand. Petrified, she waited not for her composure to return but for his laughter to erupt.

But when he opened his mouth, it was only to say that she had sand on her lips. He took her hand and leaned even closer. She held her breath so he could not smell it, but he waited so patiently that in the end she had to gasp for air. Without a warning he plucked the anxiety from her lips. She began to tremble, still not wholly aware of what was happening. All that felt real was the taste of sand and sweat, passing from his mouth to hers like the breath of life.

Neither of them could later recall how they tumbled to the sand or how long they kissed before their mouths ran dry. When they finally got up, their clothes were rumpled and the sun was down to its last shimmer. On the sand where they had grappled lay half-formed circles and triangles, each one left by the impassioned movements of their limbs. The evening wind rose and made Meridia shiver. Her pale yellow skirt was dripping seawater.

"This is the real omen," she said to herself. "Not the fawn, but this."

Daniel came up from behind and circled his arms around her. "I'm sorry, did you say something?"

She tilted her neck and brushed her cheek against his smooth chin. "I said we should bury the fawn," she said.

They turned at the same time to the spot where they had left the chest. There was nothing there. Hurrying back, they could not locate a single mark or indentation in the sand. Dumbfounded, they searched up and down the beach until a sharp glimmer in the water caught Meridia's eye. The chest was floating in the middle of the sea, drifting toward the sun with all the calm and contentment of dusk. They watched it without speaking, and after a time, the chest vanished in the rippling surface of the sea.

SEVEN

Three months from the day they met, Meridia walked the breadth of town, shining, and the dogs followed. Ten in all, they caught her shine from alleys and doorways and noiselessly marched single file behind her. Encased in a sleeveless blue dress with embroidered peonies and a high collar, Meridia noticed neither the dogs nor her shine, nor the mournful chime of the town bell that quarterly measured her progress. She walked with her chin high and her back straight, making no stop until she arrived at 27 Orchard Road. Even then, she paid no attention when a large mastiff from next door flew past her and attacked the shadowing dogs. Daniel was already approaching from the terrace.

"Don't be nervous," he cautioned, oblivious of the brawling dogs himself. "Heaven help them if they think you're not perfect."

"Heaven help *me* if they think I am," she answered with a smile.

The house was an unassuming two-story of wood and exposed brick. It sat—or rather squatted—on flat ground, and the first impression it gave was of immitigable disorder. Dry grass sprouted from the eaves, a bird's nest roosted on the roof, and moss and lichen ruptured over the bricks like angry boils. A wilderness of red roses smothered the front lawn, filling it to the edges with barely space for a clump of marigolds to survive. And yet, though it had nothing to recommend it in the way of grace or beauty, the house pulsated with undeniable warmth. The windows were wide and inviting, caged birds sang merrily from the terrace, and below them two rocking chairs nodded to each other as if engaged in an animated argument. A closer inspection suggested that loving hands had nurtured the wilderness of the roses without leaving anything to chance.

Entering the front door, Daniel led Meridia down a narrow hallway overlaid with faded carpeting. A haphazard arrangement of shoes lined one side, yellowing stacks of magazines the other. The walls were a dark shade of sage, bare save for an askew photograph of an imperial garden. Daniel paused and gave Meridia a kiss.

"For good luck," he said, "in case you need it."

Meridia smiled and realized it was he who was nervous.

They entered the living room to the resounding sound of a slap. A little girl in a bottle green dress lifted a hand to her cheek and began to cry. Standing in front of her was an older girl with eyes so furious they set her pretty face ablaze.

"That's enough, Malin," said Daniel from the door. "You've been torturing Permony all day."

"She broke my figurine!" exclaimed the older girl. "The ballerina with a pink bow! You know Mama gave that to me for my birthday."

Daniel walked over to calm the weeping girl. "That's no reason for you to hit her. Especially after Papa told you not to. I'm sure Permony didn't mean to do it. You didn't, did you, Permony? Tell your sister you're sorry and be more careful next time."

The younger girl did as she was told. "I can glue it back," she pleaded. "It will be as good as new."

Malin rolled her eyes with impatience. "But I'll still know it's broken, won't I?" Then to Daniel: "She's never happy until she smashes something of mine. Even a mule can be trained to do things properly, but not Permony. She's so fat and clumsy she'll never find a husband!"

This last bit appeared to be addressed to Meridia, although Malin had not once glanced in her direction. To her surprise, Daniel made no reply, but introduced both girls as his sisters. Malin, who was twelve, scowled while she shook Meridia's hand. Ten and bashful, Permony managed a smile through her tears.

"Mama's upstairs in her room," said Daniel pleasantly. "Why don't you sit down and talk to the girls while I fetch her?"

As soon as he left, Malin crossed her arms and sat on the farther side of the sofa. Under her glare, Permony collected the porcelain shards from the floor and put them in the wastebasket. Meridia navigated her way among more magazines and settled on an armchair that smelled faintly of burnt sugar. From there she observed the sisters with curiosity. Apart from their long braided hair, which was tied with organdy bows at the ends, they hardly resembled each other. Malin had a tight, thin mouth and a snub nose. Permony was plump and broad-faced, with soft lavender eyes that drooped like flowers. Reclining against the sofa, Malin acted as if she could not be bothered. Permony directed shy glances at Meridia, who promptly rewarded her with a wink.

The sisters resumed their play. Permony knelt in front of the coffee table, facing Malin and a carefully laid row of figurines. When Malin pointed to a chimney sweeper, Permony picked him up and cleaned him with her skirt. Seeing that her sister's hands were trembling, Malin sucked her teeth with relish. After the chimney sweeper had been cleaned, Malin pointed to a shepherdess and the same ritual was repeated. Dumbstruck, Meridia watched the game without knowing what to make of it. Before she could ask a question, a sweet silvery voice drifted into the room like a summer breeze.

"I hope my daughters haven't shocked you with their behavior."

At once Meridia was on her feet. The woman with the silver voice was smiling warmly.

"I'm Eva. I had the misfortune of giving birth to these monsters."

Daniel's mother was not a particularly tall or large woman, yet her presence filled the room with authority. Broad of shoulder, with a full bust and matronly hips, Eva brimmed with such energy and resilience that anyone would be hard-pressed to imagine her ill. Her form-fitting print dress, shapely belted at the waist, revealed firm and robust arms, darker even than Daniel's, as though she made no qualms about exposing them to the sun. Her almond-shaped eyes were alive and alert, framed by high cheekbones and steel blue hair like glittering stars.

Suddenly nervous, Meridia stammered to introduce herself, but Eva stopped her with a wave.

"I know everything about you. You're the siren who has stolen my boy's heart."

Whether or not this was meant as a criticism, Meridia had no time to discover, for Eva's hand was already on her waist and drawing her gently to the sofa.

"Please sit down. Could you move to that chair, Malin? You mustn't let Meridia think you have no manners."

The girl glared but obeyed her mother.

"I told Daniel to give me ten minutes alone with you," continued Eva breathily. "You must tell me, in all honesty, what you think of him."

Meridia cleared her throat, but Eva had begun talking again. "We're a modest family as you can see, and that little jewelry shop on Lotus Blossom Lane is our pride and joy. Daniel's grandfather started it many years ago with just two gold rings and four silver bangles. In his lifetime, the shop suffered so many hardships it almost went under twelve times. Then Daniel's father, my husband, Elias, took over and grew the business into the success it is. It took a lot of sacrifice on our part, but we managed to pull through. Daniel is second in command, naturally. When my husband retires, he'll hand everything over to our son. It will be a comfortable future for my Daniel."

Eva smiled with evident pride, and without drawing a breath, she went on to talk about the girls. "Malin is an outstanding student, always first in her class and beloved by all her friends. Permony has a blessedly active imagination—you can just tell from the extraordinary color of her eyes. They're both good girls and very devoted to their brother. Whenever Daniel catches a cold, Malin waits on him hand and foot, and Permony pampers him by making all kinds of remedies. One time, Daniel pretended he was getting worse after eating Permony's sesame soup. The poor dear cried for hours, blaming herself even after Daniel assured her he was as hale as an ox!"

Eva's laughter erupted pure and infectious. Her rounded chin, which was giving signs of turning into a double, shook delightfully from the effect. Meridia laughed along, though she noted that the two sisters did not share in their mother's merriment. Permony pinched her mouth as she went about wiping a matador. Malin's hostile stare was trained at her mother for all it was worth.

"I'm sorry my husband couldn't leave the store to meet you today," said Eva. "I'll tell him you are much prettier than Daniel has led us to believe. Look at you, you are practically shining!"

Thoroughly disarmed, Meridia turned bright red. Eva went on as if she had not noticed her embarrassment.

"Tell me about your family. What does your mother do? Do you have a good relationship with your father? Daniel said you're an only child. What was it like growing up without a sibling?"

The speed with which these questions were raised thrust Meridia's anxiety to the forefront. Although she had anticipated Eva's inquiry and had carefully prepared her answers, she remained convinced that somehow, despite her efforts to restrain them, the ghosts and the mists would find their way into the room. Their stories would not bear up under Eva's eyes. Meridia shuddered to think that the whole foundation of her existence might crumble at the flick of the woman's hand.

"Papa is a scholar," she began as if reciting a lesson. "Mama, Ravenna—"

She never finished her sentence, for at that point Eva had turned to stare at the coffee table.

"Malin, where is that pink ballerina I gave you for your birthday? Are you tired of it already? You practically begged me to get it for you!"

Without blinking, Malin tossed her chin at her sister. "Permony broke it. Right before you came in."

So many things suddenly happened at once. Eva's face shifted, almost imperceptibly, and with that, the room darkened although the light remained bright. Malin sat up straight, savoring the moment with such delight that her complexion turned the same peach color as her dress. Permony was displaying the most alarming symptoms. She buried her eyes in the matador's red cape, fidgeting like a mouse, and when the intensity of her mother's stare nearly caused the figurine to leap from her hands, she trembled mightily as if from a chill.

"Careful, dear," Eva said without changing her gentle tone. "You don't want to break another one, do you? Oh, what am I going to do with you?" She sighed and turned to Meridia. "You must forgive my Permony. The child takes after her father, always breaking everything within reach. I wish she could be more like her sister, tender and ladylike. Permony is perhaps the only girl in the world who can't sit still for more than five minutes."

Unable to bear Malin's sneer a second longer, Meridia gave Permony a conspiratorial smile and uttered the first thing that came into her head.

"Neither could I when I was little. My mother used to say I could never finish a meal without walking through all the rooms in the house."

She was surprised at how smoothly the lie rolled off her tongue. Ravenna had never said anything of the kind. Hearing Malin snort, she thought the effort was well worth it, until her gaze returned to Eva and her smile froze on the spot. There was no mistaking it. The grave slant of Eva's head told her she had committed a blunder.

"Please do not encourage her. I'd only be too glad if Permony turned out half as fine as you. A girl her age should know how to handle glassware without crushing it to pieces." Eva shook her head as if ridding herself of an unpleasant thought. "Now. Tell me more about your family. What is it that your father studies as a scholar?"

Meridia was saved from further fabrication by Daniel's entrance. At his approach, she felt light and brightness rushing back into the room.

"Is Mama giving you the third degree?" he teased, sitting down next to her. "She said she won't rest until she squeezes every drop of information out of you."

"I said no such thing!" protested Eva. "Meridia and I are having the most wonderful talk. Did you tell Patina to bring in the tea?"

At that moment an old woman hobbled in with a wooden tray. Everything in her appearance—gnarled, hooflike feet, sparse white hair, liver-spotted arms—indicated decay, except for her eyes, which were clear and youthful. As she drew close to Eva, her limp became more pronounced, causing Meridia to fear that she might fall.

"Thank you, Patina," said Eva. "You may place the tray on the coffee table. Don't worry about serving the tea."

The old woman did as instructed. The smile she gave Meridia upon leaving was the toothless grin of a child.

Eva poured cinnamon tea into three glasses, stirring sugar and ice cubes with a long spoon. She picked up a plate of plum sweets from the tray and offered it to Meridia.

"Please try these. They are my favorite."

Meridia took one and then, at Eva's insistence, another. For the next twenty minutes, Eva regaled her with more stories. "You're spilling secrets too soon, Mama," Daniel objected in jest. "Let Meridia find out a few things on her own." Eva scolded back, said that nobody who lived under her roof had anything to hide. Meridia laughed. Easing into her surroundings, she took pleasure in the crowded room with its twin bay windows and antique furnishings, the shelves loaded with not just books but brass-framed pictures of the family. Adding to the charm were the birds twittering on the terrace and the sisters' now peaceful play. A warm, delightful feeling overtook her as Eva talked on, urging her to eat and drink more.

Later, alone with Daniel on the terrace, she told him, "Your mother is wonderful. Do you think she approves of me?"

Daniel took her hand and kissed it. "Approves of you? She's ready to worship you! Don't worry, they'll come to a decision sooner or later. It's getting dark. Let me walk you home."

Meridia shook her head. "It's all right. I can find my way."

"Are you sure?"

She lifted her eyes and nodded. As their lips met, she stifled the urge to tell him that she wanted to walk alone because she had fallen under a spell. The house with its crowded rooms had seduced her, as did the wilderness of the roses and the explosion of moss over bricks. But most of all, it was the vision of Eva she wanted to cherish, privately and without intrusion, for in that bold and confident figure she had glimpsed a refuge from the ghosts and the mists. The music of Eva's laughter, her strong arms and steady gaze—these, she believed, held the power to dispel neglect, loneliness, and the unremitting curse of forgetfulness.

THAT NIGHT, WHILE THE rest of the house slept, Elias the jeweler was kept up by bees. Sullen with doubts and imagined slights, the insects tirelessly buzzed inches away from his face. Elias was an anemic man who was prone to headaches after a sleepless night, but as the bees chipped away at the hours, he knew better than to try to swat them. At two o'clock, when he staged his first snore, the bees flew in closer circles and increased the volume of their buzzing. At four o'clock, when he pretended to be sullen himself and hid his face under the blanket, the bees shrieked like mad and stung him wherever they could. All Elias could do was toss and turn, hoping the roosters would soon crow and put an end to his misery. Unbeknownst to him and the bees, his older daughter, Malin, was stand-ing outside the door in her nightgown, pressing one inquisitive ear to the keyhole.

When morning brought not only breakfast but also a migraine, the bees cleared from the air as though they had never existed. As Elias sat facing his poached eggs and ham without appetite, his wife uttered a few words to which he could give only a distracted nod.

"I'll consult the fortune-teller today," said Eva. "If he thinks the signs are auspicious, I don't see any reason to oppose the match . . ."

EIGHT

Four days later, Meridia was dressing for school in the perpetual chill of the house when the front door opened with a bang. A violent scuffle rattled the porch, sending a tremor along the house, and a second later, something heavy tumbled down the stone steps. More shouts followed, and by the time Meridia looked down from her window, an oddly dressed man was dusting himself up and shaking his fist at Gabriel. He was wearing a red silk robe with wide sleeves, a golden sash across his chest, and a conical black hat that made him look like a messenger from the afterlife.

"There is no need for this kind of behavior, sir!" cried the man angrily. "I came in good faith, bearing a most excellent intention . . ."

Gabriel stood inside the ivory mist, folding his arms and laughing his grim laugh.

"Watch where you blow hot air. Next time, I won't be so gentle."

"But sir, at least consider what I proposed!"

"I've heard enough! My daughter is of no age or condition to marry. Now leave before I do something I'll truly enjoy and you'll bitterly regret!"

Gabriel went in and slammed the door. The matchmaker, for there was now no question of who he was, went after him with his last shred of dignity. One thing the man did not count on, however, was the ivory mist picking him up by his sleeves, twirling him like a marionette, stripping him of his hat, and sending him rolling across the lawn. For the second time that morning, the man peeled himself off the ground. Cursing the mist loudly, he slapped his hat back on his head and stormed away.

In an instant, Meridia put together the chain of events. The matchmaker must have arrived while she had taken her morning bath, for she had not heard the front door open since the blue mist deposited Gabriel a half hour ago. Their discussion, then, had lasted no more than ten minutes, which did not at all bode well for her chances. Thinking quickly, Meridia paced the narrow space between bed and window, alternately clasping and flexing her hands. Outside, the sky was gray and leaden, as the sky always looked when viewed from inside the house.

She made up her mind in seconds. The shoes came off first, then the socks, followed by the school clothes she let drop on the floor. Shivering in her undergarments, she went to the closet and selected a knee-length black dress with a teardrop cutout below the neck. She put it on with an almost military precision, smoothing the bodice, puffing the sleeves, fastening the two back buttons in one continuous motion. Sitting before the dressing mirror, she stared at the apparitions with such solemnity that they all departed without a gibe. Next, she unpinned her hair and shook it loose. She applied powder and blush to her face, mascara, lipstick, and a dab of perfume behind each ear. For a finishing touch, she pinned a camellia pendant on her chest, a treasure Daniel had found in a secondhand shop. Studying her reflection, she was pleased with her effort, for she now looked twenty-six instead of sixteen. She had just enough time to strap on a pair of patent leather heels when an urgent knock came at the door.

"Your father asks to see you, Miss," said a flustered maid. "If I may say so, he looks like he's just swallowed a toad."

"He always does," said Meridia. Without another word she swept past the maid and flew down the stairs in ten steps, reciting Ravenna's lessons under her breath. She entered the study without knocking and, without giving in to a moment's doubt, marched past the towering books to the massive desk in front of the window. The air was dense as mud, but determinedly she pushed her way in. It was not until she found herself staring at the back of Gabriel's head that her heart pounded like a hammer.

"I want to marry him, Papa."

Gabriel, who had been staring out the window, spun around in his chair. The floor had not betrayed her footfalls.

"You're a child. You're in no position to know, let alone tell me, what you want."

His eyes narrowed with rage, but for the first time in her life, she confronted them head on. The collision released a shiver into the air, and in the crucial second that followed, it was Gabriel who felt the greater impact. Standing before him was not the little girl he could familiarly disparage, but a young woman inflamed by passion. Her beauty, a thing he had never previously valued or acknowledged, suddenly dazzled his vision with a lover's shine. Gabriel, resenting this, held back none of his disdain.

"You think you can fool me with that cheap dress and that vulgar lipstick? You think I can't see how your heart is beating so pitifully in your throat, or how your knees are trying their hardest not to shake? You were never a clever one, and when you try to deceive me, it only shows what a truly foolish child you are. Go to your room and wipe that paste off your face! I will let you know when you can take a husband."

Meridia quivered visibly but took hold of herself. "I'm not a child, Papa. You can't stop me from marrying him."

Gabriel burst into a laugh. "Yes, I can. And if you force me, I will."

"What have you got against Daniel?"

"For a start, his father is a middling tradesman, and his mother has a reputation for being a pest. You have nothing in common with them."

"It's not them I'm marrying. Besides, I have met his mother. She's a perfectly lovely woman."

"Then you are even sillier than I thought. Your young man, this so-called Daniel"—Gabriel crinkled his nose in distaste—"has no higher education and no money of his own. How do you expect to start a family with someone who still lives on his father's bounty?"

"We'll get by, Papa. We'll get by."

Gabriel scoffed loudly. "Sure you'll get by. With my assistance."

Stepping forward, Meridia placed her palms on the surface of the desk. "I swear I will never ask you for a penny, even if it costs me my life. We're in love, Papa. You have no right to stand between us."

Gabriel appeared to relish this. Like a scientist entertaining an impossible theory, he leaned back against the chair and locked his hands behind his neck.

"Ah, love . . . Tell me, what do you know about it? Judging from the way you speak, you're barely capable of forming a thought. But please, don't let that stop you from expressing your mind. What do you know about this love?"

Meridia shook with anger, but his mocking smile drained all words from her lips. Relenting slightly, Gabriel unlocked his hands and eyed her with a milder gaze.

"Here is what you'll do. You will finish school, go on to the university, break a dozen young men's hearts, and become a real woman. I'm far from being old-fashioned, you see. I give you permission to have as many suitors as you like—I encourage it actually, seeing that you are no longer chaste and can do no more damage to yourself. But by the grace of heaven, do not bore me with talk of love when you don't have the slightest idea what it is."

Meridia reddened. This time, before she could stop them, words had sprung to her lips. "I know that whatever it is, I didn't learn it from you!"

Gabriel did not leap to his feet and strike her. On the contrary, his eyes scarcely flickered, and not a muscle moved on his face as he continued to regard her with amusement. This was the moment when she no longer doubted that he was made of ice.

"You're right," he said calmly. "I don't know the first thing about love, nor do I understand why people lose their heads over it. And if you ask your mother, she will tell you she is cut from exactly the same cloth. Neither of us is capable of loving anyone, or each other, and certainly not you. Given this unfortunate pedigree, what makes you think you can do better with your young man?"

It was the cruelest thing he had ever said to her, and his smile drove the blade deeper into her flesh. Under his wintry gaze she felt her heart collapse against her ribs, but something inside made her go on.

"You can't deny me the happiness you denied Mama. I won't let you break me the way you broke her!"

Gabriel considered this by cocking his elegant head a fraction to the left. "Many things have been said about your mother, but one thing she isn't is broken. If you think I'm cruel and heartless, then you don't know what your mother is made of. We both know she does nothing but plot my death every second of her life."

It was on the tip of her tongue to cry out, She wouldn't hate you if you hadn't taken a mistress! but she checked herself in time, seeing how it would not help her cause. Instead, she asked him simply, "Why do you hate me, Papa?"

It was a question she had been dying to ask all her life. As an answer, she received an unequivocal silence. Imploring him with her eyes, she detected a droop in his right shoulder. His hand unconsciously rose to it, tried to correct the imbalance without success. All of a sudden his contempt seemed to desert him, leaving behind a fatigue that charred his countenance of ice. As she watched a lone vein throb on his forehead, the revelation came to her without a warning.

"She did this to you, didn't she? The blinding flash and the tumble. It was Mama who put that stoop in your shoulder!"

Gabriel stood up to his full height, and instantly she knew she was losing him. Like a thing of majesty, his face shut in upon itself, sealing the lines and the tremor, and with a single innocuous blink, his eyes became as inexorable as night.

"You have wasted my time," he said. "As long as you are still a child of this house, I forbid you to marry that boy."

"Tell me about that night, Papa!" she persisted. "What happened in that room between you and Mama? Papa, tell me!"

Even before her voice cleared from the air, Gabriel had banished her into a desolated corner of his memory. Meridia could not focus her eyes, could not feel her breath, could not hear her voice. Her perspiring palms, when she finally lifted them from the desk, left no visible prints on the surface of the wood.

RAVENNA'S KITCHEN WAS NO easier to penetrate than Gabriel's study. From the doorway, Meridia inspected the iron knot on her mother's head and hoped that her ear would be more yielding than her back. A glance around the room told her what she was up against: a knife furiously beheading cauliflowers, a teapot shrilling like a banshee, shallots frying on a hot pan, the eyes of a flounder staring in deathless rage. Imperious in solitude, Ravenna reigned over them with her dark and private language, bewitching the shallots, entrancing the cauliflowers, casting a spell over the flounder to preserve her bitterness from the rust of time.

"Rattling the house like dice before breakfast settled in his stomach! If he wanted to raise the dead with all that racket, he should have warned me to plug my ears! What will the neighbors think? They're already laughing at him for slinking around every night to see a woman who actually looks worse than a warthog! And now that someone is asking for his daughter's hand in marriage, he makes himself even more of a laughingstock! Who will want to propose after this? I gave him a clever and beautiful daughter when everyone thought he was as barren as the desert, but did he ever thank me for my trouble? Oh no, he said he wanted a *son*. Well, he should have advised me of this before my womb dilated so I could make a little arrangement with God! The next thing I knew, before his child could pass her first gas, off he went to suckle that gorilla's breasts, mounting and riding her like she was the last humpback whale in the sea—"

"Mama!" Meridia stepped into the kitchen.

"—Anybody who's got no more sense than to impale a primate's ass should be hanged on the street for crows to feast on—"

"Mama!" Meridia turned off the stove so the banshee would stop shrieking, covered the flounder so the eyes would stop glaring.

"—Does he think she's going to give him a son? How can something so old and desiccated produce anything but its own shit—"

"Mama!" Meridia sidestepped the vegetable crates scattered on the floor and tossed the hissing shallots onto a plate, all the while trying not to breathe that reek and stink of solitude she had come to associate with forgetfulness.

"—He's got no shame carrying on like a lecherous goat now that his daughter is old enough to marry—"

Meridia placed a hand on the small of that ramrod back, not a moment too soon, because the furious chopping of the knife was beginning to sound like thunder.

"Mama!"

Ravenna turned in surprise. Holding the knife to her waist, she regarded Meridia without the faintest awareness. Her tense eyes were ringed with shadows, and her frown deepened the imminent network of wrinkles she never once fought with creams other mothers purchased by the jars. Despite the strong aroma of shallots, her scent of lemon verbena dominated the air. A full minute passed before her frown eased in recognition.

"Is everyone in this house trying to burst my eardrums?" she chided, the sleet in her voice slowed into a gentle rain. In the next breath she was off again, registering Meridia's face for the first time: "Child, you look miserable! Are you unhappy?"

Meridia tried to speak, but a painful rush of emotion stopped her. She could not remember the last time she had stood this close to Ravenna, breathing her scent and reading her face as if it were a map of another world. There was so much to be said, so many questions unasked, yet already she found herself thrust into the same vacuum that had bound her inside the ivory mist. There was no stopping it. In a second Ravenna would fade, retreat behind her veil of forgetfulness without a trace for her to follow.

But the veil did not descend. For once in her life, she had her mother's attention.

"What is it?" Ravenna laid down the knife in alarm. "What is troubling you?"

Unable to collect herself, Meridia began to tremble. The words she wrested from the depth of the vacuum sounded frail and hollow.

"Papa. Why does he hate me, Mama?"

Ravenna, far from surprised, replied instantly. "Have you gone mad? You know very well he doesn't hate you. Your father hates me."

Her tone was not dismissive, her gaze even tender and patient. Yet it was with a deeper chill that Meridia greeted the distance between them.

"I'm not a child anymore, Mama. When I was little you always told me that some things are better left as dreams, but I'm old enough now to know the truth. What happened between you two? Why did you stop loving him?"

"Because he stopped loving me," said Ravenna on the dot. Then jerking her eyes wide, she raised a hand to Meridia's temple. "Are you unwell, child? You look rather flushed. What's gotten into you? Why are you carrying on in this manner?"

Her heart sinking, Meridia understood that the veil, without her noticing it, had indeed fallen after all. Ravenna would guard her secrets to the grave. What happened next took place in a heartbeat. The sweet scent of lemon verbena, combined with Ravenna's ghostly look, her shoulders thin as paper and her hair twisted so tightly in a knot, became too much for Meridia to handle. Against all instructions, tears spilled from Meridia's eyes.

"I need to know why . . . you . . . and Papa . . . Why, Mama, why?"

"Child, you're crying! Have I taught you nothing? Pull your shoulders up. Tilt your chin. Keep your spine stiff." Ravenna was scouring her daughter's face with narrowed eyes when the idea hit her like a bolt of lightning.

"Holy Mother of Heaven, you're in love!"

Startled by the tumultuous mechanism of her mother's mind, Meridia put her hand out blindly. Ravenna took it at once.

"You do love him, then? This young man the matchmaker proposed?"

Meridia nodded.

"Does he love you?"

She nodded again, propelling tears to slide from her chin.

Abruptly, Ravenna raised her eyes to the ceiling. Her long, pale throat contracted as she swallowed, and when her eyes returned to Meridia, they were not those of someone absent and forgetful, but of a woman strong enough to drive a stoop into a man's shoulder.

"Stop crying this instant," she commanded. "If it's marriage you want, then it's marriage you'll get."

Ravenna turned to the chopping board and pointed her implacable knot at Meridia. Before the knife resumed its beheading, she threw one last lesson over her shoulder.

"Whatever you do, do not repeat my mistakes."

Too stupefied by the turn of events, Meridia could only watch as the dark and private language once again flooded the kitchen. In the midst of her bafflement, she realized that Ravenna had not asked for the name of the boy she wanted to marry.

❧

THAT EVENING, AS SOON as the yellow mist whisked Gabriel
away, Ravenna went down to the kitchen in her plain black dress and
stayed there for the next twelve hours. All night long the stove
groaned and the oven rumbled, countless bowls clanged, knives clattered, skillets jangled. At midnight, awakened by the commotion,
the two maids appeared in the kitchen with metal pokers in their
hands, but Ravenna shooed them away with a stern warning not to
disturb her. More terrified of their mistress than of thieves, the
maids scurried to their beds and drew the blankets up to their heads.
The steep drop in temperature told them that the house was bracing
for something momentous, and they did not sleep for fear of missing it. Upstairs in her room, Meridia heard nothing, though she
spent the night anxious without rest.

In the morning, when the blue mist delivered Gabriel in his long
coat and top hat at the door, Ravenna was waiting for him in the
dining room. In sixteen years he had not missed a single breakfast
she had prepared for him. Although it was never voiced, their pact
went as follows: As long as she still cooked and served him breakfast
without the aid of her maids, and he still ate whatever she gave him
without burying some in his napkin (these dishes, after all, might
contain poison, ground glass, urine, or anything else Ravenna's
resentment and Gabriel's suspicion could think up), they would
remain as husband and wife. During this exercise, neither one
spoke or looked at the other. In sixteen years they never modified or
questioned their habit, so inured to its rhythm that they no longer
knew who held the upper hand on a given morning.

Gabriel took his seat, spreading the napkin on his lap in one
lordly gesture. Ravenna brought the first dish from the kitchen, a
broiled snow fish sprinkled with nutmeg. Gabriel raised a quizzical
brow, missing his customary ham-and-paprika omelet, but the flat
line of her lips silenced him. No sooner had he raised his fork than

Ravenna swept up the dish and dumped both plate and content into a large trash can she had set up for that purpose.

"One year of lies and illusions," she said calmly without looking at him.

Before Gabriel could object, Ravenna vanished into the kitchen. A few seconds later she reappeared with a steaming bowl of lentil and octopus soup. Gabriel was about to dip into the creamy surface of the soup when Ravenna snatched the bowl and hurled it into the trash.

"Two years of sheer and utter waste," she said.

Gabriel sat still, uncertain which was troubling him more—the fact that his wife was speaking to him, or that she was discarding good food and expensive china without the slightest pang. A succession of rock cod in lemon-and-pepper sauce, veal garnished with peaches and palm sugar, and cubed chicken simmered in coconut milk soon joined the mass burial in the wastebasket. When Ravenna reached the ninth dish, Gabriel leaned back against the chair. For the first time in years, he stared openly at his wife.

"Is there a point to this inanity?"

"Nine years of misery, futility, and devastation," retorted Ravenna, letting each word sprout its own blade as she relegated the roast lamb to rubbish. Then, serene as a dove, she sailed impassively toward the kitchen.

Gabriel waited until the next dish met its doom before roaring, "I'm asking you, is there a reason behind this madness?"

"Ten years of deceit, treachery, and disappointments," returned Ravenna icily. "What other reason do you need?"

Gabriel slammed his fist against the table, causing the silverware to leap in trepidation. "What do you want, woman?"

Ravenna did not shrink, but fixed him a look that drove nails into his eyes. "She wants her freedom, and you will give it to her even if it's the last thing you do." And then without wasting another breath, she swept majestically into the kitchen.

When she reappeared, Gabriel struck again. "I won't let her marry that good-for-nothing boy. His whole family reeks of commonness and mediocrity."

Ravenna slapped a tureen of boiling lobster broth onto the table, prompting Gabriel to retreat lest it overturn. Her eyes blazing with intensity, she told him, "Eleven years of pain and disenchantment. Eleven years of shame and despair and absolute humiliation. She's a grown woman who knows what she wants, capable of bearing children, responsible enough to merit freedom. Do you think you have the right to decide her life for her?"

"I most certainly do!" shouted Gabriel, but Ravenna ignored him. She baptized the trash can with the broth and solemnly withdrew into the kitchen.

For the next six courses, Gabriel fumed while Ravenna remained indifferent. When she placed the eighteenth dish before him, the customary ham-and-paprika omelet, he immediately understood that it was the last. Eighteen dishes, one for each year they had been married.

"Eighteen years of grief and regret," said Ravenna. "You owe me that and much more."

"I will not deliver her into the hands of these people!"

Ravenna waved her finger with a withering ease. "She won't end up worse than I am. Nobody can be damned as low as you have damned me."

Gabriel recoiled as if she had exploded a hole in his being. Without thinking, he picked at the omelet, expecting it to be whisked away, but Ravenna made no move.

"I don't approve of this," he said at length. "Don't expect me to give her money or blessings."

Ravenna leaned in and told him in her iciest voice, "What you owe me, I will use to buy her freedom. I will add up all the damage you've caused to purchase her passage out of this madhouse."

It was at that moment when their eyes met, and the great wings of a feathered thing began to beat in his stomach, that Gabriel felt deceived by the fickleness of his own memories. For sixteen years he had not allowed himself to think of his wife as anything other than vengeful, but at that inexcusable moment of nostalgia, she again became the woman he had loved before the cold wind blew and froze the house over. Despite Ravenna's older and more gaunt appearance, those were the same lips he had kissed, the same arms and legs that had twined him so intimately that he knew the location of every vein and freckle. Slowly, mournfully, like a man savoring every moment before death, Gabriel dragged the fork to his mouth. In this way, Meridia became engaged to Daniel.

NINE

They were married in the summer of brides, two weeks after Meridia completed secondary school. On the afternoon of the banquet, when the sun was at its hottest, an enormous eagle descended on the roof of 27 Orchard Road and upset the abandoned nest that had roosted there for years. First to sight the disturbance, Eva rose from her seat in the garden, gathered the train of her champagne-colored dress, and rushed to assemble the waiters. Pewter with vivid speckles of green, the bird supervised the crowd from its eminence, refusing to take flight even when the waiters yelled and shook brooms at it. It was Eva, with her invincible hostess's smile, who devised the idea of pasting a colorful paper onto a balloon and releasing it in view of the bird. The trick worked. The eagle soared, stabbed the balloon with its beak, and showed no interest in returning to the roof. The guests clapped. Eva bowed. Suckling pigs and grilled mutton were served.

On Eva's command, the exterior of the house had been subjected to an extensive makeover. The walls were coated pearl white, the bricks rid of moss and lichen, the wilderness of the roses in the front yard pruned to a charming disarray. Gold and emerald canopies dotted the back garden, sheltering tables of food and gifts, with one awning devoted to the stunning cream wedding cake that had taken Ravenna three days to bake. In the center one hundred guests sat at white linen tables decorated with candles and roses, while above them crisscrossed lanterns and balloons swayed in the gentle breeze. On the stage, a woodwind quartet played waltzes, their performance repeatedly interrupted by the conductor urging everyone to dance.

Meridia went through the festivity with the conviction that she would awaken at any moment. The diamond ring on her finger did not feel real, and her exquisite wedding gown, made from twenty-four meters of Duchess satin and thirty-two meters of Chantilly lace, seemed to belong to another bride. Many times she was directed to pose for the photographer, to kiss when the guests demanded, and to shake hands with people whose names she forgot as soon as they were uttered. From this confusion only a handful of impressions emerged: One of the bridesmaids, Malin, had yet to crack a smile, while the flower girl, Permony, had sauce splattered all over her dress. Garrulous in his evening jacket, Elias the jeweler captivated the town dignitaries with his knowledge of gems and precious metals. Eva, dripping with diamonds, made her way from table to table, her face flawlessly made up, her long lashes quivering with laughter as she made sure that every plate was heaped to the brim.

Gabriel and Ravenna were seated next to each other, but by some mysterious trick or illusion, they were never seen together. When one sat down, the other vanished. And despite the photographer's persistence, he was unable to capture them in the same frame. In contrast to Elias's liveliness and Eva's hospitality, Ravenna and Gabriel kept their distance from the guests. Ravenna sat through the ceremony with the impassivity of a stoic, eating little, speaking even less, though she nodded often to herself. Gabriel talked only to his friends, ignored Elias's attempts to introduce him to others. A number of Meridia's teachers were also in attendance; as soon as they congratulated her parents, they all fled to seek the friendlier company of the groom's.

But none of this mattered when Meridia looked at Daniel. Her heart swelled at the sight of him, his thick hair slicked back, his face joyous, his long body graceful in a trim black suit. At a sign from the conductor, he took her hand and whispered something she could not hear. Before she knew it, the crowd was shouting and up she scrambled to her feet. On the stage, the blind violinist from the plaza had replaced the woodwind quartet. Later, she would remember nothing of their dance, only that she moved and spun with abandon. Whenever the thought nagged her that Monarch Street would cease to be her home at the end of the day, she smiled and held Daniel tighter in her arms.

Despite Gabriel's objection, Ravenna had made sure that Meridia received a suitable dowry. The sandalwood trunk displayed under one of the canopies was packed with money, four jewelry sets, two diamond watches, sterling silverware, antique laces, and luxury linens. The groom's gifts to the bride were equally extravagant. Eva took care that every guest had a chance to admire the one hundred meters of fine silk, six pairs of pearl earrings, eight gold bracelets, ten evening gowns, and a magnificent sapphire brooch. Another canopy hosted the guests' gifts, which included silk tablecloths, crystal flutes, enamel tea sets, bone white china, and lamps of hand-wrought gold. Presiding over these was the same matchmaker Gabriel had tossed out of the house, now calm and dignified as though success had come to him without a sweat.

After the newlyweds were forced to share the same bite of cake, eight of the burliest matrons, led by Eva, stampeded toward Meridia and tied a blindfold over her eyes. The crowd went wild. Under a shower of rice and paper streamers, the matrons carried their quarry to the bridal chamber, pinched and tickled her without mercy before tossing her onto a bed perfumed with gardenias. Weak with laughter, Meridia submitted when strong hands unfastened her gown, unpinned her hair, and bundled her in a thick robe. Eva cautioned her not to remove her blindfold until Daniel arrived, and then laughing, shouting last-minute wishes for many healthy sons and daughters, the matrons departed and left her alone.

No sooner had their footsteps died than Meridia ripped off the blindfold and slipped back outside. Evening had fallen, but the wind was still warm with the heat of the day. Ducking around the canopies, Meridia circled to the front of the house and hid behind the roses. The bright light from the terrace bounced off the petals without reaching the stalks. Gabriel, always the first to leave a party, appeared before many minutes passed, arguing loudly with his friends. As soon as they had vanished, Ravenna appeared. Midway through the lawn, she turned in Meridia's direction as if she had known her hiding place all along. Before Meridia could reveal herself, Ravenna swept to the curb, wet eyes bent from the light, and walked quickly in the direction opposite Gabriel's.

"Thank you, Mama," said Meridia, feeling suddenly more alone than she had ever been. As she crept back to her room, the wind turned cold and stung her own tearful lashes.

WHILE DANIEL SLEPT, a rustling noise kept Meridia awake. The guests were long gone, the lanterns in the garden extinguished hours ago. Sweaty from their lovemaking, his face was buried in her neck, his breath on her collarbone slowly relighting desire in her blood. In the dark she walked her fingers across the taut plain of his belly. She kneaded his chest, teased the left nipple surrounded by a few hairs until she heard him moan. Lifting his hand from her hip, she recalled its salty taste in her mouth. Earlier, sensing her urgency with him inside her, he had moved his palm in time to stifle her cry. Only then, with her lips wrapped around his finger, had he groaned and shuddered his own release.

She got up without waking him and put on her robe. The noise was getting louder, closer, as if coming from outside the door. Quietly she tiptoed past the bed and went out. The hallway was dark except for a dim moon seeping through the skylight. The rustling was by then a murmur, a low, monotonous droning of flies or mosquitoes. Meridia tightened her robe. Minding the piles of shoes and magazines that lined the hallway, she drifted past the sisters' room to the foot of the stairs. The droning was coming from the second floor, where Eva's sitting room and the master bedroom were located. Meridia gripped the banister and listened. There was no doubt about it. The noise was that of bees buzzing, hundreds and hundreds of them, needling each other in rage. Suddenly, before she could venture another step, the bedroom door opened with a jerk. A greenish light spilled down the staircase. Quickly, Meridia retreated to her room.

SHE HAD SLEPT FOR two hours when a hammer struck inches from her head. Gasping, she awoke to discover the hammer muted into a knock on the door. Already Daniel was stirring, demanding the intruder to explain the disruption.

"Your father wants to know if you're going to the shop today."

It was Patina, the old servant, sounding sorry and uncertain. Daniel looked at the clock and grumbled.

"Tell Papa I'll go later."

He burrowed his face on Meridia's shoulder and fell back to sleep. Tottering steps receded in the hallway, but soon returned with another knock.

"Your father says there's too much work to spare you this morning."

Daniel grumbled more loudly but said, "Tell him I'll be right out." He wiped sleep from his eyes and rose from the bed. Meridia hastened to follow, but he stopped her. "Get more sleep," he said. "I'll be back for lunch." At random he put on a white shirt and gray slacks, splashed water on his face in the washroom, stumbled toward the door, back to kiss her good-bye, and was gone.

Not expecting to be separated from him so soon, Meridia returned to bed. The sheets, deprived of his heat, no longer smelled of gardenias. As she lay there with a blanket clutched to her breasts, she examined her surroundings for the first time. It was still Daniel's old room, transformed into a bridal chamber by new linens, laundered curtains, and a fresh cream paint. Next to the bed was a wooden desk finished in dusty white, a cushioned chair with a high back, and prints of the seven wonders of the world on the wall. A door led to the hallway, another opened to the back garden. Kicking the blanket aside, Meridia was divining Eva's hand behind the transformation when the lady herself burst into the room without knocking.

"Good morning, blushing bride! Still sleeping when your husband is already off? I wish mine were as understanding. But he insisted on having *me* serve him breakfast come hell or high water. Now up, up, up! We have serious business to attend to."

Eva vanished as quickly as she appeared, betraying not the slightest hint that she had caught her daughter-in-law in the nude.

Meridia got up in a hurry and performed her morning routine in the adjoining washroom. Ten minutes later, she emerged to the cluttered hallway in search of Eva. In addition to the two bedrooms, the ground floor consisted of a living room, a dining room, a kitchen, and the servants' quarters at the back. Meridia was about to knock on the sisters' door to ask them where their mother was when she realized someone was standing behind her.

"The misses have gone off to school, Young Madam."

She turned with a start and saw a servant girl hardly older than herself in a dirty white uniform. The girl's frank smile and guileless face made Meridia like her on the spot.

"Could you tell me—"

"Madam is waiting upstairs."

Meridia nodded and headed for the stairs. This time, there was no sound of rustling. In the vivid morning light, the creaky wooden steps were far from menacing, though they looked worn with numerous scratches. No sooner had Meridia reached the landing than Eva called to her, "Second door on your left, dear. What's taken you so long?"

Meridia walked past the master bedroom without spotting a single bee. The second door opened to a small room of mismatched chairs and hanging geraniums. Eva was sitting on a purple armchair next to the fireplace, smoking a cigarette attached to a long ivory pipe. Seeing Meridia, she expelled a blue stream of smoke and got up eagerly.

"You look more stunning than a gem!" she exclaimed. "Daniel must have spent all night polishing you to perfection. I'm sorry he had to go to the shop this morning. I begged my husband—you must call him Papa now—to spare him, but there is just too much business to attend to today. Come to the table. All these beautiful things are your wedding gifts. Look at them!"

Coloring a little from Eva's comment, Meridia drew near. On the table was a set of gold jewelry, two scrolls of lace, a pair of pearl earrings, and a sapphire brooch. The jewelry set and the lace she recognized as part of her dowry, while the earrings and the brooch were Daniel's gifts. She looked around for the other items—the luxury linens and sterling silverware, diamond watches, gold bracelets, not to mention the money lining the bridal trunk and the one hundred meters of fine silk. Baffled when she did not find them, she turned to Eva for an explanation.

"This is all of them?"

Eva's smile instantly clouded with confusion.

"Oh, dear, you're not happy with the presents? Did Daniel not tell you? It's the custom in our family that the groom selects what his bride should keep before the rest is donated to charities." Eva drew on her pipe and furrowed her brows in concern. "Daniel will invest the dowry money as he chooses and he has selected these presents especially for you. I myself added the jewelry set and the lace because I thought you might like to keep something from your family. Oh, what a horrible mix-up this is! Should I tell Daniel you disagree with his decision?"

Eva stubbed out her pipe on an ashtray, her matronly bosom heaving in her eagerness to be helpful. Meridia, red with embarrassment, silently reproached her own rashness. The last thing she wanted was to cast doubt on Daniel's judgment.

"Of course I'm happy with the presents. Thank you for your kindness, Mrs.—"

"No, no, you must call me Mama. We are a family now."

Eva smiled broadly. Pinning the sapphire brooch on Meridia's dress, she remarked that it was a priceless family heirloom, given to her on her own wedding day by Elias's mother.

"I'll have Gabilan bring the presents to your room. Now, if you'd follow me . . ."

They went downstairs arm in arm, Eva talking about how fortunate they were to have Meridia as a member of the family. When they entered the dining room, Meridia welcomed the thought of breakfast, for she had not eaten a bite since the previous night. But instead of inviting her to sit at the table, Eva guided her into the kitchen.

Patina was hard at work. Her hooflike feet dragged from stove to counter, where she sprinkled sugar and marzipan over a pan of dough before inserting it into the oven.

"Patina is dying to teach you Daniel's favorite recipes," said Eva. "As they say, a woman who is goddess in the kitchen will keep her husband faithful for life."

Meridia knew for a fact that this was not true, but kept her silence. One thing she had not noticed before had absorbed her attention: Patina's hobble was becoming more pronounced the closer Eva came to her.

"You'll see there's no better teacher than Patina." Eva let go of Meridia's arm and pushed her steel blue hair behind her ear. "I will be in the garden if you need me."

She left to oversee the workmen dismantle the canopies. As soon as the door closed, Patina offered Meridia a bowl of vegetable soup and a generous slice of bread.

"You must be hungry," Patina said with her toothless grin. Her brown eyes were as soft as a baby's, yet something in those fathomless depths seemed ravaged by grief. Meridia thanked her and ate standing up. After she finished, Patina fetched an apron from the side of a cabinet and tied it around her waist. At that moment, Meridia began to understand her standing in the family.

TEN

Meridia began her new life with the best of intentions. After the cold of Monarch Street, Orchard Road was warm and bustling, practical in habits, definite in aims, and simple in structures. Although Ravenna had never trained her to cook, embroider, plant bulbs, or polish silverware, she picked up the skills readily from Patina and Gabilan. In early morning and late afternoon, the three worked together in the kitchen, making lunches and dinners according to Eva's instructions. Midday was reserved for gardening, afternoon for cleaning, evening for sewing. Patina never said more than the necessary words, but her guidance was steady and reassuring. It was she who taught Meridia to bring Eva chrysanthemum tea every morning, and at mealtimes, to serve everybody in the family first before she ate. In this way, Meridia was inducted into a world of customs she now saw as the backbone of every family but Ravenna's. Her victories, though small, were concrete: the smiles Eva gave her, Patina's nods, the proud gleam in Daniel's eye when Eva announced that his wife was to be thanked for the beautiful dinner they were about to consume.

Elias, she thought, was a curious head of household. A short bald man with drowsy eyes and a lazy mouth, he deferred all domestic matters to Eva and desired nothing more than to be left alone. After work, wrapped in a blanket and accompanied by the caged birds, he would sit in his rocking chair on the terrace and immerse himself in books. As hours passed and the birds grew hoarse from singing, he remained engrossed in his reading of metals and minerals, flora extinct and fauna exotic, volcanoes in faraway lands, and famed discoveries of oil and gold. With the same insatiable hunger he studied the topography of the moon, inspected ancient navigation charts, and devoured tales of heroic expeditions until the dinner bell rang. Eva, armed with a basket of knitting, often tried to speak to him, but it required a great deal of effort on her part to extract an answer out of him. It was not uncommon that she had to chase him across seas and continents, tunnel through layers of earth and labyrinths of caves, to impress upon him the fact that Malin had come down with a cold or that the roof needed replacing before winter. The only person who could rouse him from his trance was Permony. All the girl had to do was call him, and he would materialize from the most remote corner of the universe without delay.

"Why do you bury your nose in books, Papa?" Permony once asked him.

"So your mother can't find me. The only problem is I can still hear her no matter where I am."

This bond between them rankled Eva to no end. Many times she complained to Meridia about how the two were always keeping her in the dark. "Every time I come near them, they act as if they'll shoot me for trespassing. No doubt it's me they're talking about. It's tragic, really. Malin is so much smarter and prettier, yet he gives her half the attention he gives Permony. Just look at them! From the way they stare at each other, you would think she's the one who wakes up smelling his farts every morning!"

Eva had a talent for finding faults, even when none existed, and no one suffered from this more than Permony. Often, when Elias was out of the way, Eva would call her younger child and point out one deficiency after another as if she were reading from a list. If she saw nothing wrong with Permony's hair, then she would take offense at her posture; if the girl's hands were disappointingly clean, she would scold her for wearing a particular dress. Permony's lavender eyes were a permanent topic of castigation, for Eva believed that this was the color most identified with sloth, selfishness, and to an indeterminate degree, satanic possession. Her tirade ceased only when she went out of breath, or became so engulfed by her own emotion that she lost all train of thought.

Permony never defended herself. Shy and gentle, she weathered her mother's storms in the manner of one overcome by a celestial vision—head thrown back, eyes awestruck, hands locked in a supplicating prayer. This "pose of martyrdom" often drove Eva to the brink of hysteria. "Don't fall for it," she sternly advised Meridia. "The guilty always keep their silence. I learned this from your father-in-law."

Eva's devotion to Malin was equally mystifying. The girl was always sullen and difficult, to Eva more than anybody else. A mealtime would not be complete without Malin pouting at her plate, and Eva's day would be uneventful without her older daughter shouting at her. Yet not only did Eva tolerate this, she went the extra distance to pacify Malin. She bought her dresses and candied fruits, added recklessly to her figurine collection, and held Permony responsible whenever Malin devastated the house with her tantrum. This devotion puzzled Meridia even more when she considered that it was Permony who took after Eva. While Malin was pale and languid, Eva and Permony had the same dark skin, animated eyes, and robust frame. They both laughed with their entire bodies, and their hands were constantly busy with one thing or another. When Meridia mentioned her confusion to Daniel, he kissed her nose and teased her for imagining things. "Mama doesn't play favorites," he said. "She loves the girls in different ways."

Malin proved more ruthless than her mother. Her favorite pastime was to recline on the sofa with a tin of butter cookies and torment Permony about her birth. She insisted that their mother almost died when she delivered Permony. "Mama was in labor for one hundred and thirty-seven hours, and her screams could be heard from desert to sea. At one point, she was bleeding so much that blood was seen trickling out the front door. On the morning of the fourth day, Papa and the midwife begged her to save herself and give you up, but she set her teeth and told them to go to hell. Twice they pronounced her dead, but just as they were about to cover her face, she opened her eyes and shouted, 'I'm still here, you fools!' When you finally decided to stop torturing her and slip out on your own, it was the midwife who nearly fell dead. 'Move back!' she yelled. 'The devil has spoiled the baby's eyes! I must gouge them before the venom spreads.' Mama was so ill and exhausted, yet she mustered her last strength to whack the woman across the face. 'I will carry *you* feet first before you do that!' she swore. This was how Mama saved you from blindness. And in return, you continue to give her nothing but pain."

Halfway through the story, Permony was guaranteed to cry, her plump body trembling with guilt and terror. If Eva was present, Permony would come to her like a puppy and tell her how sorry she was. Impatient, Eva always stopped her on the spot.

"Don't be ridiculous, Permony! How could I bleed for one hundred and thirty-seven hours and still be alive? It was eighty at most."

Following Eva's tirade, Permony would weep quietly in her room while she pretended to read. It was here that Meridia discovered the girl's passion for fantastical tales and, reminded of her own lonely upbringing, did her best to nurture it. In the beginning Meridia read to her, acting out characters until they became flesh, but soon she ran out of books and resorted to inventing her own stories. She recollected those magical images she had seen with Hannah during the Friday night projections at Cinema Garden, and from them she fashioned her own elf kings and dragon queens, mermaids and pirates, love-torn statues who embraced in the night, and preternatural princesses who lost their souls in ice and rediscovered them in fire.

The sisters' room, with its unsettling collision of colors, seemed the perfect setting for these tales. Malin had laid claim to three-quarters of the room and decorated it in smoldering orange: bedspread, carpet, and lampshade blazed with the ferocity of the two o'clock sun while her figurines commandeered a massive tangerine shelf. In contrast, Permony's side was fitted in apple green, her favorite color, the lacy drapes and pillows bringing to mind the tranquillity of arbors and pastures. Thus Meridia flew her preternatural princesses over the valley of the girl's bed, charged her knights to scale the shelf, and set loose her dragon queens upon the burning plain of Malin's carpet.

Inevitably, the well of her imagination would dry up whenever Malin walked into the room. Perhaps sensing the girl's surliness, the elf king froze with his scepter in midair, and no amount of persuasion could make the mermaids flap their tails again. Despite Meridia's efforts, Malin remained cold toward her. The girl answered her inquiries with studied politeness, was never openly rude, yet her most casual gesture seemed laced with hidden hostility. After some time, Meridia left her alone. When she hinted to Daniel about his sister's behavior, he told her it was nothing to worry about. "Give her time. Malin was eight when she first cracked a smile at me."

One Sunday at the end of August, Eva and Elias came home from a long afternoon of shopping. Attired in a floral dress and a multicolored stole, Eva was in the best of spirits, while Elias, his dark suit rumpled and soaked with perspiration, retained just enough energy to sink into his rocking chair. Clutching her packages, Eva bustled into the living room, where Gabilan was painting Malin's nails. She greeted her daughter happily, placed the packages on the table, and then sent Gabilan to fetch Meridia and Permony. A minute later, the two emerged from the bedroom, a dozen long-haired nymphs still dancing in Permony's eyes. Eva smiled and handed Meridia a necklace of turquoise beads.

"Something I picked up. It will match your blue dress splendidly."

Meridia gasped in surprise. "It's beautiful!" She took the neck-lace and admired it. "Thank you, Mama."

Eva insisted that she put it on. Visibly moved, Meridia fastened the clasp behind her neck. Then she heard it—Malin, without moving her eyes from her nails, let out a faint snort, audible only to Meridia, that sounded even more disdainful than Gabriel's.

"There," said Eva, twirling her around. "You look fit for a ball. Now, girls, don't think I've forgotten you!"

Eva turned back to the parcels and took out a velvet-trimmed handkerchief, a satin purse, a heart-shaped orange hand mirror, and a picture book ablaze with colors. She lined these on the table before Malin and explained to Meridia, "Since Malin is older, she gets to select first."

Malin lifted her long lashes and glanced at the offerings with boredom. Permony, who had been holding her breath since she sighted the picture book, averted her eyes. Malin smiled thinly, and with excruciating slowness chose the handkerchief, the purse, and the mirror. Permony sighed with relief.

"Then the book's yours, Permony," said Eva. "Now, if everyone is happy—"

"I want the book," said Malin, tossing the handkerchief back on the table.

Eva was unfazed. "Changed your mind already? Fickle girl." She clacked her tongue in mock exasperation. "In that case, you may thank your sister for that handkerchief, Permony. I prefer it myself to the book."

When the girl, crestfallen, failed to speak or move, Eva reproved her at once.

"What's the matter? Aren't you happy with your present? If you don't want it, there are plenty of other girls who do. Why, Meridia, have you ever seen such an ungrateful child in your life?"

Permony quickly took the handkerchief, but her eyes held no glimmer. When Eva excused her a moment later, Permony went to her room and sat on the edge of her bed. "Malin doesn't even like books," she repeated in confusion. Meridia tried to distract her with her wittiest elves, but Permony remained inconsolable, until the door opened and she heard her father's voice from the hallway.

"I think I know what will make my dove smile again."

Elias went in with a grin and another picture book in his hand. Permony sprang from the bed, squealing with joy, and threw her arms around her father.

Elias hushed his daughter but lapped up her kisses. "Shh, don't tell your mother," he chuckled. "She won't let me rest if she thinks I'm spoiling you."

He coughed when he saw Meridia, then stroked his bald head with embarrassment. The impression, however, had sunk in. In the years to come, even when circumstances insisted otherwise, Meridia would remember that moment as an unbreakable testament to the good in Elias. As she turned to leave the room, another revelation hit her. Elias was aware of Eva's treatment of Permony, but for reasons known only to himself, he thought it best to leave it be.

WITH THE FIRST DRENCHING rains of August, Meridia found herself alternately baffled and seduced by her mother-in-law. A woman of epic impulses, Eva possessed the talent to summon winter with an arch of her brow, and then dispel it with summer with the first crackle of her laugh. It was not unusual for her to weep when she learned of a stranger's death, and, in the same breath, to refuse Patina medication for the pain in her legs. When she was happy, she made the whole house laugh with her; when she was upset, everyone suffered twice as much. At times she was superstitious to a fault, consulting fortune-tellers for the smallest matters, and at other times she made important decisions at the drop of a hat. Permony was the most frequent and unfortunate recipient of her extremes. When the girl least expected it, Eva would clutch her to her bosom with all the force of her maternal passion, but as soon as she began gasping for air, Eva would scold her, saying no man would look at her twice if she kept breathing with her mouth open.

In her mission to save money, Eva religiously scanned house-keeping magazines for coupons and cost-cutting tips, which explained the stacks cluttering the hallway, since her hoarding instincts prevented her from throwing anything out. From these she learned how to make a bar of soap last longer than advertised, to devise meal plans for six on a budget for three, and to use ammonia and vinegar for cleaning instead of patented products. Eva's inventiveness at first shocked and then impressed Meridia, for Gabriel and Ravenna, though they disagreed on other matters, had reared her on this principle: "People lie, but money doesn't. When in doubt, purchase the most expensive item." When she confessed their viewpoint to Daniel, he gently took her aside and told her, "Don't mention it to Mama. You'll be better off spitting on her directly."

No place in town showcased Eva's bargaining prowess more than the market square. Twice a week, arms bared to the sun and basket wielded like a shield, she would take Meridia with her. When Eva approached a stall, she never browsed or wavered off course, but told the merchant straight out what she wanted. She would snort like a bull at his opening price—no matter how low it was—plant one hand on her hip, and tell him may God have mercy on him if he thought she was born yesterday. She would not budge until the merchant discounted his price several times, and even then, she would take out less money from her purse than was asked. "That's all I have," she would say, shrugging her handsome shoulders indifferently. The merchant, more often than not, would bellow that she was robbing him blind but still take her money.

In the beginning, Meridia was mortified by Eva's behavior, for Ravenna had never bargained for anything in her life. But when she saw how Eva got the butcher to give her the best cut of meat for half the price, and the grocer to throw in free flour with her purchase of sugar, she thought no one was smarter than Eva. One day, after she watched the fruit vendor capitulate with six extra oranges, Eva surprised her by saying, "We need trout for dinner. You do the haggling."

Before she could protest, Eva steered her right up to the fish-monger. Meridia choked, stammered over her words, but Eva firmly coached her from behind. The pressure of Eva's hand on her elbow was like a current that left her breathless. She had no idea what she said, but before she was aware, money had changed hands, the trout were placed in her basket, and Eva's nod told her that she had done well. At that moment, without feeling the slightest disloyalty to Ravenna, she glowed with pride and embraced Eva with her whole heart—her tenacity and boldness, her prodigious energy, her extraordinary power to convince and make herself heard. But most of all, she embraced the sound of Eva's laughter, warm and free and exultant as it erupted from the depths of her bosom.

NOT LONG AFTER THAT day in the market came Meridia's first brush with the bees. Early one evening, Daniel came home from work and called her into the bedroom.

"Mama's upset. She's talking to Papa on the terrace. What do you say we go out for dinner?"

Meridia took his suit and hung it behind the door. "Why is Mama upset? She just woke up from her nap a moment ago."

Daniel shook his head. "I don't know. Something about a mongrel from hell. If we don't clear out before the storm breaks, I won't have any appetite left."

He winked and slipped into the bathroom, leaving his wife to ponder his remark. Meridia picked up his shoes and went out to the hallway. She was about to polish them in the kitchen when she heard a noise coming from the terrace. The front door was ajar, and as she crept toward it, she felt the air shiver with foreboding. She cocked her ear and listened hard, and stopped in her tracks when she recognized the noise. It was the bees buzzing, drilling and persistent and just below range, the same noise she had heard coming from the master bedroom on her wedding night. She put the shoes down and stole up to the door, passing the sisters' room on the way. Both girls were doing their homework, and neither one seemed bothered by the noise. On the terrace Elias was sitting in his rocking chair, Eva standing behind him, both their backs facing her. The sound of buzzing was coming from Eva's mouth, causing the caged birds to twitter with fright.

"How much longer must I endure this agony? For two weeks that cursed dog next door has been barking at my windows every afternoon, causing me an immeasurable mental anguish, not to mention the rudest disruptions to my afternoons. For how can I run the house and pay the bills in the sitting room, care for my family and take my rest in the bedroom, while that relentless noise born in the bower of hell tears at my nerves every chance it has? That hellhound is destroying my comfort in my own house, assassinating all prospect of quiet and serenity, and what's worse, the second I think it's finally wearied and dropped to sleep, up it barks all over again, sending me, I'm sure, to an early grave, and if you, Elias, think I will put up with this for a minute longer, you are sorely mistaken. I did not marry you and bear you children only to live next door to a dog pound, owned, I've no doubt, by a despicable man who clearly has so little respect for you, Elias, the esteemed jeweler, that he dares to mount this insult on me, your loving wife and devoted mother of your children, and expects you to take it lying down like a coward and an idle. You must not let this pass, not while the honor of our family, the very status and dignity we have labored so hard to attain, is at stake, is at this very moment being butchered and stomped on and spat at as if it matters less than cow dung . . ."

A loud creak from Elias's chair sent Meridia back to her room. Once inside, she sat down at the desk and waited for Daniel to finish. She had heard the neighbor's mastiff bark on occasion, but did not recall hearing it more than usual in the past two weeks. Eva's windows, however, were the only ones facing the neighbor's yard, so it was possible the noise disturbed her more than anyone else. When Daniel stepped out of the bathroom, hair damp and skin ruddy from washing, Meridia decided not to say a word about what she had heard. She laid out a fresh shirt and trousers for him and dressed herself.

When they passed Eva and Elias on the terrace, the two did not notice them at all. Eva had taken the second rocking chair, confronting Elias at a right angle, while he determinedly buried his nose in a book. The air was oppressive with the sound of buzzing, yet the only concession Elias gave to the bees was to flick them irritably every few seconds. Eva gave him no reprieve, charging the insects to hunt him in every gorge and ravine of his book. Meridia, dumbstruck by the spectacle, could not move until Daniel pulled her wrist and rushed her to the street.

The couple dined modestly on tomato soup and egg sandwiches at the bookshop café. From the moment they sat down, Daniel began talking volubly. An eccentric customer, he said, wanted to purchase twelve bracelets that differed in styles and sizes but weighed exactly the same. "Down to the ounce! I spent the entire afternoon weighing every bangle in the vault and found only three that met her standard." Before Meridia could sympathize, he was off telling her about a man who had been coming to the shop for ten years to look for an engagement ring. "Until he finds the perfect ring, he won't ask any woman to marry him. Papa thinks he should try asking a man." And so it went, Daniel tense and racing to the next topic. Once when Meridia mentioned the bees, he waved his hand and told her, "Don't worry. It will blow over when we get back."

The terrace was lit though empty when they returned. The birds' cages were shrouded in black, the two rocking chairs nodding to each other like exhausted souls. Entering the front door, Meridia quickly brought her hands to her ears. Inside, the sound of buzzing had reached a deafening pitch, coming from the living room, where Eva and Elias usually sat after dinner. Before Meridia knew what was happening, Elias had flung a book at the wall, jumped out of his chair with the violence of an awakened giant, shot past her and Daniel out the door, down the steps of the terrace, over the cobble-stone wall, and disappeared into the unlit part of the neighbor's garden.

"Papa!" Daniel called after him.

"Leave him, son," ordered Eva from her seat. And with these three words, the bees suddenly cleared from the air.

A furious round of barking shattered the night, followed by a low whimper and then silence. Eva picked up her knitting calmly. When Elias returned a minute later with his face scratched and his sleeves torn, she did not say a word to him. Elias yanked a battered atlas from the shelf, collapsed on the sofa, and lost himself in the map of an ancient continent. Without a sound, Daniel led Meridia to the bedroom.

The next morning, the kitchen was abuzz with Gabilan's news. "There were no wounds or bruises, Young Madam," she whispered incredulously. "The maid said that every part of the dog is intact, but he can no longer bark as if his tongue has been cut or burned. All morning long he's done nothing but stare up dumbly at Madam's windows. I'm going to miss waking up to his barking at dawn."

On the other side of the kitchen, grinding peppercorn into a pot of soup, Patina lowered her head in silence.

ELEVEN

September arrived with a flurry of blossoms. On the day the wind shifted, all the flowers on Orchard Road shed their petals and showered the ground with rainbow snow. Roses, magnolias, and petunias danced in the air for hours, blinding passersby, buffeted by the fragrant wind like endless paper streamers. By the time the wind eased, the sky was a clear blue desert, and all the mistresses on Orchard Road were ordering their maids to rake the blossoms off the lawns. Collectively they lamented the despoiled flowers, the products of so much diligence and patience, now bald and piteously shivering in the sun.

When Orchard Road awoke the following morning, it was astonished to discover the flowers restored. Overnight, the petals blossomed, fuller and sturdier, and by morning the dew had minted them with unprecedented freshness. Awed by this miracle, all the mistresses except one looked to heaven and crossed their palms in gratitude. Eva alone let out a scream, rolled up her sleeves, and recruited Meridia to help her. The little clump of yellow marigolds had multiplied and spread into the wilderness of the roses.

"We must pluck them out," she cried. "My roses! I can't allow anything to happen to them!"

It took until noon to clear the marigolds. When they stopped for lunch, Meridia had scratches on her arms and legs from the roses' thorns, but Eva was curiously unharmed, although she was the less cautious of the two. After lunch, coming out to the terrace to inspect her work, Eva let out an even louder scream than before. Not only had the marigolds regenerated, but they now towered over the roses and were soaking up all the sun.

Joined by Patina and Gabilan, they toiled for the next three hours. But for every marigold they ripped out, two more sprouted in its place. At four o'clock, Eva threw up her hands and told everyone to stop. "It's no use," she panted with exhaustion. "An evil spirit is possessing these flowers."

In the next six days, Eva summoned twelve holy men to perform exorcisms on the front lawn. One sprinkled ashes to destroy the marigolds, another petitioned cutworms to do the job, yet the flowers kept breeding. On the seventh day, exterminating her last marigold, Eva admitted defeat. "Let them do what they want," she sighed. "I've done everything to stop them."

She fell into a dark mood after this, and the house suffered. She reduced Permony to tears at every conceivable chance, decried Patina's cooking as unfit for sow, and threatened to dismiss Gabilan for an alleged affair with the grocer. She made Elias's life impossible by disrupting his habits. She rearranged his books so he could not find them, rang the dinner bell early to abridge his reading time, and dragged him out for impromptu strolls when all he wanted was to sit in his rocking chair. Behind his back, she trained the caged birds to shriek at her command, priming them to yell "Thief!" or "Fire!" whenever she deemed he was too absorbed in his book. Not even Malin was exempt from her temper. During one historic outburst that shocked the house, Eva sent the girl to her room for playing with her food, brusquely telling her to keep her long face to herself.

Daniel she burdened with money matters. She complained that

despite her parsimony, there was still not enough money at the end of the month to keep the house afloat. "All it takes is one miscalculation," she said, "and we'll all end up in the street."

"Don't worry, Mama," Daniel tried to humor her. "We're not quite there yet."

"Why am I the only one who is worried about this family?" she retorted.

To prevent their unthinkable fate, she had Daniel review their expenses until late into the night. The result was a drastic tightening of the purse strings. Eva ordered Patina to put more vegetables and less meat into the meals, clipped more coupons, became a greater terror in the market square, and insisted that all purchases, no matter how small, be cleared through her. She reduced everyone's allowance by ten percent, including the salaries of the servants and the shop assistant, and contemplated doing without sugar and cream at breakfast. When she started frequenting thrift shops to purchase undergarments, Elias drew the line and had it out with his wife. Eva relented only after he promised not to purchase any more books until their condition improved.

Daniel's finances also took a hit. Meridia had thought that he received a monthly salary for his work at the shop, but instead, Eva gave him money whenever she felt he needed it. From this stipend, Daniel put aside a certain amount each month for Meridia, which she used to purchase personal necessities. Soon even this was curtailed. Eva's reply to Daniel's requests followed the same pattern. "We're not a wealthy family, son. Perhaps you could be more careful with your money. Last week alone you dined out on Tuesday *and* Saturday nights. And have you asked Meridia to watch her spending? I saw her with a new shade of lipstick just the other day . . ."

Immersed in her tasks, Meridia found little time for herself or for Daniel. All day long Eva occupied her with cooking, cleaning, shopping, sewing, gardening, and, if there was nothing else to do, dictation of letters. In the beginning, Meridia did not mind this; in fact, intrigued by the novelty of her married life, she was eager to learn whatever Eva had to teach her. As the months passed, however, her mother-in-law's constant faultfinding began to chafe her. Eva criticized the way she arranged her room, the powder she used, her weak tea, her spending "so much time with Permony and so little with Malin." In those early days Eva was not outright critical, but made sly, insinuating comments to underscore her points. When she disapproved of Meridia's dress, she lowered her lashes dejectedly and remarked, "Heavens, I didn't know they make them in that cut." When Meridia saw something at the market that delighted her, Eva would chime in, "I don't know, dear. I saw a charwoman wearing the exact same thing yesterday."

Though she had no proof, Meridia suspected Eva of keeping Daniel from her. In the evening, after the plates were washed and the silver polished, Eva often called him to her sitting room upstairs and occupied him with the account books until late. The few times that Meridia invited herself up, Eva made it clear that she was not welcome. As soon as she saw Daniel greet his wife with amorous looks, Eva blew out a stream of smoke and rapped the stack of books irritably. "Focus, son. There will be time for lovemaking later."

One evening in late September, Meridia took the opportunity to slip upstairs while Eva was scolding Patina in the kitchen. In the sitting room, Daniel was swearing at the ledger, his index finger jabbing the paper as though accusing it of deceit.

"These figures don't match," he said in frustration, motioning her to sit on his lap. "I've gone over them half a dozen times and there's no way they add up."

Meridia settled herself between his knees and added the columns of numbers in her head. "There," she said before long. "That should be an eight instead of a three."

Daniel redid his computation on a piece of paper.

"I'll be damned," he said. "Fix this one then if you're so smart."

She came up with the answer quickly. Daniel, incredulous, scribbled more figures on paper. Meridia was once again correct.

"Where did you learn this?" he asked in amazement.

"It's nothing. My nurse used to say I have a knack for numbers."

"Why, I've never seen anyone—"

Just then Eva walked in, her almond eyes ablaze from admonishing Patina.

"I've married a genius, Mama," said Daniel excitedly. "You see these numbers? Meridia can add them up faster than I can! Let her help me do the books from now on."

Without changing her expression, Eva picked up her ivory pipe from the ashtray. "Don't be silly," she said. "Meridia has enough responsibilities around here. Now enough fooling around. If you'll excuse us, dear, we have a lot of work to get to."

Two days later, Eva made a detour to Lotus Blossom Lane on their way home from the market. Meridia had visited the shop once during her courtship with Daniel, but now the sight of the white-and-yellow awnings and flower boxes at the windows aroused a new affection in her heart. Hanging above the glass door were a cluster of roses—a new bundle was cut by Eva every Monday morning from the front lawn and placed there for good luck—and a golden bell that jingled every time a customer walked in. Inside, the tall ceiling was painted blue and the granite floor checkered white and green. There were cushioned stools for customers, a long row of display cases, and behind it, a desk and a small room designated as an office.

Eva went into this room to speak to Elias. Since Daniel was occupied with customers, Meridia strolled behind the counter to the desk. Her attention was immediately absorbed by a tray of precious stones. She put down her shopping basket, picked up a green and a pink stone, and held each of them up to the light. Their raw brilliance dazzled her; in a flash she experienced again the thrill that had once drawn her to Gabriel's desk. She began to see potentials to which the stones could be put, and wished she knew what they were called. To her surprise, the answers came to her at once.

"The green one is tourmaline, the other pink topaz. If you want, I can tell you the names of the others."

She turned and found Elias standing behind her. "I'm sorry, I didn't mean to . . . but yes, I'm curious—"

Eva's melodious laugh voided the rest of her sentence.

"Don't bore her, dear," she said to Elias. "What makes you think Meridia's interested in those trinkets? Come, my girl, put them down. We have work to do at home."

Meridia cast a regretful look at the stones before returning them to the tray. From this and the incident with the account books, it became clear that Eva did not wish her to have any involvement with the shop.

A FEW DAYS LATER, a high-pitched wail ruptured the tranquility of dawn and snatched Meridia awake. She sat up abruptly, groped the bed in the dark, and was relieved to find Daniel at her side.

"That impossible woman," he muttered.

"What is it, Daniel?"

"Nothing. Mama will take care of it. Go back to sleep."

Daniel covered his ears with a pillow and promptly began to snore. Guided by a light from the window, Meridia pulled the blanket over his chest, got to her feet, and threw on her robe. When she opened the door that led to the back garden, the wail pitched to a higher range. Her heart stood still, then pounded harder than before. It was unmistakable; the cry was coming from the wilderness of the roses.

A golden dawn had broken, the air restive from the crow of roosters. The wind swept hot and dusty, griming sky and windows in its sightless passage. Without a noise, Meridia crept to the front lawn and halted before the roses. Shrouded in fog, the marigolds were shivering. Tottering among them like a lost sibyl was the crumpled figure of Patina.

The old servant was parting the flowers with one hand and holding her stomach with the other. Her hooflike feet made her progress difficult, yet she did not seem to notice as the roses' thorns cut her with every move. Streaked with tears, her childlike eyes were searching the ground blindly, while from her throat poured the saddest and most inhuman lament Meridia had ever heard.

"Patina!"

Meridia rushed toward her. But instantly her shout was drowned out by the violent crash of the front door. Without thinking, she dropped to her knees and hid behind the marigolds. Eva burst out of the house with her hair undone and her robe unbelted, reaching the wilderness of the roses in six angry strides.

"What now?" she thundered at Patina as the flowers parted.

"My child . . . my baby . . ."

"Have you lost your mind? Stop this nonsense right now!"

"Please . . . my child, my baby." Patina buckled to the ground and tugged at Eva's robe. Patches of scalp glistened through the sparse white of her hair.

"Get up and get back in the house!" Eva firmly whisked away her robe. "Have you no shame? What will people think if they see you?"

"My child . . . my baby . . ." Convulsing with tears, Patina continued to wail. Eva lowered her voice to the hiss of a python.

"How many times do I have to say it? If you're unhappy here, you may leave whenever you wish. But don't you dare embarrass me like this! There is nothing that's keeping you chained to this house. Say the word and I'll pack your bags myself!"

Patina shook her head despairingly. "My child, my baby . . . Please . . ."

All of a sudden Eva swooped down and struck Patina across the head. The sound jarred Meridia's stomach loose from her spine.

"You ungrateful woman!" cried Eva. "What haven't I done for you? What haven't I sacrificed? I put a roof over your head, feed you, clothe you, take care of you when you're sick. And this is how you repay me? When will you stop shoveling up the dead and throwing their bones in my face?"

Patina whimpered and dipped her head to the ground. "I didn't mean to be ungrateful. Please forgive me. Please . . . my child, my baby . . . forgive me . . ."

Indignant, Eva swung on her heels and strode back into the house, slamming the door behind her. Before the vibration ceased, Meridia leapt up and ran toward Patina. At once the roses moved to block her, erasing the spot where the old woman had knelt. "Patina!" she whispered urgently. The wind replied by spitting dust in her face. When she opened her eyes, she was alone in the yard. Only the shivering marigolds told her that what she had witnessed was real and not the trick of ghosts adrift from another time.

MERIDIA NUDGED DANIEL AWAKE and bombarded him with questions.

"What happened between them? Who is Patina calling her baby? What did Mama mean by saying 'When will you stop throwing the dead in my face?'"

Daniel rubbed his handsome face drowsily. "Can't this wait until morning?" he protested. "Look. There's a long history between Mama and Patina. I don't know much about it, and I prefer to keep it that way. Trust me, the last thing they want is for someone to come between them. Now, be a good wife and let me sleep."

"Daniel!"

Yawning, he pressed his index finger to his lips and rolled away from her.

That afternoon, Meridia waited until Eva retired to her room before cornering Gabilan. The girl was sweeping in the back garden, humming a dance tune and tapping her feet to it on the sly. She blushed with self-consciousness when she saw her young mistress approach. Meridia decided it was best to be direct.

"Did you hear Patina crying this morning, Gabilan?"

"Jerked me awake like a ghost's breath, Young Madam. Every time."

"This has happened before?"

"Oh, yes. Many times. Whenever she misses her."

"*Her?*"

"Yes. Her daughter. Have you never heard the story?"

Meridia shook her head. Gabilan looked around warily before gesturing with her eyes. Meridia followed her behind a mulberry tree.

"She lost a child," whispered the girl, leaning her broom against the tree trunk. "Many years ago. Malaria, I think. But to this day Patina believes that she was responsible for her daughter's death. Sometimes she weeps while sleeping. 'I've wronged my child,' she'll say. 'I've wronged her and no power on earth can absolve me now.' When it gets too awful, Patina sits up in bed and cuts her arms with her nails. Saps the soul right out of me when she's like that. And no one's more surprised than she is when she sees her own blood on her fingers!"

"What about Madam?" said Meridia. "What is her role in all this?"

"People said it was Madam who pulled Patina out of her grief," said Gabilan. "I don't know the particulars, but I find this rather hard to believe. Madam can be so"—she looked around anxiously—"hard and unforgiving. Don't you think so?"

Not replying one way or the other, Meridia gently examined Gabilan's face. "How long have you worked here?" she asked.

Gabilan counted on her fingers. "Six years. Patina is like a mother to me."

"Do you have any family?"

The girl shook her head. "My parents passed away when I was little. I lived with my uncle for a few years—he was a gardener here—but then he, too, died from consumption. Madam said I could stay and work for her, so Patina took care of me. Whenever I felt low, Patina would take me in her arms and tell me that the dead will eventually tire of the living. I wish it was only true in her case."

Gabilan lowered her eyes and resumed sweeping. The late sun had left a crimson gash in the sky. Having nothing more to say, Meridia walked slowly back to the house.

TROUBLED BY WHAT SHE had seen on the front lawn, Meridia began to notice things that had previously escaped her. For one, Patina was always given the shabbiest things to wear, her dresses patched up with rags and her shoes tattered with holes. For another, she was allowed to eat only after everyone in the house had finished, and by then, there might be nothing left but soup and bones. For a room, Eva assigned her a tiny windowless space behind the kitchen, and even this she shared with Gabilan. On hot nights the two abandoned the narrow cot for the floor and slept with the door open, their skin sticky with foul-smelling ointments in order to repel mosquitoes.

Nevertheless, Patina seemed oblivious to her conditions. Despite her advanced age, she worked harder than a horse, fulfilling Eva's demands from dawn to midnight, subsisting on her scraps of food without complaint. Her hobbled bones ached in the morning, but not once had she protested when Eva refused to refill her medication. The loyalty she showed her mistress baffled Meridia to no end. Since Patina spent most of her time in the kitchen, it would be so easy for her to set aside food for herself, but the thought never seemed to cross her mind. It was Meridia who pilfered for her, stowing away cakes and dishes in silver canisters, but Patina quickly put a stop to this. When Meridia used her allowance to buy her clothes, Patina declined them. "Madam provides me with everything I need," she said. "Please give these to those who are less fortunate." Often, Meridia was moved to wrap Patina's thin body in her arms, but even this small comfort, she was sure, would only distress the woman further.

TWELVE

October brought no relief from the marigolds. With every drop of autumn rain, the intractable flowers intensified their assault on the roses. Eva developed a headache whenever anyone mentioned the marigolds, and to console herself, she succumbed to long baths perfumed with aromatic oils. Convinced that the marigolds posed a direct threat to the family fortune, she turned her superstitious habit of cutting fresh roses every Monday morning to hang above the shop door into a daily ritual. "The business will fold without my roses," she warned somberly at dinner. "This table will serve its last meal when they all have been eaten alive."

Despite Elias's assurances, she was convinced that their customers were abandoning them by the droves, and sooner rather than later, they would have to sell the house, move to the dark heart of town, and live next door to strumpets and lowlifes. It was this fear that prompted Eva one day to turn the house upside down in search of things she could sell. For the first time in years, she cleared out the stacks of magazines that cluttered the hallway and sold them for a good price to a much-harassed junkman. She also harvested old china from the hidden corners of the kitchen, exhumed dusty records from the attic and surplus linens from under the bed, and turned them into money. Emboldened by her success, she told her husband and daughters the following:

"Tomorrow I'll look through all our things. The only way to survive this hardship is to stand together as a family. I promise I won't touch anything that's dear to you."

Eva did not directly enlist the newlyweds in her campaign, but that night when they were alone, Daniel said to Meridia, "We should help Mama as much as possible. There must be a few things in that closet that we can spare."

Meridia contributed Daniel's old suits and a number of her dresses to the cleaning. On that rainy Saturday, starting with the sisters' room, Eva dredged out every item she could find and determined its fate without consulting its owner. The first to go were old uniforms and childhood toys, shoes, hairpins, ribbons, and boxes of school crafts. Malin escaped with two fewer dresses and all her figurines intact. Permony did not blink when her dolls were sentenced to the pile, but when Eva began rifling through her picture books, she turned at once white and shuddered. "I'd like to keep those, Mama," she pleaded. "They're dear to me."

"Aren't you a bit old for these books?" said Eva, forgetting her promise and tossing them into the pile. Permony bit her lip and did not dare look. It was Meridia who used her quick hands to save many of the books, hiding them under the bed when neither Eva nor Malin was looking.

Although Elias guarded his bookshelves like a sentinel of death, Eva managed to walk away with a dozen encyclopedias. From the living room she swung the campaign upstairs to her room, where she yanked Elias's ties and belts from the hangers with the zeal of an avenging angel. She then fed the pile with clothes she had not worn in years, shoes that seemed to have come from another century, and scarves so colorfully patterned they cast a dizzying spell on Meridia. For every three of Elias's possessions, Eva sacrificed one of her own. Her dressing table she left completely alone—her bottles of perfume, her brushes and jewelry box, and those powders and miracle creams so indispensable to her skin. Faced with such riches, Meridia wistfully recalled the monastic contents of Ravenna's dressing table— a bowl of pins to construct her implacable knot in the morning, and a boxwood comb to undo it before bedtime.

From the back of the closet Eva produced several hatboxes. One box, decorated with drawings of ladies in muslins, was covered in dust so thick the elegant dames must have been tempted to sneeze for years. Seizing this, Eva vigorously blew on the dust.

"Heavens, I thought I'd lost them years ago!" She sat on the floor and dumped the contents onto the rug. Faded family photographs, some colored, some black-and-white, spilled all around her.

"Would you look at them? How priceless they are!"

Meridia, sitting down next to her, lifted one by the edge. "Is that Permony?"

It was indeed Permony, crawling on the floor naked with drool hanging from her chin. In countless photos, Malin varied from scowling to hissing at her own birthday candles. Meridia laughed at one of little Daniel in a clown's suit, his hair green and his face painted with grinning monkeys. There were pictures of Eva and Elias in their early years—she was slender with dark-rimmed eyes and elaborately made face, and he was fit, dapper, and thick-haired. "What silly lovebirds we were!" Eva roared with laughter when she found one of the two of them embracing. "I believe we kissed for the last time that night, a good two years before Daniel was born."

With nostalgic tears, Eva rescued more pictures from oblivion. Listening to her talk, Meridia came across a black-and-white photograph of a young woman with a little girl on her lap. The woman wore a high-collared dress with banded sleeves just above the elbows. The girl, no more than three or four, had on a white summer frock. Their heads were tilted to the same angle, their wide smiles brighter than the pearls around the woman's neck. Meridia identified the woman as Patina, for no one else had eyes as pure as hers. The little girl, then, must have been her daughter, the one she had lost to malaria. Just as she was about to show the picture to Eva, something froze Meridia on the spot. She glanced at Eva, looked back at the picture, and felt a chill shoot through her spine when she saw the smile vanish from the little girl's lips.

"Look at this." Eva extended a picture in her direction. "Daniel in primary school. Wasn't he the gangliest little boy you have ever seen?"

Forcing herself to laugh, Meridia slipped the other picture into her pocket.

SHE SHOWED THE PHOTOGRAPH to Daniel as soon as they were alone.

"Why didn't you tell me Patina's your grandmother? That girl sitting on her lap is Mama, isn't it? I never realized until now how much they resemble each other."

Startled by her directness, Daniel took the photograph and examined it.

"Where did you find this?"

"In Mama's hatbox when we were cleaning. If Patina is your grandmother—"

"Stepgrandmother," he corrected. "Mama's only her adopted daughter."

"*Only?* But wasn't Patina the one who raised Mama?"

"She was."

"And she took care of her as she would her own?"

"She did."

"Then I don't understand. Why does Mama treat her like a slave?"

Daniel, who had not seen his wife in this state, was taken aback. "Why are you upset? For one, I don't think Mama treats her like a slave."

"How can you not? She keeps Patina on her feet day and night, dresses her in rags, and gives her scraps to eat. And have you seen the inside of Patina's room? It's hardly fit for a cat to live in, let alone your grand—pardon me—your stepgrandmother."

"But it was Patina's idea to stay here and help Mama," said Daniel. "She refused to be paid, and whenever Mama bought her clothes, she declined them outright. Patina decided that everyone in the house should eat before she does, and it was she who refused to sleep in the sitting room upstairs, saying that the storage room was good enough for her. Mama never forced her to do anything. Ask Patina and she'll tell you the same."

"Who told you this? Mama?"

"Yes."

"And you believe her?"

"Of course. She's my mother."

"I see." Meridia studied him a moment, unable to argue with his simple loyalty, and then said, "You're hiding something from me. I've seen how Mama treats her. Besides, why would Patina do this to herself?"

Daniel smiled and gave the photograph back to her.

"Do you know how pretty you look when you're agitated? It reminds me of the time we found that coffin on the beach. Your cheeks were all aflame then, too, and I couldn't resist kissing you. If only I'd known that I would be marrying a woman with such boundless curiosity . . ." He laughed good-naturedly and reached for her waist.

"What did Patina do that was so unforgivable?" Meridia went on, ignoring both his touch and the amorous twinkle in his eye. "She behaves as if she's doing penance. But for what?" Meridia frowned, then met Daniel's gaze intently. "It's the other baby, isn't it? Her real daughter, the one who died from malaria."

"I told you there's a long history between Mama and Patina." Daniel knotted his hands on the small of her back and brought his lips close to hers. "Leave it alone."

For the first time in their three months of marriage, she pulled back and pierced his boyish good nature with candor.

"I won't leave it alone," she said. "So you might as well tell me."

Daniel cocked his brow and smiled, yet her burning gaze resisted his effort to capture her. After a moment he sighed and untied his hands from behind her back.

"Very well. But don't tell me I didn't warn you." He drew her to the bed and sat down. "You want to know about Patina's daughter? The poor thing died when she was a year old. For weeks, Patina couldn't eat, couldn't sleep, couldn't speak, except to howl out her loss. In his despair, her husband, a goldsmith, consulted a diviner. The man told him that unless another baby girl could be produced within three days, Patina would die from heartache. Terrified, the goldsmith scrambled about town looking for a baby girl, and by a stroke of luck managed to procure one. That baby was Mama. The second she laid eyes on her, Patina dried her tears and became a mother once more.

"For sixteen years they lived happily. Then one morning, eight days after Patina's husband died, a mysterious woman showed up at the house when Mama was at school, claiming she was Mama's mother. Patina screamed and shooed her away, threatening to have her arrested if she ever set foot in town again. Mama later heard about the incident from a disgruntled maid. She was furious when she found out that she wasn't Patina's real daughter, and that Patina had kept her mother from seeing her. She suspected that Patina's husband, the goldsmith, had procured her through some despicable act. When Mama confronted Patina, Patina denied everything. That day Patina's feet began to twist like vines—from guilt, Mama said. Since then Patina has been devoting herself to Mama, to earn back the love she had squandered. But a broken heart is difficult to heal, and Mama's a woman who doesn't forgive easily."

Something cold and sinuous fastened around Meridia's heart while Daniel spoke. When he finished, she shook her head in disbelief. "I don't think Patina is capable of meanness," she said. "That woman doesn't have a cruel bone in her body."

"You asked me, that's all I can tell you."

"Do the girls know?"

"Malin might suspect something. She's a clever girl. But I don't think Mama's told them yet. She didn't tell me until a few years ago. I always thought Patina was just a maid."

Meridia stood up and stared at him with narrowed eyes. "It doesn't trouble you?"

"What doesn't?"

"That your stepgrandmother is slaving away to atone for a wrong she committed years ago?"

Daniel sat back, an arm folded behind his head. "Then you don't understand Patina. Can't you see the joy in her face when she works? You call it penance, but I call it love. Patina is happy where she is, close to Mama and taking care of her every need. Leave her alone."

"If she's so happy, then why does she wail for her dead daughter?"

Daniel leapt from the bed suddenly.

"Let's not talk about this anymore. It's such a miserable story. I can think of a better way to spend the afternoon."

With a grin he wiped every unpleasantness from his mind. Slipping one hand beneath her skirt, he traced her leg up to her hip and then moved his fingers to the space between her thighs. "Daniel," she protested. His knowing smile slid between them like a bolt of iron. In the second before his lips silenced her, she was disturbed by the idea that many future arguments would be ended in this same way.

On the bed, the forgotten photograph rustled, although there was no wind in the room. Without anyone noticing, the smile had returned to the little girl's face.

TWO DAYS LATER, MERIDIA saw Patina whispering to a woman in the backyard. Dressed in a yellow tunic, the stranger looked to be in her forties, tall and slim with long white hands and upswept hair the color of grain. As they talked, Patina darted anxious glances at the house; before many minutes passed, the stranger slipped a small package into Patina's hand and drowned her objections with a hug. Visibly distressed, Patina hobbled back into the kitchen. The stranger watched until the screen door closed before exiting to the front of the house.

Meridia went after her. Though she had no idea what she would say, some unnamed instinct compelled her to action. She did not at once catch up with the stranger, who kept her head down as she hurried past the battling flowers to the street. The woman only slowed once she turned from Orchard Road, signaling for Meridia to approach.

"You must be Daniel's wife," she said. "You're more beautiful than I imagined."

She had a wistful oval face, apricot-shaped eyes, and a tiny crescent birthmark on her chin. She spoke in a quiet voice, and her tunic of bright yellow silk gave off the pleasing scent of lilac.

"You're too kind," said Meridia. "Forgive me if I startled you."

"Not at all. I'm Pilar, Patina's sister. I have been hoping to meet you for ages."

Her handshake was firm and steady. Her prolonged glance gave Meridia the impression that there was more to her words than she revealed.

"Patina never told me she had a sister."

Pilar smiled grimly. "Of course not. *She* makes well sure of that."

Meridia drew forward with alarm. "What do you mean?"

"I'm talking about that ungrateful, cruel, treacherous, two-faced viper. If you only knew what my sister has sacrificed for that reptile!"

"Do you mean Mama?" Meridia whispered.

"The very child my sister loved more than if her own had lived! To think that snake had fed on Patina's milk and nestled for warmth in her bosom! Do you know that she was nothing but a street baby, condemned to die in the gutter if my brother-in-law hadn't taken pity and brought her home? Oh, you should have seen the care my Patina lavished on her! She wouldn't let that baby cry, and she gave in to all her demands instantly. Every morning she rubbed coconut oil into her hair, massaged her skin with almond milk and rose powder, and worried if a crumb of dirt got between her toes. Patina had just then lost a child, you understand, so when this one showed up—this blasted serpent slinking in from the darkest pit of hell—Patina confused it with a gift from heaven. Little did she know that it would grow to bite the hand that fed it!"

Pilar's voice had grown sharp, each breath labored as she brushed her tears angrily. Meridia, with utmost delicacy, gambled her chance.

"I heard a strange woman came looking for Mama one day, claiming she was her mother. Is it true Patina turned her away before she could speak to Mama?"

Pilar's scoff exploded loud and clear. "Some mother it was! Do you know what she was? A whore! A gutter harlot! Even dogs wouldn't sniff her, so vile and odious was she. And she didn't come looking for her daughter, she came looking for gold! Threatening she would take the baby away if Patina didn't give her money. Patina flew into a rage and drove her out. Scared the woman enough that she never came back. Whatever your mother-in-law tells you is not true. That snake is incapable of saying anything but lies!"

Meridia was struck speechless. She recalled Daniel's earnest face as he recounted the story, and wondered if he believed he was telling the truth.

Pilar turned to look at the house. The distant chirping of the caged birds reached them, followed by the rich breath of the roses. All at once, Pilar began scratching the crescent birthmark on her chin.

"My poor sister," she wept. "Who could have guessed that she would spend the rest of her days as a slave in her own house?"

Meridia's mouth fell open. "Patina—Patina owns this house?"

"She certainly does!" spat Pilar. "And that jewelry shop, too! Her husband left them to her when he died—he was a prosperous goldsmith, you see—but she gave up everything to that snake. Oh, my poor, foolish sister!"

"What do you mean, she gave up everything?"

Scratching madly, Pilar winced as if some dark and bitter thing was twisting inside her. "Your mother-in-law accused Patina of deceiving her. Day and night she made Patina feel guilty for having driven her mother away, for not telling her she wasn't her real daughter. The lies she told were brazen and vicious, but they worked. For a whole year she cast such a heavy guilt on Patina, my sister grew convinced that she had sinned. On the day your mother-in-law turned eighteen, Patina signed over the house and the shop to her, convinced that the act would win back her love. Oh, I tried everything to stop her, but that snake had turned my own sister against me! When she married a year later, she put that lazy, shameless coward in charge of the shop and banished Patina into the kitchen. All these years she never gives Patina one cent, and whenever Patina falls ill, she has the nerve to say, 'It's what you deserve. Don't expect me to foot the bills.'"

At the same time that a chill entered Meridia's bones, the wind picked up and stifled her with the intoxicating breath of the roses. She remembered Patina lying on the ground, her cheek burned by Eva's hand and her voice hoarse from supplicating the dead. While the marigolds shivered, the roses had stood tall, silent like executioners. Pilar, as if seeing this same image, resumed her furious scratching.

"And that's not all," she said. "That viper was so heartless she didn't even allow the grave to remain in peace."

"The grave? What grave?"

"Why, the one where Patina buried her daughter! It once occupied the center of the front lawn, because my sister couldn't bear the thought of her baby being buried far from her. But after that snake wrested possession of the house, she had men tear down the gravestone—literally smash it to bits—dig up the coffin, and remove it to the Cemetery of Ashes. She complained that for years she hadn't been able to sleep with that grave screeching in the front lawn—lied outright that the very thought of it gave her shivers and nightmares. Ha! But Patina let her do it. And that snake didn't stop there. She planted red roses where the grave used to be and nursed them with her spite. Those abominable flowers bloomed and bloomed like nothing you have seen, erasing every trace that Patina's true daughter had once rested inside that earth!"

The chill in Meridia's bones intensified as Patina's words echoed in her memory. *My child . . . my baby . . .* Patina had been wailing on top of her daughter's grave.

Pilar stopped scratching and lowered her head in defeat. A drop of blood oozed from the birthmark on her chin.

"For years I've asked Patina to come live with me. I'm a poor woman, but as long as I can put food on the table, she's welcome in my house. She doesn't have to lift a finger there, I'll take care of her. But what does she tell me? 'I can't leave my daughter alone. She needs me, and I need her.' I say, 'What she needs is a heart, and nobody but God can give it to her.' But she gets angry when I talk like that. All she's willing to take from me is a little money, and even that I suspect she spends on *her*. You don't know how much it grieves me every time I see her, my own sister, refusing to take help from me!" Unable to control herself, Pilar covered her eyes and sobbed.

Gently, Meridia prodded, "What happened to her feet?"

Pilar let her hands fall to her sides. The spot of blood grew and darkened.

"She wouldn't tell me. One morning when I paid a visit after the baby's grave was torn down, her toes and ankles had already curled inward. It was as if someone had taken a hammer and smashed every bone in her feet."

The pain and outrage in Pilar's eyes caused Meridia to shudder. "Why haven't I met you until today?" Meridia asked.

Pilar half laughed and half scoffed at the simplicity of this question. "Do you think I'm welcome here? For twenty-five years your mother-in-law hasn't been able to bear the sight of me. She tells everyone I'm venom in her blood. There will be trouble if she knows I've been talking to you."

Meridia looked at Pilar a moment and then offered the only consolation she could. "You will let me know if I can help?"

Blotting the blood from her chin, Pilar smiled bitterly. "All these years I've been asking Patina the same question. I don't believe she will ever say yes."

She nodded at Meridia and hurried down the deserted street. The three o'clock sun glared off her bright yellow dress and left the image burning in Meridia's retina long after her footsteps faded.

On her way back to the house, Meridia covered her nose as she skirted the wilderness of the roses. Sitting on the terrace, calmly rocking herself in Elias's chair, was Malin. Her stare smashed into Meridia before she got up with deliberate slowness and went into the house. Entering the front door, Meridia caught a glimpse of the girl's feet at the topmost step of the stairs before they disappeared into Eva's room.

THIRTEEN

Except for Eva's lament that the marigolds' stench was decimating her appetite, nothing happened until the following Wednesday. That afternoon, Meridia was sewing alone in the living room when she felt a pair of eyes watching her from behind. She looked around, but to her surprise, there was no one in the room. She cleared her throat loudly and was about to resume her task when the same pair of eyes tore a hole in the back of her neck. Meridia turned around more sharply, but again saw no one. Spooked, she put down her needle and went to the hallway. There was no one there. From the clatter of spoons she knew Patina and Gabilan were in the kitchen, and at that hour Eva would be resting upstairs. Suddenly, turning back to the living room, she heard Malin laugh, a cold, wet laugh that doused her like a pail of water. Outraged, Meridia walked the ten steps to the sisters' door and flung it open. No one there. In that instant she remembered that Malin was at school; she had seen her leave that morning and the girl would not be home for another hour. Scratching her head in confusion, Meridia returned to the living room.

From then on she felt and heard Malin everywhere. Whispering outside the bathroom door while she bathed. Glaring at her from across the dinner table. Sniggering when she turned her back. But no matter how quickly she moved, she could not catch the girl red-handed. When Meridia opened the bathroom door, Malin was not there. Looking up abruptly from her plate at dinner showed her sister-in-law staring in the opposite direction. When she swung around to catch her sniggering, Malin's mouth was perfectly still, and no one took notice of the sound.

It did not escape her that since Malin saw her speaking with Pilar, Eva began to treat her differently. As early as late October, three months after Meridia stowed her bridal dress in the sandalwood trunk, Eva's initial warmth gave way to briskness. She no longer smiled and hinted when she gave orders. When Meridia accidentally dropped a spoon while setting the table, Eva did not refrain from scolding her in front of everyone. "Careful, dear!" she cried. "A husband has no need for a clumsy wife!" Now, when they went to the market, Meridia had to carry Eva's basket in addition to her own. "Gout," said Eva curtly. "I'm not to carry anything that might jeopardize my joints."

Eva's brusque treatment extended to Daniel. She demanded that he contribute his share to the household expenses, now that he was married and had more responsibilities to shoulder. At the same time, she denied his petitions for a regular salary with mounting irritation. "I've spared every penny I can, son," she said, fixing her eye on what she thought was a new pair of cuff links. "If you're truly pressed for money, I'm sure Meridia won't mind selling some of her jewelry. She hasn't laid a hand on her dowry, has she?"

Daniel shrugged off Eva's refusal as "a passing tantrum," assuring Meridia he would try again once his mother's mood improved. His strategy worked at first, but as Eva's tantrum persisted without passing, the newlyweds were forced to alter their habits drastically. They went out less and less, often having to choose between a meal from a street vendor and an inexpensive show at Cinema Garden. Daniel refrained from going to the barber until his hair swept down to his eyes. Meridia did away with purchasing lotions and perfumes. Still, Eva criticized them for spending too much. She frowned when she saw them leaving the house, even for just a stroll around the block. She scrutinized what Meridia wore from shoes to hairpins; if there was anything she did not recognize, she grumbled out loud that she wished she could afford such extravagance. Soon, Meridia learned not to browse at the market, for Eva would use this as ammunition when Daniel asked her for money.

Increasingly, Meridia aired her uneasiness to Daniel. "How long can we go on like this?" she asked him. "You must make them give you a fixed income."

"Patience, dearest," said Daniel with a smile. "Mama will come around. She always does. Besides, I don't see us starving yet."

"It will be too late once we starve. Can't you bring it up with Papa?"

"It's no use. Papa leaves every decision to Mama."

Malin, troubling Meridia further, stuck to Daniel like a shadow. The girl walked him to work every morning on her way to school. Waited for him when he came home from the shop. Sat with him upstairs while he fussed over the account books. Meridia was certain that Malin was slandering her behind her back. Through walls and across distances she could hear the girl laugh, feel her condescending glance flay her like a razor. It was this glance that brought things to a boil one Sunday afternoon, three months, two weeks, and four days after Meridia's arrival on Orchard Road. The battle that followed was simply inevitable.

That afternoon, Meridia walked into the living room and found Daniel sitting with Malin on the sofa. A pool of shadows encircled them as they talked, their voices so low they might as well have been whispering. Noticing Meridia, Malin shot her a haughty glance. Something in the girl's eyes pushed snow into Meridia's blood. The thin snort that followed—Daniel's—gave her the proof she needed.

"Dearest," said Daniel, sighting her for the first time. "Come and sit with us."

Without a word, Meridia left the doorway.

"Meridia!" Daniel leapt to his feet and ran after her. "What's the matter?"

Halfway through the hallway she fixed him a look he had never seen before.

"What did she tell you?"

"What do you mean?"

"Just now. What did Malin tell you?"

Daniel lifted his shoulders. "A boy has a crush on her. Everyone says she should be flattered. She thinks he should get a haircut and a new set of teeth."

Daniel laughed, rubbing his thumb on her chin. Meridia was not convinced.

"Was that all?"

He furrowed his brow in surprise. "Of course . . . what else?"

"Be honest. Was she talking about me behind my back?"

"Whatever made you think . . . ?" His eyes suddenly beamed with glee. "Are you jealous of my spending time with Malin? Yes, you are! I can see that clearly. Very well. From now on, I'll pay attention to you only."

Meridia stopped his teasing instantly. "Be serious, Daniel," she said, her voice rising a little. "I've watched your sister and I know she's been saying disagreeable things about me—"

She did not finish. From the stairway Eva's voice forced them to draw apart.

"Has a war broken out here? Permony! I'll toss your coat out myself if you can't hang it properly. Son! Those account books aren't going to settle themselves upstairs. Meridia! We're going to the market. Silly Patina forgot we need flour to make bread. Malin, would you like anything from the baker's, dear?"

Darting up and down the hallway, Eva dissolved all tension from the air. The newlyweds traded stares, then separated as told. At the last second Malin came out of the living room. The look she leveled at Meridia was sharp and loaded with disgust.

THE NEXT AFTERNOON, MERIDIA was dusting in her room when a pair of eyes again tore a hole in the back of her neck. This time, more to her relief than to her astonishment, she turned to find Malin standing at the door. The girl still had on her blue school uniform, her long hair secured by a band and her eyes the only things alive in her bloodless face.

"If you have something to say, then say it," said Meridia. "I know you've been talking to Mama behind my back."

A smile slow and calculating parted the girl's lips. The liveliness in her eyes extended to her mouth, which now took on a delight almost too fiendish for her thirteen years.

"You're wearing her necklace."

"I beg your pardon?"

"The necklace Mama gave you. You wear it three, four times a week."

Meridia looked down and touched the turquoise beads around her neck.

"What if I do? I happen to like it."

Malin clacked her tongue as if something were caught between her teeth. "You're just like the rest of them. So easily fooled. When I first met you, I thought you had it in you to stick it to her."

Meridia dropped the dust cloth on the floor and faced her squarely. "What are you talking about?"

Striding into the room, Malin kicked the door shut behind her. "Can't you see how cheap that necklace is? I wouldn't be surprised if she fished it out of a garbage bin. And yet you wear it like it's the most precious thing you own."

"I wear it because I like it. Mama was generous enough to give it to me."

"Have you listened to yourself lately? Every other sentence you say is Mama this and Mama that. It makes me sick to hear you go on! Well, she's not your mother and she never will be. Why do you bend to her every wish? Why does everyone? If you only knew the things she says behind your back."

Rapidly, Meridia advanced toward the girl, but Malin did not flinch. The shrewd, calculating smile resurfaced, transforming the rest of her face into stone.

"I don't believe you," said Meridia. "I know it's you who has been saying despicable things about me."

Malin's smile twisted deeper. "How can you be sure? Maybe it's her voice you've been hearing all along."

"Why would Mama—your mother—talk behind my back? I've done nothing to displease her."

"Are you really this stupid? She's resented you from the day she met you."

Meridia stopped short of seizing the girl by the shoulders. When she spoke, her voice did not betray the needles tearing at her skin.

"What do you mean?"

Relishing every second, Malin looked Meridia over from head to foot. Her cruel smile widened, compressed, then altogether vanished.

"The evening after your first visit to the house, I stood outside her door and heard her complain to Papa. All night long. Your forehead was too proud, she said, your nose too uppity, your mouth too stubborn. 'I suppose she could pass for pretty, if you go for that sort of look . . . ' She said your hips would bury the family name on the spot—they were barely wide enough to pass a pea, let alone a baby. She said she could tell from your soft hands that your mother had spoiled you and never asked you to do anything in your life. 'If they marry, she'll waltz into this house all high and mighty and expect everyone to serve her. No, this one won't do, so we might as well keep looking . . . '"

The room had grown hot and oppressive. Clawing at her necklace, Meridia let each word fall heavily. "I don't believe you. I don't believe a single word you said."

Malin ignored this and went on with a greater relish. "The night of your wedding, she sat up till dawn fuming about your father. 'What an arrogant man! He talks to no one, is stingy with the dowry, yet thinks we're not good enough to wipe his boots!' Your mother fared even worse. 'Take one look and you know something's come loose in her brain.' In the morning, it was she who forced Papa to take Daniel to the shop. And later, after she showed you the wedding gifts and you dared ask for the rest, she almost wore my ear out by saying how ungrateful you were, how impertinent, that any other bride would be happy with half of what she gave you. Did you ever wonder what happened to the rest of the presents? I can assure you they were *not* donated to charities. What she hasn't sold will reappear when she thinks you've forgotten. Just imagine, a few months from now, you'll see your mother's precious linens spread over Mama's bed!"

"Why are you telling me this?" demanded Meridia, her eyes tight with anger.

The girl shrugged as if the answer could not have been more obvious. "To see what you'll do. What *will* you do?"

"For a start, I'll march upstairs this minute and tell your mother everything!"

Malin's laugh rang with such contempt that Meridia itched to slap her.

"What makes you think she'll take your word over mine? Here's what you'll do. In half an hour, you'll go out to the garden and stand under the sitting room window. Do not move until you hear everything she says. Do you understand?"

This time it was Meridia who laughed. "You're out of your mind if you think I'll take orders from you."

"Then don't," said Malin with a yawn. "But have the good sense to stop wearing that necklace. I've no doubt she's had it bewitched by one of her fortune-tellers. You'll never see anything clearly with it choking your neck . . ."

THIRTY MINUTES LATER, MERIDIA went out to the garden and stood under the sitting room window. It was nearing five in the afternoon, and in a short while, Daniel and Elias would be coming home from the shop. Patina and Gabilan were preparing dinner in the kitchen, and from where Meridia stood, she could see Permony studying at her green desk. The garden—littered with leaves and overgrown grass—did not seem the same place where spirited feet had danced, where gold and emerald canopies had sheltered mountains of food. Now everything was yellow, crippled by autumn, and the only scent permeating the air was the drunken breath of the roses. Meridia fidgeted a moment. Convinced that Malin had deceived her, she was on the verge of leaving when the hinges of the sitting room window squealed. All at once Eva's voice rolled down loud and clear.

"Have you noticed how much fatter and lazier Permony has gotten since Meridia came here? I could hardly get her out of bed the other day, and last night at dinner she easily put away half a chicken by herself! Heaven knows what that woman does to your sister when they're together—I once overheard her telling a story about flying cows and meditating giraffes and I was sure she was teaching Permony witchcraft! I hope to God she hasn't laid a hand on your sister, if you know what I mean. It's bad enough that she gossips with Gabilan around the clock, nosy about this neighbor and that, and neglecting their chores. I saw them whispering in the garden the other day, hiding behind the mulberry tree, and I wouldn't be surprised if they were kissing, knowing she's always in heat. Even your brother tells me he can't keep up with her, if you know what I mean, although I'm *shocked* she can still stand and walk after all those noises she makes. From the way the walls rattle you would think she's being impaled by a horse! No wonder your brother always looks wan and tired. Yet still it isn't enough for her. It's a shame her generosity doesn't carry outside the bedroom. Did you see what she gave me when I asked her to donate a few measly things? Four ratty old dresses, when her closet is full of things she never wears! I'm telling you, she's no good for this family. One of these days, if we don't watch out, she'll turn your brother against us. A woman like her is only happy when she takes what belongs to others . . ."

Meridia had heard enough. Without a sound she crept back to her room and bolted the door shut. As her head pounded against the jamb, she felt as though bullets had rained down on her body.

FOURTEEN

Her heart swelled with fury. Her pride mandated she confront Eva without delay. Recollecting every false smile and gesture, she tore the turquoise necklace and sent the beads flying across the room. To think that she had trusted Eva, served her, admired her, done all she could to please her! In her blind desire to belong, she had ignored all the signs and allowed herself to be reduced to a servant—she, the daughter of Ravenna, without a penny to her name! The more she pondered Eva's words, the more furious she became. Did Daniel know—and condone—his mother's behavior? Why did Eva let them marry if she resented her from the start?

By the time Daniel came home, Meridia had assumed something of Gabriel's detachment. She kissed him as if nothing had happened, asked how his day was with a face as inscrutable as the moon. Smiling, she did not give a hint that suspicions were even then gnawing at her, that as he spoke and she listened, she kept turning it over in her mind if he was capable of saying one thing and whispering another. Had he betrayed her by telling Eva the private moments they shared in the dark? She decided it was possible.

"What's all this?" Daniel pointed to the beads scattered across the floor.

"A mistake," Meridia replied, making no move to clean the mess.

At dinner, she put on the great performance of her life. For the first time since she left Monarch Street, she resurrected Ravenna's lessons from the dust of memories and observed them to the letter. All through the meal her chin was up, her spine stiff, her smile unassailable despite it never reaching her eyes. She scrutinized Eva with the ironclad caution of a strategist, never once betraying her desire to let her hand fly across the table and rip the mask off the perfidious woman's face. Observing the other members of the family, Meridia bit down the howling terror that every one of them might have conspired against her from the start. Were Permony and Elias aware of Eva's slander? What thought was flitting through Daniel's mind as he asked his mother to pass the salt? Malin's eyes, the only ones she avoided, were alive with taunt; like a spectator at a gruesome match, the girl perked up when Eva criticized Meridia's lamb as "tasteless." Without breaking her smile, Meridia tossed back the bait: she served herself a generous chunk of lamb and said, "Mama's right—it *is* absolutely bland," and ate it up with relish.

That night she grappled with Daniel in restive love. His touch by turns assured and alarmed her, and as she hunted for deceit in the depth of his kiss, she heard his blood murmur what could be either a curse or an endearment. At times she felt suspended between bed and ceiling, watching two strangers wrestle for the sake of friction. At other times she felt so rooted to him her skin could anticipate his hand a second before he touched her. One thing she did not allow him to do—the first since she became his wife—was to cover her mouth with his hand. When her moment came, she let out a cry so loud it vibrated all the walls of the house. Eva could do with it as she pleased.

Afterward, wrapped in her husband's arms with the disquieting sense that he had never been farther from her, Meridia brought up the question: "What happened to Patina's feet, Daniel?"

A pause in his heartbeat, or so it seemed to the ear patiently pressed to his chest. A hint of annoyance rumbled in his throat.

"Guilt twisted them. I told you. For deceiving Mama all those years."

"I met Pilar the other day. She painted quite a different picture of your mother."

A longer pause, followed by a huff that sounded more forced than indignant.

"I wouldn't listen to what Pilar says. She isn't a woman to be trusted. Why didn't you tell me you met her?"

Meridia raised her head. "I'm telling you now. Why isn't she to be trusted?"

"Because for years she's been spreading lies about us. Just ask Mama."

"Ah, your mother. Of course."

"Pilar lives in the dark part of town. You know no reputable woman lives there unless she's got no choice. People say she's a harlot who'll do anything for money."

Meridia frowned and weighed this a moment. "You're keeping something from me," she said finally. "It wasn't guilt that twisted Patina's feet."

To her surprise, he shifted her head off his chest and answered without delay.

"You're right. It wasn't guilt. It was a rock from the sky."

"A what?"

"A rock. Dropped from the sky and landed right on her feet. Mama said she saw it falling and there was nothing she could do. Why are you asking all these questions?"

Meridia kept her eyes hidden from him as if from a bright light.

"Tell me, out of all the wedding gifts, why did you choose those things for me?"

"What things?"

"The gold jewelry set from my father. The lace and the pearl earrings."

"Mama picked those out. She thought you'd like them best."

"What did she do with the rest?"

"Gave them to charities. Didn't Mama tell you? It's a tradition in our family that the bride keeps only a few things for herself."

Slowly, slowly, she slipped her eyes over his face. "What about the money?"

"Papa invested it in the shop. Mama made the suggestion and I agreed it was the best option for us."

"They took it from you?"

He laughed. "Of course not. I can withdraw it anytime, with interest."

"Anytime?"

Meridia's jaw had the tightness of stone. Pushing up on her elbow, she broke away from his arms and trained her eyes on him. "I overheard your mother talking about me to Malin this afternoon. Horrible, appalling things. Has she said anything to you?"

"Mama?" Daniel scratched his naked belly and blinked sleepily. "That's impossible. She's got nothing but praise for you."

"I heard every word myself."

"Maybe you misunderstood."

"I'm not stupid, Daniel. What's there to misunderstand?"

Her tone threw his eyes wide open. "Yesterday you said it was Malin who was saying things about you. Now it's Mama. Who will it be tomorrow? Papa?"

"I was wrong about Malin. I'm not wrong about your mother."

"What did Mama say?"

Meridia told him. Halfway through, Daniel began to laugh.

"Come on. Mama was obviously joking. Do you really think she's out to get you?" His laughter gained force, louder and deeper until it chewed up her words. "But now that you mentioned it, Permony has *indeed* put on weight since you came here."

His teasing brought things home to her, and what she saw made her drop her eyes. He was not on her side. Only time would tell if he would be. What if his carefree good humor was merely gloss, surface shine, a boyish negation of the difficult and the objectionable? And what lay beneath it frightened her even more. Bound up with his simple and unquestioning loyalty was something she had not been able to penetrate—the innate and unspoken bond between mother and son. With a shudder Meridia realized that one of these days, either with a kick or a hit to the neck, she would have to jar this resting thing inside him.

"Mama's wrong, by the way." Daniel grinned and laid a hand on her breast. "I can keep up all night if you want me to."

Saying nothing, Meridia peeled off his fingers and turned to the wall. Her mind was made up. No matter what the cost, she would show him his mother's true face.

THE FOLLOWING MORNING, AIDED by mud and shopping baskets, Meridia set off her first act of rebellion. From the house she carried the two baskets without complaint. At the market square she let Eva load them to capacity with meat, vegetables, eggs, and flour without complaint. It was on their way home that she stumbled over a puddle of mud and dropped one basket from her hand.

"How clumsy of me!" she cried, extracting the vegetables from the mud.

"Careful, dear," scolded Eva. "Thank God nothing was broken."

When they reached the next puddle, Meridia stumbled again and dropped the other basket. This time, the flour burst hopelessly from the bag.

"Careful!" yelled Eva. "That's a week's supply down the drain!"

"I'm sorry, Mama. The baskets seem particularly heavy today."

Eva grumbled and moved on. Had she paid attention, she would have noticed the marks of Meridia's nails on the flour bag.

Less than a block later, Meridia feigned her worst fall yet. Both baskets flew for ten feet in the air before smashing against a tree, breaking the eggs for sure.

"What's gotten into you?" cried Eva angrily. "Do you think money drops from the sky? I'll carry them myself from now on!"

Meekly Meridia assented. Collecting the baskets from the ground, Eva suspected foul play, but could not find proof on her daughter-in-law's face.

Back at the house, Meridia continued her rebellion. Having learned from Gabilan that Eva had again refused to refill Patina's medication, she racked her brain to help the old woman. Her opportunity came after lunch, when two friends of Eva's stopped by for a visit. Minutes into their talk, Meridia burst into the room with her best distressed face.

"Patina's in pain, Mama, and there isn't a single tablet left! The pharmacist said he hasn't been paid and refused to refill. 'But this is a mistake,' I told him. 'Mama's never late on such things.' Oh, what should I do? Patina's in awful pain!"

Eva, glaring, responded as she had predicted. "Why, you silly goose, pay him, of course! Get my purse over there and take what you need." Then indignantly to her friends: "That harebrained pharmacist must have me confused with another customer. I have never paid a day late in my life!"

Hiding her smile, Meridia rushed out of the room with the money. In this way, she not only secured a two months' supply of medicine for Patina, but also discovered that Eva would do anything to save face.

With nothing to lose, Meridia grew more daring in the next five days. Increasingly, she defended Permony against Eva, fabricating excuses, drawing Elias into the fray, and, when nothing else was to be done, snatching the girl outright from her mother's talons. More and more she disregarded Eva's instructions, and always had a dozen replies ready to back her up. When told to put more salt in the soup, she sprinkled pepper instead and proved the flavor enhanced. When ordered to prepare a dish for six, she made it for eight, to make sure there would be leftovers for Patina and Gabilan. She was clever enough not to engage Eva in an out-and-out war, but outfoxed her gently and skillfully. Foremost on her mind was the dowry money. One way or another, she would have to force Eva's hand and recover what was left.

At around this time, the dying stench of the roses began to afflict her while she slept. Her nose clogged, her throat rasped, eyes watered, face swelled, lungs pounded with coughs. Even odder, this malady seemed to infect only her and never lasted beyond dawn. On the second night of torment, bathed in cold sweat and coughing her lungs out, Meridia nudged Daniel awake and asked if he was troubled by the stench. "What stench?" he growled from the far edge of sleep. "Smells just like Mama. It's your hacking that bothers me."

On the sixth day of her rebellion, Meridia found herself alone in the kitchen with Patina. It was early on Sunday. Except for Gabilan, who was mopping the living room floor, the rest of the house had not moved from their beds. Hunched over the stove, Patina was stirring a pot of red bean soup when she surprised Meridia by speaking.

"Please stop. Upsetting Madam isn't going to get you what you want."

Putting aside the ginger she was peeling, Meridia proceeded with caution. "I'm defending myself, Patina. I heard what she said about me, and from Pilar, what she did to you. You know she won't stop until she wears out every inch of me."

Patina turned. For the first time, her childlike eyes clouded with displeasure.

"Pilar spoke to you? She promised me she wouldn't."

"I'm grateful she did. Everyone else has kept a secret and played me like a fool."

The cloud in Patina's eyes grew heavy. "My sister is a good woman. A loving, generous woman. But she has very confused ideas about Madam."

"She didn't sound confused to me," said Meridia. "On the contrary, it's that woman upstairs who's been deceiving me from the start. Everything Pilar said about her has turned out to be true."

Patina winced as if the words had physically hurt her. "Don't say such things. You don't know her the way I do. She made my milk flow again. No one but she could make my milk flow again."

Meridia's eyes flew open. "What do you mean?"

Patina bowed her head. "My milk dried when my baby died," she said softly. "When I thought I'd never nurse another child, she came along and made it flow again. I rocked her and she laughed and she drank my milk and it flowed. Don't tell me that wasn't a miracle! How could she be false if she made my milk flow?"

Too astonished for words, Meridia put her hand on Patina's shoulder. The old woman began sobbing and went on. "It was my fault. I was the one who let her down. My love fell short when she needed it most."

Patina ran her fingers through her scalp, tearing out a great clump of white hair in the process. Horrified, Meridia took hold of her wrist.

"That's not true! You loved her more than any mother ever could. It wasn't your fault she turned out to be cruel and deceitful."

"My baby . . . my daughter," wept Patina. "Please. My child, my baby."

Suddenly, Meridia realized her mistake. All this time Patina had not been crying for her buried child, but for Eva. Eva alone was her baby, her blood, the one she had searched and mourned for that morning among the roses. With this came another realization, so shocking and unthinkable that Meridia almost reeled from the impact. Daniel had spoken the truth after all, if only a part of it.

"She maimed your feet." Meridia managed to keep her voice from shaking. "She maimed you with a piece of the gravestone after she ordered it smashed. The rock from the sky. Is that how she did it? With a stone bearing your own daughter's name?"

On the stove the red bean soup was boiling. Patina turned to stir it, her thin hands shaking, her eyes never answering Meridia one way or another.

"Hand me that bowl, please," said the old woman weakly.

"Why did you let her get away with this, Patina?"

"The white bowl. Hand it to me, please."

"You owned this house. And the shop. She's got no right to treat you like this."

"The white bowl. Please."

Meridia handed her the bowl. Patina, now trembling all over, ladled soup into it, splashed by the tears she was powerless to hold back.

"Take this to her." Patina placed the bowl on a tray and lifted the tray toward Meridia. "There's no need to apologize. She'll understand."

Meridia was more shocked by Patina's insistence than by her suggestion. "I won't do it! I've done nothing wrong."

"Please. Take this upstairs."

"I won't submit to her, Patina. My mother did not raise me to be a slave!"

Patina's trembling intensified to such a level that Meridia had to relieve her of the tray. At this point, a warm and carefree laughter erupted from the doorway.

"Did not raise you to be a slave! Ha-ha! What a flair you have for language, Meridia. Did you learn this from your mother? If I didn't know any better, I'd say she's one remarkable woman."

Blood drained from Meridia's face. Turning slowly, she gripped the tray with all her nerves so they would not betray her. Eva stood in the doorway, calm and apathetic as though she were merely looking in on her way to the market. At the first glimpse of her mocking smile, a hard thing knotted up inside Meridia—the closest she had ever felt to hatred. Somehow, gathering the pride and dignity she had inherited from Ravenna, she caught Eva's stare and flung it back across the room.

"My mother *is* a remarkable woman."

Eva's laugh had the soothing touch of springtime. It was when she spoke that she took on the menace of winter.

"Shall I tell you about your precious mother? You accused me of maiming dear Patina. Have you ever accused your mother of maiming your father? You see, I did my homework before I let my son marry you. A skilled fortune-teller, blessed with access to the right spirits, can tell you the past as well as the future."

She paused to regard Meridia's clenched face with imperturbable amusement. The fearsome blade that was her mouth gleamed and sharpened by the second.

"Would you like to hear what the spirits told me? Your mother, they said, lost all interest in your father three days after you were born. Apparently, she became so disillusioned by the thing she ejected out of her womb—you—that the thought of being touched by her own husband repulsed her to the core. One day, when your father demanded pleasure, she chased him from her bed like a flea and threatened to shear off his manhood if he so much as made another move. To retaliate, your father did what any degenerate would—found a perch between another woman's legs. Your mother discovered this soon enough. One night—dark and stormy it must have been—she lost her mind and attacked him while he slept. If you think this is sordid melodrama, guess what her weapon of choice was. An ax! Ha-ha! She must have read one too many potboilers and fancied herself a jilted, ax-wielding lover. Your father awoke in time to save his life, obviously, but not his shoulder. The blade hacked through his bones and left him with a stoop. Tell me, dear, do you find this as amusing as I do?"

Meridia did not hear the last words, for everything was rushing at her all at once. The kitchen was spinning, the floor bobbing, the ceiling plunging, and in the midst of the commotion she saw a blinding flash leap up from the haze of nightmares. Lit by the moon, traveling at great speed in the dark of night, the ax swung to its lethal destination. Meridia heard the crash and the familiar tumble, followed by the terrible scream that could have come from no other throat but Gabriel's. Spinning, spinning, the haze dissolved and her eyes flew from Patina hunched by the sink to Eva laughing in the doorway. Eva. Soaking up every twitch of pain that coursed through Meridia's face.

Collecting herself, Meridia strode toward the door. Eva met her halfway. Before either one knew it, they were glaring at each other with only the length of a grown man between them. Meridia felt no fear as she lifted the tray and smashed it to the floor. The porcelain bowl jumped, made an arc toward Eva, and shattered to bits. Eva shrieked and drew back, but not before the red bean soup splattered her white dressing robe. For an instant there was only silence. Then Eva's battle cry set everything into motion.

"How dare you!"

Patina rushed to help, but Eva shoved her to the floor. Meridia stood still with eyes dark as night.

"You insolent girl! I knew you were trouble from the day I met you!"

"Yet the size of my dowry was enough to silence you. Isn't that why you let Daniel marry me? Well, you can fool *him* but you can't fool *me*. Don't think for a second you can do with the money as you wish."

"How dare you accuse me of stealing from my own son! Daniel knows very well he can take back the money anytime he wants."

"Then give it to him this minute."

"As soon as I hear him ask."

"He'll ask for it, all right."

"No, he won't."

"I'll make him ask!"

"He won't say a word."

"What makes you so sure?"

"Because he trusts me more than he does you."

The words hit Meridia harder than a blow. Before she could retort, Patina began wailing with such anguish that the two women jerked apart.

"Leave her alone!" cried Eva, seeing Meridia hasten toward Patina. "That old crow doesn't need you to take care of her."

"Neither does she need you in her life," returned Meridia. "Heaven knows why she loves you when you don't deserve an ounce of her goodness."

"Keep talking. Before the day is over you'll be eating your own words."

"Very well. I'll let you know how they taste."

Enraged, Eva stormed out of the kitchen. Gently, Meridia lifted Patina from the floor. "Don't worry," she said. "I won't let her hurt you anymore."

It was after they were both standing that Meridia realized her own legs were bleeding. She lifted her skirt and found pieces of porcelain stuck to her flesh.

SHE HAD NO TIME to examine her feelings or ponder the consequences of her actions. When she returned to her room, Daniel was already dressed in his work suit.

"Mama wants me to go to the shop," he explained.

"Today's Sunday."

"Papa has a meeting scheduled but he's unwell. I'll be home at two."

"I need to speak to you, Daniel. It's urgent."

"Can it wait, dearest? The partners don't like to be kept waiting."

She detected no difference in his manner, but neither did he notice the cuts on her legs. As he kissed her good-bye, a wave of worry nearly drowned her on the spot. While Meridia was consoling Patina, Eva might have come up with a move that could seal her doom.

Master and mistress did not come down at breakfast or lunchtime. When Gabilan knocked on their door, Eva sent her away with a sharp word. All morning long, Meridia kept her ears attuned to the noises upstairs, but heard nothing. Malin's cunning glance was her sole indication that the bees were in full session, and Elias, in all likelihood, had been placed in the executioner's box without the possibility of escape.

After lunch, Meridia retired to her room. Too anxious to do anything, she sat on the bed and prepared herself for the worst. Ten minutes later, Eva's door slammed open, angry steps slapped down the stairs, and Meridia's four walls at once shook from the tremor. She got up without hurrying and bolted both the hallway and garden doors. The furious sound of Elias's breathing reached her before his fist met the hallway door.

"Open up!"

Meridia sat back down on the bed with her hands calmly knotted in her lap.

"Open the door, goddamn you!"

A whisper in the hallway. Footsteps around the room. And then Eva's loud curse when she found the garden door was also locked. Now both doors were being pummeled mercilessly, the bolts and hinges straining to break. And yet, though it sounded as if a hundred rifles were going off at once, Meridia did not stir from her seat.

"Come out and show your face, you coward!" yelled Elias from the hallway.

"Who do you think you are to insult us like this?" cried Eva from the garden door.

This went on for some time until Eva, thwarted, rejoined Elias in the hallway. The master of the house proceeded to throw his shoulder against the door and kick it. Both were screaming loud enough to wake the dead.

"You rotten ingrate!"

"Just wait until I get my hands on you!"

An eternity seemed to have passed before Daniel's voice rose in the hallway.

"What's going on, Papa?"

"Your wife insulted your mother! Calling her things you wouldn't wish on your worst enemy!"

"I beg your pardon?"

"She called her a liar and a cheat—"

"A thieving, two-faced snake," clarified Eva.

"—and accused her of abusing Patina! Where would that old woman be without your mother's generosity? Yet your coward of a wife called her vile and heartless."

"And to spite me further—"

"She threw a whole steaming pot of soup at your mother! Look at her legs all scalded and her dress bloody like she's been butchered!"

"I don't believe it," gasped Daniel.

"Are you calling me a liar?" Eva stifled an indignant sob. "Has she turned you against me? My own son, my flesh and blood?"

"It's obvious her insane mother and depraved father never taught her how to respect her elders," said Elias. "It's time she learned we're not barbarians in this house!"

The bedroom door flew open, startling Eva and Elias into silence. Bathed in a flame of fury, eyes wild with animal courage, Meridia was both fearsome and glorious to behold.

"Leave my parents out of this. You're not good enough to wash their socks."

"Listen to her talk, more arrogant than a queen," said Eva through her tears.

Elias lunged forward. "You owe my wife an apology."

"I owe her nothing."

"Then how do you explain this?"

Eva, crying and wincing, still had on her white dressing robe, now splotched in big red stains that did not previously exist. Her feet displayed wounds the soup could not possibly have caused.

"I take no responsibility for her make-believe," said Meridia.

Daniel took her elbow. "Dearest, did you say those things to Mama?"

"She certainly did. Patina saw everything. Patina!"

Like a terrified child, Patina hobbled in from the kitchen. Instantly Eva and Elias were upon her, asking so many questions with such rapidity that the old woman could only stare from one to the other in misery.

"Did she or did she not throw the soup at me?"

"Speak up! Why are you standing there shaking like an idiot?"

Meridia would not tolerate this. "I threw the soup. And I don't regret it one bit."

"She admits it!" exclaimed Elias triumphantly. "You see what kind of demon you've married, son?"

Meridia gave her father-in-law a look so cutting that any other man would have smarted from the slice. But Elias—she saw right away—was not himself. Bloodshot and haggard, he looked as though he had not slept in days, and there was a ruthlessness to his movement that told her he was demented enough to do anything. Only once had Meridia seen that look, the night Eva got him into a rage over the neighbor's mastiff. All of a sudden it hit her with a bolt of panic. Eva's bees had put in more than one morning's work on Elias. In the flush of her rebellion, Meridia had misunderstood one thing: the dying stench of the roses was not meant to afflict her sleep, but to mask the bees' insidious drone. For five nights, while her eyes watered and her throat rasped, the abominable insects had been laboring overtime—accusing, distorting, toting up every act of disobedience. She could only imagine the damage they were causing Elias.

"Is it true, Meridia?" asked Daniel. "Why did you do it?"

She had avoided his eyes until then. What she saw now confirmed what her heart already knew. He looked baffled and wounded, yet though her whole being ached with tenderness for him, she recognized him for the boy he still was.

"What does it matter?" she said. "You won't take my word over theirs."

"Dearest! What are you saying?"

"Don't listen to her, son," said Eva. "Can't you see how she's toying with you?"

"If she doesn't apologize, Daniel, there's no room for her in this house."

"What do you—but that's absurd, Papa!"

"Put her in her place, Daniel. Who will defend your mother if you won't?"

Eva backed this with a wracking sob.

"We need to calm down, all of us," said Daniel. "I'll take Meridia out for a walk. When we get back, we'll discuss this rationally."

Elias looked as if he was ready to explode. "Has she turned you into a woman? Robbed you of manhood *and* dignity? Tell your wife she's got two words to choose from. Sorry or good-bye. Which will it be?"

Daniel was speechless. It was Meridia who made the decision for him.

"I'll leave," she said. "There's room for me in my father's house."

For a few seconds no one said anything, realizing the challenge had been thrown and taken too far. And then Eva looked at Elias until he roared in anger.

"Then leave at once! I won't tolerate your impudence a moment longer. And don't you dare take anything that doesn't belong to you!"

Not deigning to reply, Meridia went into her room for the most precious thing she owned. At the bottom of the sandalwood trunk, hidden beneath layers of her bridal dress, was the gold jewelry set Gabriel had given as part of her dowry, the same one Eva had decided she could keep. She had no time for anything else. Lashed by the voices behind, Meridia took the velvet box and returned to the hallway.

Daniel moved toward her, but Elias pushed him back.

"Stay where you are," he warned.

"Papa! You can't do this to us."

"Don't call me Papa if you're stupid enough to defend that varmint. In two months' time, I'll marry you to a wife who knows how to respect you."

"Papa!"

Eva, flooded in tears, enfolded Daniel in her arms. "It's all my fault, son. I knew from the start she wasn't right for you, and yet I let you marry her. It's best to let her go."

"*You* let go, Mama. Meridia isn't leaving without me."

Without warning, Elias punched the wall two inches from Daniel's head.

"Enough! Follow her out that door and you won't see the inside of this house ever again."

Meridia watched in silence as Daniel, who stood well above his father, stepped back. The air had grown so still that his heart was pounding audibly in her ear. When their eyes met, she laid bare with all her soul the gentle memory of their caresses, and when it did not draw him to her, she began to pity him without anger. He looked so pained and aggrieved that she thought she must take it all back, take back her words and her pride as long as he was spared this anguish. Yet no sooner did the thought occur than a steel rod slid up her back and made her say the one thing Ravenna never could to Gabriel.

"Good-bye, Daniel."

Meridia turned. Silenced Eva with a look. Sailed past Elias as if he did not exist. Clutching the velvet box to her chest, she strolled past the door where Permony sobbed and Malin stood openmouthed, transfixed with awe. She did not look back when she reached the terrace and the front door slammed behind her.

There she waited.

The caged birds were silent and the marigolds clamored and she waited.

She waited and still he did not come.

FIFTEEN

Ravenna had been mute for three months, three weeks, and three days, and not a soul knew it. The morning after Meridia's wedding, she had been midway through addressing a bowl of pea shoots when she realized that her mouth was making no sound. For the first time in sixteen years, her dark and private language failed to animate the kitchen. Astonished into silence, the knife cut without zest, the bread did not rise, the kettle refused to boil. The maids, by then accustomed to their mistress's odd habits, took little interest in the sudden quiet. Gabriel noticed nothing. Since the morning she outraged him by smashing eighteen dishes in the dining room, he had yet to spare her more than a moment's glance.

Muteness had a way of beating Ravenna. By the end of the first week, she had grown so weary she could not shake her fist when she saw the yellow mist swirl up the stone steps. When morning came, a gulp was all she could muster when she smelled the baboon-faced mistress on Gabriel. Meridia's absence had done it. Took away her speech and rusted the hate she had so meticulously preserved. Despite her years of training, Ravenna missed her in the dreadful quiet of the plates, in the empty doorways—she missed the footfalls that no longer filled the house. She missed Meridia as if she were missing a limb; the only thing worse was the certainty that her child was gone forever.

Many times the silence nearly drove Ravenna to Orchard Road. Before her feet started, however, a memory stopped her: a flash of metal slicing in the dead of night. Along with this came shame and sorrow. She would slap her hands over her tears, twist her knuckles deep into her eyes, but not once, not ever, would she allow doubt and regret to come between her and her daughter.

Ravenna remembered the night the cold wind knocked her to the ground. All she did was fasten the window, but before she knew it, she was pinned helplessly against the wall while Meridia's bassinet flew across the room. That night the world suddenly teemed with dangers, herself helpless and a stranger in it, and in the days that followed she lost her reason and her strength. For months after, she saw Gabriel shiver and she could do nothing. He could not sleep a wink, he said; the bed was colder than snow, and she could not help him. Even when she saw ice forming on Meridia's lips, she could do nothing. "The wind will run its course," she had assured him. "Try to keep warm a little longer." He gave her his word that he would stick by her. Three months after the wind turned the house upside down, the yellow mist appeared. The next day she twisted her hair into a knot because she knew he had not kept his promise.

She tried her best to exonerate him. Failing that, she gave him ample opportunities to explain. But Gabriel said nothing. He sulked and watched her nurse Meridia and went out into the mist and said nothing. Her pride revolted. She had asked for understanding, and in turn, he had let another woman desecrate what belonged to her. There was nothing in the world that would make her forgive.

When she suspended the blade above his head, her only wish was to forget. Shush the anger that was howling in her heart. Obliterate his lies and the damage they caused. When she swung, she did not think of it as an end, but as a beginning. Of all the things that happened next, she only remembered one—Meridia howling in her bassinet, a second before the metal struck. That cry had saved Gabriel's life, but not her own. The blade might have missed, but her child had witnessed what she should not have. After what she had done, Ravenna could only view her daughter through a curtain of forgetfulness.

The passing years diminished neither her shame nor her anger. By degrees the curtain thickened, made opaque by misunderstandings and stifled intentions. To vent her rage, she stormed the mist and took up a dark and private language. Neither of these brought her closer to Meridia. Gabriel's ultimate victory was not in smashing her heart, but in condemning her to watch their child grow without feeling adequate to love her.

When the girl asked for her freedom, Ravenna thought it was the least she could give her. Little did she know that the days of muteness would be long and vengeful. Not since she wrestled with the cold wind had she felt so tired, so exposed and beleaguered by the tenacity of memories. Not even the thought of Gabriel's mistress stirred her. In the night she no longer had strength to storm the mist. The stillness that answered when she called for Meridia convinced her that she was shouting from beyond the grave.

Then three months, three weeks, and four days after Meridia left, the muteness came to a halt. That afternoon, seasoning a goose in the kitchen, Ravenna seized up all of a sudden and dropped the pepper mill she was holding. Someone was approaching the front door, and from the way the mist bellowed, she understood it was no ordinary visitor. Sharply, she lifted her chin and tossed back her shoulders. Before her brain could articulate the miracle, her feet had flown of their own accord. Reaching the front door, she threw it open and was overcome by the sight of a nymphlike figure shambling up the stone steps. She ran on ahead of the mist and pulled the limping phantom into her arms.

"Child!" she cried, just before Meridia's knees scraped the earth.

WHEN GABRIEL HEARD ABOUT his daughter's expulsion, he did not burst into laughter or throw her out of the house. Instead, he shattered a table with his fist and swiftly dispatched an ultimatum to Orchard Road. Meridia, moved, observed his reaction with gratitude, even though a part of her suspected he was outraged chiefly for his own name.

That night, the first in her memory, Gabriel let the yellow mist drift by. When the doorbell rang, he emerged from the study in a solemn black suit and took his place in the center of the hall. "Go to your room," he ordered her sternly. Meridia climbed the stairs and hid behind the banister. A moment later, a maid ushered Eva and Elias into the hall, followed by a terrified Daniel. Eva was high-colored and defiant, Elias pale and frazzled. Before they said a word, Gabriel lunged for Daniel, seizing his collar without ceremony.

"Son of a bitch! I wouldn't wish a cockroach to have you for a husband!"

Reeling with terror, Daniel sputtered for breath.

"Control yourself, sir," said Elias. "There's no need for this kind of behavior."

Though he sounded grave, Elias made no move to help his son. It was Eva who jumped and placed herself between the two men.

"My son has done nothing wrong! It's your daughter who's perverse and impertinent! She said she couldn't care less if we live or die."

Gabriel's violent turn forced Eva to step back. For a moment it seemed that he would throttle her as well. Spying from the top of the stairs, Meridia was seized by affection for her father.

"Watch what you say, madam. I can spot a lie from miles off."

"She's dishonored us!" shouted Eva with equal violence. "She abused me in my own house and refused to apologize. I don't know what kind of daughter you think you raised, but it's clear she's selfish, spoiled, callous, and arrogant. It's a pity you never took a whip to her back when she was little!"

Before a word could escape Gabriel, a thin shadow sliced in between him and Eva. Twice the room exploded, stunning the men and jolting Meridia from behind the banister. The next thing they saw was Eva nursing her face. Towering over her with a splendid calm was Ravenna.

"How dare you!"

Livid, Eva turned to Elias, who stood immobile with his jaw open.

"Are you going to stand there and let her assault me? Do something!"

Eva's narrow eyes were gutting him. Seeing no reaction from Elias, she turned to Daniel with a deathly aim.

"First the daughter, now the mother. Brand this moment into your memory, son. Tell your sisters they weren't conceived from the seed of a man, but from the sap of a coward!"

Elias shuddered. Slowly a faint smile surfaced on Ravenna's lips. Gabriel, who had been watching his wife with a mixture of wonder and disbelief, hollered with laughter at the other man's expense. It was this laugh that snapped Elias into action.

"Let me handle this!" Looking at the far wall behind Gabriel, avoiding Ravenna's eyes at all costs, Elias bellowed, "Your daughter must apologize to my wife. I don't see any other way to resolve this."

Gabriel smirked. "What if she doesn't?"

"But she must!"

"What if I forbid her? What are you going to do?"

Elias swallowed hard. Sidling up to his side, Eva declared decisively, "Then we won't take her back. She can stay here and look for another husband."

"You've gone too far, Mama!" Daniel broke his silence for the first time. "Meridia is accountable to no one but myself. I intend to have her back at any price."

"Quiet!" rebuked Elias, suddenly emboldened. "That woman you married is more trouble than she's worth."

"Don't bully me, Papa. I'm taking my wife home no matter what you say. If I lose her then you'll lose me. I'm prepared to fight anyone who comes between us."

A slow and chilling applause stunned the room for the second time. Without losing her calm, without even clenching her eyes, Ravenna inspected Daniel as if she might reduce him to ashes.

"How noble of you," she said. "If only you had delivered that speech before it came to this. You're mistaken now if you think I'll let my daughter return to hell."

Gabriel stared at his wife as though he had never seen her before. At that moment something he had condemned to die stirred suddenly within him.

"You heard the mistress." Gabriel said. "Meridia stays here. I'll send for her things in the morning."

Eva gasped furiously. "What do you take us for? Have we no say? No weight in this matter? So be it. From now on, your daughter can consider herself a free woman."

Meridia was on the verge of exclaiming, but Daniel beat her to it.

"Have you all gone mad? She's my wife, for heaven's sake! I'm not leaving this house without her!"

Ravenna swung on him without a warning.

"Listen to me, little boy! I delivered her to you once, and you failed to honor and protect her. I'll be damned if I should do so again. Now leave my house and never enter it while I still have breath in my lungs."

Eva was screaming now, spurring Elias to defend their name, but to Daniel, all else had become silent. Ravenna's eyes had cut him, deep in a place he could not heal. In the years to come, it was those eyes he would remember and refuse to forgive.

Gripping the banister, Meridia bit her lip to keep her tears from falling. The staircase reared, galloped to the roof, and suddenly a thousand steps stretched between her and the mayhem below. From that great distance she began to shout as she watched the speck that was Daniel leave without a single glance in her direction.

EVA DID NOT WAIT for Gabriel to carry out his threat. Early the next morning, she dispatched Gabilan to Monarch Street with a sack full of Meridia's clothes. Sweaty and breathless, the servant girl barreled right through the mist and hollered for Meridia.

"Oh, Young Madam, they turned your room upside down as soon as you left!"

"Slow down, Gabilan." Meridia took the sack and stowed it in the hallway. "What happened?"

"Master ransacked all your drawers, even pried the ones that were locked. He snatched your dresses from the hangers, your undergarments from the drawers, tossed them to the floor, and spat on them. Madam egged him on. She made him smash your dressing table and your jars and powder bottles. Miss Permony cried and cried in the hallway, but Miss Malin went up to Madam and shouted at her. She tried to rescue your wedding pictures, but Master was like a man possessed. Madam had him go at it for a good hour, then she took some of your things and carried them upstairs—your brooch, your lace, your gloves, the pearl earrings she herself had given you for your wedding!"

Gabilan was in tears and Meridia found it increasingly difficult to swallow. Had she not taken the jewelry set at the last second . . .

"And Young Master?" she forced herself to ask. "Where was he during all this?"

"Young Madam, I haven't told you the worst of it. It was wrong and cruel, what they did to him . . ."

Gabilan, overcome by sobs, needed a minute before she could speak again.

"When Young Master tried to chase you, Master grabbed him by the throat and wouldn't let go. 'You weakling!' he shouted. 'No son of mine runs after a woman like a whipped dog!' He began calling him names, things too ugly to come from a father's lips. Whenever Young Master tried to speak, Madam drowned him with her cries. Provoked to the limit, Master then did something unthinkable. He dragged out your wedding dress from the bridal trunk, wrestled it to the floor, and began clawing it like a mad beast. It was the ghastliest sound I ever heard, all that cloth and lace screaming in pain. Young Master backed away from the room and stood very still and I could see something go out of his eyes. He looked as if he was watching an animal being gutted."

While Gabilan continued to sob, a cold sensation clamped down on Meridia's spine. She could not speak, could not move, could not locate the outrage she ought to have felt. All she could see was Daniel's face, lost and wounded, washing itself up on the plundered wall of her heart.

TOO RAW, TOO BROKEN, Meridia would not see Daniel that day. Though he knocked and pleaded, she did not allow the front door to open. Angry on her behalf, the ivory mist attacked him, and finally succeeded in driving him away by yanking off all his clothes and sending him to chase after them. He did not give up. When the next day found him standing with three layers of clothes on the stone steps beneath her window, it was another force that came charging to her defense.

It seemed he had stood there for hours. She could hear him arguing with one of the maids when a furious voice blasted him like a whirlwind.

"Why are you still here? Can't you see she doesn't want you? Whatever claim you had on her, you gave it up when you proved yourself a coward!"

Ravenna wielded a broom, chased him off the steps as she

might a stray pup. As Daniel scurried, mortified, into the street, the ivory mist pelted him with laughter. Then and there, though she did not know it, Ravenna made herself his enemy for life.

Up in her room, eyes swollen from crying, Meridia let the curtain fall from her fingers. How long would it take until his name was erased from her lips, his face reduced to a shimmer of a dream?

SIXTEEN

The impasse continued for weeks. Despite threats made on both sides, neither house was willing to back down. When Eva declared to Monarch Street that she had engaged the services of a renowned attorney, Gabriel gave her three days to produce the divorce papers. When Eva shot back that Meridia's transgressions required more than three days to tabulate, Gabriel laughed in her face and said that he could have the marriage annulled in half the time. More arguments followed, more vituperative exchanges, during which no one noticed that the newlyweds themselves were silent.

Immersed in the task of forgetting, Meridia paid little attention to the stalemate. She nodded carelessly to Ravenna's plan of sending her abroad, ready to sign whatever document was put under her nose. She had no desire to eat, speak, or do anything that might make her remember. At times she was without emotion, almost without consciousness; at others she could not stand up without trembling. In the loneliest hours she folded her knees to her chest and rocked without sound. The wound was deep, immeasurable. The pain of knowing he had not come to her rescue.

Despite her attempt to foil memory, she started remembering

how they met. The Festival of the Spirits. The Cave of Enchantment. His reckless and fatal disregard—she knew it now—of the seer's warning. She remembered their first dance in Independence Plaza, their clandestine meetings around town, the kiss on the beach when his touch had allayed the horror of the gutted fawn. She remembered that glorious day in spring when Eva's laughter had seduced her, wrapped her so tightly like a quilt that she traded the cold of Monarch Street for its warmth. How could she have expected happiness when every room in the house reeked of deceit?

She found comfort in shadows. In foundering doggedly into gloom. Nothing mattered then, not the recollection of his smile or his hot breath on her nape. And she would have been content to sink, for fifty or a hundred years perhaps, had she not been roused by a melody from another time. It happened one night when visions of him burned like live coal in her eyes. Part humming, part singing, the lush and vibrant song that had lured her into the Cave of Enchantment now drew her toward the window. "Nothing but a cheap trick," Daniel had scoffed at the seer. But just as she did not feel swindled then, she did not refrain from lifting the curtain now.

It was nothing short of a siege. There he stood, just outside the reach of the mist, shamelessly appealing to her sentiment. Despite the wind, he wore neither hat nor coat, his pose plaintive, hair tousled, face handsome and penitent. There was no drizzle that night, yet he appeared wet to the skin. Torn by a hundred feelings, Meridia pulled the curtain shut.

The next evening he was back. No sodden clothes, no music, only flowers in his hand. The banality of the gesture made her grit her teeth, yet tears stubbornly sprang to her eyes. How many nights had he spent out there? How many more was he prepared to stay?

Twenty-seven, she counted. Perhaps twenty-eight. He stood there waiting in fog and heat, taking his post after the yellow mist departed and deserting it before the blue arrived. It was too late, she thought. She did not know how to trust him again. What did he think he might accomplish, wooing her with songs and flowers? When she needed him most, he had not been there for her. And yet, as he continued to disrupt her sleep with phantom kisses, she began to crave the weight of him, the sun-and-sea smell of his skin. In league with cicadas and moonlight, he assailed her with a mood so rapturous she began to feel his touch across the distance. His gaze never wavered from her window. She knew this, too, without having to lift the curtain.

On the last night of his watch, the wind pounded the window like an angry hound. Just when it dawned on her that this might be the same wind that years ago had knocked Ravenna to the ground, the window blew open with a great force. A cold gust punched Meridia flat on the bed, penetrated her stomach, hardened inside into a knot. The blow stilled her for an instant, not painful but vital enough for her to understand. The next second she was flying out of the room, racing down the hallway, thumping the banister, reaching the front door in six steps. The massive oak swung without being touched. The ivory mist whisked to the side. Daniel was running with his arms out.

"Please forgive me," he said. "I'll do anything to win you back."

She gasped hard for air, filling her lungs to the brim. It was too much, his arms around her, his heart in her ear, pounding along to her own intractable rhythm. She lifted her head quickly and kissed him.

"Why did you stay away?" he said. "It was winter here without you."

She dug her fingers into his shoulders, looked at him sternly through her tears.

"To put back what you broke. Did you think it was easy to do?"

His pale eyes gleamed with remorse. "I swear I'll never hurt you again. Will you take me back? Will you give me another chance?"

She did not answer but allowed him to hold her. By degrees the howling died to a soft moan. Telling herself it was not the same wind, she guided his hand to her belly.

WHEN RAVENNA DISCOVERED THAT Meridia was with child, she broke her vow of decades and marched straight into Gabriel's study.

"The child's still in love and she's carrying his baby."

Sitting behind the desk, Gabriel suspended his pen midsentence. It was impossible to tell if he was more alarmed by his wife's words or her sudden materialization.

"I beg your pardon?"

"Did you not hear me the first time? You're going to be a grand-father."

Gabriel let go of the pen and leaned back against the chair. Without betraying his surprise, he tried to match her blank tone word for word.

"She told you this herself?"

Ravenna nodded. She seemed then a creature born of water or ether, marvelously unaffected by human trials. In spite of himself, he felt her unflappable attitude begin to irk him.

"What does she propose to do?"

"Go back to that boy. On her terms, of course."

"And you'll let her go—'return to hell,' as you said?"

His mocking tone hit a nerve. He took pleasure in watching her jaw clench, in disarranging her, and for a moment she seemed to retreat behind her veil of forgetfulness. But then a tremendous change swept over her face. At once she righted herself, so cold and soldierly he could not imagine a single capillary of warmth to exist inside her.

"I won't stand in her way. But neither will I allow that larcenous woman to lay a hand on her."

Gabriel sat still. Even as it dawned on him that this was the most she had spoken to him in months, their eyes clashed like daggers, scourging the deep in each other. It was Gabriel who looked away first, aware that neither of them would emerge a victor.

"Let me hear it from her mouth," he said.

A moment later, Ravenna left Meridia in front of his desk without a word. His daughter's face, in contrast to his wife's, was ennobled not by frost but by love.

"Is it true what your mother said? You wish to return to your husband?"

Meridia nodded. It did not escape Gabriel that her cheeks had the wild flush of berries.

"You want to go back to that house?"

"I want to be with Daniel."

"Even when you know his family can toss you whenever they feel like it?"

"Daniel won't let it happen again. He swore."

Gabriel's scoff was something she had more than expected.

"If you believe him, then your brain is far more addled than your mother's."

Meridia bowed her head. She realized they had been here before, hurling the same arguments, the day the matchmaker came to the house. And once again, just as on that day, she found herself dueling the onset of invisibility as his glare raked her. Whatever made her think she could sway him to her side?

And then she felt the kick in her belly. The knowledge that she was no longer fighting for herself lifted her chin and made her inspect the man who had never loved her. There was no doubt he looked older, grayer, but every line of his majestic face still retained its cruel and scrupulous hardness. Meridia decided she had nothing to lose.

"I have to believe him, Papa. He's the man I love, the father of my baby. Please don't sneer at me. Say what you want, but he's the only person who ever cared for me, who comforted and held me when the rest of the world was determined not to see me. Before I met him, I didn't know what it was like to be happy. I've forgiven him, Papa. That's also something you and Mama never taught me."

She said this with tears in her eyes. To her absolute shock, Gabriel winced and raised a hand to his shoulder. His stoop, courtesy of Ravenna, now inflamed with pain. After what seemed an eternity, he replied in a voice gentler than she had ever known.

"I'll let you go back to him. But you won't live in that house again."

Meridia drew up in surprise. "Then where will we live? You can't mean—here?"

His contempt returned to blast her. "And let his family wash their hands of him? Don't be stupid. He's still their responsibility. I won't have him live off my bounty."

"Then where do you want us to live?"

Gabriel sharpened his stare cruelly.

"I want you to understand that if you return to him, you'll be on your own. I won't give you money, you'll have to suffice on what you make. Should you find yourself out in the street again, do not expect me to provide you with shelter. Give me your word, and I'll settle the rest."

Meridia turned very pale. In the long pause that followed she came to grasp the full extent of his condition.

"Why don't you want me in your life, Papa?"

His gaze, for once, was wistful and full of pity. His answer, however, was not.

"Because your mother destroyed all the space I had for you."

Biting her tears, Meridia nodded. He did not have to ask her a second time.

"If I find myself in the street again," she said, "you'll be the last to hear of it."

GABRIEL FULFILLED HIS PROMISE. Without leaving any room for negotiation, he declared to Elias the following:

"My daughter will no longer live under your roof. Neither will she abide by your wife's rules. If you want your grandchild, you will provide your son with a separate house and sufficient capital for a business. You are to give him your unflagging support, but never orders. Your wife will limit her interactions with my daughter, and

she will cease interfering in their household affairs. Should you fail
to comply with my demands, I will adopt the baby myself and wash
your name off its blood forever."

Gabriel did not stop here. After grilling Meridia with the relent-
lessness of a prosecuting attorney, he discovered Eva's deception
with regard to the dowry and the wedding presents.

"What a stupid, stupid girl you are," he berated her sharply.
"Didn't your mother teach you anything? It's too late to reclaim the
gifts, but I'll get the money even if I have to pry it from her teeth."

Thus, he added a final clause to his list of demands: the dowry
money must at once be returned to Meridia in its full amount, plus
interest.

Overjoyed upon learning he was to become a grandfather, Elias
would have accepted all of Gabriel's terms in the blink of an eye.
Nonetheless, anticipating his wife's reaction, he kept his happiness
to himself and acted up an indignant storm in her presence. He
cursed Gabriel with a perfectly livid face, calling the man "presump-
tuous, ridiculous, unconscionable, toxic, and predatory." For days he
made a big show of going to Monarch Street in a huff and coming
back hours later claiming he had at last beaten some sense into his
in-law's skull. In truth, he spent those hours conferring with his
business partners and scouring the town for a suitable place to
house his grandchild.

Eva's resistance was nothing less than epic. Day and night her
bees needled Elias, demanding that Gabriel put up the money for
the house and provide half the capital for the business. But the jeweler, for once in their marriage, found the words to thwart her. "That
man won't yield—you know how stubborn that family is. If we don't
do as he demands, he might drag us through the mud and say all
kinds of filth about us. People will talk. People will say we're mean
and heartless and stingy. There will be a scandal. Are you ready to
have the town gossip about you around the clock?"

Eva, always in dread of losing face, grumbled some more before
relenting.

"Fine, we'll do as he said. But rest assured I won't let that impudent upstart cheat us out of a single penny!"

And so in the first brilliant day of winter, while the sky sparkled and the bees went into retreat, the newlyweds moved into a tiny house on Willow Lane, ten blocks south of Orchard Road. Unbeknown to Eva, Elias had secretly furnished the rooms with secondhand furniture, hung clean cotton sheets for curtains, and spread a new rug in the hallway. A small unit connected to the house had been turned into a modest jewelry shop. It was agreed that the young couple would manage without a servant.

SEVENTEEN

The house at 175 Willow Lane wheezed with an old man's lungs. The rafters sniffled in cold, the floors in heat, and the walls never stopped coughing from their blistered paint. There were leaks in the roof, holes on the floorboards; opening a door triggered an avalanche of dust. The air, trapped by the low ceilings and narrow rooms without an outlet, smelled as if the asthmatic old man had been bricked alive in his own bed.

Yet nothing made Meridia happier. She flung the windows open, beat the air with perfumed sheets, squashed giant spiders with a broom, poured vinegar over cockroaches, scrubbed the bathroom floor until every tile gleamed. Refusing help from Monarch Street, she swept and washed and dusted for three days, polishing even Elias's threadbare furniture with a care befitting an heirloom. The house was hers. Hers. She was mistress of it as much as she was wife to her husband.

While she cleaned the house, Daniel set up the store. He painted the walls a bright yellow, sanded the floor, fitted in a window, coated the battered display cases with a brilliant varnish. He spent an entire day consulting a manual on how to arrange the space to bring the most luck, factoring into consideration the flow of air and the position of the sun at every hour. For wall decoration, Meridia pieced together an embroidery of mermaids and elf kings, magical creatures she had retained from her days with Hannah and Permony. Her work was at best elementary, yet Daniel praised it to the sky, saying it would bring them more fortune than a holy charm.

Their first dinner was both a delight and a tragedy. Without Patina's supervision, Meridia burned the rice and overcooked the pork. The mushroom soup tasted strongly of lead, and the fried bananas she had planned for dessert emerged limp and defeated from the skillet. While she contemplated her failure at the dinner table, Daniel cut out a large piece of the pork. He chewed it thoughtfully before declaring, "I've never tasted anything better in my life." Bursting into laughter, Meridia threw her napkin at him and shouted, "And I've never met a worse liar in mine!"

A few days later, Ravenna made a surprise visit to the house. Resentful, Daniel removed himself to the shop. Ravenna did not seem to mind, and began putting the lilies she brought into a vase. Refusing Meridia's offer of tea, she walked through the three rooms in the house with her absentminded grace, fluffed a pillow here, straightened a chair there, and made a lone comment on how Meridia should cook the chicken and not the fish. In five minutes Ravenna was gone, but instantly the house felt brighter, the air no longer smelling of dead flesh. An hour later, dressing a catfish for dinner, Meridia noticed that it had indeed gone bad. She scratched her head, looked around the kitchen, and sighted a chicken she had not bought sitting on the counter.

That night Meridia received another surprise. Opening the back door after dinner, she found a large, cloth-wrapped parcel lying on the doormat. The night was crowded with stars, yet the tiny yard was deserted. Meridia bent to lift the parcel and, finding it heavy, dragged it with some difficulty into the kitchen. No sooner had she untied the cloth than the sweet scent of verbena escaped into the air.

"Daniel! What on earth are these?"

Daniel quickly joined her on the floor. "Gold bars," he declared in amazement, lifting one and then the other. "They look solid, at least a kilo each."

"Gold bars? Are you sure?"

"I'm a jeweler, dearest. Who do you think put them there?"

"Smell the cloth," Meridia said without hesitation. "Who else can it be?"

He said nothing but helped her carry them to the bedroom. A day earlier, she had discovered a loose floorboard under the bed while cleaning, and had hidden the dowry money and the gold jewelry set there. To these she now added the two bars. "How did she—" Overwhelmed with gratitude, Meridia let the question drift unfinished.

When the first batch of jewels arrived from Lotus Blossom Lane, she pestered Daniel to tell her what they were. Aquamarine pendants, he said. Jade bracelets, tanzanite rings, garnet necklaces. She rolled their names off her tongue like a prayer, committing each one not just to memory but to heart. The next day she had Daniel instruct her on how to spot defects in diamonds, how to appraise gold by taste and spot genuine pearls from the counterfeit. Keeping a chart of precious stones by her bed, she recited nightly the properties of ruby and topaz, agate, amethyst, opal, and others. The thirst for knowledge lit her face like a fire in the sky. No one stopped her this time. No one took away the gems she studied with such rhapsodic fascination. After lovemaking one night, Daniel teased her that the moonstone was making her passion more unbridled. "Don't be silly," she retorted, pinching his buttocks savagely. But in her blood she knew that their future lay in the hands of those jewels.

Three days later, the shop opened with little fanfare. A few loyal customers from Lotus Blossom Lane, along with friends of family. Ravenna sent a gold-lettered banner and a basket of oranges for good luck. Elias beamed with pride, Eva found fault in everything. However, wary of Gabriel's conditions, she directed her criticisms only to Daniel. Meridia pretended not to hear. From Gabriel she received no acknowledgment.

Despite their high hopes, the next two weeks went by without a sale. The number of people who stopped in to browse could be counted on two hands.

"What are we doing wrong?" Meridia asked Daniel one night after closing.

"Patience," he answered serenely. "Our luck will turn when the time is right."

When another week went by and still nothing was sold, Meridia decided she had to do something. That afternoon she left the store early and went for a walk. How long would the drought continue? Even then Eva was already crowing to see profits. The idea that the shop would fail was unthinkable. She could not go back to Orchard Road, and Gabriel had made it clear she was not welcome on Monarch Street. They still had the dowry money to live on, but how long would it support them if things went on in this fashion? Rambling from one alley to another, Meridia battered her brains for a way out. There must be something she could do. Something to stand the business on its feet.

The answer came to her less than a minute later.

"Look up. You won't solve anything by staring at your toes."

Meridia looked up. A woman no more than twenty, fitted in boots and bangles and a revealing carmine dress from overseas, was speaking to her. Stouter, slower in movement, but with the same flowing red hair Meridia would recognize anywhere.

"Hannah!"

Her mouth fell open. Before she recovered, her old friend had enfolded her in a kiss. Time stopped then, or rather unwound to the day they had last seen each other.

"What are you doing here?" she shouted with joy.

"Keeping my husband on his toes," said Hannah with a grin. "My father retired a year ago, and out of sheer perversity, I pledged my life to another traveling merchant. So here I am, on the road once again."

Meridia laughed. "You haven't changed. How long will you stay this time?"

"Months. Years. But let's eat first. All this talking is making me hungry."

Their feet tacitly agreed on the same place: the bookshop café next to the courthouse. They walked with their arms twined, recalling nonstop the adventures of their girlhood days. Hannah told her the many countries she had visited, the strange spectacles seen and stranger characters befriended. She had just returned to town last week, she said, and had been searching high and low for her dearest friend ever since.

"You're pregnant, aren't you?" Hannah said as soon as they sat down. "Does your husband treat you right? I'll skin him alive if he doesn't."

Snacking on grape soda and strawberry sandwiches, Meridia acquainted Hannah with her married life. "Daniel's a good man," she said. "He will make a wonderful father." She painted her in-laws in broad strokes, never once alluding to Eva's behavior or her own ousting, and became specific only when she talked about the difficulty the store was facing. Shoppers, she said, did not seem to notice it when they walked by.

"Make them see it then," said Hannah simply.

"What do you mean?"

The spirited redhead gave a broad wink, followed by a vigorous shaking of her bangles. "Meet me here in the morning and I'll show you." Then, more seriously, she added, "You haven't always been happy, have you? Yet prettier than I remember."

For the rest of the day, Meridia was walking on air. Daniel, watching her break into smiles for no reason, finally asked, "Why are you so excited?"

"I ran into an old friend," she said coyly. "We haven't seen each other in ages."

"But you're blushing," he said with a twinkle in his eye. "If you aren't careful, people might think you're in love."

When Meridia returned to the bookshop café the next morning, Hannah was waiting for her. A simple white dress this time, no boots, no bangles, her wild hair neatly framed with a schoolgirl's headband.

"Take a deep breath," she told Meridia. "I'll show you how to get people into your shop."

So for the second time in their friendship, Hannah introduced the town to her. With her old self-confidence, the imperturbable woman made Meridia approach complete strangers in the streets, made her compliment them and then tell them about the magnificent new shop on Willow Lane. Meridia, shy at first, quickly learned her lesson. That day she covered Majestic Avenue from end to end, shaking hands with so many people whose names Hannah insisted she memorize. "Young or old, each one is special. Next time you see them, make sure you greet them."

The next day they repeated their rounds in the commercial neighborhoods surrounding the market square. "We'll focus on the retailers and the servicepeople," explained Hannah. "You need customers, they have plenty of them." Meridia purchased two dozen tins of cinnamon toffee and wrote down her address on elegant business cards. That day she made the acquaintances of three hairdressers, seven dressmakers, two teahouse owners, a florist, four milliners, six storekeepers, and one proprietress of a beauty parlor. Thanks to the toffee and Hannah's instructions, many of them happily agreed to mention the shop to their customers.

On the third day, Hannah met her at the most curious of places—around the corner from the jewelry shop.

"Why here?" Meridia was baffled. "Hardly anybody walks this way."

"Know your own turf," replied Hannah coolly. "Don't expect your business to take off before you shake hands with every one of your neighbors."

Without waiting for an answer, the redhead marched straight to the nearest door and began knocking. For the next four hours they visited every home in the area. From these conversations, Meridia learned that Willow Lane was a developing neighborhood, comprised mainly of hardworking tradesmen and their young wives, most of whom sewed or took in laundry for extra income. Only a handful of businesses serviced them—a smoke shop, a newsstand, a fabric shop, and a little café with a light blue awning. The young wives expressed hope that the jewelry shop would inject new life into the neighborhood.

Finished with their rounds, the two friends walked over to 175 in great spirits. One arm fastened around the other's waist, they talked animatedly about how kind the neighbors were and how welcoming.

"I can't thank you enough," said a beaming Meridia when they reached the shop. "Please stay for dinner. Daniel would love to meet you."

She had opened the shop door partway, but Hannah pushed it shut again.

"Stay a minute. There'll be time for that." Hannah's voice had changed, low and feverish. Without a warning she pulled Meridia in an embrace. When they drew apart there were tears gleaming in her eyes.

"I behaved shamefully last time," said Hannah. "All these years I wanted to explain why I left without telling you."

"There's no need," said Meridia quickly. "I understand."

"But I want you to know—"

"There's no need," Meridia firmly repeated. "I know." Against her will, a single tear tore its way down her cheek. The door was opening from inside.

"Are you coming in?" asked Daniel. Meridia wiped her cheek and turned.

"Yes, Daniel. This is—"

She felt Hannah's hand pressing hers with urgency. When she turned, her friend was nowhere to be seen.

"Why are you standing here all alone?" said Daniel. "I swear you were talking to yourself just now. Where is this mythical friend of yours? I must have a word with her for hogging you these three days."

"I was—didn't you see—" She could not speak. "It's nothing. Are you hungry? I'll get dinner ready in a minute."

The next morning, when Meridia saw a letter from Hannah waiting for her on the kitchen table, she did not open it. Neither did she toss it into the wastebasket. Instead, she hid it carefully in a pile of dresses, a memento of need and loss, along with the part of her that had once again shut.

EIGHTEEN

Two days after Hannah's departure, Meridia sold her first pair of earrings. From that point on, a growing number of customers came into the shop, paltry by Lotus Blossom's standards, but many left with purchases in hand. Heeding Hannah's advice, Meridia not only greeted each one by name, but urged them to return with friends and families. Pleased with the results, Daniel could not help bragging one day.

"I told you our luck would turn. Do you believe me now?"

Meridia tried her best not to grin. "Of course, dearest. Heaven must have sent down a spirit to help us."

Before long, he discovered her talent for selling. Her gift did not come in the form of bargaining or persuading, but from listening carefully to her customers' wishes. One morning, he saw her help a young man pick out an engagement ring. Reserved and bashful, the young man had no idea what he wanted. Meridia began not by showing him rings, but by asking about the woman he loved. The man's face instantly brightened.

"She's the gentlest of souls," he gushed without restraint. "She speaks only when necessary, but even when she's quiet she fills the room with peace and happiness."

Meridia considered this thoughtfully. "You want something like this then, a simple ring with a square diamond. It's quiet and under-stated, yet shines with purpose and authority. What do you think?"

The man took one look and bought the ring.

"Who taught you to do that?" asked Daniel after.

Meridia shrugged her shoulders. "Everything was written plainly on his face."

Her friendships with the women of Willow Lane developed rap-idly. Tossing aside any feeling of awkwardness, she baked orange and vanilla pastries for them, invited them over for tea, and inquired after their children with fondness. Drawn to her intelligence and honesty, they repaid her advances by spreading a good word about the shop to their relatives and employers. Two of the younger women—Leah and Rebecca—Meridia was particularly fond of. Round and broad-hipped, Leah was the garrulous wife of a printer. Rebecca—thin, freckled, quieter—had been married to a successful mechanic for three years. Both women were sensible and resource-ful, wise about the ways of the world. It was their idea to create three different posters for the store and paste them all over Independence Plaza. "One for the men, one for the women, one for the in-betweens," they explained. Meridia saw the logic and did it.

In this way the business began to grow. Every night Daniel counted the profits, and though small, they were always more than the previous day's. Yet somehow money remained scant. The more they sold, the more difficult it was to meet expenses. The problem was Eva, who carted the money off to Orchard Road as soon as it was made.

DESPITE HER AGREEMENT WITH Gabriel, Eva watched the couple like a hawk. Two or three times a day, she blustered her way into the shop without being invited, always at the most inconvenient hour, and made it her business to know everything. Every evening she in-spected the account books to see how many items had sold, and then copied each transaction in her own ledger while her tongue clacked in displeasure. At the end of the week, she totaled the numbers and made sure Daniel paid Elias sixty percent of the proceeds. This was the figure they had agreed upon, but Eva, when it suited her, sometimes raised it to as much as ninety. Her excuses were innumerable—"The shop loan is due this week," "Your sisters need new uniforms"—and Daniel, not wishing to aggravate his mother, grudgingly relented. Meridia did her best to hold her tongue, knowing she was still dependent on Eva no matter how much she hated it.

At the beginning of each month, along with a fresh supply of inventory, Eva also delivered the small stipend Elias had agreed to give the couple until they became independent. She did this as if it were the greatest of sacrifice, loudly cautioning Daniel that "your poor father worked very, very hard for this, so please don't spend it unwisely." She only had to arch her brow to reduce Meridia to a charity case, a pauper pleading for crumbs, and the experience was among the most humiliating in memory. Still, Meridia followed her reason, not her emotion, and said nothing in return.

Eva's menacing did not stop at the shop. Soon her bees were all over the house, spoiling the food, suffocating the air, even swarming Meridia's growing belly. One afternoon, she showed up at the house while Meridia was cutting a pear. Eva did not say a word but marched straight into the shop. "I'm glad you're putting your father's money to good use," she said curtly to Daniel. "If only he could live as extravagantly as you, eating imported pears every day. But we're just humble people. We count ourselves lucky if we could eat watermelons once a month."

Daniel's ears burned as he listened to his mother. "I'm sorry, Mama," he said. "Meridia bought that pear for me. I'll tell her it won't be necessary in the future."

At another time, a grocer's boy delivered a bottle of milk to the shop during one of Eva's visits. Meridia, ringing up a customer, felt a nail clawing at her throat when she saw Eva frown in disapproval.

"It's for the baby," Daniel explained. "To make it strong and healthy."

"Of course," returned Eva acidly. "I'm sure you know more about it than I do. I wish somebody had pampered *me* while I carried you in my womb, but nobody did, and you turned out just fine. But if *your* baby needs it, who am I to say anything?"

From then on, Daniel had the milk delivered in the morning before Eva came.

Meridia consoled herself by outwitting Eva in money matters. Through Daniel, she learned that despite Eva's being married to a jeweler for almost three decades, her knowledge of jewelry was at best superficial. Meridia exploited this as follows: When she sold a piece of jewelry, she would replace it with an imitation she bought from a street vendor for a fraction of the price. The account books still listed the item as unsold, Eva was unaware of the difference, and Meridia put away the profit under the loose floorboard in the bedroom. In order to avoid suspicion, she did this only when she could find a truly good imitation. Furthermore, when a customer brought in an item to sell, she would record the purchase at a price higher than what she paid and pocket the difference. Daniel, catching on to what she was doing, quickly followed suit. In this way they saved up little by little, adding whenever they could to the stash under the bed.

Inspired by her craftiness, Daniel came up with the idea of cluttering the account books. His reasoning was simple: "Mama's never been very good with numbers. You are." Meridia did not need to be told twice. That day she began to ensnare Eva in endless columns of numbers, turning the books into an impenetrable maze where ten times ten did not equal a hundred, but ninety. "What does this mean?" Eva asked a few days later, sliding off her spectacles in frustration. Daniel, armed to the teeth with explanations, pulled out so many receipts so rapidly that his mother, in order not to lose face, had no choice but to nod. "Yes, yes, of course," Eva said with the impatient air of an expert. Behind her, Meridia began coughing so as not to laugh at Daniel's solemn face.

AS HER BELLY ROUNDED, Meridia grew weaker. Her skin lost its shine, her appetite waned, and her body defected into a territory whose laws she no longer understood. Some days she walked as if trudging through a swamp, her feet so swollen they felt cast with lead. Some mornings she looked at her reflection without knowing what she was— not a woman, barely a life-form, with grotesque alien stumps posing as limbs. Daniel constantly fussed over her, adamant that she eat even when her tongue could not tell sweet from sour. "Stay in bed," he said. "Rest whenever you feel like it." Meridia shook her head, knowing too well what Eva would say if she found her napping.

But neither could she sleep. In dreams, the bees pestered her, their stink churning her stomach more than the dying roses. One night, they chased her to the edge of a cliff; rather than surrender, she took a leap into thin air. She was falling, falling, the rocks below springing to meet her, when a hand jerked her back into the sky. For a moment there was nothing. Only breeze and a blur of sun. Then suddenly she was back on the ground, covered in so many scarves and underclothes her skin broke out in a rash. The same rescuing hand was now herding her toward Cinema Garden.

"Nurse," she said from her little-girl body, "why did you never come back?"

The good woman had not aged. The same stout figure. Robust cheeks. Vast breasts exhaling interminable sighs.

"You don't think I tried? Your mother thwarted me every inch of the way."

"But you'll stay this time? Please tell me you'll stay."

"I'm afraid I can't, my dear. My last wish is to see you before I die."

The little girl began to cry. "Please stay. Don't leave me again. Please."

No sooner had she said this than the mists appeared. Blue, yellow, ivory. The nurse bore down and looked at her intently.

"Shh! What would your mother say if she saw you? Listen carefully. The next time you see the three mists together—"

The nurse never finished her words, for the mists had pounced with a roar and whisked her into the sky. Screaming, the girl ran after them.

"Come back, Nurse! Come back!"

"Wake up." Daniel was shaking her shoulders. "You're having a bad dream."

Meridia panted in the dark and arranged her arms frantically around her belly. "No—no—not a dream," she stammered. "The nurse—*my* nurse—was saying good-bye."

Then she remembered. What would happen the next time the three mists appeared together? The thought pinned her head with needles and kept her up for hours.

MEANWHILE, NOT ONE OF Elias's gestures was lost on Meridia. The fumbled, diffident smiles. The apologetic looks. The awkward hemming and hawing. While the cold war raged between her and Eva, Elias was trying to make amends.

One day, she saw him smuggle a crate into the shop and then leave without a word. Inside the crate were a dozen imported pears and a large jar of medicinal roots, known to boost the appetite of expectant mothers. Attached was a note for Daniel: *Your wife mustn't lose more weight. Hide these from your mother.* When Meridia tried to thank him the next time they met, Elias blanched and walked away. From then on, he dropped by every Sunday when Eva was not visiting and quietly left a present behind. A silver baby rattle one week. A remedy for swollen ankles the next.

One Sunday, he brought Malin and Permony with him. After Meridia proved she could stand up to Eva by leaving Orchard Road, Malin no longer treated her with contempt, but with a grudging respect that sometimes passed for admiration. Malin was still cold, still indifferent, but her sneer, once an indispensable part of her armory, was now kept to a minimum. Meridia smiled to herself when she saw the girl drink the tea she had poured for her. Malin would not have done this a few months ago.

Permony, on the other hand, made no pretense of missing Meridia.

"I'm sorry Mama made you leave," she confided in secret. "Will you still tell me stories after the baby comes?"

The look of longing and regret in the girl's eyes went straight to Meridia's heart. Eva must be hard on her, now that Permony had no one to protect her.

"Of course. We'll make up stories together for the baby. You know you can come here anytime . . . when things aren't pleasant at home."

Permony understood and was grateful. Before Meridia could tell her about the golden phoenix that eclipsed the moon once every two hundred years, Elias cleared his throat and shook hands with Daniel.

"I knew you'd turn this place into a success, son."

"Thank you, Papa. Meridia has been a tremendous help."

"I know." Elias smiled, caught himself, and turned to the girls. "We'd better go," he said, then added, quite unnecessarily, "before your mother gets any ideas."

"WHAT EXOTIC DELICACIES IS your wife craving today?"

The question, whispered none too softly in the living room, was addressed to Daniel, but Meridia had no doubt it was meant for her ear.

"Honeyed venison? Plum roasted goose? With dishes that fancy she'll not only spoil her uterus, but burn a hole in your pocket and leave the baby with nothing."

"Meridia hasn't been craving anything," said Daniel. "But if she wants plum roasted goose, then she'll get it, even if I have to make a pact with the devil."

Eva pretended to ignore this.

"Are you her servant? Why were you fixing her lunch just now? You're too kind, too soft, and I'm afraid she's taking advantage of you. I wish your father was half as understanding, but he wouldn't stand any laziness from me. Even when an iron stick was prodding my womb, he still insisted I make him dinner!"

"Meridia's been ill all morning," said Daniel curtly. "I told her to rest a little."

"Are you sure? A woman has ways to make a man work for her. Trust me."

By this point Daniel was clearly irritated. "Yes, I'm sure, Mama. If you'll excuse me, I have a million things to do."

Meridia was lying in bed with a migraine. A wall separated her from the living room, yet she could hear Eva as clearly as if she were standing next to her. How did the woman do it? Still, even with her head splitting, Meridia could not deny that she was pleased by the note of irritation in Daniel's voice. Lately he had acted brusque around his mother. If Eva was smart, she would give Daniel space to breathe.

A chair suddenly scraped in the living room.

"She's coming—that odious woman!" hissed Eva. "I can smell her even with my nose pinched. I'd better leave before she hits me again."

Meridia winced in pain as Eva's footsteps slapped the floorboards. The front door opened, slammed with a crash. Hurriedly Daniel withdrew into the shop. A minute later the door opened again. The scent of lemon verbena drifted into the bedroom. Meridia closed her eyes. Now that Ravenna was here, it would not be long before her migraine subsided.

The incident planted an idea in her head. The next day, she went to a perfume shop and purchased a bottle of verbena essence. Back at the house, she waited until she heard the faintest buzzing of bees coming from a distance. Then she took the bottle from her pocket, walked to the curb, and sprayed a few drops of perfume into the wind.

"What are you doing?" yelled Daniel from inside the shop.

"Magic. Just you wait and see."

That day Eva did not come. When Meridia explained her ruse to Daniel, he nearly fell off the chair with laughter.

"Clever girl," he said. "Why didn't you think of it sooner?"

"I thought you enjoyed your mother's company."

Daniel's laughter turned into a groan. "She's my mother. But sometimes I'd rather be trapped in a cave with a mountain lion than speak to her."

"What was that woman doing here yesterday?" Eva grilled him the following day. "Insanity is catching, son—do you really want it to rampage freely under your roof?"

Daniel put on his game face and assured her it was not so.

THOUGH MERIDIA WAS CAREFUL to use the perfume only when necessary, Eva quickly wised up to her ruse. Furious that she had been tricked, the mother-in-law heightened her surveillance to an uncanny degree. When Meridia bought a dress on the sly because her old ones did not fit anymore, the next day Eva said to Daniel, "A dress from that store must have cost an arm and a leg. Your father will be thrilled to hear how she's spending his money." A few days later, during a particularly hot afternoon, Daniel bought two bowls of shaved ice from an itinerant peddler outside the shop. The next morning, Eva walked into the house with her bees clouding around her. "Guess what I did yesterday? Sweltering in the garden weeding while your father patched a leak in the roof! Oh, sometimes I wish I could forget all about work and responsibilities and stuff myself silly with shaved ice!" Meridia overheard this and frowned. How did Eva know?

She solved the mystery by accident. One morning, having tea with her new friends from the neighborhood, she happened to glance out the living room window and see a boy standing across the street.

"Do you know who that is?" Meridia said.

Leah and Rebecca approached the window. The boy looked no older than twelve, wearing a shabby military jacket and a cap drawn low over his eyes. Aware of the women's stares, he pretended to lace his shoes before walking away.

"Of course," said Leah, who knew everyone in the neighborhood. "His father operates the newsstand around the corner."

Rebecca's freckled nose wrinkled in disapproval. "A delinquent, from the looks of him. Why did you ask?"

"Never mind," said Meridia. "I thought he was someone else. Would you like some more biscuits?"

After her friends left, Meridia dragged her swollen feet to look for the boy at the newsstand. He was standing alone inside the kiosk, reading a magazine. Meridia crept up to the entrance and blocked it. The boy looked up in shock. Although she had nothing more concrete than a suspicion, his guilty face at once gave him away.

"How much did she pay you?" Meridia was trying to keep calm.

"I—I don't know what you're talking about."

"How much?"

The boy stammered out a sum.

"What did she ask you to do?"

The boy shrugged, took a hard swallow. "Watch the house. Keep track of where you go. What you buy. If you have visitors."

Meridia seized both his shoulders. "Come with me this instant."

"I can't leave the kiosk." The boy shook his head. "My father will kill me."

Meridia did not hold back her anger. "You come this minute or I'll tell your father what you've been doing. *Then* he'll kill you all right."

The boy stared up in fear and nodded.

DANIEL WAS OUTRAGED. HE grabbed the boy by the collar before he could finish speaking and lifted him off the floor.

"Tell my mother you won't work for her anymore. If I ever catch you loitering outside the house again, I will thrash you silly. Do you hear me?"

The boy cowered in terror. Daniel dropped him, smacked the back of his head, tossed him out the door.

"Damn her!" cursed Daniel, his eyes tight with anger. "What did she think she was doing?"

Meridia went up to him and took his hand.

"What are we going to do?" she said. "I know we're still dependent on your mother, but this cannot go on. We can't let her dictate how we should live our lives."

Daniel clenched his jaw. "Leave her to me. Don't upset yourself. It won't be good for the baby."

An hour later, Eva's laughter preceded her entrance into the shop. From her jubilant mood, Meridia concluded the following: One, she had not spoken to the newsstand boy. Two, a number of merchants at the market square were kicking themselves for yielding to her.

"You'll never believe the bargains I found!" Eva exclaimed to Daniel. "This serving dish is sixty percent off. This beef flank, seventy. And these lobsters—"

"Mama."

Something in Daniel's tone silenced her excitement. Bewildered, Eva shoved her purchases back into the basket and stared at him across the empty shop.

"You're exhausting yourself, Mama, coming here two, three times a day. Why don't you stay home and let me bring the books in the evening? Don't worry. The shop is doing well. Why, we made a dozen sales just this morning! Isn't that right, dearest?"

Meridia, her heart pounding in her ear, was ready.

"Fourteen, actually, if I counted right."

Eva, caught off guard, was silent for a moment. Then her laughter rang shrilly.

"Don't be ridiculous. It's no bother at all. I'm happy to look in as often as I can."

Daniel was not finished. This time, there was no mistaking his meaning.

"I'm serious, Mama. It makes no sense for you to be here. Go on. It's a beautiful day. Why don't you shop some more? I'll make sure the store turns a huge profit by the end of the day."

Eva's face darkened at once. "You mean I'm not welcome here?"

"That's not what I said. There's simply no need for you to be here."

"Son! What's the matter with you?"

"What's the matter with *you*, Mama? Why did you hire a delinquent to spy on us? Don't try to deny it! I can drag him here if necessary."

Eva's mouth dropped open, and her hand flew to her stomach as if she had been punched. Bristling with menace, she lifted a finger and pointed at Meridia.

"She's behind this, isn't she?"

Daniel walked to the door and opened it. In those seconds Meridia realized that she had never loved him more.

"Son!"

Eva was not about to leave without a fight, but a customer walked in. Huffing with rage, she snatched her basket and stormed out. It was not until her feet hit the curb that her bees began to scream.

"Thrown out by my own son! Who would have thought that someone who had nursed from my breasts would stick a knife into my back! Oh, don't think I don't see your hand in this, you arrogant fiend! Turning my own flesh against me when I have nothing but love for him! Just you watch. As my son has made me weep today, that baby in your womb will be your anguish. When the time comes, it will refuse to go in or out until you drown in your own blood!"

Inside the shop, Meridia alone heard the curse. Even as she tried to dismiss it, a shiver already ran down her spine and settled in her womb.

NINETEEN

Two months later, six weeks earlier than anticipated, Meridia went into labor. Dawn had just broken when a panic-stricken Daniel pounded on Leah's door and sent her to fetch the midwife and the two grandmothers. Not knowing what to do while he waited, he stood anxiously beside the bed, holding Meridia's hand and wincing when a contraction seized her. After what seemed an eternity, Rebecca came and led him out of the room. "Don't worry," Meridia assured him with a smile. "The baby will come before you know it." He kissed her hand again and again until she teased him, not once suspecting that the next time he saw her, her bravery would be replaced by terror.

Ravenna was the next to arrive. Without saying a word to anybody, she burned three sticks of incense, placed fresh towels by the bed, stripped off Meridia's dress, and helped her slip into a robe. A strange chant issued from her lips while she worked, a toneless, meaningless incantation that effectively put Meridia at ease. She positioned Rebecca outside to keep Daniel company. When the midwife arrived with her ancient bundle of instruments, Ravenna did not beat around the bush.

"I'll kill you if anything goes wrong."

The midwife, a small, pleasant woman with an abundance of silver hair, laughed good-naturedly. "That won't be necessary, madam. Your daughter has more good luck than she knows what to do with."

Nobody could have foreseen the disaster that was about to occur. After reciting a prayer, the midwife spread open her bundle of instruments. The hairsbreadth needles went into Meridia's arms, the sacred oil on her head, chest, and stomach. In order to invoke the aid of benevolent spirits, the midwife hung a colorful wooden amulet on the bedpost. "The womb is opening in good time," she announced brightly. "You'll have the baby in your arms before noon." Meridia grimaced with each thrust of pain, but they were not great and she bore them without sound. Along with the midwife's words, Ravenna's self-possession continued to give her strength.

Much later, she would blame her memory for setting off the catastrophe. While everything was going smoothly, she suddenly remembered Eva's curse. *The baby will refuse to go in or out until you drown in your own blood.* The words awakened all her fear, and at once Meridia spotted dangers everywhere in the room: the crooked angle of the bed, the spider crawling across the ceiling, the amulet swinging above her head. The midwife, not yet alarmed, tapped more needles into her arms. But Meridia knew something terrible had happened. She had conceded room for the bees to enter.

The next thing she remembered was seeing Eva in the room. Meridia did not know when she arrived, who had let her in, or if she had simply materialized out of thin air. Dressed in heavy crepe and dull black kid gloves, Eva looked every inch the angel of death as she hovered near the door away from Ravenna's reach. One glance at her amused face sent pain coursing through Meridia's body.

"Mama, what is she—"

Her question turned into a scream. Something sharp was piercing her eyes, and when she opened them, a legion of bees had surrounded her from head to toe. Shrill and wrathful, the insects jabbed their wings into her face, stung her throat, pried her legs, undid her robe, bit her breasts and belly. The air was rotten with their stink. Desperately she tried to slap them away, but her movement only increased their fury. Meridia screamed, struggled, screamed again. Away in the corner, Eva's smile was growing wider.

"What is it, child?" cried Ravenna, pinning her to the bed. "Keep still if you can."

Meridia yelped when the baby began to twist. Daniel was pounding on the door, begging to be let in, but no one heard him.

"Steady now, steady," said the midwife. Though her voice spoke of control, sweat was transforming her brows into a beaded landscape. Ravenna shook Meridia's face and told her to keep breathing. Her authority prompted the bees to retreat, but only for a short time. Ravenna could not see them, did not hear the racket they made.

Meridia stopped moving when blood began oozing from her womb. The baby was kicking inside, pushing with impatient fists for a way out. She tried to scream that the bees were blocking the passage, but managed only a whimper. Was Eva planning to kill her, or only to frighten her?

Suddenly a shout erupted from the doorway. The midwife turned, gasped, covered Meridia's bloody parts with a cloth. Standing in the open door was Daniel. Eyes wide, jaw slack, face drained of color. Leah and Rebecca detained him on each arm.

"Get out!" barked Ravenna, rushing to the door without seeming to notice Eva. "This is no sight for a man to see!"

She pushed him out to the hallway, but Daniel put up a struggle.

"She's my wife—let me stay with her!"

Ravenna was unmoved. "Keep him calm," she charged the two neighbors before bolting the door. In the hallway Daniel raged, pelting his mother-in-law with curses. Impervious, Ravenna swept back to the bed and rebuked the midwife for not locking the door. But Meridia knew better. It was Eva who had let Daniel in and branded the image of horror into his brain.

"Push, child, push."

Meridia was worn down. The bees kept up their attack, and no
matter what method the midwife pursued, the bleeding continued.
When another spasm wracked her, she could barely whimper, so
tired had she become from the struggle.

"Push, child, push."

Meridia shook her head feebly. Clear the bees, Mama, she wanted
to say. But her tongue had swollen to fill up her whole mouth.

"It's lying feet first," said the midwife, wiping her brow. "The
baby's blocking its own way out."

"Then reach in!" said Ravenna. "Grab the brute by the heels and
drag it out!"

The midwife shook her head. "She's losing consciousness. If I
reach in now, only the baby will survive."

The midwife had not even finished talking when Meridia heard
it: a laughter so thin and ghostly it might as well have been a fig-
ment of her imagination. Nobody else heard it, or seemed troubled
by it. And if Eva had refrained from speaking, the bees might have
accomplished their mission then and there.

"Some monster it is, refusing to go in or out. So stubborn, just
like its mother. To think that she might not be around to raise it herself . . ."

Startled, Ravenna whipped around, noticing for the first time another person in the room. Eva, peeling off her gloves slowly, took no
trouble to conceal her delight.

"Get out," said Ravenna.

She moved so rapidly that Eva did not realize she was being
ejected out of the room until Ravenna's fingers cut into her arm. Eva
dropped her gloves. Her cry of pain rang louder than Meridia's.

"Don't touch me, you lunatic! I don't give a damn what you did
to your husband, but it's my grandchild you're murdering!"
Ravenna shoved her out the door. "Son! They haven't a clue what
they're doing in there. I tried to help but they wouldn't let me. If
you don't stop them, the only way your wife will leave this house is
feet first!"

Daniel shot out of the living room, where he had been pacing and sweating while Leah and Rebecca consoled him.

"Stop," said Ravenna staunchly. "Before you listen to your mother, consider all the lies she's told you. If you want your wife and child alive, keep her away from them."

With that, she flung Eva at him and slammed the door shut. At once Eva commenced shrieking as if she were being butchered alive.

"Tell me what to do, woman," Ravenna told the stunned midwife back in the room. "Nobody is dying today. Not on my watch."

Gulping, the midwife looked at her in fear and collected herself. "Keep your daughter awake, madam. I have to cut her open. That's the only way."

Ravenna bent and slapped Meridia on the cheek. "Wake up, child. Look at me."

Meridia could not open her eyes. Her lids, though no one registered the change, had grown as swollen as her tongue. Now the bees were twice as vicious, lustful and furious on Eva's behalf. Feeling their sting deep between her legs, Meridia was convinced her next breath would be her last.

Ravenna snatched a brass jug from the nightstand, parted her daughter's lips, and poured water down her throat. Caught unawares, Meridia choked and coughed, opening her eyes a fraction. Light hit her like a blast of sun. Daniel was pounding, pounding on the door while Eva urged him on. In panic, she saw the midwife spreading ointments on her abdomen, preparing it for the knife's passage. Don't! Meridia wished she could shout. The bees will get to the baby if you cut me.

"Those bees! What are they doing here?" Ravenna suddenly screamed.

She ran to open the window, but the latch stuck fast. She smashed the glass with a chair, ran back to the bed, and beat the empty air with all her might. The midwife stared at Ravenna as if she had gone mad. Shrieking, the bees flew helter-skelter, knocking against wall and ceiling before scattering out the window. A torrent of cold air burst into Meridia's lungs. She sat up on her elbows, and for the first time heard the sound of two hearts beating inside her. "Don't give up on me," she told the baby, finally out loud. "I want more than a yowl from you, do you hear?"

"What are you waiting for?" Ravenna scolded the midwife. "Cut her already!"

The midwife snapped into action. In the hallway Daniel's pounding slowed and then became completely silent.

A LONG TIME PASSED before she heard the first cry. A long time in which no amount of cutting, tearing, shifting, extracting, or stitching measured to the earlier pain inflicted by the bees. While Ravenna and the midwife went about their task, she felt only an overwhelming urge to hold her child. When the first indignant cry pierced the room, her arms were ready, weary as she was. "A boy," announced Ravenna, wiping the baby with a towel. "No wonder he put you through hell."

Meridia received her son with tears streaming down her face. Touching the little nose and delicate lips, she shuddered when she realized how closely they had come to danger, and eluded it. What if Ravenna had failed to beat back death with her two hands?

"Mama," she began to say, wrenched with gratitude. The woman with the implacable knot took one look at her, sensed what was coming, and shook her head.

After Meridia was made presentable, Ravenna quietly opened the door. Daniel stormed in and gave his mother-in-law a dirty glare. The second he laid eyes on his wife, however, all the hardness melted from his face.

"Are you all right?" He rushed forward in alarm. "I'll never forgive myself if—"

"I'm all right. Look."

He was struck speechless. Taking the baby from her, he nudged and teased and poked him gently as if to make sure he was real. He kissed the round pink cheeks and the thick midnight-colored hair, cooed and chuckled and kissed and chuckled again before proclaiming, "What a handsome little devil!"

Leah and Rebecca came in and doted over the baby like two proud aunts.

"He's beautiful," gushed Rebecca. "He's got his mother's pretty little nose."

"And he's got your eyes," Leah told Daniel. "The freckles, I'm afraid, are his aunt Rebecca's."

Smiling through her pain, Meridia thanked them for their help. Soon, the kind neighbors took their leave, promising they would return later to look after her.

Meridia took the baby from Daniel the instant Eva walked into the room. Though she was weak and in pain, anger at once blazed from the pit of her womb. She dared her mother-in-law to look her in the face, and when Eva failed to do so, dark words at once surfaced to her lips. Yet instead of firing them like bullets, Meridia burst into laughter, a pure, thunderous laugh that cut Eva deeper than the sharpest knife. Holding her newborn son, Meridia was seized with such love, such wonder, such joy, that she wiped her tears and laughed all the harder. For the first time in recorded memory, Eva's mouth pinched shut. Meridia was transformed. She laughed and laughed and laughed until she drove Eva out of the room.

A SHORT TIME LATER, thinking Meridia was asleep, the midwife stole up to Daniel and tapped him on the elbow. He was standing over the bassinet with his eyes glued to the baby, a position he had occupied with little change for the past half hour. Ravenna was in the kitchen brewing a tonic. Eva was nowhere in sight.

"May I have a word with you, sir?"

Daniel turned and looked at her in surprise.

"It's not enough, the money in the envelope?"

The midwife quickly shook her head. "No, it's not that. You and your wife's mother have been very generous. But there's—something—"

She glanced sideways at the bed, then returned her anxious gaze to Daniel.

"I did the best I could," she whispered, "but her womb took quite a beating. I'm afraid that baby will be her last."

The smile vanished from Daniel's lips. His face turned very pale, and for a long time he simply stood and said nothing. Then turning to the bassinet, he lifted his son and held him as if he would never let go.

"Can you keep this to yourself? There's no need to upset my wife."

The midwife promised. Unbeknown to either of them, Meridia was not only awake, but heard every word. She kept her eyes closed, still as a corpse, while an image of horror rose from her memory and cleaved her. On the day she surrendered herself to Daniel, more than a year ago, a gutted fawn had washed up on the beach—bluish of skin, frothing with worms, innards splayed like ribbons. Now she knew what it meant. It was her womb she saw that day, pecked to pieces, tossed in a coffin, cut up by bees.

Standing outside the door, Eva, too, had caught every word. Her laugh as she walked away was one she could barely keep to herself.

And so Noah was born on the evening of June 6, eighteen hours after the labor began.

TWENTY

For six days Ravenna appeared with the morning dew. Fetching the paper from the porch, Leah would see her stiff black cloak plodding through the fog, face veiled, shoulders erect, basket swinging from one arm. Rebecca would see the same woman but in a billowing white dress, head bared and feet riding on a rapid sailor's breeze. Once or twice they greeted her, but Ravenna never seemed to see or hear them. Later in the day, when they went to visit 175, they would find not only the house clean and in order, but tins of food spread on the table and baby Noah fed and bathed. Meridia would be sitting in her bed, still too weak to stand, sipping a tonic Ravenna had brought in her basket.

On the seventh morning, fetching the paper with hair up in rollers, Leah did not see the black cloak trudging through the fog. Nor did Rebecca the white dress, try as she might to crane her neck out the window as she made breakfast. When they got to 175, Meridia was on her feet, nursing Noah while studying the account books. "What are you doing?" they scolded her with concern. "You're not well enough to be up!" "Yes, I am," she replied without delay. "I've never felt readier to get back to work." Trading glances with each other, the two neighbors kept their astonishment to themselves.

One night, walking home with a pile of sewing work from a local
seamstress, they spotted a yellow vapor lingering outside Meridia's
door. They made nothing of this, until a man with a stoop surprised
them by appearing out of the vapor. He looked well dressed and extremely dignified, with streaks of gray hair visible in the moonlight.
Yet like a thief he crept around the house and looked through all the
windows until he came back to the front and found what he was
looking for: Meridia's bedroom.

"Who is it?" whispered Leah in alarm.

"I don't know. He's looking at the baby."

They came closer, making as little noise as they could. Sensing
them, the man stepped back into the vapor and glided away.

When they broached the incident to Meridia the next morning,
her breath momentarily stayed in her throat before she answered.

"A stray peddler, I'm sure. A lot of them have been coming to the
house."

"He seemed to be looking for Noah. Aren't you afraid he might
come back?"

She laughed at this outright. "What for? There's nothing here he
wants."

In her ordinary voice she began asking them about their husbands. But in that moment where her breath stayed, they had read
her longing, before she snuffed it with all her will, to believe otherwise.

LEAH AND REBECCA ALSO bore witness to the mysterious habit of
another visitor. Early in the morning or late into the night, the man
they soon learned to be Daniel's father would approach the house
like a convict on the run, hiding behind trees and under shades as if
the sky might fall on him. And yet, there was no denying the happy
spring in his steps, his irrepressible smile, or the light that illuminated his eyes from within. He stayed long enough to elicit a laugh
from Noah, entertain him with silly faces, or simply stroke his hair if

the baby was asleep. He was never without gifts. Sometimes he would bring one or both of his daughters; the older one bored and unsmiling in pretty orange dresses, the younger thrilled as a freed bird. Leah was the first to notice how fond Noah was of his grandfather. The baby could sense his arrival from a distance, and if he was crying, he would stop before Elias entered the house.

"Why is he skulking around to see his grandson?" asked Rebecca one day.

Meridia creased her brow as if the answer could not have been plainer. "You would, too, if you were married to my mother-in-law."

The two neighbors wished she would elaborate further, express a grievance, if not articulate a secret. True to her character, Meridia said nothing more on the subject.

TO MERIDIA'S DELIGHT, NOAH did not take to Eva at all. No matter how hard his grandmother tried to wheedle him, Noah cried angrily when she came near. He greeted her kiss with a gush of saliva; every time she held him in her arms, he relieved himself all over her. He refused to touch her, never gave her a smile, and broke into alarming hiccups when she sang to him. Meridia, who never left Eva alone with the baby, felt her heart swell with pride as she watched him.

To save face, Eva pretended it was *she* who chose to stay away from the baby. He would only ruffle her dress, she said. Undo her hair, and heaven knows how unhygienic babies could be. She endlessly cautioned Daniel to air Noah out in the morning sun, to sanitize him by scrubbing his skin at least three times a day, and to have him sleep enclosed by two layers of curtains so his germs would not fly about the house. She recounted innumerable parasites and diseases that a baby could host, citing anecdotes of massive epidemics caused by filth-ridden infants. Meridia ignored her. It was Daniel who gave his mother a long, steely glare that would have daunted a less resolute critic.

Two weeks after the birth, Eva sent Gabilan to the shop with a gift for Noah. Wrapped in butcher paper and tied with kitchen twine were half a dozen baby clothes—moth-eaten, yellowing, with seams frayed at the edges. From the lace and flower patterns Meridia suspected they were Malin and Permony's baby clothes. Her first instinct was to throw them into the garbage, but Daniel told her to save them.

"What for?" she asked.

"Magic. Just you wait and see."

When Elias came around the next morning, Daniel dressed Noah in these clothes and paraded him before his grandfather.

"Why are you dressing my grandson in rags?" asked an outraged Elias. "A baby girl's rags, for that matter."

"They're from Mama," said Daniel blithely. "Fit him well, don't you think?"

Elias patted his head as if he had hair and went off. An hour later, he returned with a boxful of new clothes, unwrapped them by the bassinet, and put some on Noah.

"Burn those," he ordered Daniel, pointing to the old clothes on the floor. "No grandchild of mine is dressing like a pauper."

A few days later, Eva asked Daniel why Noah had not been wearing the clothes she gave him. "They're too nice, Mama," he said. "We're saving them for special occasions."

FOR THE NEXT SEVERAL months, baby Noah tormented Meridia to the limits of her endurance. Sleeping little and crying nonstop, he bruised her nipples without taking her milk, screamed when put down in his bassinet, and slept only when one parent rocked him and the other sang. Daniel solved the eating problem by taking money from under the floorboard to buy costly milk formula. The sleeping problem, however, left him dumbfounded. No matter what trick he tried, both parents ended up awake all night, taking turns between rocking and singing. In addition, Noah was always too hot or too cold, always sweating or shivering regardless of how he was dressed. One time, he had a case of diarrhea that lasted three days. When the illness finally ran its course, the parents looked a good deal more depleted than the baby.

Having no siblings, Meridia was ignorant in the subject of child-care. She did not know how to calm a peevish child, and instead relied on her instincts to guide her. In the beginning, she had her mother to count on. However, when Ravenna inevitably withdrew behind her veil of forgetfulness, she was left to fend for herself. Leah and Rebecca tried their best to help, but not having children themselves, they knew little more than she did. In her most helpless hours, Noah's crying sounded so much like Eva's bees that she wondered if those insects had gotten to him after all.

At the same time, Meridia's own emotions were turning against her. She was often befuddled, unable to recall what task she needed to complete. Sadness, fear, and anxiety plagued her without end. She would burst into tears for no reason, then plunge into a restlessness so great it made her irritable. Her breasts ached to be emptied, and the baby's rejection of them hurt her more than she cared to admit. When alone with Noah, she felt herself lost in an ocean of darkness. It was absurd to think that she, in her bumbling youth and inexperience, was responsible for his care, his well-being, for the flow of blood and pump of heart that kept him alive for another day!

As Noah's demands multiplied, she tolerated Daniel's advances less and less. In the little time they had away from the baby, she shuddered when Daniel touched her. The heat of his breath reminded her of the bees, of the womb they had destroyed and the child who would start bawling the instant she closed her eyes. To ward him off, she pleaded headaches and exhaustion, and then guiltily watched him retreat to his side of the bed. Her failure as both wife and mother crushed her like a mountain of steel. Was it possible that she had caught it, too, the cold wind that had knocked Ravenna to the ground and turned Monarch Street upside down?

Once the thought took root, Meridia pursued it to its conclusion. Attempting to calm a furious Noah one morning, she cobbled up a possible reason for Gabriel's resentment toward her. Perhaps Ravenna's story was not that of a wife betrayed and abandoned to disillusionment, but of a mother worn down by her child. Perhaps it was not the cold wind that had turned Ravenna against Gabriel, but Meridia's own demands as a baby. As she wiped bits of Noah's vomit from her hair, she wondered if she herself had absorbed all of Ravenna's attention at Noah's age, worn thin the love between her parents, chased Gabriel into the arms of another woman. The rest was easy to fill in. Ravenna and Gabriel would only take so much before arguments began, all leading to the inexorable devastation of the ax. What if she was doomed to repeat their fate? Once her bed frosted with ice, how long would Daniel wait before he looked for warmth?

The question had no sooner formed than it shamed her. Daniel was not Gabriel. Since their reconciliation, he had given her no cause to doubt his devotion. In fact, the opposite. One evening, while Daniel had gone to present the books to Eva, Noah began crying and would not stop. Meridia, armed with little rest the night before, was at the end of her tether.

"Please," she begged the child. "What is it you want?"

Noah screamed louder. Her patience exhausted, Meridia left him in the bedroom, went to the kitchen, crouched next to the stove, and burst into sobs. She did not stop crying until a pair of arms lifted her and carried her to bed. By then she was too tired to open her eyes. When she awoke, the room had come alive with sunlight. She got up and went to the living room. Daniel was on his feet, holding the baby. His wearied face told her he had been up all night.

"He's asleep now," he whispered. "I'll hold him a while longer just in case."

At that moment, she realized he had become a man.

MEANWHILE, THE SHOP WAS declining in profits. Eva, aware that the couple had been flourishing, stiff-armed Elias to furnish them with second-rate inventory. Through her interference, only items that had not sold in months were transferred to Willow Lane. Her answer when Daniel tried to reason with her: "A man must rely on his own resources, son. Do you expect your father, who has sacrificed so much, to rescue you yet again? If only your wife knew how to economize, you wouldn't be in this jam today. I'll tell you what, doesn't she still have that jewelry set from her father? Why don't you tell her to sell it to me? I have no use for it but I'll buy it as a favor to you."

"Tell your mother I'd rather saw off my own arms," said Meridia when Daniel told her.

Following the incident with the newsstand boy, Eva no longer came to the store every day, but still found ways to assert her presence. Apart from limiting the inventory, reducing the couple's stipend, charging Daniel with miscellaneous expenses while increasing her own share of the profits, she began using Patina as a pawn. The old woman turned out to be her most effective weapon to date.

Every morning Eva sent Patina to Willow Lane with an order to purchase food from restaurants in the surrounding neighborhoods. "Grilled calamari and coconut beef for lunch today," a shamefaced Patina would whisper to Meridia. "For dinner, seared abalone and fried octopus with mushrooms." Eva never wrote these orders down on paper, and she told Daniel that they were to pay for them from Elias's share of the profits. However, when it came time to settle the bills, she would deny she had ordered most of it. During one of his nightly visits to Orchard Road, Daniel showed his mother the receipts, but Eva only grew furious at Patina.

"Come up here, you deceitful hag!" she thundered down the stairs. "When did I ever ask you to buy a grilled flounder stuffed with roe?" she attacked as soon as Patina hobbled into the sitting room. "We are a simple family—our stomachs turn at the mention of such a dish! You know what's going on here?" Eva turned to Daniel, broiling with wrath. "This old woman must be scheming with the restaurant owners! I asked her to buy plain roasted chicken, they billed you for tangerine duck. Now confess! What have you done?"

Patina blanched, shaking from head to toe. Unable to bear the sight, Daniel interrupted.

"I'm sure it's a simple mistake, Mama. There's no need to accuse Patina. Meridia and I will pay for these dishes."

The next morning, Patina showed up on Willow Lane with welts on her face and cigarette burns on her hands. Seeing these, Meridia cried out in alarm.

"Did she do this to you?"

"It's nothing," said the old woman. "I fell and scalded myself on the stove."

Meridia's eyes flamed with anger, but she knew she could not fight Eva on this ground. Fearing further consequences on Patina, she motioned to Daniel to open the register.

"It's all right, Patina," said Daniel. "Buy Mama whatever she wants today."

The old woman began to cry. "I'm so sorry. You both are too kind to me. I know how much you need that money for Noah. Let me go home without the food. I'll make up some excuse. I'll tell her I was robbed on the way to the restaurants."

Meridia firmly pressed the money into her hand. Shocked to feel Patina's bone-thin wrist, she wondered if the old woman had again fallen ill.

"Don't worry yourself, Patina. We'll find a way to manage."

From that day on, Daniel stopped disputing Eva's bills. When there was not enough money in the register to pay for them, Meridia reached under the floorboard for her dowry. Each time it felt no less painful than cutting her own flesh.

TWENTY-ONE

The decline of summer amplified the demands for money. Growing Noah needed milk, clothes, vitamins, lotions, and shoes. The old house demanded a new roof, the cold bed a second blanket, the walls a thicker insulation against autumn. One afternoon, an endless stream of cockroaches erupted from under the shop, chasing away half a dozen customers before they could make a purchase. When a home remedy of vinegar and quicklime failed to work, Daniel was forced to hire an exterminator, and the process of annihilation required the shop to close for three days. They were yet to recover from this setback when Eva dealt them her next blow.

In addition to the dishes, she now included rice, flour, tea, and spices in her daily demand. At the same time, she continued to supply the shop with obsolete inventory: garish rings and necklaces, impure gold, tarnished silver, stones the color of mud and ditch water. The young couple would be lucky to make two sales a day. Yet when profits plummeted, Eva's look became no less excoriating than her words.

The dowry money kept them afloat for two months. Then one morning in October, reaching under the floorboard to pay for Eva's grocery, Meridia counted only a small amount left. Another week at most, and they would have to sell the gold bars. Tasting panic in her throat, she fished out two crisp bills and gave them to Patina in the shop. As soon as the old woman left, Meridia rested on Daniel the full weight of her gaze. He needed only one look to grasp the thought whirling through her brain.

"What if Mama finds out?" he said.

Meridia allowed a quiver to betray her panic. "Our heads. The chopping block."

"We can ask Papa for a loan."

"For how long? If your mother hears, our heads will be on that block even sooner."

Daniel shifted his eyes to the bassinet in the corner. For a long minute he listened to Noah breathe before assenting.

Meridia had come up with the idea one night. At first they both had dismissed it as too risky, too difficult, too outrageous. In recent weeks, however, Eva's behavior increasingly warranted a drastic maneuver. Compared to the prospect of living indefinitely under her rule, the idea no longer seemed farfetched. Now that the dowry was almost gone, they could not afford to waste the gold bars in the same way.

The plan was to establish a partnership with another jeweler, without Eva or Elias knowing. Once they had a steady stream of quality inventory, the couple could hope to make profits and gain independence from Orchard Road. Daniel had cautiously approached a handful of trusted merchants with this idea. Some expressed unwillingness to work with a young jeweler with no independent means, others wondered why the partnership had to be kept a secret. The risk was great, the return uncertain. But Meridia believed that if they could find the right partner, the plan would pay off handsomely.

Four days after their agreement, Daniel came into contact with a renegade dealer in jewelry. The man lived in another town, had no acquaintance with Lotus Blossom Lane, and was known for taking risks in fledgling businesses. Although his endeavors met with mixed degrees of success, his daring resourcefulness had much to recommend him. He acted solely as a dealer and had no shop of his own. As initial capital, he required at least two kilos of gold. Daniel's preliminary assessment of the man was positive. Before they made a decision, Meridia wished to meet him in person.

To prepare herself for the interview, Meridia carefully reviewed Eva's masterful ways at the market square, borrowing the words but tempering the tone with Gabriel's elegance. She rehearsed what she would say if asked this or that, armed her weak spots with bullet-proof arguments, and examined her position from every conceivable angle. She went through this process for hours, quiet yet unstoppable, so that by the time Noah was ready for bed she was as exhausted as a farm laborer.

The following afternoon, a barrel-chested man with coal-dark skin and thick black beard came into the shop. From his well-tailored suit and confident gait, there was no question that he was successful, yet his manner carried no trace of arrogance. His long black eyes were especially audacious. He was about Gabriel's age, patient and round whereas the other was brusque and angular. The man introduced himself as Samuel.

They sat down in the living room while Noah slept a few paces away. After pouring him tea, Meridia asked the dealer about his family.

"My wife and I have been together for twenty-five years," Samuel said proudly. "We have two daughters at the university. The older one is engaged to a civil engineer. We hope to become grandparents by the end of next year."

Pleased by his answer, Meridia inquired about his business. She put him at ease by posing her questions lightly, yet there were no stones she left unturned. In twenty minutes she ferreted out of him his various enterprises, his discipline and work ethics, his knowledge of jewels. Never once forsaking her smile, she spread her questions wide like a net, hoping to catch him in a lie, but his story remained consistent. By chance, the conversation turned to a recently bankrupt jeweler, who happened to be a friend of Samuel's. The dealer admitted that he had been given the opportunity to purchase his friend's assets far below market price, but he had declined.

"Why did you refuse?" asked Daniel. "Reselling the assets alone would have made you a lot of money."

"It's wrong to profit from a friend when he's down," said Samuel. "The way I see it, money takes a backseat to loyalty."

This made up Meridia's mind. Satisfied, Daniel, too, nodded.

"Do you have a question for us, sir?" Meridia poured Samuel another cup of tea.

"Only one. Have I passed the examination, madam?"

The three of them had a good laugh. Daniel, hearing Noah stir in his bassinet, rose to pick him up while Meridia excused herself to the bedroom.

"Your wife is a clever woman," said Samuel, stroking his bushy black beard. "If she were a jewel, there would be no price to her worth."

"I can't and won't argue with you," said Daniel with pride. "I knew her worth from the moment she stomped on my foot."

A few minutes later, Meridia reappeared with the two gold bars. She handed them to Samuel and shook his hand.

"There's one more thing," she said. "My husband has explained that we would like to keep this a secret. Will you give us your word?"

The dealer nodded. A gleam in his audacious eyes gave away his wonderment that somehow, without his being aware of it, this pretty and soft-spoken young woman had not only outsmarted him but also bent him to her wish.

After Samuel left, Daniel asked his wife, "Where did you learn to talk like that?"

"From your mother," said Meridia, taking Noah from him.

~&~

THEY LIVED OFF THE rest of the dowry while they waited. The fact that those gold bars were no longer hidden under her bed gave Meridia frequent chills. What if the partnership failed? Or Samuel turned out to be a swindler? And if Eva found out . . . She held the thoughts at bay by keeping busy. At least she still had the jewelry set from Gabriel. If worse came to worst, she could always pawn it.

A few days after the interview, Meridia was on her way home from the market when she sensed someone following her. She glanced over her shoulder, holding her packages tighter, but saw no one nearby. Majestic Avenue lay languid in a lambent haze. In the distance children were running, men smoking, women whispering. Meridia picked up her pace. Soon she was threading in and out of alleyways, moving as fast as she could, yet the sound of hurried breath persisted. When at last she turned into the brick-paved sanctuary of Willow Lane, a winded feminine voice appealed to her.

"Wait, please!"

Meridia whipped around, squinted her eyes at the approaching shadow. It took her a moment to recognize who it was.

"Pilar! You scared me!"

Patina's sister was pale, thinner, quivering. The same bright yellow tunic she had on last time now looked dull and shabby.

"I've been waiting since sunrise," she explained breathlessly. "I was awake all night—I didn't know if I should talk to you."

"What's the matter?" Alarmed, Meridia placed the packages on the ground and took the older woman's hand.

"It's Patina. She's ill."

A cold wind blew and fluttered the long hems of Pilar's dress. The scent of lilac that had previously perfumed her was now replaced by something akin to naphthalene.

"She's been complaining of a sharp pain in her chest. I thought nothing of it, because who wouldn't have a sharp pain if they had to live with that snake? But one day I was with her when the pain hit.

One second she was fine, the next she was doubled over in agony. I begged her to let me take her to a doctor, but she refused, saying the money would be better spent elsewhere. I kept pleading and pleading, and after many weeks of pain and sleeplessness, she finally consented. The doctor who examined her said there's a lump near her heart. It's not too late to remove it, but it will be costly. This is the part where you won't believe your ears! Patina didn't even want to tell your mother-in-law about it, let alone ask her for money. 'She's got enough problems,' Patina told me. 'This is my fate. Let me bear it on my own.' For once, I lost my patience with her. I stormed into the house and demanded to have a word with that viper. But your mother-in-law wouldn't listen to me! She threw me out of the house and screamed for the whole world to hear that I should stop extorting money from her. Me! The one who used to make sure she wasn't bitten by mosquitoes while she slept! If I had known she would turn out like this, I would have crushed her little skull when I had the chance!"

Pausing for breath, Pilar began scratching the crescent birthmark on her chin. The sharp lines around her mouth shivered like cobwebs in the breeze. In the one year since Meridia first met her, her grain-colored hair had turned a drab shade of gray.

"I don't know where else to go," Pilar said woefully. "It's my last wish to bother you, now that you have a child to raise. But that demon has taken away Patina's feet—don't let her take her heart, too! If you have anything to spare, anything at all . . ."

Meridia did not hesitate. "How much do you need?"

Pilar named a sum that took Meridia by surprise. "Wait here," she said, gathering her packages and disappearing into the house. A few minutes later, she returned with a diamond bracelet, a necklace, and a pair of earrings in her palm.

"Take them."

Pilar stopped her scratching. At once tears came and blurred and smothered.

"They're so beautiful. Are you sure?"

Meridia gave her the jewelry. "Please don't tell anyone."

All of a sudden Pilar seized her hand and kissed it. "You dear, dear angel!" she choked. "May heaven repay you a thousand times for this!"

Embarrassed, Meridia withdrew her hand. "There's no need. Patina has always been kind to me."

After Pilar left, Meridia stood in the street and bit her lip. The back of her blouse darkened with sweat the length of her spine. No one knew that under the loose floorboard in her bedroom lay a velvet jewelry box, the only thing she had taken with her when Eva ousted her from Orchard Road, but the contents of that box now occupied the front pocket of Pilar's dress. With the dowry and the gold bars gone, she decided it would be wise not to tell Daniel.

THAT SAME EVENING, DANIEL returned from Orchard Road with news that Patina had a lump in her heart. Pilar, to everyone's surprise, had agreed to pay for the surgery.

"It doesn't add up," he said, bewildered. "Where did she get that kind of money? As long as I've known Pilar, she could barely afford to buy herself shoes."

Meridia went on feeding Noah, leaving Daniel to his confusion. The next morning, Eva and Elias came to Willow Lane to visit the baby. Meridia was making lunch in the kitchen when she heard Eva's bees hard at work inside the shop.

"Who knows where she got that money. Probably stole it from an old letch after he deflated inside of her. I offered to pay for the operation, but she refused, saying it was her responsibility to take care of her sister. The way I see it, she just wanted to show off. In thirty years that vulture has done nothing but poison Patina against me, and now suddenly she's a model of virtue and generosity. I'm telling you, there's something fishy behind this, and I don't like it one bit!"

Noah was laughing in his grandfather's arms. For a long time it was the only sound competing with the bees.

TWENTY-TWO

They were cautious, perhaps overly so, and they made little. All around the house they hid Samuel's inventory in flour sacks and shoeboxes, in tin oil drums and cookie canisters, exhibiting it only to customers who they knew shared no connection with Lotus Blossom Lane. They shuddered to imagine Eva's wrath were she to find out, the curses she would rain down on them, and the unleashing of bees that would propel Elias to unimaginable deeds. Even when night fell, sleep did not come to them easily. They did not know when Eva or her spies might burst into the shop and catch them red-handed.

No matter how frugally Meridia budgeted, there was hardly money at the end of each month. Some days she felt capable of pawning her soul for a new pair of shoes, a tiny bottle of perfume, or a five-minute hair wash at the beauty parlor. It shamed her to see holes in Daniel's socks and patches in her own nightgown, but to purchase even an extra bar of soap was out of the question. When money became truly scarce, she took to selling some of her better dresses. One evening, when Daniel returned from Orchard Road carrying a paper bag of his father's hand-me-downs, she locked herself in the bathroom and wept. Noah, thankfully, was spared this. Elias saw to it that his grandson was handsomely clothed without exception.

During this period, Eva dressed to the nines whenever she paid them a visit. Among her arsenal were a pink tweed jacket with gold buttons and a matching hat, a shimmering silk skirt edged with antique lace, and a diamond watch consulted every five minutes. Some of these items Meridia recognized as her own wedding presents. She gritted her teeth as Eva inspected her threadbare skirt and shoes, and quietly bore the knowing tilt of that perfectly made face that at once said nothing and everything. Her own skin was dry and rough. She had not allowed herself the luxury of a bottle of lotion.

One afternoon, Eva was about to leave the shop when she took a jar of cream from her purse and set it down grandly on the nearest table. "Use this," she said with a flourish, to no one in particular, before departing. A day passed, then two, then three. Meridia left the cream alone. On the fourth day Eva returned, and finding the jar still untouched, she swept it into her purse in a fit of fury.

NOAH CONTINUED TO BE difficult. Between taking care of him, keeping the house, running the shop, and fending off Eva's bees, Meridia was rapidly wearing herself out. Her figure diminished into a spare geometry of bones; her movements, once so light and nimble, slowed with exhaustion. The face of a stranger dwelled in her mirror, one whose eyes had dulled and whose cheeks drooped with pallor. One time, pleading with this reflection to smile, she was rewarded with a gashlike grin. Her horror knew no bounds when she noticed the resemblance between her face and that of the ghost of Monarch Street. How was it possible that being a mother made her less of a woman?

She recoiled further from Daniel's touch. During the nights when she could not keep warm, she dreaded his embrace more than a rainstorm. Sometimes he caught her short without excuses, and out of guilt and duty, she yielded. She took her part without zeal or pleasure, touched him where he liked to be touched, even uttered her cry without missing her mark. But he was not fooled, and she knew it. In the feeble heat of her moan he detected winter. At such times it appeared that no matter how long he chipped at it, he would never break the ice at the center of her being.

Afterward, always, she turned to the wall and hid from him. When he asked, she smiled and told him she was worried. The shop. Noah's eating habits. Eva's demands. "I might have to beg Papa for money soon." What she did not say was now that she could give him no more children, the last thing she wanted was to look in his eyes and wonder if he remained unchanged.

A REPRIEVE CAME ONE cloudy morning in November. After a long absence, Ravenna emerged from the solitude of her kitchen, put on her winter coat (black according to Leah, white to Rebecca), and set off through the fog to 175 Willow Lane. Her arrival chased Daniel into the shop, but Meridia, breathing in the scent of verbena from her bedroom window, was overjoyed.

"Child, why are you starving yourself?"

From her basket Ravenna produced food in red lacquer boxes, toys for the baby, avocado oil for Meridia's hair and jojoba cream for her skin. Noah—the little imp!—behaved like an angel in front of his grandmother. When she chanted to him in her guttural voice, he fell asleep right away. That day, Meridia learned to feed the baby sugared water to calm him, to massage the soles of his feet when he was restless, and to cure mosquito bites with warm eucalyptus paste. Before leaving, Ravenna told her, "Bring him to the house when he's six months old. It's time he met his grandfather."

After dinner that evening, Meridia found a blue envelope tucked under the mat outside the kitchen door. In it, she counted enough money to last them a month. There was no writing, no scent, no signature. Slipping the envelope into her pocket, Meridia whispered to herself the thanks Ravenna would never claim.

On the morning of December 6, she dressed Noah in his finest clothes and took him to Monarch Street. Ravenna was nowhere to be seen, but a maid she did not recognize told her that Gabriel was in the study. At the door, Meridia paused to take three deep breaths, then walked in with Noah propped high on her arm. Seated behind the monumental desk in a fawn linen suit and a luminous brown tie, Gabriel did not spare her a glance until she greeted him. Even then his handsome gray head was slow to lift, his hard eyes regarding her as if she were no more than a blur. "Let me hold him," he ordered her. She went around the desk and gave him Noah. Gabriel took his grandson by the armpit, shook him once, and held him at arm's length. Terrified, Noah made pitiful faces, but let no sound escape his lips. Meridia remembered how she herself had been studied and dissected until her blood, rebelling, spilled onto the rug. Wishing to spare Noah of this, she began to reach for him when Gabriel's chuckle stopped her.

"He's a fine boy," he said. "Bring him here every year on his birthday."

Gabriel then did something unthinkable—he drew the baby close and kissed him on the brow. Meridia's eyes welled up. It was a kiss he had never deigned to give her.

Noah continued to make no sound until they were outside. Only then did he cry and wet himself, a long golden stream that did not stop for two full minutes.

THREE MONTHS AFTER THE partnership started, Samuel the dealer expressed his disappointment with Willow Lane's performance.

"These pieces need to be displayed prominently, not hidden in sacks and cookie canisters. Why, they're more valuable than those trinkets you have out front! I don't care what kind of a family crisis you're in, but when we agreed to do business, I was under the impression you were going to do your best to make it a success."

"Give us a few months," pleaded Daniel. "We have a plan but it takes time."

"I'll give you one month," said Samuel. "Thirty days from now, if I don't see those jewels sparkling from the window, I'll find myself a new partner."

The couple panicked. How were they to avoid Eva's discovery? For sure they would be denounced as liars. Thieves. Ingrates. They would lose Orchard Road's backing, the stipend, the shop, the house. Adding to the murk was Gabriel's threat that Monarch Street would keep its doors shut. Quickly, the weeks passed without a solution. Three days before Samuel's deadline, an accidental discovery blew their cover for good.

That afternoon, Elias came to Willow Lane alone to visit Noah. He was watching the baby sleep in the living room when he had the sudden urge to drink tea. Not wishing to disturb Daniel or Meridia at the shop, Elias went into the kitchen and boiled himself water. Rummaging through the pantry, he found a large tea tin next to a flour sack and opened it. Instead of tea leaves, small velvet boxes lined the inside. He took one out and opened it—a ring of diamonds and cabochon rubies. He opened another—a pendant with four pink pearls. His trained jeweler's eyes instantly recognized the craftsmanship.

He attacked the flour sack next, the cookie canisters, the lidded ceramic jars labeled innocuously as COOKING OIL. All concealed jewelry in their bellies. Shutting off the stove, Elias gathered a handful of the boxes and returned to the living room. For a long time his gaze alternated between the sleeping baby and the boxes, smiling at one, glaring at the other. And then he went into the shop.

Hiding his hands behind his back, Elias waited until all the customers left before he spoke.

"You shouldn't leave these lying around in the kitchen." He dropped the boxes on the counter and saw color drain from his son's and daughter-in-law's faces. A crazed, manic gleam flashed through his eyes, charging the air with something irreversible.

"Papa, I can explain," said Daniel.

"I've seen enough," Elias said, stopping him briskly. "I will tell your mother that from now on, as a favor to my friend Samuel, I'll allow him to sell his jewelry here at your shop. I'll tell her that I will settle the accounts directly with that bushy goat."

It took Daniel and Meridia a while to grasp this.

"Papa, what are you saying?"

"Don't be dim, son. Dig out those pieces and display them, front and center, where they belong."

Elias headed for the door. Daniel followed him. Before he could speak, Elias wheeled around and cut him with a glare.

"Don't say a word to me. This is for Noah."

And so on the thirtieth day, when Samuel returned to Willow Lane, he had nothing but smiles when he saw his jewelry sparkling in the display cases.

"Do you know my father-in-law?" asked Meridia.

"Only by name," said Samuel. "Why do you ask?"

"You may call him a friend if you wish," she replied cryptically.

SOMEHOW, AGAINST ALL EXPECTATIONS, Elias managed it. When Eva next came to the shop, she looked positively irritable, but not murderous. For the better part of an hour, she stood in front of the display cases patronizing Samuel's jewelry with a scowl.

"Your father said he owed this man a favor from ages ago, and now he's demanding him to repay it. He had some nerve asking your father to carry his trinkets at Lotus Blossom Lane, but your father told him outright they didn't belong there. 'My son's store will be a more suitable place,' he said. I must say, for once, that I agree with him. Look at that topaz ring—it screams tasteless from here to next week! Your father is sorry you're burdened with them. I hope they won't be too difficult to get rid of."

When Eva left, the house turned quiet and stayed quiet. Along with Eva's voice, some other great noise seemed to have been muted.

For the rest of the day, Meridia went about her chores listening for the missing sound. The pipes still bewailed their ancient joints, the stove whirred, the rafters grunted. The wind puffed between the trees and buffeted the roof in endless gusts. What was it then that had been silenced? It was not until nightfall that the answer hit her. Noah had not cried since Eva left. Laughed he had, belched even, but cried, no. Unable to control herself, Meridia swept up her son from his bassinet and kissed him, once, twice, twenty times, laughing, crying, spinning with him around the room until the fire in her heart threatened to consume her. His difficult days were over. She was sure of it just as she was sure that the bold, bright thing she glimpsed in his eyes was the future, stretching its hand toward her.

TWENTY-THREE

The next two years were marked by caution, surreptitious success, and innumerable compromises. Given Elias's backing and Samuel's inventory, the store yielded considerable profits, so that slowly the couple filled the space under their bed with money. Every night with the door locked and the window closed they nourished their dream of independence; every morning they spoke in muted voices of living in their own house and running their own shop. For even at their most brazen they remained wary. There was no telling where Eva's bees were stationed, what grievances they were nursing, or when they were going to pounce out of hiding. Meridia lost count of the number of times they slandered her to the limit. Always, just before anger goaded her to strike, Daniel would interfere. "Not yet," he would say, drawing her from the fray. Over time, she came to resent these two words as much as the bees.

Meridia took refuge in devising ways to drum up business. It was no coincidence that her most daring plans were conceived when the bees were at their worst. In the summer of her nineteenth birthday, entering her third year of marriage, she came up with the idea of photographing babies alongside jewelry from the shop. She hired a photographer at a bargain, rounded up the neighborhood babies with the help of Leah and Rebecca, and had the man snap pictures of them playing with bracelets and crawling among rings. She persuaded Samuel to run a series of these pictures in the paper. The combination of happy, smiling babies and beautiful jewelry proved to be irresistible. Customers, many of them young mothers, flocked to the shop. One photograph in particular, that of Noah nibbling a large emerald pendant, became the talk of Willow Lane for weeks to come.

In January, coinciding with the next Festival of the Spirits, Meridia dressed Leah, Rebecca, Permony, and herself in celestial costumes from a bygone century. The long muslin gowns she borrowed from two dressmakers, the wigs from a hairdresser, the spangled wreaths from a milliner—all businesswomen she had met with Hannah with the aid of cinnamon toffee and whose friendships she continued to cultivate over the years. To these outlandish costumes she piled on the most eye-catching jewelry. Rebecca and Permony could not stop giggling on their walk to Independence Plaza, but as soon as they sighted the solemn mix of prophets and exorcists, they played their parts to perfection. Ethereal in those watery gowns and waist-long hair, they modeled the jewelry to the crowd like spirits from another world. Bewitched by these creatures, spiritualists came to the shop for weeks after, curious about the rings and necklaces that had lent them such an empyreal grace.

IN THOSE YEARS, THE couple did all they could to deceive Eva. Six nights out of the week, Daniel went to Orchard Road with his most honest face and showed his mother the books for Elias's inventory. Eva digested the numbers skeptically, always hoping to unveil a dishonesty, yet her rudimentary arithmetic was no match for Meridia's sly intelligence. On occasion, she insisted on seeing Samuel's books as well, prompting Elias to yawn in dismissal. "The old goat's meager stake isn't worth your time," he said. To this, Daniel added that Samuel's inventory was causing him no end of headaches. Customers, he said, neither requested nor desired the pieces. Elias played along. "I'm sorry, son." He shook his head ruefully. "I owed the man a favor."

Before Eva could ask questions about the photographs in the paper or Meridia's antics at the festival, Daniel threw her off the scent by putting on a shamed face.

"We're desperate for publicity, Mama. A lot of good it did us. We made even less money afterward."

"What did you expect?" Eva replied with a huff. "Jewelry, babies, spirits. The three don't even belong in the same sentence!"

WITH NOAH NO LONGER difficult, Meridia steadily regained her vigor. The ghost in her mirror disappeared, taking with it the roughness of skin and unsightly protrusion of bones. Her own emotions ceased to hold her hostage. Those episodes of hopelessness that had often paralyzed her now occurred but rarely. Once again she took pleasure in work, in cooking, and in caring for her family. And as their income grew, they allowed themselves small and secret indulgences. Daniel bought a pair of fine cowhide boots, hiding them the second he glimpsed his mother strolling down Willow Lane. One Saturday out of the month, Meridia had her hair and nails done at a beauty parlor, careful that she was not followed on her walk there. Early on Sunday mornings when only the dead were awake, they took Noah to the market and gorged themselves on salted plums, sticky buns, sweet bean curd in steaming ginger soup. Each time they ate quickly, standing in shade or behind trees so no one could see them.

One thing that helped Meridia greatly through those years was Ravenna's infrequent yet indispensable visits. To inhale the scent of verbena drifting from a distance, and then to behold her mother's face and implacable iron knot, was enough to bolster her for weeks. Ravenna stayed an hour at most, just long enough to put the house in order. On the evening of each visit, a blue envelope awaited Meridia outside the kitchen door. Not once in the years to come would Ravenna allow her to mention this.

One night after such a visit, a blast of heat pummeled Meridia awake. She sat bolt upright, eyes and cheeks afire, and blinked rapidly in the dark. Next to her, Daniel was snoring. Noah was asleep in his bassinet. Suddenly the heat in her face shone like a bright yellow sun, spun down her limbs, and lighted with yearning every vein and capillary on the way. Her breath caught in her throat. Her lips turned dry. She tossed the blanket aside and found the frost gone from her bed. For the first time since Noah's birth, she turned to Daniel and squeezed him in her arms, dug her fingers into his back, kissed his eyes, nose, lips, and desired him so urgently he woke up in confusion. Careful not to meet his stare, she buried her mouth in his shoulder and bruised it with a hunger she had never before known. It was not enough. His grunt as he tore off her clothes resurrected feelings she thought the bees had slain. She shut her eyes, she willed him to pull her deeper. The presence of Noah did nothing to deter her. That night, she cried out Daniel's name without needing a mark. All she was aware of was the taste of his skin, the lips sealed over hers, the heat that enfolded them where for so long there had only been cold.

THE REKINDLING OF PASSION gave birth to arguments at the dinner table. Eva, naturally, was at the root of them. Mistaking Meridia's silence for compliance, the mother-in-law became bolder with her demands, sending not only Patina in the morning for food, but also Gabilan in the afternoon for oil, candles, and soap. As Noah grew older, Eva's unwelcome advice also multiplied: what he should eat and wear, how he should be reared, why an evening bath was more beneficial than a morning one. In most instances, Meridia pretended deafness, but there were times when she turned dinner with Daniel into a battlefield. Their biggest argument, in fact, revolved around a piece of fruit.

One Sunday afternoon, Eva was watching Noah play on the living room floor when she had the idea of feeding him a banana. She took the fruit from a glass bowl on the dinner table, peeled the skin, broke off a generous piece, and mashed that piece between thumb and forefinger. She was in the midst of inserting this pulp into Noah's mouth when Meridia came out of the bedroom and saw her. Appalled beyond description, Meridia rushed to her son and snatched him. "Time for his nap," she announced sharply, taking him into the bedroom. Daniel, occupied with bills at the dinner table, had scarcely registered the skirmish when Eva exploded.

"Do you see how your wife treats me? I'm not even allowed to come near my grandson! Don't tell me you're going to sit there and do nothing!"

More angry words followed. Refusing to be drawn in, Daniel made no reply. That night, it was Meridia who confronted him at dinner.

"Why didn't you say something to your mother this afternoon?"

"About what?"

"About feeding Noah that filth. Heaven knows where her hands have been."

"That's how she fed me and the girls when we were little."

Meridia widened her eyes in disbelief. "Are you condoning her behavior? Her revolting, unsanitary behavior?"

"I'm saying that's how she is. Don't you think you were the slightest bit rude, snatching Noah from under her nose like that?"

A bowl jumped from Meridia's hand and banged against the table.

"Your mother is meddling, Daniel, after she promised my father she wouldn't. You must take a stand and draw some boundaries."

"I have taken a stand. Yours. Dearest, aren't you overreacting? It's a banana."

"But what are we waiting for? I ran the numbers in my head thousands of times. We have enough. We can purchase a place of our own."

Sighing, Daniel shook his head. When the dreaded words came, Meridia could not bring herself to look at him.

"Not yet. You know very well that if we break now, the slightest setback will put us in the poorhouse. Wait a little longer and we'll be home free."

Frustrated, yet unable to refute his logic, Meridia pushed her plate and got up from the table. "I'm beginning to think that's a miracle I won't see in my lifetime," she said.

A MIRACLE SHE DID witness in those years left her baffled to no end. Three months after the surgery, Patina's sparse white hair grew thick and black, her flesh filled out, and all the wrinkles in her face vanished without a trace. Her eyes regained their vivid youth, and as if a yoke had been lifted, her shoulders straightened from their hunch to elevate her above Eva. Healed also were the hooflike bones of her feet. Her toes, strong now and uncurled, permitted her to walk for the first time in decades without pain or hobbling.

One morning, amazed by the mystical joy suffusing the old woman's face, Meridia asked her, "You look so happy, Patina. What's your secret?"

Patina smiled brightly. Her teeth were white, even, complete.

"Can you keep it to yourself?" she said, carefully looking around the shop before whispering, "My child, my baby—she gave me back my heart."

Meridia raised her brow. "Your child? What do you mean?"

Then it hit her all at once. For an instant she felt like laughing, but instead she shuddered, dropping her eyes to avoid Patina's.

"You think she paid for the surgery?"

Patina was beaming. "Pilar refused to disclose the donor, but who else had that kind of money? Or cared enough about me? People can say what they want, but nobody knows her like I do. To the world she shows a hard front, but inside she's loving and generous. She made a big show of saying no to Pilar because she didn't want attention drawn to herself. Do you see? She's forgiven me! After all these years!"

Meridia, handing her money for Eva's food, had no heart to tell her otherwise.

The miracle did not stop there. Over the course of the year, a phosphorescent glow illuminated Patina's skin from within, so brightly that her bones became visible like glass. Little by little her features blurred, first the nose and lips, then the eyes and ears, transforming her face into one transparent incandescence. With every abuse Eva heaped on her, Patina's diaphanous state intensified until she was no longer discernible to the naked eye. One morning, precisely two years after the surgery, Eva searched for her everywhere and could not find her. Eva turned the house upside down, looked under stairs and inside cabinets, but not a trace of Patina remained. "Has someone misplaced that miserable old crow?" she shouted angrily at Gabilan and the girls. That day, Eva's steel blue hair began to turn white.

TWENTY-FOUR

It so happened that Pilar, indiscreet, was the one who precipitated their freedom.

A week after Patina vanished, Eva ran into her old foe at the butchers' aisle and accused her of hiding her sister. Pilar, though she betrayed no shock at the news, denied the charge vehemently.

"If you're so concerned, then why don't you alert the authorities?"

"I told her she could leave whenever she wanted to. Why should I lift a finger if she'd rather stay with you in the gutter?"

"Very well then. Patina's much happier in the gutter than she was with you."

Swinging her basket like a weapon, Eva retorted that she knew exactly how Pilar had obtained the money for the surgery.

"The whole town knows what you do to earn your bread. The whole town has had a whiff—in one form or another—of that foul cave between your legs."

Enraged, Pilar spat out the truth. "It was Meridia who gave me the money. Yes, that generous, thoughtful, kindhearted woman who is too good to be married to your son. She was the one who gave me her jewelry and saved your mother's heart."

"My mother died a long time ago!" Eva shouted in full hearing of the butchers. "And I never got to know who she was, thanks to your sister!"

More bitter words flew before Eva stormed off, for once paying for her meat without haggling. That afternoon she summoned Daniel to Orchard Road and besieged him with her bees.

"Your wife's conduct is nothing less than an outrage. Did she consult you, her husband, the father of her child, before she made her decision? That proves how little she values your opinion. And for her to assume I wouldn't take care of dear Patina myself! That gentle, devoted woman raised me, for heaven's sake! God knows she'd made her mistakes, but I'd be the last to let her suffer in pain. I'll tell you what's cooking in your wife's vain head. She's dying to show off who wears the pants in your house. Oh, you should hear the dreadful things Pilar said about you at the market square! 'One crook of Meridia's finger and Daniel will do anything. He'll jump if she tells him to jump. He'll drop his trousers if she wants him to service her, but only when it's convenient for her, of course.' Pilar even said that you wouldn't have the guts to do anything if you were to catch your wife with a lover! Son, this sort of talk did not come out of nowhere. Your wife must have said something, bragged somewhere about her power over you. Now the whole town is laughing, thinking you're not man enough to be her husband. After what happened today, I'm convinced your wife plotted with Pilar to steal Patina from me."

For the first hour Daniel laughed and smiled, shrugged his shoulders, and was successful in swatting the bees off his face. But as the second hour droned on and the insects showed no sign of fatiguing, his vision began to blur along with his judgment. Cunning and vicious, the bees uncovered every crack in his marriage, exposed every insecurity a husband might harbor toward his wife. Those nights when Meridia refused his advances because she felt "indisposed" . . . her insistence to break from Orchard Road when he told her they were not ready . . . her refusal to understand that Eva was his mother and he could not altogether cut her out . . . the banana incident when she felt she had to have the last word on everything . . .

When Daniel returned home that night, his face was long, his arms covered in small dark marks, and his clothes reeked from a stench Meridia would recognize anywhere. For the first time he was cross with Noah and did not speak to her at all. Having witnessed the bees at work on Elias before, Meridia guessed what had happened. She waited until they were in bed before asking.

"What did your mother say?"

He turned to her slowly. The single dim light on her side of the room allowed him to observe her more than she could him. Under her steady gaze, the bees swirled and clamored in his head.

"She said you gave Pilar the money for Patina's surgery."

Meridia nodded without surprise. "I asked Pilar to pawn my jewelry set. I take it your mother was displeased?"

Garbled by the bees, her cool, collected tone shot straight into his vein. Had she sounded less certain, guilty even, he would have thought she had realized her mistake and was sorry for it. But this calm, unruffled confidence, this look of utter irreproachability, gave her the appearance of premeditation.

"Why didn't you tell me? I would never object to it, but the least you could do was ask. That jewelry set was our last safety."

Again, Meridia's reply sounded too pat to his ear. "I wanted to spare you the worry. I swore Pilar to secrecy—I never meant for anyone to know—and it's unfortunate that you had to find out this way." She leaned across and reached for his hand. "Don't fall for it, Daniel. This is another one of your mother's ploys to divide us."

The bees screeched the instant her fingers found his. Deafened by the noise, Daniel jerked back his hand.

"Did you have anything to do with Patina's disappearance?" he asked.

She looked at him. Her beautiful face, with the light behind her, seemed like a riddle he could neither solve nor understand.

"Of course not. I didn't know Patina was gone until your mother informed us."

Daniel lay flat on his back. Kissing him good night, Meridia felt a fence going up between them. She pressed her palm against it, gave it a little push, but he closed his eyes and did not open them again.

ANGERED BY MERIDIA'S ACTION, Eva looked for a way to retaliate. She began by dropping small hints, harmless enough to the casual ear, but when she deemed Elias sufficiently primed, her bees struck without mercy where he was most vulnerable.

"She's grooming Noah to scorn us. Did you notice how that child pouted at me when I saw him the other day? Two years old and his nose already up in the clouds! Let's face it. She thinks we're not good enough for her child. I've seen how she sneers at you when you play with Noah, making fun of your bald head, I'm sure! Who knows what poisonous things she pours into his ear when you're not there. Did you notice that Noah threw up on you twice this past week? Gabilan was just saying she's been washing too much vomit off your shirts lately. I wonder if she's trained him to do that, making your grandson allergic to you. Malin was there the other day, and she overheard *her* telling Daniel that you're unclean! 'Noah's always itchy after your father holds him.' And instead of defending you, Daniel agreed with her. Our own son, turning his back on us! You must do something. Our dignity is hanging by a thread, and before she snaps it altogether, you must stop her. How can you face your father and grandfather if you let a woman mock you, piss on your honor, defecate on your manhood? The next time we pay them a visit, notice how Noah puckers his nose when Permony comes near him . . ."

Elias endured the onslaught for twenty-one days without a single night's rest. On the twenty-second morning, nerves strung to the breaking point, he staggered out of bed and threw on a coat. Eva quickly dressed and followed him. She said nothing during their walk to Willow Lane, but her bees did not let up their torment inside his head. Elias's pale, harassed face contrasted horridly with his red eyes, enough to send a few schoolchildren fleeing in fright. When they got to the house, Noah was having a tantrum in the kitchen: He wanted his mother, who had gone off to the market. Daniel, doing all he could to calm the boy, was relieved to see his father.

"Grandpa's here," he told Noah, handing him to Elias. "Stop that bawling now."

"Go open the shop, son," said Eva calmly. "We'll look after him."

Too preoccupied to notice the signs, Daniel left the three of them together.

There was nothing Elias could do to pacify Noah that morning. The boy refused to greet him, howled and flopped about when Elias held him, kicked his feet irritably when placed on the floor. Once or twice he stuck his tongue out at his grandfather. Elias did not remember that Noah had displayed the same tantrum a few weeks ago, and he had responded then by tickling the boy into laughter. Now he burned with anger and humiliation. Seeing her opportunity, Eva jumped in with a cry.

"Are you convinced now? She's turned him against you. Look at him!"

Out of Elias's sight Eva glared at the boy, keeping him anxious and petulant. Twenty-one days' worth of bees droned on and on in Elias's head.

Noah, seeing how red his grandfather's face had become, suddenly pointed and laughed. In Elias's sleep-deprived mind, the laughter exploded like a terrible insult.

"He's mocking you!" seized Eva triumphantly. "This is what his mother's been teaching him behind your back."

"Shut up, you monkey!"

Elias's roar, followed by a plangent smack to Noah's head, shocked the boy into silence. Even Eva withdrew a little. Frightened, Noah dropped to the floor and scrambled under the dinner table.

"Come out this instant!"

"Mama! Mama!"

Noah receded deeper. Angered beyond reason, Elias dropped on all fours and stuck his arms under the table. He took hold of Noah's legs, but the boy, flailing in panic, kicked his knuckles with all his might. "Goddamn you!" Elias roared again, grabbing the boy's ankles. In full force he began to drag him out, Eva goading from above, Noah screaming, twisting like a trapped animal. And then they heard it: the sound of bone smashing against wood. The dinner table jolted from the impact. Elias released his grip. A second later the boy whimpered, not daring to scream out loud.

"Noah!"

Drawn by the noise, Daniel ran in from the shop, pushed the dinner table aside, and gathered Noah in his arms. There was blood on the boy's face, a gash on his right temple. Before Daniel could press a towel to the wound, a shout erupted from the door.

"What's going on here?"

Rushing in with packages in hand, Meridia dropped everything on the floor. As soon as he saw his mother, Noah burst out crying.

"Keep him calm." Daniel handed the boy to her. "I'll run and get the doctor."

He dashed out to the street. Murmuring, Meridia began the impossible task of quieting the boy. It did not escape her that Noah had raised his index finger, to point not at Elias but at Eva, who was standing by the stove with a horrified expression. Meridia had only to glance at her father-in-law to confirm the labor of the bees.

Elias, who had not risen from the floor until then, started to stammer, more to Noah than anyone else. "It was an accident, you understand . . . an accident . . ." The instant the grandfather got to his feet, Noah cried louder.

"Don't come closer," Meridia said sharply, more to Eva than anyone else. Giving her mother-in-law her deathliest look, she carried Noah into the bedroom and laid him down on the bed. Hushing, comforting him, she held a towel firmly to his temple and wiped the blood with another. The interminable wait began. Noah cried and cried and there was no sign of Daniel.

Meridia did not leave her son's side until the doctor Daniel brought home assured her that the wound was not deep. If there was to be a scar from the stitches, it would fade away with time. Only then did she go out to the living room, extract Eva from her seat, and hurl her against the wall. Eva's bloodcurdling scream brought Daniel running out of the bedroom. Had he not moved quickly, Meridia's fist would have loosened a molar or two.

"It was an accident," said Daniel as he held her back. "Nobody meant to hurt Noah. An accident was all it was."

"Don't bother hiding your dirty hand," Meridia spat at Eva. "You can try to harm me all you want, but leave my child out of this. If you ever lay a finger on him again, God help me, I'll tear you apart with my own hands!"

She trembled with rage and hatred. Daniel, who had never seen her in this state, released his hold silently. Eva, for once, said nothing in return. She stood with her back flat against the wall, lips pursed, palms curled, eyes downcast. Meridia swung on Daniel.

"I won't live like this anymore," she said.

She narrowed her gaze when she saw him waver. Hardened her jaw when he shook his head. At last, realizing that her will was stronger than his, he took a breath and cleared his throat. She did not seem like a woman then, but a man far more determined than he was.

"We won't need your help anymore, Mama," he said. "From now on, Meridia and I will make our own way."

It was done, their dream of independence put into words. Like a bolt of lightning, the news pried Eva off the wall and set her tongue to work.

"And how do you propose to perform this miracle? 'Make our own way.' You have no money, no shop, no house of your own. How will you survive without your father's name to back you up? Have some sense, son. Noah banged his head against the table. It's unfortunate but it happens to children every day. Why must you turn this into a crisis? Your wife, on the other hand—"

A groan interrupted her, prolonged and anguished. It was coming from Elias.

"Say nothing more, please. Let them do as they wish."

Eva turned to her husband and was shocked by the change in him. She was aware that he had been sitting quietly at the dinner table, removed from the scuffle, and had not stirred or spoken in some time. But now he stood with his head bowed, away from the light and contemplating his hands as though something in them were stirring his disgust. Lifting his eyes a fraction, he met his wife's glance and shuddered in horror.

"Did you hear what I said, Papa?" asked Daniel.

Elias nodded but made no reply. Before Eva could rally her bees, Meridia spun on her heel and returned to the bedroom.

TWENTY-FIVE

Twelve blocks east of Willow Lane lay the burgeoning neighborhood of Magnolia Avenue. Property number 70—two-story, plain, but full of light—stood in the middle of the shop-lined street. Formerly a bakery, the ground floor hosted a retail space with a kitchen, a dining room, and a little garden tacked to the back. Upstairs were three bedrooms, a bath, and a living room. Counted among the surrounding shops were a confectionery, two booksellers, a clockmaker's studio, clothing stores, eateries, and specialty boutiques. At sundown the white lanterns strung between the two sides of the street came on, and performers rushing from Independence Plaza joggled for space in the sidewalks to compete for coins.

Meridia bought new furniture for the house. Putting Eva's haggling skills to good use, she acquired a handsome dining set at a deep discount; a sofa, chairs, coffee table; a four-poster bed for the master bedroom. Noah's room she decorated with a bright blue rug, an ancient toy chest, stenciled animals along the walls, and a bed built to resemble an ark. The garden she planted with orchids and bougainvilleas—a cramped yet quiet retreat from the hullabaloo of the street.

The shop was an instant success. The high quality of stock and service, combined with aggressive pricing and strategic location, worked not only to retain old customers from Willow Lane but to draw new ones off the street. Unable to handle all the demands, Samuel introduced them to two renowned dealers, both trusted and longtime friends of his. New partnerships were quickly established. Three months after opening, the shop became one of the most frequented businesses on Magnolia Avenue. In this way, the couple began to accumulate wealth, which they no longer stowed in a hole under their bed, but in a venerable bank on Majestic Avenue bearing the flags of seven nations.

As much as the change in fortune delighted Meridia, it was nothing compared to the taste of freedom. The absence of Eva's daily requirements—in fact, of Eva altogether—was a perpetual source of wonder and celebration. For the first time in her marriage, Meridia felt liberated from the bees. The anxiety, the tension, the petty arguments between her and Daniel disappeared. Her house was now her own, a sanctuary where Eva exerted no more influence than a visitor. She could dress and raise Noah as she pleased. She could eat any food she liked out in the open. She could stop glancing over her shoulder when she went to the market or the beauty parlor.

Meridia hosted her first dinner party the following spring. Leah, Rebecca, their husbands, and four other neighbors from Willow Lane. She spent the entire day cooking and cleaning. When night fell, nothing could stop her from exclaiming in horror—the dessert was not ready, the guests were due in fifteen minutes, she had not had time to sweep the stairs or clean the windows. "Relax," said Daniel, grabbing a broom from the hook. "They won't notice a thing once they see that mustache on your face." Shrieking, Meridia brushed her hand across her lips and saw it smeared with molasses.

The guests declared the house lovely and welcoming. Rounder now that she was expecting her first child, Leah found much to admire in Meridia's new furniture. "I want that chair before the baby comes," she threatened her husband. "And I don't care what your

mother says, that curtain will look divine in our living room." Rebecca and the other two women focused their assault on Noah.
"How handsome you look in that suit! And how grown up! Tell your
mother you're going home with Aunt Rebecca tonight." The boy
acted indignant, not to mention scandalized, but it was evident from
his reddening ears that he was pleased.

At dinner, Meridia earned raves for her dishes, especially the
seared golden prawns and the duck roasted in a clay cooker. Daniel
took a bite of the duck and told her, "It's better than Patina's." Meridia beamed, pleased that she now could turn flour into delicious
pastries, stew meat without spoiling the vegetables, and add just the
right amount of salt to any dish. All through dinner good humor
abounded. While the women clamored for recipes, the men made
sure that not a drop of sauce was left on the plates.

Later, while the guests were departing, Rebecca pulled her friend
to the side and whispered, "You must visit us often. Willow Lane is
haunted without you."

Meridia laughed. "What are you talking about?"

"It's true," Leah joined in. "Numbers 173 and 177 swear there's a
woman living in your old house, though the agency claimed no one
has rented it since you left. They say she has the wise look of an old
woman, but the unlined face and thick hair of a little girl's. Evidently
she likes to cook. The house smells of food at all hours of the day."

"I heard her skin is like water," said Rebecca sensationally. "So
clear you can see right to her bones."

Meridia felt hairs standing on the back of her neck. "Have you
seen her yet?"

"We waited for an hour one night, hoping to catch a glimpse of
her. Smelled the cooking all right, but the house remained dark and
there was no one inside."

"They'll never get another tenant for it," said Leah. "Not with a
ghost that looks like she's settling in for good."

"Just as well," said Rebecca. "Any neighbor after Meridia will be
a letdown."

∽

AFTER PUTTING NOAH TO bed, Meridia went to her room and saw Daniel waiting for her with a blue velvet box in his hand.

"I found an old friend of yours," he said. "Say hello."

"What is it?" Meridia took the box and opened it. Her jaw dropped the instant she recognized the contents.

"How did you find it?"

"Pilar." Daniel grinned. "I ran into her the other day and scared her into talking. It's a shame the pawnshop already sold the bracelet and the earrings."

He took the diamond necklace from the box and put it on her.

Meridia's voice was breaking, but she blinked back her tears. "I didn't think I'd see it again," she said. She took Daniel's face in her hands, moved forward, and kissed him, so hard he thought he might bleed.

Later, entwined and exhausted in the dark, Daniel tugged at the necklace and said, "Where do you think Patina went?"

Meridia considered this a moment before answering. "A place far away where good souls rest. Even if I knew where she was, I would never disturb her."

IN THOSE YEARS, NOAH was an easy child in all ways but one: he became extremely sensitive when teased. One time when he was four, he saw a pretty rabbit doll in a shop near Cinema Garden and could not take his eyes off it.

"The little fellow wants the rabbit," Daniel said to Meridia with a wink. "Shall I get it for him?"

Playing along, Meridia replied, "Only if he kisses his mama on the cheek."

Noah instantly turned away. "Who says I want an ugly thing like that?"

Back at the house, Daniel surprised the boy with the doll, having purchased it without his knowledge. Noah took one look and tossed it to the floor.

"I told you I didn't want it! I won't play with it!"

Meridia put the rabbit on top of the ancient toy chest. That night, after Noah retreated to bed, she heard strange noises coming from his room. Together with Daniel, she approached the boy's door and opened it without sound. Sitting on the floor with his back to them, Noah was playing with the rabbit, laughing joyously as he burrowed his nose on its belly. The parents traded a smile and returned to their room.

To Ravenna, Noah behaved like the perfect gentleman. On those special days when Meridia caught her mother's scent drifting in from the window, the boy would run to his room to comb his hair and change his shirt. As soon as Ravenna walked in, he greeted her with a formal bow he had learned from a street performer. "Grandma," he would say brightly. Her wild-eyed expression did not scare him, nor did her gaunt face when it came so near he could see her wrinkles. When she patted his cheek, he grinned wide with pleasure. Her scent of lemon verbena lingered on him long after she was gone.

Gabriel was a different matter. Every year on the boy's birthday, despite the number of presents he unwrapped at breakfast, there was no curbing his tears as Meridia dressed him in his new clothes. "Stop that," she said. "I won't have your grandfather think I'm as bad a mother as I am a daughter." Unmoved, she led him downstairs and out to follow the sun. During their walk Noah raised no objection. When they entered Gabriel's study, he held his shoulders up the way she had trained him. Together they walked past the towering shelves, his hand digging into hers but his eyes looking directly in front. Stopping before the desk, he uttered the greeting he had carefully practiced. "Come here, boy!" bellowed his grandfather. Though his knees quaked, Noah covered the remaining distance by himself—so small, yet so brave and determined. Gabriel lifted him from the floor and placed him on his lap. Being so close to that terrifying face could not have been pleasant, but Noah answered all his grandfather's questions without a tremor. When they left the study, his shirt was always damp. As soon as they reached the sanctuary of Ravenna's kitchen, Meridia loosened his collar and hugged him. "I'm so proud of you," she whispered again and again, laughing and crying at the same time.

WHILE HE FEARED GABRIEL and worshipped Ravenna, Noah remained unimpressed by Elias's repentance. For a long time after the accident, he howled like a kicked dog when he saw his grandfather, cupped both hands over the scar on his temple, and refused to be pacified until he drove the jeweler out of the house. Elias brought him gifts, sang, read, walked like an ape, bleated like a goat. The only thing he accomplished was annoying his grandson.

Over time, Noah developed the skill to ignore the jeweler. Meridia had little idea how deeply this affected Elias until one afternoon in the boy's fifth year. Elias, seated on the sofa, was reading aloud from a book. Noah, occupied with his toys on the floor, paid no notice. Meridia was dusting a shelf behind the sofa when she heard Elias's voice stopped in midsentence. She turned, surprised, and regarded the back of her father-in-law's head. It was still and oddly bowed, two birthmarks on the smooth, glossy surface. She inched closer until she stood behind him. Looking over his shoulder to the book he held, she saw tears dropping onto the page. Quietly she retreated from the room.

That night Meridia sat down with the boy and talked to him.

"You're being cruel to your grandfather Elias. That scar was an accident—he will never hurt you again. Why don't you be kind to him?"

"He never leaves me alone, Mama! Always asking if he could play with me. Sometimes I don't want to play with him."

"He's sad because he thinks you're angry."

"Then tell him to stop making those noises. He doesn't sound like a goat."

Meridia sighed deeply. "Be kind. Your grandfather's a good man."

"How can he be good if he gave me this scar?"

At a loss for an explanation, she placed one hand on his cheek and stroked it.

"Few people can stand up to your grandmother Eva. One day you'll understand."

"Are you one of those people?"

"Absolutely."

"Papa?"

"When he chooses to."

"What about me?"

Meridia pushed her nose against his. "By God, I hope so! Now go to sleep."

TWENTY-SIX

Eva's mistake had been grave, and no one knew it better than herself. Without intending to, the blow she had aimed for Meridia had missed and struck Noah. At present, Magnolia Avenue did not welcome her. When they met, Meridia spoke no more than two words, barely troubling to conceal her displeasure. Daniel acted curt, full of insufferable excuses. He no longer came alone to Orchard Road as in the old days, but brought his wife and child with him. Did he think he needed protection from his own mother? There he would sit in her living room, drinking her tea yet consulting *her* opinion every three minutes as if he had none of his own. "What do you think of this, dearest? Should we do as Mama suggested?" Though Eva was too proud to breathe a word, his behavior wounded her. Why was he punishing her for something that was clearly an accident?

Noah added to the insult by refusing to greet her. Every time they met, he kept his lips pursed and his expression hostile. And every single time, his blasted mother had to make a production out of it in front of everyone. "Where are your manners? I didn't raise you to be a savage. Greet Grandma. Don't you see her? She's right there.

Repeat after me. 'Good afternoon, Grandma.'" And the boy just stood there, mortified, and gaped! Eva had no doubt this was a routine they had rehearsed often and to perfection.

They had deceived her, of course. Somehow, all her vigilance notwithstanding, they had pilfered money from Willow Lane. Or rather, *she* had pilfered money. How else could they afford a house and open a shop? Something was amiss. Daniel said Meridia had received a loan from her father—a plausible but unlikely story, given how that adulterous boar had declined to fund Willow Lane in the first place. Oh, if only she could expose their treachery and breathe life back into stupefied Elias!

For he was no longer the same man. Since the accident, he had been spending more time glued to his rocking chair on the terrace, not to read those tiresome books that were now collecting dust on the shelves, but to contemplate his hands. He lost interest in his caged birds, and the bees swirled round and round without even stirring him. One by one, the birds died from neglect, the bees dropped from exhaustion. Elias began to limp, and his face took on the look of a shriveled fruit. From the few roses left on the lawn and the odious sea of marigolds surrounding them, Eva gathered that Lotus Blossom Lane was in trouble. But what did the shop matter to Elias when the memory of Noah's scar so tortured him he had to knuckle his eyes raw to stop it?

Exasperated by her husband, Eva turned to her daughters for comfort. She took immense satisfaction in the fact that Malin, almost twenty, had caught the interest of a handsome suitor. The son of a wealthy silk merchant, the young man wooed Malin so ardently that the indifference with which she treated him only served to fuel his passion. Judging from his spellbound look and the number of gifts he sent to the house, Eva predicted marriage before the year was over.

Without Patina to abuse, she concentrated her faultfinding on Permony. The girl's face, weight, and manners became permanent and delectable topics of castigation. Given the severity of her censure, it was a miracle that Permony grew up to be a charming and complacent young woman. Now in her seventeenth year, she was no longer shy or awkward, but carried herself with an easy grace. After Patina disappeared, an armor seemed to descend and isolate her from the bees; however ripe with spleen, their droning went into one ear and fell out the other. Permony alone possessed the magic to roust Elias from dejection. All this was lost on Eva, who resented the girl more when she realized she no longer took her scolding to heart.

Once she realized the futility of cutting more roses for the shop, Eva took to casting her eyes vindictively in the direction of Magnolia Avenue. There to the southeast, in that plain two-story house cramped with nondescript others in that noisy street, they neither needed nor respected her. Her son and grandchild, corrupted by that detestable woman to scorn her. How could she right this wrong? Remedy this gross injustice? After months of consorting with fury, the answer came to her loud and clear.

ONCE SHE MADE UP her mind, Eva was unstoppable. Aware of Meridia's opposition, she came up with ironclad excuses to visit Magnolia Avenue. One day she brought sweet rolls filled with condensed milk, which she knew Daniel liked; the next, she brought Permony to play with Noah. Shrewdly leaving her bees at home, she made amends with her grandson by giving him coloring books and jigsaw puzzles, things she knew Meridia would not object to, and feeding him milk candies and lemon cookies on the sly. She learned from Elias's mistake not to become a nuisance to the introverted boy, but to flatter him with a few choice words and then withdraw. One morning, three months after her campaign began, Eva reaped her first reward. When Noah saw her climb the staircase from the shop, he broke away from his mother and ran to her. "Grandma," he said warmly. Meridia looked as if a thunder had struck her deaf.

Soon, other victories. When Eva deliberately stayed away for a few days, Noah grew restless and pestered his father to inquire if she was ill. The next time Eva showed up, he welcomed her with a hug, causing Meridia's heart to leap to her throat. Sensing the enmity between his mother and grandmother, the clever boy used it to his advantage. When Meridia forbade him to play past his bedtime, Noah retorted, "Grandma Eva will let me. She says I can do anything if I live with her." Too taken aback for anger, Meridia let him stay up another hour.

"Your mother is plotting something," she told Daniel that night. "Noah is always irritable after her visits."

In bed, Daniel raised his brows but did not close the book he was reading.

"I think it's good she's making an effort to befriend him. Would you rather they bicker like enemies?"

"She never came near him before. Now suddenly she can't get enough of him."

Daniel cocked his head and regarded her with amusement. "Noah seems to take to Mama. You're not jealous, are you?"

"Of course not," she said, a little abrupt. "I don't trust her, that's all."

"She won't dare harm him again. She knows we're watching her."

"Are you? Watching her? I know I am."

He smiled wryly, then fixed on her the helpless look he used to humor Noah.

"What do you suggest I do? I can't tell him to stay away from his grandmother."

His teasing tone aside, Meridia knew this was fair. Particularly since she had not heard the slightest buzzing of bees. Before she could reply, Daniel's smile had widened.

"Why are you smiling like that?" she asked.

"You know I love you, dearest," he said. "But just now, you sounded exactly like Mama."

To make his point, Daniel snapped open his book until the spine cracked. Meridia, reminded of how Eva used to pester Elias to the most remote corner of his encyclopedias, hurled a pillow at Daniel.

"Laugh all you want," she said. "But the second your mother slips, I'm going to be all over her."

A few days later, Noah asked her if he could have a bird for a pet.

"Like Grandfather Elias's. I want it to talk to me when I'm bored."

"A bird?" said Meridia, intrigued. "But you can talk to me when you're bored! Believe me, once I put my mind to it, I can be more entertaining than a bird."

Noah, thinking he was being teased, kept his face long for the rest of the day.

When Eva showed up with a white cockatoo in an antique brass cage the next morning, Meridia realized it was her mother-in-law who had put the idea into Noah's head.

"I hope you don't mind, dear," said Eva. "Noah's been telling me how much he wanted a talking bird. I managed to get one with the voice of an angel."

As if on cue, the cockatoo trilled out Noah's name. The boy ran into the living room and hollered, "Grandma! What did you bring me today?"

"Just a minute . . . Ask your mother first if you could keep it."

"Oh, Mama! Could I keep it? Please . . . please . . ."

Aware that she had been trapped, Meridia could do nothing but nod.

"Give Grandma a kiss," said Eva. "The other cheek, too." Smiling broadly, she handed Noah the cage. "Careful, don't scratch your mother's beautiful floor. Shall we put it in your room, right next to your bed?"

Holding the cage high, Noah shot his mother a triumphant glance. Had he forgotten it was Eva, too, who had branded him with the scar?

In no time, Meridia grew convinced that the cockatoo had been enchanted. Enslaved by the same sorcery Eva had once practiced upon Elias's caged birds. But instead of shrieking "Fire!" or "Thief!" the bird declaimed, "Who loves Noah dearly? Grandma Eva . . ." The mischief did not stop here. Fueling Meridia's suspicion that black magic was at play, the bird could sense, from any position in the house, every single time she undressed to bathe, and would shrill "Filthy! Shame!" at the top of its lungs before whistling innocently the instant she charged out of the bathroom. Daniel heard nothing, stared as if she had gone clean out of her mind with only a towel around her. Once again, Eva had kept her alchemy hidden from him.

The change in Noah was startling. Bewitched by the bird, he no longer called for Meridia when he awoke, shunned her kisses, and preferred the cockatoo's lullaby to her bedtime tales. He developed a rash when she tried to hug him, stopped speaking to her for three days, and could only swallow her cooking with the utmost difficulty. At the same time, he ate everything Eva brought him and insisted she spend every morning at the house. The grandmother, jumping at the invitation, settled herself comfortably on his bed until dinner. All day long they laughed and whispered, arms linked around each other while the cockatoo squawked obscenely. Even without the bees, Eva's pearl white smile was enough to darken her daughter-in-law's blood.

Meridia's attempt to remove the bird met with a scream more deafening than gunshot. Feet thumped angrily on the floor. Hands clawed at the scar as if the boy wished to reopen it. Meridia had no choice but to withdraw. Eva wisely stayed away for two days until the heat cooled. When she returned, Noah ran to her and squeezed her with all his might.

Daniel was not the slightest bit troubled. "Noah is proving to be a good influence on Mama," he told her with the air of one who had been right all along. "I've never seen her so happy and active. Now that she's taking care of him, you have some free time for yourself. Didn't you say you wanted to plant more flowers in the garden?"

Meridia looked at him with eyes that could freeze fire.

More humiliations followed. Even as she refused to believe that Noah had sided against her, her head swelled to the width of a pumpkin. Her face clouded with angry purple pustules, which burst and multiplied painfully at the touch of a finger. Not willing to be outdone, her neck sprouted a hard lump the size of a peanut, which in a day's time grew as big as an egg, and later still, a gourd. An alarmed Daniel sent for a doctor. The man needed only one glance at Meridia to declare that she had fallen victim to a viral plague overtaking the town.

"All you need is a week's rest until the virus clears," the doctor assured her. "Funny, the ailment only afflicts strong-willed young mothers in their twenties."

Swallowing with agony, Meridia did not question him. After he left, she whispered to Daniel hoarsely, "It's the bird. It's been cursed to make me ill."

"Half the women in town have your symptoms!" he replied with impatience. "Are you saying that harmless little bird brought on the epidemic? Enough suspicions. Mama had nothing to do with this. The sooner you rest, the quicker you'll feel better."

For the next four days Meridia could not leave her bed. Alternating between feverish sleep and oppressive wakefulness, she vomited twelve times in half as many hours—red and green bile, though she had consumed nothing but water. As her face continued to swell, ponderous thoughts clamored behind her eyelids, and all her muscles ached as though she had performed a tremendous labor. One afternoon, kept awake by the cockatoo's mocking cry, she overheard Eva saying to Noah outside her door, "You can live with me if your mama doesn't get better. I have a beautiful room all prepared for you." Meridia scrabbled to get up, a scream and a curse knotted in her throat, but what she heard next drained the anger from her head. Noah was laughing, clear and bell-like, accepting Eva's offer as if it was the one thing he had been hoping for.

On the sixth night of her illness, a giant birdcage dropped on her chest and smacked her awake. Neck thick as a pillar, shoulders sore, she squinted her eyes in a stinging daze and craved water. The lone dim light pressed heavy around her. It was not yet midnight. Daniel must still be doing the books in the office downstairs. Next to the clock on the nightstand was a half-filled glass, which she could not command her hand to reach despite her thirst. Her hearing ebbed and flowed—one second revelers whooped in the street and then the next there was nothing.

Suddenly she realized she was not alone. With difficulty she rolled on her back and faced the door. Noah. He made no move when their eyes met, but studied her with Gabriel's old expression as though she were a specimen in a glass. Had he come to laugh at her? Inspect and report back to Eva? *She's half blind because her nose is swallowing her eyes, Grandma.* How long had he stood there recording her deformity?

"Mama," he said.

The cockatoo shrieked. The revelers whooped louder. Meridia could not speak, could not lift her head. Fire raced across her lungs as tears dampened her cheeks.

"Mama!"

His voice was stern now, angry. Before she could make a sound, he slammed the door and was gone. She scrambled to get up, thinking now or never, but the giant birdcage flew back out of nowhere and crashed down on her head.

In a dream, the cockatoo shrieked and shrieked and shrieked.

Meridia awoke the next morning as if she had never been ill. Along with the swelling, the pain and pustules were gone. Her mind cleared and strength restored, she sprang from the bed and went outside. Golden light flooded the hallway. She opened Noah's door and found him sitting in bed.

"Where's the bird?" she said, overwhelmed by the silence.

"It flew away," he replied. "The cage door was open when I woke up."

He did not break into a rash when she hugged him. Asked even if he could have eggs for breakfast.

"Of course," she said. She bolted the cage door shut and went back to the hallway.

Stepping out of the bathroom, Daniel greeted her brightly. "Up already? It's just as the doctor said—seven days for the virus to clear."

Meridia did not trouble to correct him.

That afternoon when Eva came, Noah marched to his room and shut the door in her face. Angry and confused, the grandmother retreated downstairs with her bribe macaroons untouched. Two days later, a neighbor's dog dug up the remains of a bird from a rain gutter. The neck was wrung; cats or rats had gotten to the wings. Noah displayed no reaction when he heard the news.

TWENTY-SEVEN

Malin's wedding took place eight days after Meridia's twenty-fourth birthday. In keeping with the bride's favorite color, the groom's father had a massive orange tent erected in the middle of Cinema Garden. Swaddling the canvas walls were twenty layers of orange silk. Draping the conical ceiling like waterfalls at sunset was sheer orange organza. A constellation of candles floated above the two hundred guests, reflecting beads and shimmering spangles on their merry faces. Each table was equipped with a towering bouquet, crystal flutes, gold-plated china, and silver candlesticks. The bride and groom sat at a table raised in the center of the tent. Surrounding them were seven pairs of groomsmen and brides-maids. The latter were made up so identically in bright violet dresses it took the guests a while to realize the bride's sister was not among them.

For months in advance, Eva had been trumpeting her daughter's good fortune. To the butchers and fruit-sellers she enumerated the virtues of young Jonathan: his wealth and upbringing, education, social position, gentlemanly manner, and devotion to Malin. To the florists and wreath-makers she professed her adoration for his family, snapping her purse shut before the carnation vendor developed any ideas. "The father listens to reason, never scowls or condescends, and is not in the habit of keeping mistresses at the outskirts of town. The mother is a delightful woman who has no violent bone in her body. I'm sure she has never scolded a cabbage in her life either. Do you know that they are providing the couple with a mansion on Museum Avenue?"

Courtesy of Leah, a tireless seeker and cataloger of news, Meridia got wind of these words two hours after they were uttered. Instead of flaring with anger, she merely laughed and continued playing with Leah's little boy in the stroller. Three months previously, she and Daniel had purchased the building next door and combined the two units together. After weeks of renovation, the shop had reopened with a splendid new look: ethereal blue walls, taupe carpeting, gilded ceilings, warm mahogany cases. Gracious wingback chairs and carved tables re-created the splendor of an old-fashioned drawing room; it was Meridia's idea to serve complimentary tea and pastries while customers shopped. Business instantly boomed. The partners, headed by Samuel, were ecstatic. To keep up with the expansion, Daniel hired a clerk and a live-in maid. In light of this success, it was easy to imagine Eva's envy getting the better of her.

Although Meridia guessed right, she failed to calculate the price imposed on Permony. Unable to wound her daughter-in-law, Eva turned on her youngest with all the force of her acrimony. "It's a pity you're nothing like your sister. Just look at you. Plain and silly, with no grace or curves to save your life. How will you find a man half as clever or handsome as Jonathan? Those evil-colored eyes alone are a guarantee you'll end up grim and unwanted. Let me spare you some embarrassment. How about letting another girl take your place as a bridesmaid? One who will live up to the beautiful dress your sister has selected? Once you're up there with all those pretty girls, you'll be sure to feel awful about yourself. Don't you agree, Malin?"

The bride-to-be, whose cruelty toward her sister had cooled into mild disdain in the ardor of Jonathan's courtship, shrugged her shoulders.

As became her nature since Patina's disappearance, Permony took this stoically. If she bled inside, no one could tell. In his chair, Elias pondered his hands and did not object, so deep was his gloom he could not rescue his darling daughter.

On the day of the wedding, a tangle of clouds obstructed the sun and threw shadows over Cinema Garden. Thick fog shrouded the jasmine blossoms, burnished the air with a chilly hue. The guests arrived in their coats, hair rumpled by wind, fearing it would rain before they returned home. Once inside the cavernous tent, however, they were astonished to find sunlight and palm trees. The parents received the guests at the entrance, all proud and beaming except for Elias, who could barely stand to mutter his greetings. The mayor came with his brother the judge, the general with his wife and four colonels. Renowned bankers and merchants took their seats—all good friends of Jonathan's father. Everyone noticed that neither Gabriel nor his wife was present.

Unbeknown to Meridia, Eva had attempted to have her ejected from the table of honor at the last minute. "Jonathan's great-aunt is coming after all," she explained to Malin. "I'm sure your sister-in-law wouldn't mind sitting away from your brother." Malin, who had silently grown to respect Meridia over the years, took one look at her mother and said, "You don't have to sit at my table but she does." Eva gasped in disbelief, turned to Permony, and berated her soundly for wearing too little rouge.

All the guests agreed on one thing—there was no denying the groom's love for his bride. Tall and bright-eyed, with lanky brown hair and a patient mouth, he followed her movement with a nearly sacramental devotion, which the bride accepted as if she had expected nothing less. At twenty, Malin had a kind of beauty that commanded worship as much as it resisted intimacy. Her visage was stunning with its jet-black hair and delicate cheekbones, yet her impenetrable air of self-sufficiency discouraged her admirers from coming closer. A splendid white gown, a sparkling artillery of jewelry—these were no match for her eyes, which remained the boldest and most intimidating thing about her.

But beauty of a different nature rivaled Malin's. Wearing a plain avocado dress Eva had grudgingly purchased at the last second, Permony managed to attract a fair share of attention. Many were drawn to her polite and disarming manners, took pleasure in speaking to her, and noted how her whole face glowed without the aid of a single diamond. One distinguished-looking foreigner with short yellow hair and a long mustache was visibly smitten. He could not stop glancing at her every few minutes.

"She's glorious, isn't she?" said Daniel as they sat down for dinner.

Meridia, watching the same yellow-haired foreigner steal yet another glance at Permony, nodded without asking which sister he was referring to.

"She is," she said with a surge of affection. "I've never seen her look prettier."

She turned to Noah on her other side and encouraged him with a nudge. "Go sit with your grandfather."

Noah opened his mouth, closed it, then got to his feet. Meridia watched anxiously as the familiar scene repeated itself. At Noah's approach, Elias emerged out of his gloom with a roar of laughter. But then just as suddenly his face darkened, the laughter stopped, and back he tumbled into the shadows. Despite Noah's attempt to cheer him, he kept his eyes bent until the boy returned confused and defeated to his seat. Elias would not look at him, would not regard the scar his hand had branded.

It was Eva who performed the heavy lifting. In order to draw attention away from Elias, she stayed on her feet all night and graced every table with her invincible hostess's smile. With skill she shrugged off his silence as "simple indigestion," spread ripples of laughter wherever she went, and urged the guests to eat and drink but "save plenty of room for the cake." Her hair was showing white, a curious and maddening condition that no dye was able to camouflage, but her figure was solid and sprightly in a cascade of ruffles. In spite of herself, Meridia felt a tinge of admiration for the woman.

At a sign from the matchmaker, the conical ceiling parted to reveal glimmering stars. Fireworks exploded, then magically simmered into a hundred white doves. The guests erupted in cheers. The sheer organza fluttered like ribbons. As the birds soared into the night, eight matrons led by the groom's mother leapt to their feet and charged toward the bride. Malin, somehow managing to retain her dignity, succumbed to the blindfold and the relentless tickling. In the midst of the commotion, Meridia noticed the strangest thing. Elias was staring at the distinguished-looking foreigner who had been stealing glances at Permony. His gaze seemed angry and troubled, as if he had placed the man's face from somewhere but wished he had not.

ELIAS'S CONDITION DETERIORATED OVER the next several months. First to go were words, slipping like sand from an uncurled hand. Then thoughts eroded, taking with them habits and memories. Every morning, Elias awoke to remember less, and his days regressed to those of an infant. If he was hungry, he fussed. If he wanted something, he drummed his fingers impatiently. Nothing upset him anymore. Everything erased in a stroke of mercy.

The doctors agreed there was nothing they could do. They said a blood vessel had ruptured in his brain, debilitating cell after cell quickly and unstoppably. One thing they could not agree on was numbers. Three, five, seven, nine. Weeks or months or years they could not say. After each prediction, Eva went out to the front lawn and wept among the roses.

Mobility was the last to go. Elias spent his final weeks in bed, eyes strapped to the ceiling in search of some impalpable firmament. He had shrunk to half his size, his body a mere hanger for loose flesh and folded wrinkles. A child's perennial smile lingered on his lips. Aided by Permony, Eva tended to him faithfully. Together they bathed him, scooped food into his mouth, wiped spittle from his lips. They held him steady in the bathroom as he went about his business.

In those weeks, Elias let his love for Permony show. As soon as the girl entered the room, he grinned foolishly like a simpleton. He would not sleep until he heard her voice, would not eat until her cool hand touched his cheek. When nightmares harassed him, it was Permony he hollered to see, all the while ignoring his wife, who fretted by his side. Like beads on a necklace Eva strung one snub after another, waiting for the right time to exact her payment from Permony.

It happened one day in the middle of autumn. Since Elias fell ill, it was Eva who had been running the shop on Lotus Blossom Lane. That afternoon, due to a lack of customers, she closed business early and went home. As she was making her way up the stairs, she heard strange, cricketlike noises issuing from her room. She crept toward the door and peered in. Elias was speaking in a peculiar language. Permony, sitting with her back to the door, was kneading her father's nape with one hand. This display of intimacy sliced through Eva like a rusted blade. She shook with pain and anger, recognizing the sounds burbling from Elias's lips as an outpouring of love.

"What is he saying?"

Permony jumped and turned to the door. Her lavender eyes were wet with tears.

"You scared me, Mama."

"What is he saying?" repeated Eva. "Is he telling you what a terrible wife I am? Is he blaming me for his illness?"

Permony shook her head as tears spilled down her cheeks. "Papa's telling me of beauty. Boundless, heavenly beauty. Immortal forest at dusk . . . eternal river . . . enchanted land where souls drift like fireflies . . . He said the air is pure there because there's no rage, no shame, no guilt. Oh, isn't it beautiful, Mama?"

Dread slithered up Eva's spine. The thought that Elias had envisioned himself passing through death's door—embraced it even—was more than she could bear. In defiance she threw him an angry look, damning those cricketlike noises he kept spitting at Permony. It hit her then, the pang of his rejection, his complete and absolute denial of her. At the end of his life, a hateful hand had knocked her right out of his consciousness. And she knew full well to whom the hand belonged.

"What is this nonsense?" she said, her voice exploding like a rifle. "Either you're making it up or he's gone insane."

Permony lowered her eyes sadly. "He said you would say that. He said you wouldn't believe me if I told you."

The girl could not have put it worse. All at once Eva stiffened. Vivid and unerring it flashed before her, the scene that had first stoked her fury and preserved it over the years. She was lying on a damp bed with blood pouring from her womb—weak, used, forgotten. She did not want this one, she had told him; she was too old and tired, but he had insisted. "It will be all right," he had said. "I'll stand by you." But he did not even look at her as she lay bleeding on that bed, absorbed as he was in the pale ugly thing he held in his arms. "This one is precious," he said, laughing. "This one will be a comfort in my old age." She knew he meant every word, because he had said nothing when he first held the other two. At the time, she had endured the humiliation by sobbing into her pillow. But now, eighteen years after the pale ugly thing stole her place in his affection, she would expose her for who she was.

"You've always been your father's whore," said Eva. "I've seen the way you look at him. Touch him like a lover. You think you can fool everyone with your innocent face and little-girl manners, but you can't fool me! I've known for years there's something going on between you two. Why do you think Malin kept away from you all these years? She guessed it, too, but wouldn't say a word. Because even God has no forgiveness for what you've done."

Permony stood still as if a thunderbolt had struck her.

"How could you say that, Mama?" She was gasping now, shaking uncontrollably. "How could you think such things of your own husband, your own daughter?"

She began to weep the way she used to as a little girl—soundlessly, head folded to chest, fingers digging into her eyes. Eva was unstoppable.

"I knew what you were from the day you were born. No mother is ever as unfortunate as I, to have carried an abomination in my womb and live to see it spite me!"

Permony protested in vain. Eva's curse rained down like hail and drowned her. On the bed, Elias's recounting of celestial valleys and mystical mountains continued. He smiled as he prophesied, a glob of spit wavering on the tip of his chin. The unseeing eyes he trained at the ceiling were glazed with contentment.

FOUR DAYS LATER, EARLY in the morning, a heavy silence fell over 27 Orchard Road. All at once the marigolds ceased their clamor, Gabilan her scrubbing, Eva her fussing, Permony her weeping. In alarm, mother and daughter stared at the father's white lips, hushed now with no more hiss of divination. Had it not been for the childlike glow of his smile, they would have taken him for dead. Immediately, Eva sent Gabilan to inform the family.

Malin had refused to enter her father's room during the final stages of his decrepitude. She was horrified by the stench, she said, by the sharp bones that stuck from his skin and the bedsores that never healed. Citing a hectic newlywed's schedule, she seldom came to visit, and when she did, she acted as if she was performing a penance. But on that fateful morning when Eva summoned her, she did not enter the house with her usual arrogance. There was a quiver in her voice, so habitually armored with distaste it was perceptible only to those who had known her all her life. She took one look at her father, blanched, and withdrew downstairs to her old room, refusing to say good-bye.

A moment later, Daniel arrived accompanied by Noah and Meridia. They were halfway up the stairs when a stricken Permony ran down to meet them.

"Tell me he's not going," she pleaded, her face worn with anguish. The silence that followed confirmed her worst fear, and she burst out sobbing.

Meridia made a sign to Daniel, who understood and took Noah upstairs with him. Holding Permony in her arms, she let the girl sob to her heart's content.

"He told me he was sorry." Permony choked on her words. "For throwing you out of the house that day. All these years he didn't know how to make it up to you."

"It's in the past," said Meridia gently. "Heaven knows he's made it up to us."

"It broke him, you know, what he did to Noah. He couldn't look at that scar without falling apart at the seams. He called himself a monster, saying it was in his nature to harm those he loved most."

Meridia tightened her clasp on the girl. "It wasn't his fault," she said. "Noah forgave him a long time ago."

Nodding like a person in a trance, Permony made her way down the stairs. Meridia watched her glide to the terrace, sit in her father's rocking chair, fold her head to her chest, and cry without sound.

Meridia was turning to climb the stairs when a low strangled noise arrested her. Alarmed, she went back down and followed the noise to the girls' room. The door was half open. When she pushed it, she saw Malin kneeling at the foot of the orange bed, rocking to and fro with her hands cradling her stomach. Seeing Meridia, she stopped crying at once. "Don't tell anyone," she warned, her haughty eyes red with tears. Meridia nodded and went back out. She understood then that Malin was with child. The girl had not kept away from her father out of callousness, but to protect her baby from the mark of death.

Upstairs, Meridia joined Noah and Daniel by the bed. Elias's body had begun to rot. Daniel shivered as he watched his father's chest rise and fall, the childlike smile odd yet stubborn, and in that second Meridia realized how these men had loved each other without ever saying a word, their needs sacrificed to please the woman who provoked every mutation in their souls with her slippery tongue and inscrutable desires.

Without being told, Noah stepped forward and kissed his grandfather good-bye. He did not shrink from the ghastly sores, did not look away from the greenish skin. Elias stirred at the boy's kiss and opened his eyes. For a second they burned directly into Meridia's. Then his smile faded and his breath departed.

A shadow closed in fast from behind, and before they knew it, Eva had pushed them away from the bed. Ravaged by anger, grief, and disbelief, she stared hard at her husband's remains and shook her head, looking at once weak and invincible. "Come back, you fool!" she wailed in a voice jagged with loss. Silent and profuse, the tears fell. Daniel put his arms around her, but she shook him off.

"If you could arrange the coffin, Malin will take care of the service," she said, wiping her tears roughly. "Gabilan! Run to the mortuary and fetch the undertaker. Permony! Get your father's blue suit from the closet and send it to the cleaners. I will deal with the florist myself. That man has been known to swindle highly emotional widows. Hah! Let's see him try putting one over on me!"

Meridia scarcely heeded this outburst. In the second when Elias's eyes met hers, she thought his lips had mouthed a plea. *Save her.* Save whom? And from what? Meridia leaned closer to the dead body, willing it to give up one more clue or confirmation, but nothing moved. She shuddered when she thought that she had misread the last and final commandment of his life.

TWENTY-EIGHT

In the third month of Malin's pregnancy, Eva commissioned a fortune-teller to eliminate every imaginable catastrophe. The man's surefire methods included burning incense for seven days, chanting, strangling a chicken, and brewing a papaya-based potion against miscarriage. Following weeks of frenzied supernatural activities, a silver banner was mounted on the roof of 27 Orchard Road, signaling to the town that all the universal elements had been realigned for a favorable delivery.

The prospect of fatherhood seemed to have knocked common sense out of Jonathan. Unable to guess the sex of his child, he turned two rooms in his house into nurseries: one painted deep blue for a boy, one pink for a girl. He placed orders all over the world for baby clothes and toys, blankets and shoes, and when they arrived, it took his servants days to classify them into the two nurseries. He summoned doctor after doctor to monitor his wife, always agreeing with one while repudiating another. From morning till night the house on Museum Avenue was packed with herbalists and acupuncturists, nutritionists and massage therapists, all tending to Malin as if she were the most fragile creature in existence. When Malin announced that the baby was kicking for the first time, Jonathan went wild with joy and bought her the biggest piece of jewelry from Lotus Blossom Lane.

Eva attended to her daughter like a crazed disciple. With unrelenting eyes she oversaw the army of doctors and therapists, made sure Malin had plenty of rest and exercise, and served her all the delicacies with which she had accused Meridia of spoiling her uterus while pregnant. When the heat became unbearable, Eva tasked the servants to fan Malin with all their strength, and when they did just that, she blamed them for creating a hurricane in the room. To anyone who would listen, she detailed Malin's struggle with morning sickness, her sore nipples, frequent urination, and impossibly hard bowel movements.

Malin herself was no longer the girl she had once been. As her due date neared, her patented sneer gave way to an uncommon tenderness. Gone were her tantrums, her endless irritations when her wishes were not met. To everyone's surprise, she was able to develop a tolerance for Jonathan's folly, humor for Eva's meddling, and patience for the servants' shortcomings. More amazing still, her contempt for Permony dissipated. For the first time in her life, Malin made efforts to befriend her sister, buying her dresses, inviting her to dinner, and even defending her against Eva. A shocked and grateful Permony responded by placing herself completely at her sister's disposal.

Ignoring Eva's protests, Malin also sought to improve relations with her sister-in-law. Ever since Meridia caught her crying in her old room on the morning of Elias's death, a tacit understanding took place between the two, and Malin no longer hid the admiration she had felt for Meridia over the years. Twice a week now she went to Magnolia Avenue for tea, always bringing a gift for Noah and sweet rolls for Daniel. As she sat in her sister-in-law's newly decorated living room, she peppered her with questions about Noah's birth. What did the midwife do to keep her calm? Were there crystals present to clear the baby's passage? Had the knife been rubbed with con-

secrated oil, could the womb have been spared from destruction?
Receptive to Malin's conciliatory efforts, Meridia put the past behind
them and answered thoughtfully. She became genuinely fond of
Malin when she realized that the girl had found her calling as a
mother.

One topic was off-limits to Malin—her father's recent passing.
Although she had a standing order with a florist to decorate Elias's
grave with gardenias every morning, she had yet to make an appearance at the Cemetery of Ashes. Whenever the subject came
up, Malin clutched her belly and withdrew from the room. Bol-
stered by her faith in the fortune-teller, Eva tried to assure her that
there was nothing to worry about. The expectant mother's reply
was short and to the point: "I'm not taking any chances, so back
off."

Malin's water broke at the precise hour the fortune-teller had
predicted. Despite a dire warning from Eva ("That woman will cause
your womb to twist!"), the girl wasted no time in sending for her
sister-in-law. As soon as Meridia entered the big house on Museum
Avenue, she knew that Eva's efforts to circumvent disaster had
failed. Malin was screaming as if she were being hacked to pieces.

"Come! She's waiting for you."

Permony did not give Meridia time to take off her coat, but
rushed her up the stairs and along the corridor where Jonathan was
pacing. Drenched in sweat and panic, the young man jolted with
every scream Malin hurled from behind the door. He lunged for Meridia the instant he saw her and seized both of her arms.

"You'll try your best to help her, won't you?"

"Don't worry," she told him while Permony pounded on the door.
"It will all be over before you know it."

There were three doctors in the room and two midwives, shouting instructions at one another in total pandemonium. The door had
no sooner closed than Meridia recognized the mark of death loom-
ing over the bed. Everything reminded her of her own labor—the
chaos and disorder, the pain, the confusion, the simultaneous yet

separate battles for mother and child. Only the bees were missing. In their place was the clicking of prayer beads—fast, unwieldy, desperate. It was the first time she saw Eva afraid.

Feeble, Malin's voice called to her above the din.

"You've lived through this before. Tell me my baby will be safe."

Fear had the girl in its grip. Her brave eyes and enormous belly aside, she looked deflated, as if all her hope was hanging by a thread. At Meridia's approach, Eva left the corner where she had been praying and placed herself in the way.

"Yes, tell her," she whispered, her voice hoarse and abnormally dismal. "Tell her nothing will go wrong."

Then Eva did something unprecedented—she stepped aside and let Meridia pass.

At once the noise cleared. For a moment there was only Malin and the two heartbeats inside her. Meridia had scarcely time to grasp the girl's damp hand when a certainty flashed through her brain: Malin would live, but the baby would not. The same premonition must have also occurred to Eva, which then explained the hysterical clicking of her beads. Repressing a shudder, Meridia smiled and affected something of Ravenna.

"Nobody is dying today. Not on my watch."

Relief surged through Malin. For the next six hours, the girl fought as if she were taking on the heavens. Finding the doctors and midwives at odds with one another, she threw out all but two from the room. She clenched her teeth like an animal at war, bold and determined through all the blood and pain. Every fifteen minutes, Jonathan lifted his knuckles to the door, only to receive the same discouraging answer. Permony waited on her sister with absolute devotion, impressing even Eva, who alternated between rallying her daughter and praying in the corner. In those hours Meridia did not let go of Malin's hand, her strong grasp somehow giving flesh to the confidence she did not feel.

Eva's scream was the signal they had all been waiting for. Permony gnashed her teeth. Meridia grabbed Malin's shoulders and blocked her view. The midwife whisked the dead thing away . . . too late. Roused by her mother's scream, Malin demanded to see it.

"No!" said Eva. "It won't do you the slightest good."

Weak and exhausted, Malin began to scream.

"It's my baby! You can't stop me from saying good-bye!"

Eva pleaded with her, and they bickered back and forth. The effort on Malin's part caused blood to erupt from the womb, rapidly emptying color from her skin. The doctor was barking orders no one followed as he tried in vain to stanch the flow. Meridia, realizing this, made a quick decision.

"Show her the baby," she told the midwife. "She's strong enough to handle it."

The force of her command stunned Eva for a moment, long enough for the midwife to approach the bed. In her arms lay what looked like a crumpled slab of stone, moldy with black pieces of meat wedged in for eyes. A network of clots covered the limbs and the genital area, from which they gathered it was a boy. Permony started sobbing. Malin took one look and closed her eyes.

"Take him away," she said.

Recovering herself, Eva turned on Meridia savagely.

"Are you out of your mind? I know you're mean and arrogant, but I never take you to be this cruel and thoughtless!"

Meridia did not dignify this. She gave Malin's hand to Permony and hurried to the midwife.

"Don't show it to the father," she said. "He's not as strong as his wife."

Dodging Eva's bees, which had suddenly filled the room with profanities, Meridia went out to the corridor. Flanked by his parents, Jonathan rushed toward her. As soon as he saw the look on her face, he realized that the bottom had fallen out of his world. He shook and staggered and crumbled on the spot. "There will be another, son," said his mother. "You are both still young." He tore from her angrily and folded in upon himself, the light swaying and then dimming on his private universe.

THREE DAYS LATER, EARTH rained on the baby's coffin. The following morning, Malin took her place in the town's annals as the 622nd mother to haunt the Cemetery of Ashes. The graveyard sweeper declared that she always appeared no later than dawn, and the flowers she carried—orange butterfly weed—set her apart from the other ghosts. Cloaked in a heavy robe the color of fall, she trudged up the hill without looking left or right, sliced through the bitter smoke that guarded the cemetery, and paused at her father's grave long enough before heading to the smaller tomb in the back. Carefully she would replace the flowers that were still fresh from the last dawn, wipe the urn with the hem of her robe, and caress all the letters on the headstone as though they contained a message from another world.

The townspeople claimed that a completely different woman now lived inside Malin. Her dressmaker said she no longer had a taste for fashion, had stopped placing orders even though all her dresses hung loose on her. This observation was echoed by her hairdresser, who said that Malin had not been to the shop in weeks and could not be bothered about her hair. The maids from the big house on Museum Avenue added that their mistress no longer showed interest in her furniture, her figurines, her husband, or the rest of her family. The mother did not know what to do, the sister was beside herself with sorrow. The husband, suffering alone and intensely, alternated his nights between the two nurseries, pacing, sighing, hoping that her door would open to admit him.

"Is it true? But they look so lovely together!"

Having relayed all this to Meridia, Leah awaited her answer with the hungry look of a compassionate gossip. Meridia looked away, did not confirm one way or the other.

TWENTY-NINE

Twenty-seven years after its first appearance, the blue mist arrived late at 24 Monarch Street. All morning long as she flayed carrots and admonished turnips, Ravenna nursed her fury. By the time the mailman completed his rounds in the neighborhood, there was still no sign of Gabriel. Ravenna threw away the carrots and attacked the pork rump, so viciously her maids did not dare come within ten feet of her. When at last the blue mist made its delivery, the sun was halfway up in the sky. Armed with a steaming plate of ham-and-paprika omelet, Ravenna entered the dining room and glared at the man seated at the head of the table. When she plopped down the plate in front of him, he did not appear to notice. Taking in his pale and exhausted color, Ravenna gave a righteous grunt, saying to herself that his mistress's erotic antics must have finally caught up with him. She continued to watch him with disdain when the unimaginable happened: Gabriel pushed the plate away, stood up, and went off to his study. Ravenna reeled as if he had punched her. The pact was broken. For the first time in twenty-seven years, he had left the food she served him untouched.

That evening, the yellow mist arrived earlier than usual. As soon as Gabriel stepped into the vapor, the knot of anguish that had been sitting in Ravenna's stomach since morning ruptured like a boil. She flew downstairs and tore into his study. She ransacked the cabinets and towering shelves. Smashed jars and flasks. Flung books into the air. She peered closely at his notebooks. Stripped the maps and charts off the walls. Rushing to the little closet where he kept his clothes, she yelped in disbelief when she found it half emptied. In rage, she turned out all his jacket pockets, netting two fountain pens, four buttons, and a handful of change. She prosecuted his remaining wardrobe next, but still could not extract an explanation for his change in behavior. Snatching a shirt from the hanger, she shredded it to pieces, took up another and another until a hill of sacrificial fabric mounted at her feet. At last, the smell of burnt meat snapped her to her senses. The pork roast! She ran to the kitchen, pushed aside the terrified maids, and put out the fire with her bare hands. That night, long after Monarch Street fell asleep, Ravenna charged up the stone steps and assailed the ivory mist. "Bastard! Coward! Son of a bitch!" she barked. The break of dawn found her standing on wet grass, grim and erect with the terribleness of a storm.

The blue mist did not turn up that morning. Ravenna waited until noon before she hurled breakfast against the wall. For the rest of the day, Gabriel neither returned nor sent news. When evening came, Ravenna stood at her bedroom window and stared far beyond the rooftops. A pale autumn sky stretched vast and benign, yet some unaccustomed movement among the stars convinced her that the blue mist would never again carry him home. All at once she felt it—the keen and irrevocable agony of loss. Closing the window and shutting the curtain did not lessen the feeling one bit.

The blue mist did turn up the following morning. But instead of releasing Gabriel from its union with the ivory, it held out a note addressed to the lady of the house. Ravenna stuck her hand into the beating heart of the vapor and plucked out the note. In the gray morning light Gabriel's fastidious handwriting glared at her. *I can no longer live under the same roof with you. You can have the house—I will send for my things.* Ravenna dropped the note as a tide of pain knocked her back. Blinking and trembling, she looked up and realized that both the blue and ivory mists had vanished. A gust of wind snatched up the note and buoyed it dancingly, first across the street, then to the tops of trees and to the sky beyond. Ravenna slammed the front door shut. Back in the kitchen, she gathered all her cooking implements, her pots and pans and knives and spices and sacks of flour, and heaped them together in one corner. To these she added fresh meat and vegetables, fish, eggs, butter, fruit, rice, and oil. The two maids watched in horror as the iron knot on the back of her head sliced about the room like a rapier.

"Take what you want and leave," she ordered them. "From this day forward there will be no more cooking in this house."

She unlocked a drawer and dispensed their wages. Before either one could object, Ravenna had herded them away.

On the third night of Gabriel's absence, she threw a thick coat over her shoulders and marched through the fog to Magnolia Avenue. A drizzle was falling, peppering the town with beads of liquid pearls. From the way the leaves bent in the wind, she predicted they were in for a season of thunder. The hour was not late; under the bright white lanterns, Magnolia Avenue was bustling with pedestrians and their umbrellas. When she reached number seventy, friendly voices drifted from an upstairs window. Ravenna hesitated a moment, not expecting others to be present, then pressed her finger to the doorbell.

"You're an hour late, Rebecca!"

Meridia answered the door in a blue evening dress, her hair stylishly swept back and eyes bright with laughter. She started when she saw her mother but suppressed her gasp.

"Come with me," said Ravenna.

It took Meridia all of one second to digest this. In a rush she went back up the stairs, and reappeared a moment later in a hooded cloak that fell down to her ankles. Daniel followed with daggers in his eyes. Before he said a word, Meridia gave him a kiss and swept out into the cold. "Go ahead without me," she said, hoping his displeasure was somehow lost on Ravenna.

Under the waning moon, they began their journey. Meridia had no idea where her mother was going, aware only that they were heading into the dark heart of town. The earth was damp and muddy, yet Ravenna walked as though her shoes touched nothing but brick. As the drizzle thickened into rain, they hustled past moldering huts and ramshackle tenements, past temples of abandoned gods and hotels tenanted by transient midnight souls. Eyes without bodies tracked them from the depths of shadows, howling, laughing at every turn of the wind. Crude letters blazed up dusty windows. For a few coppers, anyone could purchase a pill for oblivion, a curse for a cuckolding spouse, a brew to abort the unwanted. Through an open doorway, Meridia saw a toothless crone standing by a fire, calling in a loud, croaking voice, "Let me erase your past, hapless one! I can deflect the future and obscure the present!" Meridia shuddered and fastened her hood. Ravenna strode on as if she did not hear a thing.

The wind lifted in a violent gust when they entered the mouth of a certain alley. A hailstorm of flowers broke out, trapping them in swirling, shivering petals that beat their skin like frenzied wings. The rain came down hard and soaked them. For a long time they could neither see nor move. When the gust receded, Meridia brushed the petals off her face and noticed that Ravenna's knot had come undone. Down her unbending spine the long strands of hair hung wet and heavy.

Mother and daughter swung into the alley. A modest cottage, which did not otherwise differ in appearance from the others, was marked by the familiar yellow mist. Seizing this, Ravenna flew at the vapor and pounded on the door. Meridia followed, her tongue coppery with panic and premonition. As soon as her skin brushed the cold mist, she understood that she had plunged into a world where men withdrew to hide their shame.

Despite Ravenna's thunderous knocks, a long time elapsed before footsteps approached. A moment later the bolt turned and the door yielded a fraction. A woman's tremulous voice reached them before her eyes appeared through the slit.

"What do you want?"

"My husband," said Ravenna.

"He's asleep. Come back in the morning."

"Open the door now, woman!"

"He doesn't want to see you. Please leave before you wake up the whole town."

Ravenna's fury suddenly found an outlet. "I've waited for twenty-seven years, you shameless old slut! Before this rain stops, that bastard will listen to what I have to say!"

Ravenna kicked the door open, smashing the woman in the face. There was a painful yelp, followed by a nasty tumble to the floor. Ravenna flung the door wide and charged into the house.

"Where is he?"

The woman had fallen on her backside, one hand supporting herself and the other clamping her nose. A shaded lamp lit the dingy parlor, spartanly furnished with worn leather chairs and a battered table. A stale yet familiar smell of lilac suffocated the air. The instant Meridia locked eyes with her father's mistress, a deep tremor took hold of her bones. She needed no help to recognize who it was.

"Pilar!"

Sinking, Patina's sister was hiding her face and weeping. "I'm sorry. I didn't mean for this to happen."

Meridia stared dumbly. Saw bright blood oozing from the woman's nose but could not move to help her.

"Come out, you pig! You rotten, good-for-nothing asshole!"

Ravenna was already storming the narrow hallway. Two doors stood to her right, one to her left. She tried the first one on the right, which led to an empty sitting room, and slammed it shut. The second door she shut even more quickly—it opened to a cramped and smelly kitchen. She made for the last door and flung it open. A second later her scream vibrated the cottage to its core.

Meridia ran for the door and found herself in a large, dusky room. At a glance she made out a garishly ornate bed, huge and imposing in the center of the room, with Ravenna bending over it. The air here shimmered with heat, as if an invisible fire were eating its way slowly across the floor. As Meridia crept closer, she began to perspire, and noticed that the bed was surrounded by iron pails full of blazing charcoal. Why did the room require such excessive heating? The question had barely crossed her mind when she saw it: a pillar of ice lying in the middle of the bed. She drew back, nearly losing her balance. She stared at the face sealed by doom and felt its coldness slicing at her heart.

"Papa!"

Under the transparent ice, Gabriel's elegant features were meticulously preserved. Thick gray locks swept across his forehead, skin unlined, lips flushed, jaws clenched in inviolate dignity. He was wearing one of his dark suits with a gardenia pinned to his buttonhole. His hands, long and well sculpted, folded regally across his chest. Only the eyes were restless, staring straight up with a bleak sense of unfinished mission. Meridia had no doubt she was looking at a corpse.

"What have you done to him?" Ravenna suddenly swung around to face the door.

Pilar had walked in with a towel pressed to her nose. The sobbing noise she emitted sounded as strange and incorporeal as a goblin's wail.

"He caught a chill a few days ago and woke up sick," she began, frozen to the spot by Ravenna's glare. "I pleaded with him to stay in bed, but he said he was fine and insisted on . . . on returning to you. That evening he came back much earlier and immediately took to bed. He looked dejected and kept muttering something about a broken pact. I made nothing of it, but all night long he complained that a cold wind was jabbing up and down his spine. I scolded him

for talking nonsense and pulled out more blankets. I never suspected—dear God, if I only knew—"

Pilar wiped her tears with the bloodstained towel. Meridia, torn
by a hundred emotions, could not decide whether she ought to pity
her or smack her.

"Go on," Ravenna demanded, immovable as the ice that swad-
dled Gabriel.

Pilar exerted herself with difficulty. "The next morning he
couldn't get out of bed. His teeth were chattering, and I couldn't
keep him warm no matter what I did. That afternoon I sent for a
doctor, who prescribed plenty of liquid and hot-water bottles. A few
hours later, the first frost appeared on his lips. I panicked and piled
more hot-water bottles on him. This seemed to reduce the chill, and
the frost slowly began to thaw. That night, he insisted on writing a
note to you. After he finished, he ordered me to change him into his
best suit. I didn't know what he was thinking, not then, and when he
asked for the gardenia, I thought he'd lost his mind. He made me
swear that under no circumstance was I to let you in this house. He
slept peacefully that night. In the morning, I woke to find him sealed
in ice. I jumped, sent again for the doctor. This time the gentleman
scratched his head and ordered for charcoal to be brought in. We
kept it going for hours but the ice did not thaw. 'Just as well, the cold
will keep him alive,' said the doctor. 'Whatever you do, do not break
the ice. It will be the death of him.' This was yesterday. Last night
the ice stopped growing, and he's been the same since."

Seeing that Ravenna had not moved, Pilar ventured a step forward. Meridia noticed that her nose had stopped bleeding.

"I'm sorry the note never reached you," said Pilar, a thumb
scratching her chin. "I put it on the hallway table after he wrote it,
thinking I would send it in the morning. But it wasn't there when I
looked the next day. I must have misplaced it. Or maybe he changed
his mind during the night and destroyed it while he still had the
strength. I wish I could tell you what he wrote, but he kept it secret
from me. I would hate to think—"

"I received the note," Ravenna said brusquely.

Pilar staggered back. "You did? But who delivered it?"

Ravenna had no time to respond, for at that moment a loud split-ting sound erupted from inside the ice. A tiny fissure appeared on the surface of the pillar, running from the top of Gabriel's head to just below the left side of his chest. Before anyone else could react, Ravenna leapt into motion.

"Get up, old man!" She grabbed a pewter washbasin from the nightstand and brought it down hard against the ice. The fissure broadened. Ravenna struck harder, creating a hairsbreadth line to Gabriel's heart.

"You'll kill him if you break the ice, Mama!" cried Meridia. Ravenna responded by increasing the force of her pounding.

Pilar let out a shriek but did not dare interfere. Meridia stood thunderstruck, thinking her mother had lost it.

"Did you think you could write me off with a lousy letter?" Ravenna shouted into the depths of the ice. "Did you honestly be-lieve this *igloo* would keep you safe from me?"

As the blows rained harder and the tangle of lines spread across the ice, Ravenna's face lit up with a madcap determination. Sud-denly Meridia understood what she had to do. She shed her cloak on the floor, snatched a brass candlestick from the top of the armoire, and smashed it full force against the ice.

"Help us, woman," said Ravenna. "Don't just stand there and gape."

Pilar looked as if she might faint at any second. "Stop! You're killing him!"

"Nonsense." Ravenna slammed the washbasin to a booming crash. "The bastard will live longer than any of us."

Pilar's mouth fell open. Without giving her a choice, Meridia thrust the candlestick into her hands. Ravenna tossed the washbasin aside and began to claw between the fissures. Soon her fingers were bleeding, an affliction she neither seemed to mind nor notice. Me-ridia took the washbasin and promptly led the demolition work on

Gabriel's feet. Sparks of ice flew to the floor, some landing inside the iron pails and stirring the charcoal into a hiss. Many minutes later, when there was only a thin layer of ice left on Gabriel, Ravenna scooped the live coals with her bare hands and rubbed them on him. Though she worked quickly, she took care not to scorch his skin. Meridia and Pilar continued to ply their weapons, the latter without once ceasing her sobs. When they cleared the last bits of ice from the doomed man, his chest faintly began to heave.

"I'm taking him home," said Ravenna.

Pilar dropped the candlestick and trembled. "He'll die for sure if you move him! I beg of you, listen to me!"

Ravenna answered her by stripping the bedsheets, wrapping them around Gabriel, and flinging her coat over him.

"Please stop her," Pilar implored Meridia, her nose bleeding all over again. "Please!"

Meridia speared her a look. "I'm sorry," she said. "You're barking up the wrong tree, woman."

And with that, she took her place next to Ravenna.

They lifted Gabriel out of bed and propped him up to stand between them. His staring eyes aside, they could not tell if he was conscious. A soft irregular breath, a vague hum of pulse—these were the two indications that life had not deserted him.

Pilar made a last-ditch effort to stop them. "You are two women! How will you have the strength to carry him across town?"

Mother and daughter countered this by transporting Gabriel easily to the door. Without so much as a twitch, Meridia managed to master her shock. The unkind and despotic man who had governed her childhood with terror now weighed almost nothing in her arm, utterly helpless. She bent to pick up her cloak and wrapped it around him.

Pelted by Pilar's wail, they carried Gabriel out of the house and into the night. The rain had doubled in strength, and the wind raged against the earth in a fierce, grudging torrent. Meridia signed for Ravenna to halt and fastened the hood of her cloak over her father's head. How would Gabriel react if he knew they had stuffed him into not just one woman's coat, but two? The same thought evidently occurred to Ravenna, for at that moment she allowed a fugitive smile to steal across her lips.

In silence they retraced their steps through the dark heart of town. While the crude letters glowered in the wind and the eyes without bodies pursued them from the black of shadows, a glorious warmth was spreading from Ravenna, traveling through Gabriel, and nestling in the coldest part of Meridia. The same warmth glowed and illuminated their path, so even with the moon dim and the lights scattered, they did not stumble in the storm. By the time they reached 24 Monarch Street, the two women were drenched to the bone, but the man they held between them was dry as a desert. Not a drop of rain had fallen upon him.

THIRTY

Ravenna and Meridia had just put Gabriel to bed when the ice awakened. Lucent flowers bloomed on his face and neck, crystal spangles on his arms and legs, propagating with such speed that the air thickened with frost. Armed with a hammer and a wire brush, the women threw themselves into combat, but the ice thwarted them by swaddling him once more. Underneath the cocoon, Gabriel's staring eyes were losing their shine. Slowly yet cripplingly, the cold seeped into Meridia and dampened her spirit.

"It's no use," she said, wiping her brow with the soiled sleeve of her evening dress. "The ice is growing too quickly."

"It's this house that's too cold," said Ravenna. "How on earth did we manage to live here for all these years without freezing?"

Meridia saw the truth in this, but kept it to herself. "We need more than just heat to stop the ice, Mama."

The words had scarcely left her mouth when Ravenna drew back with a jolt. The brush ceased scraping. The hammer fell from Meridia's hand. At once mother and daughter hid their eyes from each other. A hissing, breathing demon had materialized between them, inadvertently summoned from the tomb of things shameful and unspeakable. Ravenna lifted her hands to her eyes. She reared. She fumbled. She backed away. Her lips began to stammer, to spin and weave the dark and private language that would return her squarely to forgetfulness.

"No!" shouted Meridia, snapping her head up. She would not let her fade this time. She gripped the hammer with both hands, and without making a single movement went after the demon who had erected this wall between them. In her mind's eye, she saw herself lifting the hammer again and again, striking the demon's neck and skull and brains until every festering misunderstanding that had alienated husband from wife and mother from daughter was shattered clean. The demon yelped and crumbled, helpless in the face of Meridia's will, and took the wall down with it. For the first time since the cold wind turned the house upside down, there was nothing hidden, omitted, unsaid.

Meridia withdrew the hammer from the cracked skull and gripped it tighter. "Go get it, Mama," she said.

Ravenna had stopped muttering. She nudged the demon with her foot and, finding it still, kicked it to the window, where it dissolved in the moonlight.

"I'll be damned, child," she said. Her puzzled eyes locked with her daughter's, and in that instant saw everything clearly. She sank to the floor, crawled forward, reached under the bed. The object she retrieved from twenty-seven years of anger and resentment was not an ax as Eva had alleged, but a short-handled shovel. The once shiny silver blade was grimed with age, rust, and what appeared to be blood.

Gooseflesh broke out all over Meridia. Nevertheless, she did not look away as Ravenna clasped the shovel with both hands, swung it above her head, and brought it hard against the ice. The cocoon gasped—shrieked—and splintered in half. Ravenna struck again and again. Up and down the silver blade traveled at great speed, catching and tossing light blindingly as it had done years ago. The irony was not lost on Meridia. The same instrument that had come close to claiming Gabriel's life was now prying him from the jaws of death.

The last chunk of ice fell to the floor. Gabriel lifted his head a fraction, coughed, and then made a weak signal with his hand. Mustering voice and breath from every vein in his body, he spoke the two words that sent shivers down the women's spines.

"My love."

IT WAS A STRANGE and startling lightness. Purged of the hatred of decades, the house jettisoned its yoke and floated on enchanted air. Ceilings rippled like waves. Walls swayed like windblown trees. The whimsical staircase morphed into an accordion of tunes. It was unsettling to take a lungful of air and not smell spite, to drink water from the fountain and not taste rage. The perpetual cold and dusk were gone. Light flooded the rooms and warmed the walls with a hundred golden shades.

The morning after they brought Gabriel home, Meridia sent a note explaining his condition to Magnolia Avenue. An hour later, as requested, Daniel showed up at the stone steps with a suitcase of her clothes. Noah came with him, but neither of them displayed any desire to see Gabriel. "Your father's door has never welcomed me," said Daniel. "I don't see why his bedroom would." Noah stared off into the distance and avoided her eyes. His eight-year-old mind was no doubt barricading itself against the memory of the grandfather whose most fleeting gaze could make him tremble. "I'll come home as soon as I can," Meridia promised. They did not hear her. She watched them disappear down the hill with a twinge in her heart.

Ravenna had moved planters from the garden into the bedroom, filled them with wood, and kept the fire going. Taking instructions from her almanac of ancient remedies, she brewed Gabriel foul-smelling tonics and rubbed his limbs with banana leaves in order to save them from atrophy. Meridia sponged, fed, dressed, and changed compresses, all while Gabriel's stare continued to elude her. The ice was by then contained. Every few hours Ravenna picked up the brush and scraped. It was clear that to Gabriel, she was the only thing alive in the room. Husband and wife exchanged no word that day, but that night, long after Meridia retired to her old bed, the torrent of their whispers juddered her awake.

"Why did you hide and leave me?"

"Because I didn't want to see your pity."

"Did you think I would pity you?"

"Look at me! I can't even wipe my own ass."

"You've always been so proud, so stubborn."

"Isn't that what first attracted you? My pride?"

"You were kind then. And gentle."

"You were beautiful. And loving."

"You are gentle now."

"You are beautiful still."

"Where did it go wrong?"

"You changed."

"It was the wind. The cold wind."

"Nonsense. Something in your eyes died and you didn't look at me the same."

"I asked you for time."

"I thought you'd stopped loving me."

"I asked you for patience."

"I thought you'd abandoned me for good."

"You gave up so quickly. I closed my eyes and you found her."

"I was cold and she gave me fire."

"Did you love her? No! Don't answer it."

"I never loved anyone but you."

"You owe me my heart. It was whole before I met you."

"You almost crushed my skull, woman!"

"How foolish we were. And you, jealous of your own child."

"Is that what she thinks? That I held her responsible?"

"You never told her otherwise."

"I can't look at her without remembering what we'd lost."

"I can't look at her without forgetting what we have."

"Tell her I love her."

"Tell her yourself. You've still got breath in your lungs."

"My time is running out."

"Hush. If I couldn't wear you out then nothing will."

"Tell her. I'll burn in hell if she doesn't look me in the eye before I go."

"Hush now. Hush. Don't talk like that, you fool. Hush . . ."

Meridia climbed down from the bed and went to the hallway. A thick haze of tears blinded her, made her place one foot in front of the other without thinking. Though Ravenna's room lay just a few paces ahead, the distance seemed endless and fraught with peril. As Meridia got closer to the door, the haze closed in around her throat. Her head was beating harder. She held the doorknob a moment before turning it.

Wrapped in a blanket, Ravenna was sitting far away from the bed, studying the window with her back to Gabriel. Tight and bone-like, the implacable knot had returned to grace her head. On the bed, Gabriel lay in the same position Meridia had left him in. There were no whispers, no words, no signs that any form of exchange had occurred between them.

"How is he, Mama?"

Ravenna did not shift from her chair. "The same. Still hasn't moved or said a word."

Without her meaning it to, a sob spilled out of Meridia's breast, soft enough for Ravenna to miss. "Why don't you get some rest, Mama? I'll keep a watch on him."

Ravenna got up and paused by the bed. Tightening the blanket around her, she opened the door and went out without another look.

Left alone with Gabriel, Meridia was incapable of separating impressions from illusions. Had they really been speaking those words, her father and mother, whispering things she had longed to hear all her life? Or had her mind deceived her in the delirium of a dream?

It must be so. Even in his condition, Gabriel was not a man to admit regret. Or was he? The more she questioned, the deeper doubt sank into her heart. In desperation she seized her father's hand and picked away the breathing layer of ice.

"I'm here, Papa. Tell me."

The handsome face remained shut and impassive. Meridia waited and waited but no movement came from either eyes or lips.

THE ARRIVAL OF DAWN brought another whispering. Female and single-voiced, it surged from the stone steps below in a helpless, pleading strain. From her window, Meridia saw a gray figure shivering in the garden. She sighed angrily and stormed down the stairs, wishing the mist was still at hand to chase the intruder away.

"Let me explain," said Pilar as soon as the door opened.

"I have nothing to say to you," said Meridia. "You have deceived me long enough. Now leave before my mother sees you."

Pilar blanched and took a hard swallow. The cut on her nose had dried into a dark blue vein, which seemed a fitting complement to the crescent birthmark on her chin.

"It was never my wish to keep secrets from you," she said. "But fate had pitted us against each other since you were a baby."

"So you've known who I am all my life? I didn't think anyone would make a career out of being my father's mistress."

Pilar's slight frame trembled from the insult. "Don't take him away from me. What we had—what we shared—allow me to hold on to it."

Meridia did all she could to curb her anger.

"What about my mother?" she flung out, suddenly appalled by the scent of lilac on Pilar's skin. "You've taken what was hers and condemned her to hell!"

"I didn't take your father away. Every night he withdrew himself willingly from this house."

"Because you cast God knows what despicable spell on him!"

Pilar began scratching her chin. "Believe me, I had no hand in it. By the time I came into the picture, something else had finished tearing them apart."

Meridia narrowed her eyes dangerously. "Do you mean *me*? Are you saying my father could no longer stand my mother because she gave birth to *me*?"

Pilar stopped scratching and reared her head back in shock. "Whoever gave you that idea? You really believe he—My dear, you were just a baby! How could a grown man blame an infant for his mistakes?"

She regarded Meridia with a tenderness that seemed at odds with the cloying lilac. Tears accrued from years of abandonment snaked up Meridia's throat, but before they could find a way to betray her, she choked them back with all she had.

"What tore them apart then?"

Pilar did not hesitate before replying. "Their love."

Meridia's laugh rang chillingly in the morning air. "Are you insane?"

"Don't you see? They are both extreme and exacting creatures. When they love, it is so complete that they tolerate no defects. Ask them to die for each other and they would drag a sword across their throats without hesitation. But ask them to blunt their edges, to endure arguments and daily imperfections, and they would despise each other to no end. It must have happened soon after you were born, this disillusionment, and somehow they believed it had killed their love for good. But the fact that they chose to stay under one roof when they had the means to separate should tell you something. I suppose that after everything had been stripped bare, another kind of love matured between them. Frail at first, deformed by confusion and disappointment, but it was there, and it grew stronger with time. All these years I thought I had won him, but now I know it's your mother he's always loved. I gave him body and soul,

my youth and my devotion, but to him I was never anything more
than a comfort. When the ice got him, it was your mother he wanted
to see. To save face, he ordered me to bar her from the house, but
why did you think he wanted to wear his best suit? And that gardenia, too? When I realized he had betrayed me, I went mad with
anger. I tried—though I failed, I tried—"

Suddenly Pilar broke off and dissolved into tears. "May heaven
forgive me."

"What is it you've done?" Meridia softened her voice but did not
relent her stare.

"I tried to keep your mother away from him." Pilar was scratching, scratching. "I tore up the note—the last thing he wrote her—
and scattered the pieces to the wind the same night the ice began to
cover him. I didn't read it, but I knew exactly what he would write to
get her to come. You can imagine my shock when your mother said
she received the note. I knew then that even the wind and the mist
were conspiring to bring them together."

The steel quickly crept back into Meridia's voice. "You were content to let him die without seeing his wife?"

Pilar cast her a guilty look. "Don't think meanly of me. You were
always so kind to me, so generous. What you did for my sister—"

"Did Patina know about my father?"

Still scratching, Pilar lowered her head as if her thoughts had
become too heavy. "I kept it from her. She always thought I was a
decent woman—poor but honorable."

A groan exploded from Meridia. "How can you be poor when
you have my father's money at your disposal? In fact, why didn't you
ask him to pay for Patina's surgery? Why did you have to come to
me, of all people, and make me give up what little I had?"

Tears came flooding down Pilar's cheeks. "It's not like that. Your
father never gave me more than what was necessary. You've seen the
house I live in."

Meridia thought back to the dingy little cottage in the dark alley.
It was indeed strange that Gabriel should have lived in such a place.

"He didn't want me to have a better life than your mother. In fact, he made sure that I lived much worse."

"Why? To punish you?"

"To punish himself. For the man he allowed himself to become."

"By making everyone else miserable? Is that his idea of punishing himself?"

Pilar sighed tiredly. "Some men can only love from a distance. But in his own way, he always tried to set things right."

"How?" flared Meridia suddenly. "What has he tried to set right? Tell me one selfless, generous thing he's done in the past twenty years! Go on, I dare you!"

Her anger, long buried without a name, shocked her with its intensity. In a flash she relived Gabriel's countless abuses, his contempt and petty persecutions, the hand he had cruelly withdrawn when to offer it would cost him nothing and comfort her greatly. It was too much to bear, too painful to remember. Red and breathless, she almost spat the words in Pilar's face: "Go on, tell me!"

Gabriel's mistress was watching her intently. "I promised him I'd never tell. But who do you think gave you those gold bars? And all that money on your doorstep?"

Meridia's jaw dropped open. "The gold . . . ? They weren't from my mother?"

Pilar shook her head. "I delivered them myself, and those envelopes, too, every time he learned your mother had gone to visit you. Sprayed her perfume on the gold bars himself. Don't you see? You take up a bigger space in his heart than I ever did."

The last words hung between them like a knife. Neither one could bring herself to look the other in the eye. By then the sun was climbing rapidly, raking the earth with silvery blades of light. With no more mists to haunt them, the stone steps sparkled like freshly polished jewels.

"Why did you stay with him?" Meridia forced the question out.

"I love him," said Pilar in tears. "Please. Let me see him one last time."

Meridia shook her head firmly but without resentment. "You owe this to my mother. You've had your time with him. Let her have hers."

All at once Pilar's face caved in upon itself. "You won't let me see him?"

Meridia met her eyes and said nothing more.

Shuddering, Patina's sister turned and shambled down the stone steps. For a moment she seemed to be melting into the sun, shedding a brighter and brighter brilliance until it eclipsed her whole. But Meridia knew better. Pilar was going where Patina had gone. The suspicion had crossed her mind before, and now she understood it clearly. Pilar had orchestrated Patina's surgery not so much as a means to cure her heart, but as an act of mercy to deliver her from Eva. Whatever sleight of sorcery Pilar had used to elevate her sister into the world of the spirits, she would now unleash upon herself. As Meridia watched the frail figure blur into transparency, she knew it was the last time she would ever see Pilar on this earth.

THIRTY-ONE

Rumors ran rampant in Independence Plaza. Speculations swirled at Cinema Garden. At the market square people shook their heads and rolled their eyes. For weeks the rumors hatched, then at once flapped their wings and rode the wind to Magnolia Avenue. Cordoning the two units that housed the jewelry shop, they splattered the roof with droppings, shed feathers all over the garden, and coated the windows with the grime of scandal.

Despite the maid's complaints that the garden had become a veritable shitting ground for invisible birds, Meridia did not notice it. It was Daniel who brought the matter to her attention. Since she began to divide her time between Monarch Street and Magnolia Avenue, an unspoken tension had manifested between them. He disapproved of her spending so many hours away from home, neglecting the shop and leaving him and the assistant to do her work.

"People are talking," he said, frowning at their filthy living room windows.

At the table, Meridia paused from correcting Noah's composition. "About what?"

"Your mother. How long does she intend to keep this going? Customers are pestering me with questions."

She stiffened visibly, then resumed her correction. "Let them. They'll tire of it soon enough."

Daniel slowly turned to face her. "Do you understand what your mother is doing?"

Meridia looked at him with bafflement. "My father is ill. If I were in her place, I would behave the same."

"That won't be necessary. I'm sure I'll be long gone before it comes to that."

The disquiet festered. A few days later, Noah, who was in his second year of primary schooling, came home with a black eye. While Meridia tended to him with a pack of ice, the boy furiously related what had happened. A classmate had taunted him in the schoolyard by yelling, "Don't let Noah's grandmother bite you! She's crazier than a mad dog!" Outraged for his beloved Ravenna, the delicate boy knocked his friend flat in two blows, but not before one landed on his right eye. A teacher intervened, but did not chastise the classmate when she learned the cause of the fight.

"Is it true, Mama?"

Meridia lifted the ice and examined the bruise closely. Meeting it just above the eye was Elias's scar, pulsing red and feverish as the boy waited for an answer.

"Of course not," she said. "The last thing your grandma will lose is her mind."

Later at dinner, Noah told his father about the fight. Giving Meridia a look she would not soon forget, Daniel told her, "Do something before it's too late." She bit her lip and continued eating as if she had not heard him.

The person who finally spurred her into action was Eva. One afternoon in March, while the day was still redolent with sunlight, Meridia was packing tin boxes with food to take to Monarch Street when she heard Eva's disgust boom across the market square, shoot up past trees and rooftops, ricochet off clouds, thunder toward her kitchen, aim for the only open window, and punch her directly in the gut.

"At least I know better than to keep mounting a man who's got no breath left in his body!"

Meridia dropped the tin boxes. Pale and reeling, she stumbled into the street and set off toward Monarch Street.

"What's the matter, child?" cried Ravenna as soon as she entered the house.

Meridia did not reply but staggered up the stairs, burst into the room at the end of the corridor, and forced herself to confront the figure stretched upon the bed. For the first time since they took him home six months ago, she was able to see Gabriel clearly. Face blue and swollen. Nostrils whiskered like a seal's. Scales crowding every inch of skin. Odor of an alien sea. In horror, she realized he looked more suitable for water than land.

Her eyes smarted as she recalled the doomsayers. "He will neither improve nor worsen," said one doctor. "Scrape the ice all you want but there's no life left inside that body." "Do as you wish," said another, "but to let him go will be a mercy." Overriding them was Ravenna's imperturbable voice. "What do those fools know? One of these days, your father will open his eyes and become the same insufferable old ass."

Six months had now passed. Autumn had turned into spring. While the trees sprouted new leaves and the flowers new blossoms, the figure on the bed had not revived. Every day mother and daughter pumped milk into the tube that snaked through Gabriel's throat. Every morning they bathed him, cleaned the little waste he secreted, and rubbed eucalyptus oil on his skin to keep him warm. In the afternoon, Meridia massaged his limbs, which had grown heavy as timber, while Ravenna tried method after method in her almanac to stop the ice.

How long could they go on like this? And to what end?

Ravenna herself looked worn down. Though she upheld her conviction that Gabriel would recover, she seldom went out of the house anymore, relying instead on Meridia to run her errands. She slept no more than two hours each night, pecked at her food, and, save for her iron back and implacable knot, had become as insubstantial as a shadow. Not for the first time Meridia wondered if her mother's persistence was simply a stubbornness fueled by illusion, a wayward unwillingness to accept what others had foreseen as inevitable.

She did not budge from the sickbed when Ravenna followed her into the room. Clearing her mind of thoughts, she looked at her father without flinching. *Give me a sign, Papa. Tell me what to do.* She took his cold hand and pressed it between her own. She willed it to lift, to strike, to shiver, anything but this slimy amphibian immobility. She stroked the mottled scales that covered his fingers and could not decide if it was blood rumbling in his veins or the roar of the alien sea. With her other hand she pressed his brow gently, hoping something indissoluble would pierce her with certainty. As tears came and smudged her vision, she told herself that he would squeeze her hand if he wished to stay, and no matter how feeble, she would feel the pressure of his will.

Gabriel remained still in his bed, Ravenna behind Meridia. In the planters, the burning logs shot opalescent flames into the air. The room had no breeze but many animate shadows. Meridia counted to one hundred, then two hundred. Nothing happened. She was on the verge of releasing her father's hand when she heard it. The familiar puffing voice of her old nurse coming from the window.

Look here.

Meridia turned. Outside the window hovered the three mists—blue, yellow, ivory—banded together for the first time in memory. At once she remembered her dream from long ago, when the good woman was saying good-bye. *The next time you see them together . . .*

All the hairs on Meridia's arms stood up.

"Papa's gone, Mama," she said at length. "Set him free."

Startled out of reverie, Ravenna laughed dismissively. "Don't be silly, child. That old fool isn't going anywhere. Oh, look how thick the ice has grown. Quick, hand me that brush."

Meridia shook her head as tears dropped from her lashes. "It's time, Mama. Set him free."

Ravenna fetched the wire brush from the nightstand. Meridia placed herself in front of her mother and wrenched the object away.

"No! Leave him alone."

"Are you mad?" cried Ravenna. They struggled. Surprised by her own strength, Meridia locked her arms around her mother and flung the brush across the room. Kicking and cursing, Ravenna fought like a woman possessed, but Meridia was too strong for her. They wept as they grappled, their screams exposing all the wounds that time was powerless to heal. Then with a roar something smashed the window. A thousand glass shards rained down on their bodies. The two women tumbled to the floor while the three mists wheeled like mad birds into the room.

A sharp pain cleaved Meridia's heart. Amid the toss and whirl she caught Gabriel's eyes flicker for the last time. "No!" Ravenna was crying. The mists jumped on the bed, shoved their talons into Gabriel's chest, and ripped the cord between worlds. Rocking and weeping, Meridia kept her arms locked around her mother. In the next instant the mists were off, carrying with them the mass of a reborn soul—peaceful now, pure and majestic—borne upward in a density of wings.

Ravenna made no more sound or movement, as if she, too, had been infected by the ice. Her bleeding arms hung without strength, and her neck gave the ghoulish impression that it had been snapped. Carefully, Meridia sat her down in a chair. She spoke to her as she picked the glass from her flesh, and when no answer came, she set to shaking her vigorously. It did not take her long to notice that something had faded from Ravenna's eyes.

A WEEK AFTER THE funeral, Meridia braved herself to enter her father's study. Without Gabriel, the towers of books looked unremarkable, the massive desk no grimmer than a toothless hound.

In six months, no one had tidied the mess Ravenna had made when she was last here. The shattered beakers lolled in the dust. The overturned tables pleaded for a restitution. There were shreds of clothes fluttering everywhere, incredulous still, it seemed, at Ravenna's fit of anger.

Meridia began her task by throwing the windows open. A crisp morning breeze flooded the sepulchral room, but did little to mitigate the stench of neglect. After she rid the floor of debris and righted the tables, she turned to the documents in the desk drawers. Over the next four hours, she tracked Gabriel's investments across two continents and seven nations, and in this way learned the true state of his finances. She took turns frowning and grimacing, and by noon came to an unfavorable conclusion—her father had much less money than anybody had suspected. All her life she had imagined some powerful beast residing inside his bankbook, smashing down doors and assuring his status in the eye of the town. Now she saw it was no great beast at all. Apart from the house and a modest sum of money, Ravenna would have little to rely on.

This revelation soon paled in the face of another: Given his financial condition, it must have cost Gabriel no small sacrifice to part with the two gold bars, not to mention the money in the envelopes. Feeling a sudden heaviness, Meridia bowed her head. He had loved her after all. In his own way, he had tried to set things right. There in that room where he had taught her terror at a very early age, she began to forgive the man she had understood so little.

The study concealed yet another surprise. As Meridia was sorting the thousands of books into boxes, she discovered that a great number of them were not scientific texts as Gabriel had led everyone to believe, but much perused treatises on resurrecting a love long dead. One whole shelf was devoted to writings on trespass and atonement, another to elaborate formularies on annihilating grief and enmity. Gabriel's notes cluttered the margins of many, and these faded words revealed his pain more than any confession he had made in life. *In the end it was your mother he wanted to see,* Pilar had said. Sadly and reverently, Meridia returned these volumes to the shelves.

A FEW DAYS LATER, the town was scandalized by tales of Ravenna scavenging the streets in broad daylight. Witnesses said she rambled aimlessly from one avenue to another, strapped inside a stiff mourning dress from another age that barely exposed her face. She spoke to no one, though her lips moved without cease, and her panicked eyes darted to and fro without catching the phantom they pursued. She looked ill and extraordinarily pale, and many who offered her water wondered how she managed not to suffocate in that punishing dress.

The following Monday, Leah brought Meridia news that an urchin at the market square had witnessed Ravenna sharing a meal with an enormous black beast. On Wednesday, Rebecca claimed that Ravenna had been spotted leading a white colt by the halter while waving a palm branch over its head. On Friday, Noah confessed that two boys in his class had seen a blind woman with snake hair sitting outside the school gate. She had laughed and licked her lips when they petted the vipers in her hair.

Meridia did not know what to make of this. Every time she visited Monarch Street, she always found Ravenna sitting in her room, staring at Gabriel's deathbed with an idol's invariable expression. The nurse she had hired to look after her attested to the same thing: All day long, Ravenna stayed in that room, saying nothing and sometimes refusing to take her meals. As the tales multiplied, Meridia began to show up more frequently at unpredictable hours, but not once did she ever catch Ravenna in her wandering. In the meantime, Daniel's displeasure deepened. She had only to examine his frown to guess the lurid nature of the tale being circulated that day.

Things came to a boil a month later. One afternoon, Meridia was writing a purchase order for a customer at the shop when a commotion erupted in the street.

"Make way for a sick woman, sirs! See for yourselves her deplorable condition!"

Meridia rushed to the curb. A crowd, lured by the noise, had gathered. A distance away, Eva was marching in the direction of the shop, head held high and shoulders thrown back, pushing a haggard and barely clothed Ravenna from behind. On seeing Meridia, she dropped her voice but was still loud enough for everyone to hear.

"How tragic it is to be a widow. I am without husband myself, and I bless heaven for giving me a stronger constitution than this wretched soul. An abandoned mother! At her advanced age! Her daughter must be too busy to look after her. Guess what she was doing just now? Scouring the latrines at Cinema Garden for food! She was so relieved to see me she wept and kissed me on the cheek!"

Before the crowd caught on, Meridia surged forward and snatched Ravenna away from Eva's clutches. She moved so lightly and swiftly that all the crowd felt was a heated breeze on their elbows. It was only on her way back to the shop, leading Ravenna by the shoulder, that they noticed her. A storm had broken over her face, and though her lips were colorless, her eyes blazed like lightning. She threw a cutting look at Daniel, who had come out to follow her, and went back into the shop. The tension between them was not lost on Eva.

"Son!" she exclaimed jubilantly. "Imagine what would have happened had I not rescued your beloved mother-in-law!"

With these words clanging in her ear, Meridia guided Ravenna up the stairs. More than a few customers stared, but she managed to dismiss them with a measure of calm. As soon as they reached the guest room, Meridia shut the door and sat her mother down on the bed. Ravenna looked lost and frightened, clucking like a hen but saying nothing. Her gaunt cheeks were streaked with dirt, her knot disarrayed, her dress torn, her mouth reeking something abominable—Ravenna, who had never tolerated a speck of dust in her house, let alone on her person! To see her mother paraded around like a circus animal, pitied and gawked at without the least amount of self-defense, incited in Meridia a sadness greater than anger. As she cleaned the dirt off Ravenna, her mind began to fashion the armor she would have to wield in order to protect her.

THAT EVENING, AS SOON as the assistant departed, Meridia went into the small office at the back of the shop. Daniel was storing the day's inventory in the fireproof metal vault, and from the way his eyes strayed from hers, she knew she was in for an uphill battle. A sleeping dog had awoken in him the night Ravenna took her to the dark heart of town. In six months, he had gone to visit Gabriel but twice, and with each hour Meridia spent away from the house, his temper, up till then mild and agreeable, became increasingly volatile. Often he turned churlish for no reason, and made vague demands that required all her mind-reading ability to interpret. When she guessed wrong, he rebuffed her with silence. When she tried to please and mollify, he stopped her cold with a gruff look.

Presently she stood before him, tall and straight-backed as a sword, and did not move until he raised his eyes from the stacked jewelry trays on the desk.

"What is it?"

The impatience in his voice made her decide on a direct approach. "I want my mother to live with us," she said.

He picked up a tray and slammed it into the vault.

"She has a house of her own. What good can come from her living here?"

"She's lonely and can no longer take care of herself. You saw what happened this afternoon."

"You already hired a nurse. And visit three times a day."

Maintaining her calm, Meridia shook her head. "She needs me, her daughter, to take care of her. And besides, once she lives here I can spend more time at the shop."

Daniel pushed the remaining trays aside and drew to his full height. The eyes he trained on her were those of a stranger.

"What makes you think you can take care of her? From what I've heard, she's quite a handful, roaming the streets like a lunatic, barking at strangers and pelting them with stones. How are you going to keep her in this house without chaining her ankles? She'll make a spectacle of herself and humiliate us again, just like today!"

Meridia felt her calm quickly slip away. "If I remember correctly, it was *your* mother who provided the spectacle."

"You should be thanking my mother for rescuing yours!"

"For parading her around like a beast of marvel? Allow me to send a dozen roses this instant!"

Daniel clenched his eyes sharply. In that moment there was no trace of the tenderhearted man she had married.

"There's no room for your mother in this house," he said.

Meridia stepped forward, keeping her eyes on him, and replied through her teeth, "Yes, there is."

A mocking smile spread across his face, chilling for a moment the flare of anger on her lips. She felt as if time had reversed, and the occurrences of the last ten years had done nothing but returned her to the exact same spot. For there on his face was the same cruel expression that had darkened Gabriel's, more times than she cared to remember.

"Then answer me this," he said. "Should my mother find herself in the same condition—heaven forbid—would you allow her to live with us?"

Meridia responded instantly. "I will never stand in the way of your duty."

Daniel burst into a gale of laughter, so brutal and belittling it would have flattened anyone with less composure. Meridia asked him point-blank: "Why do you resent her so?"

"Because she treated me worse than a flea when I had nothing to my name!"

"She did it to protect me."

"To protect you? From *me*?"

"From despair and adversity." She drew a deep breath and wished she could locate the man she loved. "It was a mistake. Forgive her one lapse of judgment."

Daniel huffed in disdain. "Why should I? She never apologized. And now, given her malady, she probably never will."

It was a cheap shot, but Meridia let it pass. "Then let me apologize for her. Please."

She humbled herself, sought him with all the love in her being, yet she could not still the beating animosity inside him. In a flash, she deduced that something—someone—had been toiling overtime to influence him. While she was busy nursing Gabriel and comforting Ravenna, Eva must have surrounded him with her bees. She had been too anxious, too preoccupied, to notice.

"I have suffered more than anyone at your mother's hand," she said, weighing her arguments to find one strong enough to blast away the bees. "But if she needed my help—if for any reason her happiness depended on my blessing—then because I love you, I would give it to her. I'm asking you to do the same. Forgive my mother as you once have been forgiven."

"How dare you throw that at me!" cried Daniel. "Mama was right. You *would* do and say anything to get your way."

Meridia saw it clearly then—the fence she had first glimpsed the night Daniel returned home from Orchard Road covered with bees' marks—now stretching and thickening in her face. Daniel had never looked angrier. Blood flushed his temples and his lungs panted for air as though they could never get enough.

"You will not bring your mother into this house!" he roared. "Am I making myself understood?"

Meridia drew back, rupturing the tension so tenderly at first that Daniel mistook it for a surrender. But nothing, nothing in their ten years of marriage could prepare him for her next words.

"Then I'll take Noah to live with me on Monarch Street."

There was nothing menacing in her voice, yet Daniel froze as if he had been stabbed. Snatching the rest of the trays, he thrust them into the vault and slammed the bolts. Meridia did not linger. For the moment she had won, but every victory, as she well knew, came at a price that no one could predict.

THIRTY-TWO

Noah was nine the year Ravenna moved into Magnolia Avenue. By that time, she had secured her place in his affection as that enchanting and elusive being who drifted into the house in a cloud of scent when he had least expected it. Though he saw her even less after his grandfather turned into a seal, he remembered every detail about her—the immemorial black dress with pearl buttons on her wrists; the steel knot on the back of her head; her long, generous nose; the bold twilight eyes and their power to defy misfortune.

He was surprised, therefore, to discover that the woman who occupied the room at the end of the hallway was not the grandmother of his memory. In her place was a befuddled creature with leathery skin, murky gray eyes, and a loose, crinkled tunic that swallowed her rail-thin figure. Her coal black hair was replaced by bristly silver wires his mother combed once in the morning and once before bedtime. She looked ancient to him, drained of energy, her hands folded to her chest like wounded claws. The only thing that remained of her old self was her scent.

For the first few days, Noah did not dare approach his grandmother. Her wracking cough frightened him as much as her bewildered stare, and his stomach heaved at the texture of her skin, which had dried and toughened like that of a reptile. But then one day, when the two of them were alone, his grandmother spoke to him. She told him, in a strange and halting language only he could understand, to bring her scents.

That day, he brought her a bottle of vanilla extract from the kitchen, which she inhaled greedily, as if it was the most pleasing aroma in the world. The next day, he ransacked his mother's spice rack and came up with thyme, clove, and nutmeg. On subsequent mornings, he brought her flowers—daffodils, hyacinths, tuberoses—plucked from his mother's garden or pilfered from the neighbors. Over the course of the month, not content with what was free and available, he used his allowance to buy frankincense, sandalwood candles, cane syrup, cinnamon pastilles, and lemongrass vinegar. In the afternoon after his father picked him up from school, he kept his nose out for the most extraordinary scents as they walked home through the market square. Seeing him dart about and brandish his coins like a little lord, Daniel cocked a brow, but the boy, warned by his keen intuition that his father would put an end to his spending were he to discover the truth, simply looked at him with his snub nose and round dark eyes and explained, "It's for school, Papa."

He cherished the moments when his grandmother drank in the scent he brought her. Her breathing might turn raspy while she imbued the aroma with meaning, but it was more than countered by her suddenly glowing skin. Sometimes he could not stop himself from hugging her. She never objected. She only looked at him with tender eyes. When she smiled, she looked neither old nor wizened but beautiful.

Every day their game would end when he heard his mother approach. Quickly, he would hide the bottle or flower in his pocket and watch his grandmother's expression revert to its state of torment. But by then she had already savored the scent he brought her, and he had already absorbed a little more of her mystery. Together they had shared a secret whose sanctity he would uphold until the day he died.

IN THE BEGINNING, MERIDIA did everything to hide Ravenna from Daniel. She did not tell him when her mother was moving in, but one day simply settled her along with two suitcases in the room at the end of the hallway. She kept the room closed up at all times, and at night took an extra precaution by sealing the crack at the bottom of the door with a towel. She personally prepared and delivered Ravenna's meals, stuffed her clothes in a sack for the maid to wash, and brewed her tonics with the windows open so the smell would not linger. Once a day, she took Ravenna down to the garden for exercise, but only when Daniel was out on an errand. Her strategy worked so well that for a full week he did not realize there was another person living under his roof.

As spring turned into summer, Meridia carefully wove Ravenna's presence into the house. Whenever she left her post at the shop, she would signal to the assistant that she would be just upstairs, making sure that her gesture was not lost on Daniel. Once a week when the doctor came, she would pause with him on the stairs before she brought him up, acquainting him in a low voice with Ravenna's progress while Daniel watched. She let slip to a few customers that her ailing mother was now living with her, and in turn, they sent her cards and flowers, all of which she displayed prominently in the living room. At dinner, she set aside a plate of food without giving an explanation, thus turning Ravenna, through a scoop of rice and a serving of vegetables, into an undeniable reality.

She found an indispensable ally in Noah. Since the episode of the cockatoo (on some nights the empty cage in his room still rattled with the bird's outrage), there was no more question where his loyalty lay. The boy proved to be as wily as she was, and much more merciless. One afternoon at the shop, he made a great show of stuffing his schoolbag with books in front of his father.

"What are you doing, son?" asked a puzzled Daniel. "Opening a library?"

"No, Papa. I'm going to do my homework upstairs in the guest room. You know, the one that smells like lemon and coughs for no reason?"

Daniel almost choked. Meridia ducked her head and pretended to be busy.

After weeks of these maneuvers, Daniel exhibited every sign of being pacified. He no longer glared at her with resentment, and seemed reconciled to his mother-in-law's presence in his house. Emboldened, Meridia took Ravenna more and more out of her room. One Sunday, she sat with her in the living room for the entire afternoon and heard not a word from Daniel. The following week, she took her down to the shop and sat her across the table from him, and still he said nothing. Every morning, she kept an ear out for the first outcry from Orchard Road, but the wind blowing from the westerly direction carried no trace of bees. Business was booming. Their finances were in order. Their lovemaking, if somewhat less frequent, remained on familiar ground.

IN REALITY, THE BEES were out in full swing that summer, but Eva cleverly kept them from Meridia. "How dare she shelter that revenant under your brother's roof!" They droned round and round Permony. "The very house whose door has never welcomed me and whose table has yet to serve me supper! I understand that the beastly woman is in mourning, but when *I* became widowed, did I receive any such pampering? I don't even remember your sister-in-law offering me her condolences! And why should that crazy woman be rewarded for wallowing in self-pity? I was the strong one. I said my good-bye, put your father in the ground, and moved on with my life, like any self-respecting woman would. And to think that letch spent the majority of his life despising her, frittering his manhood in the arms of a harlot, and probably sowing enough bastards to mobilize

an army! Hah! One time she slapped me until my ear rang for three
days, and now she can't even slap a mosquito. Heaven's justice,
wouldn't you say? But why your brother's peace of mind should be
mixed up with her lunacy, I don't see. She's rich enough, she can
hire someone to coddle her in her own house. What kind of an upbringing will my grandson have with an ax-wielding grandmother
breathing in the next room? If your brother doesn't put his foot
down, Noah will soon start chanting to houseplants, or worse, hacking off our limbs while we sleep!"

Nettling the bees over time were three additional injuries. One,
Gabilan, after years of enduring abuse in silence, skipped town in
the middle of the night with a fellow maid. She left behind all her
belongings, but took half a dozen copper pans from the kitchen. Eva,
apoplectic with rage, threatened to have her arrested. "For what,
Mama?" counseled Permony wisely. "Stealing battered skillets? God
knows why she wanted them in the first place." But secretly Permony understood. For years Patina's hands had handled those pans
every day; as a matter of fact, they were among the few things in the
house that Eva never touched.

Two, the town's gossiping of Malin was reaching a new low. At
the market, Eva could not walk from one stall to the next without
being harassed by whispers. *Jonathan hasn't touched her in months,
wouldn't kiss her, wouldn't make love to her. And who can blame him?
What good is a wife who prefers a gravestone to her husband's flesh?* Indignant, Eva scowled. Yet even haggling and hectoring did nothing
to stop them.

The third injury was the most galling. When not gossiping
about Malin, the town picked apart the shop on Lotus Blossom
Lane. *It's gone downhill since Elias died three years ago. Thanks to his
widow's incompetence, customers are leaving by the droves and the inventory is as musty as its carpeting. If only Eva would hand over the
shop to Permony. The girl has an eye for jewelry and a good head for
business. But her mother always chases her to the background as if she is
jealous . . .*

Eva listened to this angrily. It was one thing to accuse her of ineptitude, but jealousy? Of Permony? Her youngest could barely pour tea without spilling it! And for their information, the shop was failing because Meridia stole all her customers! If only she could get her hand on some money, she could give the shop a face-lift, an updated inventory, and squash that bloodsucking cockroach once and for all. She thought of borrowing money from Daniel, but the idea of Meridia's discovery was too humiliating to bear. Borrowing from Malin was out of the question; these days the girl could do little more than gather flowers for the cemetery.

What could a mother who had been forsaken by her children do?

The answer, as it happened, came walking into the shop one sluggish afternoon in August. Working alone, Eva was about to close early when the door swung and the golden bell jingled. For a second all she saw was sunlight, brilliant yellow, and a headless man in a military-style jacket standing in its midst. Then he stepped away from the light. Pale skin, long mustache, eyes the color of cobalt. Because his hair had the same radiance as the sun, she had not been able to see him before. Suddenly, as her mind rushed to excavate him from memory, Eva knew why he was there. The townspeople were right. Permony might yet be her one saving grace, but not in the way they thought.

WITHOUT PATINA AND GABILAN, Permony was left with all the bees. At first, she was able to rely on her cheerfulness to fend them off, but as summer descended into autumn, her optimism gave way to restlessness and despair. How would she ever escape her mother? She had no money, no skills or training, and her education was incomplete since Eva saw no point in keeping her in school after Elias's death. For the past three years, she had been assisting her mother at the shop, an occupation that hardly qualified her for the workforce. The other prospect, to wed and start a family, seemed equally impossible. Though there was no lack of suitors, their interest evaporated quickly when they learned she had no dowry to speak of. What if she was doomed to spend her life on Orchard Road, enslaved by Eva's temper and married to her outrageous demands?

On occasions Permony was tempted to confide in Meridia. However, when she saw how burdened her sister-in-law was with Ravenna, and how fraught with tension Magnolia Avenue had increasingly become, she decided to spare her. In the same way, though their relation had greatly improved since childhood, she could not penetrate the grief in Malin's heart to speak to her. The only person she could approach was Daniel. But even he, as she soon found out, had his mind saddled with other matters.

She noticed that he had been coming to Orchard Road more frequently since Ravenna moved into his house. For hours, he would shut himself with their mother in the upstairs sitting room, and afterward would leave the house looking grim and extremely vexed. Permony could only guess the nature of their meetings until one night in September when she decided to question him. The instant he opened his mouth, she felt her blood go cold. There were bees in his voice. Bees in his breath. Bees shooting out of his eyes like needles.

"I know she thinks I'm nothing without her. She thinks it's her talent, her cleverness, that made the shop into a success. Do you know what she did to let her deranged mother in the house? She threatened to take Noah from me if I refused! She knows how much I abhor that woman, yet she parades her in front of me every chance she has. You remember how she went behind my back to give money to Pilar, when that money was all we had to keep us from the poorhouse, and then she had the nerve to tell everyone that Patina would have died had it not been for her charity. Mama is right. She thinks she's better than I am. That day when Mama was kind enough to rescue her mother, she gave me a look that cut me down in front of everyone. Why does she always try to humiliate me? I have tried my best to be a good husband and father, but she behaves as if any other man would do just as well. I know how people talk.

I've seen the stares they give me. They say she's prouder than a queen because I let her wipe her feet on my face. Mama told me so herself! And now she's got Noah to back her up. They're always scheming together, spending hours locked up with that infernal woman in my house. Well, I won't be her fool anymore! One of these days, I'll make her sorry for taking me for granted!"

Shocked and distressed, Permony recounted this outburst to her sister-in-law the following day. Meridia listened without interrupting, but it was clear that her mind was elsewhere. Every so often, face drawn and eyes tired with worry, she kept glancing at the door at the end of the hallway.

"I've heard them all before," she said after Permony finished. "They're your mother's words. Let her say what she wants. Daniel knows better."

"But he sounded so angry!" objected Permony. "Aren't you at all worried . . . ?"

A moan rose from the end of the hallway. In an instant Meridia was on her feet.

"I appreciate your concern, Permony, but your brother is a good man. He may feel resentful at the moment, but he knows what's right and what's wrong. This will pass. I trust Daniel—he will never hurt me intentionally. So no, I'm not worried. Nothing your mother throws will stick between us. Now you must excuse me. Mama isn't feeling well today."

Meridia's confidence was a quality both rousing and maddening. As Permony walked home in the dusk, slowing her steps so she could postpone her encounter with the bees, the girl wished she could have a piece of it for herself.

JUST WHEN THE BEES were getting the better of her, Permony began seeing the foreigner everywhere. Always in his long military-style jacket, patent-leather boots, and a square of white silk peeking from his breast pocket. At first she ran into him by chance, crossing

Majestic Avenue or strolling through Cinema Garden. And then she saw him browsing the same stalls and exiting the shops she was entering. He never spoke to her, never acknowledged her presence. Had he done so, she would have thought he was following her.

After two months of running into him in public, he smashed into her private space in a way she could never have imagined. One afternoon, while she and Eva were at the shop waiting for nonexistent customers to show, the foreigner swung the glass door open and advanced directly toward them. He had no greetings to offer, simply looked at Permony with bulging blue eyes as if he wanted to consume her. It was Eva who saved her from embarrassment.

"Heavens! What have I done?"

The tension broke as beads of pearls hopped wildly across the floor. Permony jumped at the noise and began chasing them. Eva, nursing the broken necklace in her palms, turned to the foreigner in distress.

"How clumsy of me! Would you give my daughter a hand, sir?"

The foreigner agreed. Together with Permony he moved chairs and tables, inspected dark, dusty corners; and with every pearl collected they exchanged a brief smile. Crawling on their hands and knees, they bumped and jostled each other, while his strong scent of sun and tobacco pleasantly saturated her nostrils. "There!" Eva kept urging them. "Please make sure you find them all."

After every last bead had been collected, Eva thanked the foreigner profusely.

"I can't tell you how grateful we are. It would have taken us a whole day to search for all those pearls. But haven't we met before? You look terribly familiar."

"So do you, madam," he replied in a raspy voice. "It was at a wedding, I believe."

"Of course! My daughter Malin's! You were a good friend of Jonathan's father."

"And you were the mother of the bride. I remember. This young lady here was the most beautiful girl at the wedding."

ERICK SETIAWAN

Permony blushed as if he had set her on fire. His crude metallic accent pricked her like thistle, sharp yet not wholly unwelcome. He was big and rugged with a sinewy build; he had corn-colored hair and mustache, and a bulbous nose that reminded her of a tulip. Judging from his puckered eyes, he could not have been younger than forty.

Reading her daughter's interest, Eva thrust her forward.

"This is Permony, my youngest."

Permony offered her hand, which the foreigner brought to his lips. Unaccustomed to such boldness, the girl was taken aback.

"The pleasure's all mine," he said. "Call me Ahab."

His smile was a pearl white gleam that lightened the puckered hardness in his eyes. It was this splash of sun that Permony seized, this field of white light that thrilled and drenched her, even as she withdrew her hand, with the nearness of hope.

FOR THE NEXT SIX weeks, she saw him every Tuesday and Saturday afternoon. If his attention at first left her tongue-tied, by the second week she could not wait for him to show up with flowers in his hand. She did not think he was handsome; unlike those of the slim and refined noblemen in her childhood tales, his features were too large, his manner too gruff, and his pale skin reminded her of a cloth that had been left out too long in the sun. But what he lacked in appearance he made up plenty in ardor. He kissed her as if he might swallow her. He spun her, twirled her, clasped her in his thick arms until she thought she might break. In spite of herself, his bumbling roughness gave her pleasure. Gradually, she viewed him as a giant who would run through fire to carry her to safety.

To her amazement, the bees turned silent from the moment Ahab harvested pearls from the floor. Stranger still, Eva conducted herself like the happiest mother on earth. Warm and lovely, she served them tea and cakes on the terrace, urged Ahab to stay for dinner, and had a smile on her face that lasted all day. To Permony she could not behave more beautifully. She addressed her with affection, bought her dresses, took her to the beauty parlor every Saturday morning. Brushing Permony's hair one night, she told her, "You won't find a better man than Ahab, dear. Kind, hardworking, determined, wealthy. Don't say a word to Malin, but I think he's a better catch than Jonathan."

Permony's fate was sealed one afternoon in November. She was walking arm in arm with Ahab in Cinema Garden when she suddenly stopped and stared at him. It was the hour when the sun gilded every surface with a million tiny lights. In those million lights Ahab's face blazed like fire, burnishing his hair more goldenly, and from this conflagration emerged the vision of another face. Permony stood transfigured. How could she not have noticed before—the lazy mouth, the same broad forehead, this man and her father? Something contracted inside her. All at once she yearned to throw herself into the center of that brilliance, to caress and cradle the miracle of the million lights for as long as she could. But before she could move, Ahab beat her to it. He swept her off her feet and closed his lips forcibly around hers. In his arms she wilted like a little girl. His hoarse grunt followed on the heels of her surrender.

"Be my wife," he said simply.

Permony replied by wrapping her fingers around his nape. His large, rough hand snaked up her belly and crushed her breasts. His mustache stabbed as she closed her eyes and slipped to a place where she could kiss him with all her worth.

FOR THE FIRST TIME in memory, Eva embraced her youngest with tears streaming down her cheeks. "Your father will be proud," she kept repeating while her head, now completely white, shook with emotion. "Will you tell him I've done well by you?" Moved to tears herself, Permony soaked up the blessing. It was the first time and might be the last, but to see her mother's eyes awash with love, proud of who she was and what she had done, touched her deeper than anything that had passed between them. Without a doubt in her mind, Permony nodded.

THIRTY-THREE

The news took Meridia by storm. Despite Permony's hints that she was seeing a man with a stiff tongue and a yellow mustache, the girl had not once spoken of marriage. Neither had Daniel said anything. Since Ravenna took up residence in the room at the end of the hallway, Meridia was no longer privy to his thoughts, and her questions, before she learned not to ask them, were frequently met with a vexed gaze. Of course there was the endless wind of gossip. "Eva's youngest and the hulking foreigner," it breezed by Magnolia Avenue on the way to the market square. "If he doesn't propose soon, she'll walk down the aisle with her stomach big as a drum." But talk of this sort, however spiced with scandal, never sustained Meridia's interest for long.

Meridia finally met Ahab when Eva brought him to the shop. In one glance she recognized him as the distinguished-looking man who gazed at Permony all night long at Malin's wedding. He was certainly cordial in a brash way, but more than that she did not know what to make of him. His accent and foreign manners aside, it was the glint in his eyes that she found odd, flashing now and then as if he was laughing at them. Daniel liked him well enough; the two were sharing business advice before tea was served. Permony looked happy and pretty, but her joy was nothing compared to her mother's. Beaming with triumph, Eva was gregariousness made flesh, her voice alive and her laughter deft against pauses. And yet, unlike her other victories in the past, this one carried no trace of gloating. Her bees were nowhere in sight, and she even seemed kind to Permony. Meridia suspected something was afoot.

Fired by curiosity, she made an appointment to see Samuel in his office the next day. The renegade dealer, who knew just about every merchant within a fifty-kilometer radius, was eager to help. He told her that Ahab owned several businesses in neighboring towns, among them a lumber mill, a rubber plant, and a sugar factory.

"He trades goods overseas for very large profits," Samuel said, stroking his beard confidentially. "From what I heard, he came to this part of the world with his country's backing. A pioneer, if you will, to see what else they can get."

"You mean a secret agent?"

Samuel laughed. "I'd call him an exceedingly adventurous businessman."

"What about his personal life?"

"He keeps to himself and doesn't have many friends. You know how foreigners are. But I haven't heard his name attached to any scandal. Is everything well at home?"

The suddenness of the question startled her. For a brief second Meridia thought that if there was anyone she could talk to, it would be patient and perceptive Samuel.

"Yes, of course," she said. "Why do you ask?"

"You look tired, that's all."

His audacious black eyes bored into her. Feeling herself weaken, she resisted him.

"My mother's a handful these days," said Meridia. And finding it difficult to believe her own words, she fumbled for her coat and took leave.

Next, she turned to Leah for information. Her friend, now pregnant with her second child, was only too willing to play detective. "I need the exercise," she explained, patting her swollen belly glowingly. A few days later, the steadfast woman returned with an even rosier complexion. She had scoured the town for news, she said, and at first could find nothing on Ahab. But just that morning, she had the good fortune of running into an old cloth-dyer who told her the following:

A few years ago, Ahab was planning to build a warehouse in a distant town. However, when he exerted pressure on the residents to sell their homes, they not only cursed his blue eyes to the sky but chased him away with sticks and stones. Three weeks after the dispute, twelve of the residents' daughters began to exhibit symptoms of hysteria. Night after night, at precisely the same hour, the girls fell into the same dream where they were ravished by a half-swine, half-human creature. At dawn they woke up screaming along with the roosters, their faces flushed, their clothes torn, their wombs bleeding painfully. The girls never left their rooms and no one had broken in. The parents, realizing their daughters were no longer virgins, were horrified. They stood watch all night long, banging gongs and swinging censers, yet the dream persisted. Soon, all twelve girls developed a scarlet flower that burned between their thighs and secreted pus. Believing it was the work of the devil, the parents sold their land to Ahab for peanuts and fled town.

"No one ever proved anything, but they suspected him all the same," said Leah, clearly relishing her role as talebearer. "I must warn you, though, the cloth-dyer mistakes gourds for chicken, so I can't vouch for her accuracy."

That evening after the shop closed, Meridia placed herself once again before Daniel in the little office.

"Permony looks so happy these days," she began delicately. "Everyone thinks Ahab is a good match for her."

Without sparing a glance, Daniel shoved the jewelry trays into the vault.

"He's better than good. Everyone thinks he's perfect."

It was too early for his back to be up. Meridia waited until he looked at her.

"Do you agree with them?"

Daniel frowned. The resulting lines mapped to an uncanny degree the turbulent nature of their recent interactions.

"He's friendly, he adores her, and he's a top-notch businessman. Is there a reason why I shouldn't?"

Meridia chose her words carefully. "I want you to tell me if I'm wrong, but I just can't convince myself that Permony is making the right choice."

His face, which he now left unshaved for days, darkened with more lines.

"Why can't you convince yourself?"

"I have a strange feeling about Ahab."

"Come to the point. What are you trying to say?"

She proceeded to tell him what Leah had told her. Midway through the story, a crooked smile appeared on Daniel's face and stayed there.

"Let me understand this," he said after she finished. "You're accusing him of ravishing virgins in their dreams?"

"I'm simply telling you what I heard."

"What you heard is an old wives' tale."

"There's truth even in the strangest story."

Daniel threw his hands up in the air. "Where are the witnesses, testimonies, proof? You need more than idle talk to implicate someone in a scandal. I've held off long enough to say this, but I suggest you spend less time with your mother. You're beginning to sound as crazy as she is."

Meridia felt her skin heat up from the attack. Daniel's irises were unusually pale, cold as snow, and in them she could read his desire to hurt her. This collision of fire and snow dredged up something irrevocable between them.

"My mother is not insane," she said, as evenly as she could.

His hollow laugh exploded in her ear. "You're the coldest woman I know. Always together, calm as marble. Do you ever show anyone what's in your fist?"

Her slender throat pulsed with emotion, yet she refused to acknowledge his taunt. Slowly she peeled her gaze off him.

"I only want the best for Permony. To make sure she doesn't make a mistake."

"I appreciate your concern. But do you honestly think I'd let her go through with the marriage if she's making a mistake? My own sister? What do you take me for?"

Angry now, he shut the vault and locked it. Aware of the dismissal, Meridia planted her feet more firmly.

"They have more than twenty years separating them, Daniel. She's a virgin and he's a man of the world. What can they have in common?"

He spun around quickly. "Have you seen the way he looks at her?"

"He's a lover, without a doubt. A ravenous one. But a husband?"

"I never took you to be a cynic."

"Everything is happening so fast. Don't you find it the littlest bit odd?"

"Find what odd?"

"Until a week ago, we knew nothing about this man."

"So naturally you suspect—"

She took a deep breath, placed her right hand on the desk between them. "Your mother is up to something. I have a feeling it was her idea to arrange for them to meet."

In a flash the fence sprang up between them and all his resentment bubbled up to the surface. "I knew it! Enough with your suspicions! Again, what proof do you have? This has nothing to do with Mama. This is about you."

Placing her other hand on the desk, Meridia leaned her whole body against the fence.

"You know very well she's capable of masterminding this. I wouldn't put it past her to sacrifice Permony for her own self-interests."

Daniel leapt forward, eyes wide and livid, and slammed both hands on the table. "My mother isn't the monster you make her out to be!"

Incredulous, Meridia charged against the fence.

"Need I remind you of what she's done over the years? To me? To Patina? To Noah?"

"It was an accident with Noah. If anybody was at fault, it was Papa."

"What about Patina's feet?"

"A lie Pilar embellished over the years. Nobody knew what really happened. Patina herself never confirmed anything."

"And my womb? Are you going to tell me she had no hand in destroying it?"

"Do you really believe she was out to murder you that day? The mother of her own grandchild? Unforeseen complications arise during labor. Why do you hold her responsible for things that clearly lay beyond her power? We're a family, Meridia. You should forgive and forget and release that bitterness in your heart."

Her astonishment was so absolute that for a moment she could say nothing. Only the movement of her dress, vigorously shivering though there was no breeze, betrayed the tumult inside her. Before her the fence towered without a dent. Meridia withdrew her hands and balled them into fists.

"You are no longer a child, Daniel. Why can't you see what others see? Your mother is a woman who'll stop at nothing to get what she wants. How many times does she have to trample you before you realize this? It's time you looked her in the eye. Let go of her skirt."

Swift as thunder, he swept his hand across the desk, hurling a lamp and a jeweled clock to the floor.

"Damn you!" he shouted. "How dare you talk to me like that! You walk around with your superior airs and you judge, you condescend, you presume to know what's best for everyone. Mind your own business! I leave your mother alone even though the house reeks so much of her I can't stand it. Why don't you do the same with mine?"

All at once she appeared to relent. Her shoulders relaxed, her eyes turned mild, and the tension that had pulsed in her throat died as her fists unclenched. Yet he knew it was the farthest thing from a concession. She could not fool him; smile as she might, she was not the same person who had returned to him after their separation ten years ago. Back then she had been made of flesh; the woman standing before him was made of flint.

"I'll drop the matter on one condition," Meridia said with a shattering certainty. "Permony must tell me it is entirely her choice to marry him."

"Then ask her by all means!" Daniel shouted, his voice choked with resentment. "But if you go back on your word, by God, I won't let you hear the end of it!"

AFTER SUPPER, MERIDIA SET off to Orchard Road with the same thoughts clanging in her head. She must knock down the fence between her and Daniel. Eva could not be trusted. Ahab was hiding something. God knows what those two were up to together. Deserted under a languorous sky, Independence Plaza rang loudly with invisible steps while the town founder waved his fist. Meridia picked up her pace. When she reached the Cemetery of Ashes, the smoke that guarded it was cold and bitter; at first whiff she turned up her collar and held her breath. The town bell chimed twice before she got to 27 Orchard Road. As soon as she glimpsed the familiar wood-and-brick structure, another thought hit her: Daniel had not taken her here since Gabriel fell ill. The front lawn was now a jungle of marigolds without a single rose left. In the moonlight, the house looked more disheveled than she remembered.

Permony answered the door on the second knock. It was true then: Eva had not had a maid since Gabilan skipped town with a dozen copper pans.

"Mama said you might be coming."

Permony looked grown up in a lime tulle dress that revealed the young slope of her breast. The brightness of her smile did not rate second to the diamond on her finger.

"How did your mother know—"

Meridia did not finish her sentence. Daniel must have warned Eva of her arrival.

Permony's smile grew wider. "Come. I want to show you something."

She took Meridia's arm and led her to the bedroom. Since Malin moved out, Permony had taken possession of the entire room and adopted the orange furniture as her own. Presently, the two beds were strewn with dresses. On the table was a vase filled with lilies of the valley. Permony picked up an olive cashmere dress and caressed it with affection.

"Isn't it pretty? Ahab said I should dress with care now that I'm to be his wife."

She posed with the dress in front of the mirror. Her joy, pure and simple, suffused her cheeks with a delicate bloom. Meridia went straight to the point.

"I want you to tell me if you're at all unhappy."

Permony turned with a perplexed gaze.

"Why should I be unhappy? Ahab has shown me nothing but kindness."

"But are you sure you want to marry him?"

The girl's color burned deeper. "Mama has nothing to do with it, if that's what you're asking. The decision is mine entirely."

The ceiling creaked above their heads. Try as she might, Meridia could hear no bees. In fact, the house no longer smelled of them.

Had she overstepped her bounds and let suspicions get the best of her? Thinking Eva might be listening in her sitting room, Meridia took the dress from Permony and laid it on the bed.

"Do you love him?" she whispered.

Permony blushed even more. "I'm very fond of him. He's strong and incredibly manly."

"But do you know who he is, his thoughts and inclinations and feelings?"

Permony bent her face as a struggle raced inside her. Placing her hand on the girl's shoulder, Meridia searched for signs of Eva's bees, but there were none. No threat, no bruise, no intimidation. From head to toe Permony glowed with powdered gold.

The girl said, "Do you remember our stories? Those gentle kings who woo their sweethearts with songs and gallantry? Ahab is not like them. He woos me by kissing me until I grow faint and beg for breath. Sometimes he is so strong and so full of desire I fear he might break me. But always I cry for more, because when he holds me and takes me I feel fire, and while that fire burns everything else stops to matter. I've spent my whole life fettered to Mama's chains, serving her whims and enduring her hostility. But then Ahab came along and burned those chains right off. Look at me! All these dresses and flowers! They're silly and immaterial, I know, but when did anyone ever think to put my happiness first? So I beg of you, if you come to tell me things I'd rather not hear, keep them to yourself. I can't go back to Mama's chains now that Ahab has set me free."

Her voice had sunk and become plaintive, yet her lavender eyes were fiercely alive. In them there was no confusion. The girl had decided to marry without love.

Meridia slowly took back her hand. "So you know? You've heard?"

Permony nodded. "I don't believe a word of it. Please give me your blessing. That's all I ask from you."

"I don't want you to be deceived. I'll never forgive myself if I fail to help you."

"And for that I'm grateful—you can't know how much—but my mind's made up. I'm going to marry Ahab by year's end."

Permony untangled a sealskin coat from the bed and put it on. She smiled, tiptoed to the mirror, and twirled. Childish as it was, it was this gesture that convinced Meridia she was no longer speaking to a girl, but a woman who knew her business exactly.

"Is there nothing I can say? Nothing to change your mind?"

Permony shook her head. "I need only your blessing."

Meridia looked at her for a long time before nodding. Permony screamed, showered her with kisses. It was then that the certainty sank in. Somehow, despite her best intention to honor it, Meridia knew she had broken a promise she could not remember making.

THIRTY-FOUR

By February, the odor of the house had become intolerable. In the beginning it had the whiff of something sulfurous, coming upon Meridia one morning as she was waking. By afternoon, the odor in the bedroom had grown so strong she had to throw the windows open. She ordered the maid to beat the rugs and wash the curtains, scrub the floor and boil the sheets, but instead of diffusing the stench, the effort merely added a whiff of offal and rotting fish. In three days, the stink permeated the entire house. Desperate for fresh air, the maid indulged in excessive pruning in the garden. Noah walked around with a hand clamped over his nose. Daniel went out and stayed out as soon as the shop was closed. Customers sprinted to the door without waiting for their purchases to be wrapped.

Only Ravenna's room was exempt, and here, Meridia took refuge with increasing frequency. In her absorption, she did not notice that the stench only grew fouler the longer she stayed in that room. Yet even this sanctuary came to an end the morning she awoke and detected the odor in her own skin. She jumped from the bed, dashed into the bathroom, undressed, scrubbed her body with pumice, but the stench remained. As the pale light of day penetrated the wooden slats of the window, she put back her nightgown and returned to bed and smelled the same odor emanating from Daniel's body. It hit her then that she had been sleeping for an eternity with her face confronting the great wall of his back. The fence, erected by the bees, had turned into a fortress. A few times in the last six months, propelled by sheer urgency, he had tossed a rope down the wall to admit her, but those moments of reunion had been as unmindful as they had been quick. In the cold morning light, she suddenly felt that if she could burrow her face in his skin, or run her lips across the span of his chest, then the stench would disappear. The arc of his naked back was long and graceful, the fuzz on his nape a tender dare. Breathless from the need, she pressed her breasts against his spine and aimed a hand at his shoulder. He shrugged them off—breasts and hand—as if they were clammy or dirty and moved away.

A FEW DAYS LATER, the wind changed direction and ushered in the winter cold. The townspeople hardly noticed, however, so enthralled were they by the sight of a glorious Eva strolling through the market square in a new mink coat. It was the first time in years that they saw her wear her triumph so conspicuously. Even back in December, the month of Permony's wedding, they had heard little from her. Not once did she brag about the couple, the fortune-teller's predictions, the lavish party at the Majestic Hotel, or the number of guests invited. Her unprecedented discretion not only boggled them but robbed them of the delicious pleasure of talking about her. And so when they saw her beam at them in her resplendent new coat on that wintry February morning, they were only too glad to welcome her return.

"I'm the most blessed mother on earth," she crowed to the fruit-sellers. "My son has made a name for himself, my daughters are married well, and the three of them are loving and generous children. My grandson, Noah, is handsome and wonderful; in fact, he adores me so much he always asks for me the instant he wakes up.

He's my only grandchild so far, but not for long! Look at this coat. My son-in-law Ahab gave it to me just this morning. Isn't it absolutely ravishing?"

Unanimous, the town concluded that Permony was with child.

When Eva appeared on Magnolia Avenue with the news, Daniel introduced her to everyone in the shop as "my dear, dear mother." Shooting Meridia a vindicated look, he told a misty-eyed Eva to select any piece of jewelry she wanted from the shop. For the rest of the afternoon, he circulated the news to all their neighbors. His smile was so bright and wide Noah could not help teasing him, "Watch out, Papa! Your teeth look ready to fall out."

At dinner he spoke his first words of the day to Meridia. "You could have at least cracked a smile. The way you act, people might think you don't care for Permony at all. Don't you think everything turned out nicely for her after all?"

Meridia refrained from replying. Thus far, her concerns regarding Ahab had proven unfounded, since the man had done nothing but worship Permony. Whenever she ran into them, they were one creature fused at the hip and joined at the head. Leah said that Ahab bought Permony a dozen lilies a day. Rebecca claimed that the seamstress they worked for had her hands tied with Ahab's orders until next year. Recently, Permony herself declared that she could not imagine leading a fuller or happier life. More astonishing still, Eva's bees had not created a stir for some time. Nevertheless, Meridia's doubts persisted; the more she strained to evict them, the deeper they lodged in the center of her thoughts.

Meanwhile, Ravenna's condition continued to worsen. Now nearly blind, she had become as frail as a moth's wing, her proud back bent and her breathing fitful. If not moved, she would sit all day in her room like a statue. If not fed, she would build a maze out of her food without eating it. When she heard someone talking, she would smile placidly at the voice without recognizing the speaker. It caused Meridia no end of heartache that Ravenna had not spoken a word to her since Gabriel died.

The morning after Eva's announcement, Meridia took her mother to view the blossoms at Cinema Garden. She led her gently like a child, sat her down on a warm bench in front of the fountain of the swans, and then tempted her with flowers from the trees. The air was crisp and smoky, the Garden empty but for a few mothers and their children. Meridia was arranging the blossoms in Ravenna's lap when a woman in a heavy robe stumbled from the direction of the cemetery.

"Malin!" Meridia started from the bench. "Are you all right?"

The girl jerked to a stop. A wilting clump of butterfly weed dropped from her hand. From her swollen eyes Meridia gathered she had met the dawn weeping.

"Permony's having a baby?" she whispered. "Permony—a baby?"

It was anguish, not envy, that lay smoldering beneath the question. Meridia took both of Malin's hands and squeezed them.

"You'll have children of your own one day," she said. "In a year's time you could have a little boy or girl to keep you up at night."

Malin shook her head and cried. "There will never be one for me."

"Don't say that. You don't know what heaven has in store for you."

Malin shook her head harder. "You don't understand. We have tried and failed, so many times. *I* have failed, that is. We've seen doctors everywhere, but no matter what they tell me to do, I can't hold the baby inside. Jonathan's given up and hasn't come near me in months. He says it's killing him to have his hope dashed every time he gets it up. He won't admit it, but I know he thinks it's my fault. I'm not a woman, you see! How can I be one when I can't bear him children?"

Meridia squeezed her hands harder. "If you're not a woman, then what does that make me?"

Malin stopped sobbing. "I'm sorry," she said. "I didn't mean to—"

"I know you didn't." Meridia released the girl's hands. A sound she did not like was pulsing through the air, barreling its way into her ear with the beastly tenacity of the bees. Meridia glanced at her mother: Ravenna was busy tearing the blossoms to pieces. Meridia glanced the other way and the sound hit her hard and clear. It was the other mothers. No longer watching their children but pointing and whispering.

Meridia began to walk and motioned for Malin to follow.

"Does your mother know?"

Malin's face suddenly twisted with anger. "I wish someone would stop her! She goes around telling everyone she'll soon be grandmother to my children. 'Malin's womb holds the seeds of ten thousand generations. Any day now they'll spill out and make the world a brighter place.' How do you reason with someone like that? Someone with such self-delusion she can fool herself into believing anything? And now she won't shut up about Permony and she tells me how everyone is *dying* to hear the same news from me. Oh, I just feel so mad and low and useless—"

"Don't let her do this to you."

"She says everyone . . . everyone—"

Malin choked on her words. The women's whispering was getting louder. Meridia glared at them. Their number seemed to have doubled in a matter of minutes.

"Listen to me, Malin. You've gone out of your way to mend things with your sister and I'm proud of you. Don't you see what your mother is doing? She's setting you up against Permony by making you jealous. If you let her, you'll end up despising your sister again and giving your mother control over the both of you."

Malin nodded without surprise. "She's done this our whole lives. All through my childhood she told me, 'Papa's got no room for you now that your sister's pushed you out of his heart.' She always said Permony was doing this and that behind my back to steal Papa's affection. I used to get so angry and make Permony's life a living hell. Then Mama would be so pleased and she would kiss me and let me have everything I wanted. If only I'd wised up to her tricks sooner."

She said this with no trace of the cruel and sullen girl who had been a terror to her sister. In that instant Meridia realized how far they had traveled to stand this close to each other.

"You did hate me once, Malin," she said.

The girl made no pretense at denial. "Mama used to tell me the most dreadful things about you, even before you were married. She said you bribed the spirits to capture Daniel's attention, and once you had him under your spell, you wouldn't stop until you took control of the house and broke up our family. At one point she filled me with so much hate I thought you were the most despicable creature who had ever lived. To this day she looks for every opportunity to do you ill. I'd be careful if I were you. You never know what someone like Mama has got cooking in her head. She's been fuming every day since your mother moved in with you."

Malin's eyes filled with concern as they reached the lone figure on the bench. "How is your mother?"

It was Meridia's turn to shake her head. "No better, no worse. I don't know if she won't speak because she misses my father or because she's angry with me."

"You did what you had to do."

"My mother doesn't seem to think so."

Malin stood still and gave back her full gaze. "You're the strongest woman I know. I want you to help me when the time comes."

Meridia did not hesitate. "What do you want me to do?"

"I can't say just yet. But will you give me your word?"

The two women shook hands and went their separate ways, Malin to the frozen silences of Museum Avenue, Meridia to the bench where her mother refused to recognize who she was.

"Come, Mama. It's time to go."

The second her hand landed on Ravenna's shoulder, the whispering pitched to a deafening level. It was armed with fire and brimstone.

Why does Malin still speak to her? If she hadn't shown her the dead baby, Malin wouldn't be so haunted by it. She did it out of spite, you know, to break the girl's womb because her own is broken. Now she's gone ahead and wrecked her mother, too. Do you know she let Gabriel die while he still had plenty of breath in his lungs? Oh, yes! Her mother tried to stop her, but she wouldn't listen. That's what broke her. Look at that poor widow, sniffing flowers like an idiot and not knowing her face from her own behind. Just be thankful you don't have a daughter like her.

Meridia shook with fury. She wheeled around and marched straight toward the women, certain that Eva—wasn't that her new coat flashing in the sun?—was among them. "Say it to my face, you coward!" Her scream cut through the air and scattered the golden swans in the fountain. Angry tears burned and blurred. The women wobbled, the children shifted. The whispering became fainter and fainter. When she reached the place where her assailants were gathered, hot blood instantly drained from her face.

There were no mothers, no children, no Eva. It was winter and the Garden was deserted.

Her breath came unglued in her throat. Her stopped heart pounded like a storm. Where had they gone? What had she heard? Those voices had sounded so real, so near. Was it possible that she had imagined them? Finding no answer in the frigid air, Meridia slowly walked back to her mother.

A FEW DAYS LATER, Eva announced that the shop on Lotus Blossom Lane would be closed for remodeling. The whole place would be gutted, she said, additional windows put in, along with new carpeting, curtains, and handsome cases made from teak. She enlisted Daniel to supervise the work, and he agreed with a hearty enthusiasm, calling it "Mama's big shot." As the weeks passed, he began spending all his spare time on Lotus Blossom Lane, skipping meals and working late even on weekends. Unwilling to risk a further quarrel, Meridia showed no opposition, but she noticed that the stink suffocating the house would become stronger the instant he stepped out of the door. It was understood that Ahab had supplied the money for the remodeling.

The shop reopened in the spring on an auspicious day chosen by the fortune-teller. Dressed in burgundy silk and starred with diamonds, Eva was at her warmest and most hospitable. She entertained the guests with endless stories, skillfully urging them to shop as she fed them champagne and crab cakes. A very pregnant Permony glowed at her right, while at her left, Ahab had never looked more distinguished. Everybody remarked on how loving Eva was with her family—she massaged Permony's swollen fingers, called Daniel "the dearest son a mother could have," and made sure Noah had plenty to eat. Her dazzle was such that it outshone even the splendid new inventory, so fiercely blinding no one noticed that neither Malin nor Jonathan was present.

Meridia paid Eva little attention, for a young and pretty assistant who was to replace Permony in the shop had caught her eye. The girl had pure alabaster skin, a laughter of tinkling silver bells, and mesmerizing eyes whose color alternated between green and gray. Ahab was clearly enthralled—he kept glancing at the girl when he thought no one was looking. His behavior brought Meridia's suspicions to the forefront—it was the same appraising stare he had given Permony at Malin's wedding.

"Her name is Sylva," said the expectant mother herself, noticing Meridia's gaze. "She's pretty, isn't she? She's been working here a month, helping with the remodeling. Mama highly approves of her. She thinks she will be good with customers."

"She's certainly attractive," said Meridia. She noticed that Sylva was smiling at Ahab in return, clearly relishing the attention given to her.

Later that evening, a banquet for thirty took place at 27 Orchard Road. With exceptional care Eva had selected the catered dishes, which ranged from glazed oysters to roasted quails and crusted tuna rolls. For dessert, she served a towering chiffon cake decorated with lemon sprinkles. Long into the night she kept the guests up with coffee and laughter, and even facilitated an impromptu dance in the narrow hallway. Shortly after midnight, Meridia excused herself and

Noah, but Daniel decided to stay. "Don't wait for me—I'll help Mama clean up," he said, loud enough for the whole room to hear.

Early the next morning, an unbearable loneliness pierced Meridia awake. She fumbled in the gossamer dawn, sat upright, and nervously reached her hand toward Daniel's side of the bed. There was no fortress, no fence, no wall. In fact, there was no Daniel. Meridia rubbed her eyes and something else hit her. The air no longer smelled of rotten things, but breezed with a familiar coldness that chilled her marrow. The room did not feel real; neither did the pale light that seeped in from the window. This was not her house, her family. Her heart was tapping anxiously when an animal-like howl ripped through the house and yanked her to her feet. In an instant, she was rushing down the hallway to Ravenna's room.

"Mama! What is it?"

She was surprised to find Noah already there, pale and stricken, with his arms tight around his grandmother.

Ravenna was standing in the middle of the room, shaking and howling without meaning. Her dimming eyes were flashing anger and disgust.

"What is it, son? What is she saying?"

Noah pointed to the window and clung tighter to his grandmother. The curtain had been torn off the rod, and the smudged pane gave out to a drab and dreary morning. Meridia ran to the window and looked out. In the distance, stealing its way swiftly toward Magnolia Avenue, was a bright blue mist, Daniel in the center and a cloud of bees at the rear.

THIRTY-FIVE

Meridia did not know how she got on in the first few days. For the longest time she could neither scream nor cry, could only watch and sigh as her world crumbled. The initial shock gradually hardened into disbelief, then from there sunk rapidly into denial. Night after night, watching the great wall of Daniel's back lengthen in her face, she tried to convince herself that everything was as usual, that the blue mist was but a trick of the mind—a hoax, a glitch, a memory from Gabriel's time she would be wise to discard. Anxious for an explanation, she turned a blind eye to Ravenna's agitation and Noah's puzzlement, and when Daniel still did not open his lips, she recriminated herself beyond measure. It was she who had allowed the stench to possess the house, she who had permitted the fence to spring between them. Had she learned nothing from the cold wind that turned Monarch Street upside down? She had been so consumed, so obsessed with her suspicions of Ahab that she had missed the shadows slithering in her own house.

It was not until the yellow mist appeared, six days after Eva's banquet, that she felt the first rush of anger. An hour after closing time, Meridia was sitting upstairs in the parlor with a stack of invoices when the window rattled. She looked up from her work and froze. The knowing eye of the mist was staring right at her. Her hand jerked; the invoices poured like flour to the floor. Footsteps hurried down the stairs, a door slammed, and a minute later, the mist coasted back down the avenue. While the window hissed, Meridia sat still. In her blurred vision the glass vase on the desk seemed to have leapt into midair. A violent impulse tempted her to grab it, to slam it against the wall and let burst the heaviness in her heart. But she stood up instead, walked to the window, laid her palm against the pane. For a moment she felt it bucking before quieting. She returned to her chair and picked up the invoices.

AT THE START, THE blue mist appeared no later than the stroke of midnight. But as the days passed, its delivery of Daniel inched closer and closer toward dawn. Meridia waited for him, trying her best to remain calm, though his excuses were feeble and insulting. He had to entertain a customer, close a deal, meet a friend, or, most frequently, help his mother with "a pressing problem." Her eyes searched him, but her mouth did not. She had no proof. If she voiced what she deep down knew, he would pounce on it as "yet another of your crazy suspicions." How was she to explain the coming and going of the mists as her only evidence of his unfaithfulness?

Then she discovered things that for a moment confirmed the deep-down feeling. One night it was a rouge-stained tie, the next the smell of perfume on his undershirt. One morning she found a love note in his pants pocket. These marks of betrayal, however, had the gall to change nature as soon as she held them up as evidence. The tie was spotless in the morning. The undershirt odorless when she waved it in front of Daniel. The love note turned into a receipt from the barber. In spite of herself, she felt her baffled mind begin to question if she was imagining it all. Perhaps she had been too overworked, running the house, tending the shop, nursing Ravenna, caring for Noah. Nobody would believe her; Eva, for one, would jump upon the opportunity to crush her. "It's a fact that insanity runs in her family," she could hear her mother-in-law saying. "Son, I've always known it would come to this."

Many times she thought of following the yellow mist, just as Ravenna must have done many years ago for a glimpse of Pilar. But her tremendous pride rebelled against it. Even as she suffered, she promised herself that she would not become one of those women who eviscerated their rivals with curses, dragged them by the hair to the ignominy of a public square, and exposed them to the judgment of others. Still, the harder she resisted, the more she was haunted by ghosts. Both male and female, they strutted before her in the most lavish clothes or nothing at all, each and every one clamoring to be Daniel's lover. These vibrant phantoms tormented her at all hours of the day, shattering her sleep, breaking her concentration, reducing her to such a state that she drew concern from the maid and the customers, from Leah and Rebecca and from half her neighbors, but not a word from Daniel.

Her condition affected especially Noah, who regarded her with startled incomprehension. "What is it doing out there, Mama?" he would ask whenever he saw the yellow mist fetch his father. Meridia would not answer him. Though words were bubbling to her lips, words she knew would cast an eternal shadow between father and son, she always checked them from spilling. "Nothing. We're having another cold day is all." Noah would stare at her in such a way that she had to turn her head quickly. For the first time since his birth, she feared that the bond between them, unwittingly forged for eternity by the enchanted cockatoo in her seven days of illness, would rip her apart and crush her. The son she could not bring herself to look at would turn ten next month.

But Noah was not fooled. He sensed the uncertainty beneath her bravery, the sadness lurking in her smile. During this time, his sensitive nature became almost clairvoyant, a feature that would set him apart for the rest of his life. Without a word, he would take her hand before it actually trembled; he would push her to keep going on their walk to school before her feet stopped. He began to follow Daniel everywhere, to inspect the papers he had been reading, the letters he wrote, the food he had not eaten, just as Meridia had done with Gabriel many years ago. He did not tease his father anymore, did not laugh at his jokes. The look he gave him grew increasingly distant. He refused to speak to him unless necessary.

Once again Meridia found solace in Ravenna. To take her out on a walk, read to her, dress her, bathe her in lemon water and almond milk—these were the only things that could quiet her anguish. By then, Ravenna was no more than a column of bones, still not speaking a word, her eyesight gone, her gait stilted, her gestures imprecise. Yet her presence worked like an amulet against the apparitions. Her room was the only place in the house where the persecuting phantoms did not dare trouble Meridia. For this reason, Daniel came home one dawn to an empty bed. When he discovered that his wife was sleeping in the room at the end of the hallway, he lost his temper and quickly left the house again.

Things went on in this fashion until Eva showed up one evening, one hour after the yellow mist whisked Daniel away. Without asking for Meridia, she handed a package to the maid. "Give this to my son," she said loudly. "And tell your madam that Sylva, my assistant, sends her regards. She really should get to know that lovely girl better."

Upstairs in the parlor, Meridia was balancing a checkbook with the window open. The name Eva had let slip so casually hit her like the blow of an oar. She dropped her pen and jumped out of her chair. She wondered how in God's name she had not guessed it before. Those stolen smiles and drifting glances at the banquet, gestures she thought had been aimed at and provoked by somebody else . . . Along with this realization came another that turned her blood colder still: it was Eva who had engineered the union between Daniel and Sylva, Eva who had lured Daniel away from home under the pretense of remodeling the shop. Eva who had come to Magnolia Avenue for no other purpose than to explode Sylva's name in her consciousness!

Meridia's head grew light, and her hands were shaking. She met the maid at the head of the stairs and took the package.

Back in the parlor, she examined the large brown envelope. It was unsealed, which told her that Eva had no intention of hiding the contents from her. For a second she wavered, wary of falling into the woman's trap, but her curiosity was too potent to resist. Like a beast famished, she tore the envelope and shook it upside down.

A batch of bills rained upon the desk. Copies of checks dating as far back as four months earlier. The bills originated from several hardware stores and a decorator, requesting payments for various labors and materials. Each bill had a corresponding check; all fourteen checks had been signed by Daniel and drawn from an account Meridia did not recognize. The signatures were all authentic. It was Daniel then, not Ahab, who had financed the reopening of Eva's store. Knowing how she felt about his mother, knowing everything his mother had done to them and their son, he had gone ahead and deceived her, had lied and concealed and used their money to betray her. What else had he done? And why? To punish her for caring for her own mother? It was too low, too spiteful, this double blow. Her love, her trust, discarded like refuse. All of a sudden the damning papers flew from her hands; with a single intent to wreck and demolish, Meridia picked up the glass vase and hurled it against the wall.

She fell back into the chair shaking with anger. She tried to breathe, but the air had turned thick with bees. All this time Eva had been watching and listening patiently, storing her opportunities and keeping her insects silent. *She* was the one who had been careless, the one who had been too sure. Permony and Malin had warned her and she had not listened. Now Eva had struck and gotten Daniel where she wanted him—on her side and hateful to his own wife. Meridia closed her eyes and slumped against the chair. She felt weak and sick to the bone. She could not lift her hand to scatter the bees. She wished the crying in her breast would stop before it choked her.

Some time later, she opened her eyes and saw a figure shining in the doorway. Half horrified, half resigned, she thought it was one of the persecuting phantoms, loosed at last from the region of nightmare to confront her in the flesh. But then the figure approached, and the bees scattered in fear. Meridia's breath caught in her throat. It was Ravenna, handsome and magisterial as she had not seen her in years. Her hair was again swept into that implacable knot, the luxuriant black pierced by a single white lily, and her slender figure was made momentous by a billowing white robe. Her shine came from inside, from that inexorable fire that had kept her chin up and her back straight through the long years of loneliness and humiliation.

"Mama."

The cry broke from Meridia with equal alarm and wonderment. There was no blindness in Ravenna's stare as it shot through the air like a current, drying Meridia's tears, stiffening her spine, pulling her to her feet. Under that unflagging gaze, Meridia felt hurled back into the midst of things, no longer frail and confused but braced with courage. She ran to the doorway, putting her arms out to embrace her mother, but all she met was air and vapor. Her heart stopped suddenly, and with a chill she understood what sacrifice was being performed for her sake. She ran down the corridor with a single thought burning in her head: She must stop her mother before it was too late.

She burst into the room at the end of the hallway and saw her fear turned into a reality. Ravenna was missing. Somebody had made the bed immaculately, and the smell of verbena no longer scented the air. Meridia tore open cupboards and drawers, only to discover that all of Ravenna's belongings were gone. Dashing to the open window, she peered up and down the length of Magnolia Avenue and startled the evening crowd with her frantic inquiries. No one had seen Ravenna. Meridia turned and looked about the room, and every object there, from the lyre-backed chair to the silver washstand, disputed that her mother had breathed among them. A hundred terrifying thoughts were swarming her brain when she spotted a single white lily lying on the carpet.

Meridia dropped to her knees to retrieve it. The instant her fingers curled around the stem, a savage cry tore from her bowels. She snatched up the lily as though her life depended on it, dashed out to the hallway, and yelled in surprise when she ran right into Noah. Earlier, the shop assistant had taken him and two schoolmates to see a traveling carnival. Meridia's heart shattered at the sight of her son's beaming face, his little hand holding up a candied apple. "For Grandma," he said proudly. Meridia patted his head. "Why don't you wash up first?" she said. "I'll be back soon with Grandma." Feeling tears scratch her eyes, she did not stay to hear his question, but pressed the lily into his hand, called to the maid to prepare his supper, and rushed downstairs and out to the gleaming spectacle of Magnolia Avenue.

Her feet covered the pavement rapidly. Under the swinging lanterns, faces swam by her, this one hazy, the next opaque, and at them she fired the same inconceivable question: "Have you seen my mother?" She walked quickly and tensely, without noticing that the path she was on was turning from stone to grass and grass to mud and mud back to stone. The hushed darkness of the residential quarters soon replaced the din and lights of Magnolia Avenue. Through a window, a woman wearing an apron was scraping dinner plates with a butter knife, and her little girl, standing on a stool and wearing the same green apron, was rinsing the plates under the faucet. Feeling a punch to her heart, Meridia traded the curb for the middle of the street. A minute later, she struck across a deserted playground and was overcome by a feeling that she had been there before. Was that her riding the swing on a summer day, a white bow in her hair and her shoes the color of teal, while Ravenna pushed from behind till she laughed and aimed her legs to the sky? She could smell the sun-warmed grass, feel the wind on her cheek, even hear the other children talk with envy, but the memory itself could not have been real. Ravenna—boiling resentment in the kitchen—would never have taken her here.

The house at 24 Monarch Street stood silent and grim. Along with the crescent moon, a street lamp provided an indifferent illumination, casting just enough light along the stone steps to prevent a fall. At the top of the steps someone had left the massive door open. Pale with terror, Meridia went in. It was much darker inside than she had anticipated. Fumbling along the wall, she shouted for Ravenna and pushed her way into the hall where Gabriel used to smoke and torment her in the morning. The air was stale and sour. Dusty white sheets stretched over furniture, stirring like ghosts waking from a spoiled dream. Suddenly there was a bright spark coming from the kitchen, accompanied by a loud explosion that shook the house. Meridia ran along the wall. A few paces from the kitchen an incandescent bullet flew straight at her face. She ducked at the last second. The bullet zoomed up, twisted into an arc, then made a slicing dive down the length of the corridor. Before she could move, another bullet followed, then another, and another. It took her a moment to realize they were fireflies.

She broke into a run. Inside the kitchen a bright swarm of fireflies hovered over the stove, hundreds of them, thousands perhaps, as if the great explosion had just given birth to them. An overpowering smell of smoke and charred meat sent her reeling with a cough. The floor was littered with Ravenna's belongings, her suitcase and dresses, shoes and powder bottles, and all the objects Noah had procured for her to smell. Meridia reached for the stove to steady herself but withdrew her hand instantly. The stove was hot as fire. The raw and horrific immensity of loss suddenly hit her. There was no trace of Ravenna anywhere, only the smell of ash and smoke and flame.

"Mama!"

Her scream set the fireflies into motion. With that one word, she said all that had eluded a lifetime of expression.

THIRTY-SIX

She knew he would wait for her, and it was for him that she returned. Under the drowning moon, the fireflies guided her passage
home, distracting passersby with their flame so no one noticed her
grief or the suitcase she was dragging. As she retraced her steps
from stone to mud and mud to grass and grass back to stone, she
did not allow herself to think what she would say to him. The fireflies did not scatter once she entered the house, but flew upward to
the roof like a thousand glittering jewels.

She carried the suitcase up the stairs and into the room at the
end of the hallway. She was not surprised to find him there, sitting
on his grandmother's bed with his profile shaded in darkness. He
was still holding the lily and the candied apple. When their eyes met,
he did not give her a chance to speak.

"She's not coming back, is she?"

His tone was steady, more a declaration than a question. Keeping
the gesture small, Meridia shook her head. He said nothing more,
but went on staring at her, his clairvoyant eyes defenseless yet seem-
ingly unruffled. It was only when he turned to the lamp that she saw

the patchwork of tears on his face. On his right temple, Elias's scar throbbed thick with blood.

Meridia pulled her son close and felt him shaking in her arms. Noah allowed her to comfort him but did not cling to her. Something in her eye had warned him of the thing to come. Over her shoulder, he noticed the worn leather suitcase at the door.

"What's that, Mama?"

Without turning, she held his wet face between her hands.

"Grandma's last wish," she said. "In the end, you see, she found a way to speak to me."

SHE PUT HIM TO bed and hauled the suitcase to her room, unlocked it, slid its sole content under the bed, and repacked it with clothes. Twenty minutes later, she went downstairs to the little office, opened the combination on the fireproof vault, and emptied into a sack all the money and jewelry there. Back in her room, she took her own jewelry box from a locked drawer and dropped it into the sack as well. She put the sack in the suitcase and hid the suitcase in the hallway closet. Only then did she slip into bed with all her clothes on, switch off the light . . . and wait.

The blue mist arrived an hour before the cocks crowed. The sequence of sounds was by then a familiar one—first the front door clicked, then the stairs thudded, then the bedroom door opened with a breeze. Light as a thief, Daniel hung his coat on the hook behind the door, pulled off his clothes, and climbed into bed in his underwear. This time, as though he knew what his wife was planning, he let his leg brush against her calf. The unexpected touch nearly split Meridia at the seams. For a moment she was tempted to open her eyes, to abandon what was stored under the bed and in the closet and walk to the pit of hell and pull at the rope he was holding. But then she smelled the heat oozing from his skin, the scent and staleness of another woman, and her anger surged. She pinched her eyes tighter, remembering Ravenna, and remained still. Daniel rolled away with a grunt. A long time passed before his breathing steadied.

She waited a few more minutes before getting up. Without a sound, she gathered his clothes and carried them to the window. She parted the curtain a finger's width, and with the aid of dawn examined the clothes carefully. The trousers had a viscous, darkish stain on the left thigh; the shirt the scarlet imprint of a mouth. No sooner did she spot them than they began to fade.

She placed the clothes on the chair by the window and reached under the bed for the object she had dragged across town in the suitcase under shelter of the fireflies. She stood up, pointed the blade of the shovel straight down, and gripped the top of the shaft with both hands. One look at Daniel was all she needed for twenty-seven years of Ravenna's anger to burn in her veins. She took three steps back until the chair stood between them, raised the shovel to the ceiling, and brought it cleanly down. The instant the blade bit through the clothes the cocks began to crow. The chair gave a terrifying shriek, but the shovel stuck. The viscous stain and the scarlet mouth glowered. Nothing could erase them now, for Ravenna's sacrifice had purchased their permanence. Removing her wedding ring, Meridia tossed it onto the bed where Daniel continued to sleep.

Noah appeared in the hallway as she was retrieving the suitcase from the closet. He was dressed and had his coat on, his own little suitcase ready at his feet. They said no words, exchanged only a look. Meridia fastened her coat and took both suitcases down the stairs. He followed her without a glance at his father's door. Outside, the morning was brisk and amber-hued, the southerly wind damp with the scent of the mountain on its back. Except for a street sweeper, Magnolia Avenue was deserted. No one kept watch as a horde of fireflies followed mother and son down the street and vanished along with them.

〜

DANIEL WOKE UP LATE from a dream. In it he was kissing a woman's nape, sweet and slender, yet interminable in length. Starting at the base, his lips must have traveled miles and miles of skin, some freckled, some dappled with hair, all tasting of berries, and still there was more to kiss. After what seemed like hours, his mouth gave out from exhaustion, but when he tried to lift his head, a steel hand clamped down and pitted him against the nape. Gasping for breath, he saw the pale freckles balloon into boils and the fine hairs sprout into darting reptilian tongues. He woke up choking with disgust. His wife's wedding ring was wedged between his lips.

"Damn you," he spat.

His first thought was that it had slipped off her finger while she slept. Seeing that she had already risen, he set down the ring on the nightstand and did not make much of it. He closed his eyes and was sinking back into sleep when the smell of blood knocked all thoughts out of his head. He sat up with a start and blinked his eyes savagely. He was already on his feet when he spotted the shovel sticking from the chair.

He saw the shirt and trousers he had worn last night pinned underneath the blade, and the smell of blood was coming from them. "What is it now?" he snapped as if his wife were standing in front of him. He was about to kick the chair away when the glowering stains caught his eye. One dark, one red, both pulsing with blood.

For a moment he stood pale and speechless. Then angrily he wrenched the shovel free from the chair and hurled it against the wall.

He hitched up his pants and threw on a shirt. In the hallway he barked at the maid, "Where is your mistress?" The terrified girl said she had not seen her, an answer that almost made him shake her out of the way. Daniel stormed into the parlor, the dining room, the guest room—smashing lamps and breaking furniture—but found no sign of either mother or daughter. His heart thumping madly, he ran toward the room he had saved for last and told himself she wouldn't dare take his boy. The door yielded before he opened it, and

at once he knew his worst fear had come true. A layer of fuzz covered the floor, mildew spread over the bed, and a fat spider was
weaving a web in one corner of the ceiling. The room looked as
though it had not been inhabited in months.

Daniel dashed for the stairs. The ground floor was deserted, and
then he remembered it was Sunday and the shop was closed. He
rushed to the little office and noticed the vault door was open. He
pulled the handle and saw that the money box and jewelry trays had
been emptied.

"Goddamn you!" he bellowed. Shaking with fury, he set off
toward Orchard Road and marched straight up to his mother's
room, where she was dyeing her hair. Without waiting another
minute, he fulminated on the spot, skipping the part about the
shovel and the stains. Eva listened solemnly, almost serenely, while
black henna dripped down her face and stained the towel around
her shoulders (it was no use; her hair would turn white again in a
matter of hours). When Daniel was done, Eva's mouth became a terrifying thing that tore at him without pity.

"Go get your boy. Show your wife no mercy. If you fail this time,
God help you, she'll have your manhood out on a platter."

It was all he needed to hear. Indignant, he stomped out of the
house with his back straighter and his head taller than when he entered. This time he'd really show her what he was made of! What he
had done—what she in fact had driven him to do—was nothing
compared to her action. The brazenness! The deceitfulness! As he
approached the stone steps of 24 Monarch Street, fresh anger jolted
him anew. More than a decade ago, when he was poor and green
and terrified, Ravenna had chased him away from these steps like a
flea-ridden dog. Well, let the blighted woman try now! Even if she
had the force of hell on her side, he would not budge until he had
his boy back!

He strode up to the door with enough resolution to fell a tree. In
the bright noon sun the house stood gray and silent. He lifted his
fist and pounded on the door. No one answered. He pounded harder.

Just when he thought his boy was peering at him from behind the window, something unimaginable happened. A hail of tiny bright bullets dropped from the sky. A blinding spark followed, and the little bullets tore viciously at his vision. Before he could move, a sharp pulsating pain seized him from head to foot. He fell and rolled down the stone steps, smashing his shoulder on the pavement. The incandescent bullets pursued him without mercy. He clambered up, screaming from the pain, and began to run. A second later he was down again, crawling and yelping, yet no one helped him, though he could hear voices talking. The last thing he remembered was bumping his head against a hard surface. The darkness swelled and spun and swallowed the earth from underneath him.

When he came to, the pain was gone and it took him some time to realize he could not see. He kept blinking his eyes, certain that something was blocking his vision, and when it finally dawned on him that he was blind, he screamed and fought like a demon condemned. He did not know where he was. Womanly hands, gentle yet unfamiliar, soothed him as he shouted over and over for his wife. He did not like those hands; they were not Meridia's and they did not know how to calm him. When he grew weary of fighting, he sank into lethargy and smelled his wife's scent emanating from the pillows. He was in his bed after all. But who had brought him home from Monarch Street? In a rough voice he asked again for Meridia, but the woman with the soft hands told him she was not there. He did not recognize her voice, and when she leaned over him, a whiff of her perfume made his bowels churn. Swinging his arm haphazardly, he caught her in the flank and ordered her to leave. The woman began sobbing.

"Wait outside, Sylva," said another voice. "I'll take care of him."

It was his mother. Applying compresses over his eyes, she told him that two of his friends had seen him lying in the street, twisting like a man bedeviled while strangers gawked because he kept flailing his arms and screaming "Get them off me!" when they could see that he was alone and fighting nothing but air. Every time they tried to help, he pushed them away and yelled that they were hurting his eyes, those tiny bullets that had dropped from the sky and exploded his eyeballs. The louder he yelled, the more he added to the confusion, because as far as anybody could tell, neither his face nor his clothes bore the dimmest trace of blood.

"You fainted after you screamed yourself hoarse," said his mother. "Your friends carried you home. The maid ran to get me."

He shook his head in total confusion. Before he could put two and two together, his mother launched into a tirade, declaring that his wife had put an evil curse on him, paralyzed him, turned him into a public disgrace, and if he did not realize this now then *she*, his mother, truly grieved for him, for she had raised him to have respect for himself, not to mention the courage and wisdom to do what was right, and if he thought he could show his face in town after this—

"Enough! Enough! Enough!" he pleaded. His fatigue was so deep he could not feel his arms or legs, only the darkness that beat down thickly upon his eyes.

THE DOCTOR SAID IT was a temporary blindness, brought on, in all likelihood, by overworked nerves and a prolonged exposure to the sun. "Keep him in bed for a few weeks with the curtains drawn and he'll regain his sight." In addition to herbal tea and honey, the doctor prescribed a variety of salves and unguents, to be applied over the eyes at different times of the day. He also cautioned against sleeplessness and extensive ruminating, a malady he claimed would prolong the blindness indefinitely.

Bed-bound, Daniel employed every trick in his possession to escape nostalgia. He added numbers in his head, counted forward and backward, composed music from the noises in the street, and pretended the humming maid was a spirit masquerading as a lark. At night, before the sleeping draught his mother gave him took effect, he fortified his thoughts with anger and resentment, reciting under his breath all his wife's offenses until they blackened his dream. Nothing worked. After three days of resistance, he realized he was no match for the memories that saturated every corner of the room. She was at once nowhere and everywhere. No matter how he struggled, he could not evade the scent of her, the taste of her. The glimpses of her that blazed up the dark edges of his sleep never failed to wake him with the terrible urgency of a desolation.

On his fifth day of blindness, he curbed his pride and asked his mother if she had received word from Monarch Street. "No," Eva said simply. When prompted, she confessed that against her better instinct, she had already informed Meridia of his condition, but that cold and calculating woman who never thought of anyone but herself had refused to see him. "'Daniel brought it upon himself and must now pay for it,' was what your wife said. And as if this wasn't enough, she then had the gall to demand her things! 'You can take them anytime you want,' I told her, 'but what about letting the boy see his father?'" To this, she, Eva, had the door slammed in her face.

He attended his mother's tears with mute bewilderment. The picture she painted did not resemble the woman he knew, yet in these days of darkness he could barely tell who he was, let alone how much his wife might have changed since she left him. And so he continued to lie in silence, incapable of wrath or repudiation, while his mother's sobs grew louder and more indignant.

After the doctor permitted him to walk, he devised a secret game to drive the loneliness out of his heart. Once in the morning and once in the afternoon, he would grope his way around the room in search of an object he had not identified before. After he found one, he would tax his memory to recall the times his wife had come into contact with that particular object. In this way, he remembered that many years ago, she had a habit of putting dried citrus peels in the blue ceramic dish he was now holding, but one day she stopped when four-year-old Noah ingested them by mistake. Another afternoon found him sniffing her boxwood comb. Her handkerchief. The squat ivory brush she used to powder her nose. Day by day, more objects occupied his universe of longing. He did not think much about it, only felt that if he could resurrect his world on top of the one she had crumbled, he might find the word to break her silence.

One thing he noticed was that he could not find her wedding ring anywhere, even when he ordered the maid to search the house up and down. The shovel and the chair were also gone, as were the shirt and trousers that had divulged his shame. He attributed this work of elimination to his mother, and soon confirmed that her effort did not stop there. Over the course of days, things that belonged to his wife began to disappear from the room. The ceramic dish vanished one morning, then her books and hats, followed by her slippers and stockings. One night, he woke up covered in sweat because the room no longer smelled of her. He snatched her pillows and buried his face in them, but the only scent he breathed was that of sun and freshly laundered linen.

On his tenth day of blindness, conquered by an uncontrollable yearning, Daniel dictated a letter to his mother and asked her to deliver it to his boy. Three days passed and no answer came. He was about to compose another letter when his mother broke down in tears.

"It's no use, son. She told Noah to his face that you're not his father. I was standing at the door when she tore up your letter."

His mother was working herself into a fit, exclaiming, "We'll get her! We'll get her!" and insisting he hire an attorney before that hound from hell stripped the very socks off his feet. He listened to her as if from the remote depth of a cave—every word reached him clearly yet dully, and despite her rage, her voice sounded tired and ancient. The only things he was aware of were the pillows that no longer smelled of his wife, and the words he kept muttering again and again like a curse.

"She doesn't want to see me, wants nothing to do with me."

THIRTY-SEVEN

From Magnolia Avenue, the fireflies led them to the Cemetery of Ashes. Noah walked in silence, stern in his Sunday vest and trousers, while behind him Meridia followed with the suitcases. As the sun rose higher, the fireflies' flame grew brighter, forming a swirling golden shield around them. The few people out at that hour stopped when they saw the spectacle, thought it was a spirit departing and raised their hats. Every time the town bell chimed, Meridia paused and muttered a prayer. The town was otherwise quiet.

When they arrived at the cemetery, Noah was the first to notice the oddity. Adjacent to Gabriel's grave, in the lot reserved for Ravenna before the time of the mists, was a mound of freshly turned earth topped by an arrangement of stones. "Look, Mama," he said, and pointed. Meridia at once recognized the mark of a primordial burial. Noah removed the lily and the candied apple from his pocket and placed them among the stones. Except for the chirping of lone birds and the bitter cemetery smoke, nothing disturbed them until the fireflies spun and settled over the mound. Startled by the motion, Meridia looked up and saw a woman in black looking at her from a

distance. It was Malin, standing before her baby's grave with butterfly weed in her hand. When their eyes met, they each looked away
and did not interfere with the other's grief. The next time Meridia
looked, only the blossoms remained, decorating the most handsome
and polished headstone in the cemetery.

MERIDIA DID NOT ALLOW herself an opportunity to sit. The instant they arrived at 24 Monarch Street, she rolled up her sleeves and
subjected the house to a cleaning more thorough than Ravenna's.
First she attacked the kitchen from top to bottom, wiping cabinets,
scrubbing walls, soaping the stove until all smell of ash and charred
meat was eradicated. Moving to the living room, she beat the dust off
the curtains, yanked the funereal white cloths off the furniture, swept
the floor, restored the indigo rug to its original position. She assigned
Noah the task of beating the mattresses, and then told him to hold
the wooden stool steady while she climbed up and harvested spider-
webs with a broom. Pulling sheets and pillows out of the closet, she
urged him to explore the house and make himself comfortable, because from that day on, "this place will be our home." The boy
nodded without comment and left to wander on his own.

At noon, shuffling about the house with a mop and pail, she
caught Noah staring out the window into the street.

"What are you looking at?"

He turned and for a moment seemed to be sneering savagely.

"A crazy man was clawing his own eyes. You should have seen
him jumping like a monkey and punching the air for nothing."

Meridia looked out the window. A few people were still scratching their heads, but it was evident that the main attraction had
ended.

"Poor man," she said. "I hope someone is taking care of him."

An hour later they went out for lunch at a café near Independence Plaza. They each had a plate of beef and mushrooms, a

chicken roll and cheese croquettes, and two scoops of cherry ice cream topped with chocolate sauce. They ate urgently as if they had been starved for days, and did not speak until they finished. Sipping coffee, Meridia told the boy that they would fix the house and make it their own; he could have her old room and his grandfather's study and decorate them in any way he wished. Noah listened with his clairvoyant look and saved his question until the end: "Will we be happy again, Mama?" "Of course," Meridia answered at once. "As long as we have each other."

After lunch, she took him to the Sunday bazaar and bought him the latest marvels. A levitating spin top. Color-changing marbles. A rectangular stone that drove away nightmares if kissed before bedtime. At a bookstall, Meridia bought a dozen novels, knowing they would be her solitary companions in the long nights ahead. After this, they went to Cinema Garden and saw a colored projection of people who lived in flying castles and airborne chariots. Noah liked it so much that he contemplated the idea of stringing his beloved rabbit doll to the levitating spin top when he got home. On their way back, they stopped by the market to purchase fish, vegetables, eggs, and oil. Deep dusk had fallen when they reached the house, blanketing Monarch Street with a formal solemnity. This alone allowed Meridia to conceal her disappointment when she found no one at the door.

That night, they ate a simple meal of fried fish and egg soup. While Noah bathed, Meridia unpacked their few belongings and hid the money and jewelry in various places around the house. At bedtime, Noah refused to sleep by himself in her old room, so they huddled under a great blanket in Ravenna's bed. He asked her to tell him a story, and for an hour she resurrected the fanciful tales she had invented with Permony many years ago. After the boy dozed off, Meridia remained awake. She forced herself to read, but her brain rejected the pages. At dawn she gave it up. Despite herself, she kept waiting for a hand to reach out from the dark and reverse her sorrow.

EVA WAS SHOUTING AND pounding before breakfast. No sooner did the door swing open than she tried to shoulder her way in.

"Give me my grandson!" she said angrily. "You have no right to take him from his father."

Meridia planted her feet and kept her out.

"I have every right to take what's mine," she said. "If he cares so much about Noah, why didn't he come to get him himself?"

Her unassailable tone had the desired effect. Eva, growing more furious, snorted contemptuously.

"What makes you think he wants to see you? My son sent me here because he wants nothing to do with you."

Meridia took her time examining her mother-in-law. In place of anger, it was pity that surged to her heart. She saw the thin white hair and the bowed spine, the graying eyes and furrowed skin, and wondered how that old, withering body was still able to contain five decades of bile.

"Daniel's certainly old enough to make his own decision," Meridia answered.

"You don't believe me, do you?" taunted Eva. "If you think he'll come here on his knees and beg to have you back, then you're far more deluded than I give you credit for. Your marriage is doomed and no power on earth can rescue it. Your husband—*my* son—has been unhappy for a long time, and it's all because of you. *You* forced him to find his comfort elsewhere, failed him so utterly in so many ways that I think you've done him a tremendous favor by leaving."

Meridia was upon her at once. "I knew you were in on it from the start. Tell me, how did you pick her from the crowd? Did you promise her she would be mistress of Magnolia Avenue? And what lies did you tell Daniel to sway him? For the love of heaven, did you let them make love in your bed while you turned the other way?"

"For shame!" cried Eva. "How dare you stand there and accuse me of baseness! If your husband sought the company of another woman, then you've got no one but yourself to blame. You spat on his love, mocked it, murdered it, and for what reason? Did you learn nothing from the mistakes of your ax-wielding mother? Daniel's done no wrong. It's you who chased him from your bed with your pride and your stubbornness, after he was kind enough to stay when he knew you could give him no more children!"

The arrow did more than hit. Detecting a quiver in Meridia's eyes, Eva sharpened her voice and added, "Hand me the boy. It's the least you can do."

Silence, yet all at once Eva knew she had miscalculated. What she took as a weakening was but a lull in the shifting of forces. The quiver swiftly sealed itself with steel. The eyes tore at her with passionate honesty. Eva had no choice but to look away.

"There is nothing here that belongs to him," said Meridia. "Not a strand of hair or a drop of sweat. If you're having trouble understanding me, I'll gladly repeat myself."

The response—delivered calmly and almost inhumanly—struck louder than a slap. Before she could stop herself, Eva backed away from the door. For a second she saw tiny bright objects swarming her vision, and her cheeks suddenly burned with the old sting of Ravenna's hand. It was the same unforgivable pain, the same crushing humiliation. Quickly she rallied herself. "I'll get Noah somehow. Just you watch!"

Meridia did not even blink. "If you ever come near him, I swear on the names of my father and mother, I'll rip your heart out and feed it to you piecemeal."

She slammed the door shut. For several minutes Eva stood staring at it, absolutely livid, but finding no courage to strike.

MERIDIA DID NOT LET Noah go to school that day. She told him that she needed his ideas on what to do with the house, but to herself, she admitted that she would not take chances with a woman like Eva. Sensing her restlessness, Noah raised no objection. She was in the midst of urging him to choose a color for his room when a note arrived from Permony. The girl, burdened with a troublesome pregnancy, excused herself for not coming to see them in person, and then continued:

"You have every reason to be angry. Mama tried to hide things, but I can read well enough between the lines. Daniel has no excuse. I'm appalled by his conduct and I never imagined he would hurt you this way. However, if it makes the slightest difference, I have reasons to believe that he is suffering deeply from his action. Mama was just here, more upset than I have ever seen her, and she let slip that he's taken to bed ill. She wouldn't say from what, but I think he's heartbroken. Even if it was impossible for you to forgive him, I thought you should at least know of his condition . . ."

Meridia did not finish the rest. Her first instinct was to laugh and shred the note to pieces. Let him suffer! Let him wallow in the hell of his own making! But then gradually, as the thrill of vindication cooled in her blood, a part of her she had sentenced to die with the fall of the shovel began to revive. The note explained why Daniel had sent Eva for Noah, why he had not come to confront her himself yesterday. He was ill, aggrieved, heartbroken. What if Permony was right and he was truly sorry? Inconsolable and wishing he could take it all back? Her rational mind felt foolish to believe this, and yet the damage was done. For the rest of the morning, Permony's words jangled in her brain, breeding hope, inciting anger, striking down resolutions already settled. In the end, she found herself in no greater clarity than when she started.

At two o'clock, she left the house with Noah and headed to Magnolia Avenue. The boy asked point-blank, "What for, Mama?" She told him she had some business to do in the neighborhood, "things to pick up and bills to settle," but of course she would not be mad enough to venture anywhere near their house. Noah lowered his head and said nothing. From this she knew he had stopped listening halfway through her excuses.

They were almost at the shop door when it hit her that she had made a mistake. A festive tune was drifting from inside, followed by a laughter of tinkling silver bells that brought her to a standstill.

Meridia did not have to search her memory far to remember where she had heard it before. A second later Eva's warm voice confirmed her suspicion. "Pour us more tea, Sylva. The lady of the house should never permit her guests to die of thirst. Daniel, come down and join us!"

Meridia stood petrified. In wave after wave, fury and humiliation swept the world from under her feet. Her vision tunneled to a single point, and all over her body her heart was trembling with a violent and unfamiliar sensation. She blinked quickly. The desire to storm and unleash, to flare up in rage and inflict severe and irreparable damage cried out with each beat of her wounds. She blinked again. In the second before she took the irreversible strides that would have vaulted her into the shop, a small hand grabbed her wrist and pulled her away. Meridia gasped as if emerging from a dream.

"Let's go, Mama," said Noah.

He led her away without another word. The pressure of his hand was enough to tell her that if she should look back with regret at the house with the flowing music and the easy laughter, or if for any reason she should remind herself of the way the sun slanted in the parlor while his father read the paper and drank coffee, then nothing on earth would save them from the heaviness of the days ahead.

OVER THE NEXT TWO weeks, Meridia did everything she could to rid the house of its grudges. She had the walls painted a sunny yellow, fitted the rooms according to Noah's approval, replaced the ghostly mirrors and moth-eaten curtains, and resuscitated the garden with tulips and hydrangeas. She hired a crew of experts to analyze the airflow of the house, and at her friend Rebecca's suggestion, she rented a machine for ridding the air of perpetual chill. The device not only worked well but also cured the staircase of mischief—there were now exactly twenty-five steps to go up or down. In order to exterminate Ravenna's rancor from the kitchen, Meridia commissioned workmen to strip the floor and ceiling, layer the walls with checkered

paper, and install brand-new cabinets and appliances. She inaugu-
rated the finished space by baking one hundred cream cakes from
Patina's recipe, and ended up stuffing herself and Noah to the point
of sickness. For hours they could not move from the sofa, sugar in
their hair and custard on their lips, and still they forced themselves to
eat until they sank into a sleep without dreams.

Unable to dismiss Eva's threat from her head, Meridia walked
Noah to school every morning and waited for him at the gate when
the last bell rang. This precaution earned the boy no small ridicule
from his friends, but he appeared impervious and did not object to
his mother's company. Around this time, the other students began
to notice his deepening air of isolation. Noah was always amicable,
ready to offer help when needed, but a barrier clearly separated him
from the rest of them. At recess, he displayed no awkwardness in sitting and eating by himself, and when asked to play, he would partici-
pate with polite interest but never zeal. Many years later, it was this
trait of solitude that kept him alive in their memories. An intense
and inscrutable boy, they would say to one another. Always peering
ahead as if he had a crystal ball to look through.

In reality, it took Noah a long while to adjust to his new life. Even
after his mother's feverish bout of redecoration was completed, the
archaic house with its autumnal rooms and innumerable shadows
continued to terrify him. After the first night, he chose to sleep in
his own room, and although his fear kept him up till dawn, he
breathed not a single word to his mother. Noah would never admit
that what he feared most was to spot his grandfather Gabriel among
the shadows. Whenever he imagined the grim paraffin face with its
sharp nose and relentless brows lurking underneath his bed, he
would break into a sweat and cover his face with a pillow.

For a long time, despite Meridia's urging, he did not dare enter
his grandfather's study. Here, year after year on his birthday, he had
stood sweating before the massive desk in a necktie and a stiff-
collared shirt, trying his best to keep still while his grandfather
passed a terrifying glance over him. For this reason, he resolved to

avoid the room at all costs. But one afternoon, it was his grandmother Ravenna who told him to go in. He was doing his homework
in the front hall when he heard her approach from the kitchen,
laughing more joyously than she had ever laughed in her lifetime.
"Go on," she said, clear as a whistle. "The bastard's got no more use
for his toys now that he's stuck with me." The moment he felt her
hand on his shoulder, he was no longer afraid. He opened the door
to the study and walked in. At once she encouraged him to play with
the compass and the globe, the writing instruments, the crystal
flasks, the alabaster jars that housed a million tiny seeds. He studied
the archaic maps on the wall, intrigued by the names of continents
that no longer existed, and then boldly added his own archipelagos
with a red pen. He took down book after book from the towering
shelves, and while he labored to decipher the arcane texts and convo-
luted diagrams, his grandmother Ravenna bustled happily around
him. At dinnertime, Meridia found him asleep in Gabriel's chair, his
mouth open and his feet flung exhaustedly on the baronial desk.

From that day onward, Noah spent all his time in the study. No
one could have foreseen it then, but it was during those solitary
hours that his hatred for his father was born. Without betraying a
hint to anyone, the boy held Daniel responsible for his grandmother's departure, for his misery and anxiety, and for the look of devastation on his mother's face. Much in the manner of Ravenna, who
close to thirty years ago was beginning to compose her dark and private language in the kitchen, Noah soon took to whispering his rage
between the pages of Gabriel's books. A few weeks after they moved
in, Meridia was dusting the shelves in the study when she discovered that a whole row of books had rotted. Some inexplicably turned
to dust at the touch of her fingers.

AROUND THIS TIME, MERIDIA witnessed the return of the fireflies. Every night, regardless of weather, they appeared at the elev-
enth hour, cascading from the sky like a trail of candles to hover

outside her window. They never stayed more than a few minutes, only long enough for her to marvel at their flame and forget her own loneliness. Leaning against the window, she would memorize the patterns they traced in the night, those swirling and looping arabesques that remained with her hours after they were gone. She believed that those patterns concealed a message from Ravenna, and if she could only put meaning to the jumbled lines, she would find a way to bring her back.

Once the redecoration was finished, Meridia grew more restless. She had made no contact with Daniel, heard nothing from him, and except for going to the school and the market, she hardly left the house at all. During a visit, Leah and Rebecca suggested that she should throw herself back into work. "It'll take your mind off things," said Rebecca. "And make money while you're at it," added Leah practically. Meridia gave the matter some serious thought. Although the money and jewelry hidden around the house eliminated any immediate financial concern, she was not content to remain idle for long. The next evening, she invited Samuel for supper. The renegade dealer, broader and bushier than she had seen him last, arrived promptly at the appointed hour. Meridia did not give him time to offer sympathy. Talking quickly and assuredly, she showed no trace of despondency as she bombarded him with ideas. She had made up her mind to open her own shop, she said, which would showcase not only the best jewelry in town, but also her own designs. After a decade in the business, she thought she had a pretty good handle on what customers wanted, and secretly, she had been doing a few sketches of her own. She planned not only to modernize the traditional pieces, but also to offer jewelry tailored to suit their owners' personality and lifestyle. She could come up with half the capital herself—would he put in the other half? Of course, this should not affect his partnership with Daniel in any way, and she would completely understand if he thought she should secure another backer. At this, Samuel, who had been listening with rapt attention, leaned forward and interrupted her.

"I'll back you up in whatever enterprise you choose, madam. Magnolia Avenue would be nothing today without you. He's one damn fool to let you slip away."

Over the next few days, Meridia focused all her energy on work. She scouted various locations around town for the new shop, interviewed artisans with potential to put her designs into execution, and began the exhilarating process of transferring her ideas onto paper. She found herself somewhat a natural at it, for she could envision clearly the piece she wanted before her pencil scratched the paper. Deriving inspiration from everything within sight, she paid careful attention to shapes and textures, to colors and outlines and negative use of spaces. One night, while observing the fireflies, she was seized by a tremendous impulse to capture both their radiance and evanescence. She sketched all night, her pencil faithfully looping and swirling, and by morning had a stack of drawings piled at her elbow. Too excited to sleep, she was about to make coffee for herself when a loud pounding rattled the front door. Still in her dressing robe, Meridia flew downstairs and answered it. Malin was standing on the topmost step with a bundle in her arms.

"Will you help me?" said the girl.

Meridia remembered her promise and let her in.

THIRTY-EIGHT

In many respects, that fateful night in July was coming to a close like any others. After dinner, Ahab retired to the library to smoke cigars and write letters. Permony, seven months pregnant, followed a minute later with a book and a knitting basket. Though she understood little of the missives Ahab dispatched to his home country, she took a great deal of pleasure in watching him work. At ten o'clock, she excused herself to bed and went to her room. As usual, the maid had placed on the dressing table a cup of bitter tonic, which Ahab insisted she drink every night to ensure an easy delivery. That evening, however, the baby gave a massive kick just as Permony was reaching for the cup, spilling every drop on the floor. Amazed at the force of the kick, Permony pretended to scold her child and cleaned up the mess. Ten minutes later, Ahab came in and helped her to bed. He asked the usual question as he fondled her belly. "Did you drink the tonic?" Permony pointed to the empty cup. "Good girl," he said. "You won't scream one bit when the time comes." He winked lustily, ripe with meaning, and with his big hands squeezed her breasts until she squealed half in pain, half in pleasure. Afterward, he covered her with a blanket and went to wash himself. As on any other night, she was fast asleep before he returned, her flushed skin smelling strongly of his sweat.

Since her marriage, Permony was given to sleeping like a log: nine hours of solid rest that no sound or movement could disturb. But that evening, four hours after she went to bed, she awoke to the sound of a great engine chuffing from underneath the house. The walls were vibrating too, and even in bed she could feel heat and steam rising from the floor. From the sound, she imagined enormous steel claws boring into the soil, pulverizing stones and plundering minerals from the earth below. Permony sat up in fright when she heard a muffled scream colliding with the noise.

"Ahab," she whispered. He was not in bed. Forcing herself to remain calm, she turned on the light and clambered to the floor with difficulty. Her limbs were shaking as she slipped on her robe and slippers and went to the hallway. The chuffing noise grew louder. It was coming from the east wing of the house.

She moved as swiftly as her swollen feet allowed. Crossing the shadowy hall, she was besieged by a terrifying feeling that she had never set foot in this house before. The prized old tapestries that had often delighted her with their flaxen-haired maidens and flower-strewn meadows were now bursting with malevolent beldams. The mirrors reflected a thousand disfigured eyes, the splendid vases leered at her like giant floating heads. Permony pressed her hand to her mouth and hurried away.

When she reached the east wing, the sound was no longer that of an engine chuffing but of a great beast panting. Down in the cellar where Ahab kept his wine and hunting rifles, something seemed to be rearing and rasping, its tail—or fin—sending shuddering slaps along the belly of the house. The muffled human scream nearly froze her with dread, but curiosity kept her going. There was something familiar in that collision of panic and outrage, something she had heard many times before in her dreams. Permony crept forward to the cellar door and opened it.

Candlelight swayed on the ceiling. A shadow rocked violently along the wall. Still without a sound, she climbed down the stairs in infinitesimal steps. The panting was by then deafening, the scream lobbed to a higher pitch. By the time she reached the floor, the baby's heart was pounding faster than her own. Permony patted her belly and looked around the staircase.

What she saw she did not at once understand. First there was the beast, naked and huge and slimy. In the candlelight it looked half swine, half human, moaning and gasping on all fours and facing away from her. The beast was furiously thrusting itself against a bed of straw. She could smell the sweat slipping down its back. She could see the enormous scarlet genitals smashing into the straw. And then the candle guttered and the whole scene altered. It was not straw the beast was mating with but a girl, then another girl, then another. Barely older than children, they kicked and screamed help-lessly with all the force of horror. Before Permony could move, the candle guttered again. This time there was no beast anywhere. Only corn yellow hair, pale white skin, muscular backside. Atop the girls, Ahab was bucking in a systematic fashion.

Permony screamed and fell back against the wall. The beast re-appeared to take Ahab's place, and without seeing her resumed its business. Too shocked to do anything, Permony stood about until she received another kick in the womb. The thought of her baby fired blood into her legs. Heavily, she trudged back up the stairs, through the door, and out to the hallway. She labored to cross the hall and made her exit through the front door. Only after she reached the street did she realize that she was in her robe and slippers. By that time her mind was made up: Not for the world would she return and chance another glance at the beast.

The warm night offered little light. There was no one in the street, only dogs baying at the sky. With each block traveled, Permony felt a fresh pain shooting up her womb, which caused her to stumble more times than she cared to count. Despite her fear, she stopped often to relieve the pressure on her knees and the more urgent one in her head. How long had this been going on? How was it possible that she had not heard the noise until tonight? The tonic! Of course! Was it true, then—the rumor about Ahab and the girls he'd violated for the sake of land? Thinking her head would explode, Permony longed for someone who would comfort her and explain away the horror.

She had meant to go to Magnolia Avenue. In her distress, however, she was halfway there before she remembered that Meridia was no longer living in that house. She considered going ahead to Daniel with her confession, but as much as she loved her brother, she decided it was a woman's counsel she needed. By this time, she was far away from Monarch Street or Museum Avenue, so she decided to seek refuge at Orchard Road. In the hours to come, Permony would regret her decision bitterly.

It was half past three when she rapped on her mother's door, breathless and drenched in sweat. A startled Eva screamed when she saw her.

"What's wrong?" She cupped both hands over Permony's belly. "Is it the baby?"

"No, the baby's fine, Mama. It's Ahab . . ."

Eva sat her down in the parlor. From the start there was no stopping Permony's tears as she relived the terror and tension of the past hour. She did not skip a single detail, but often became confused as she spoke, shaking her head, losing her voice, visibly overwhelmed by emotion. Eva listened without interrupting. After Permony finished, she stayed silent for a minute before replying, "I don't believe it."

"Neither do I," sobbed Permony. "I never suspected he was that kind of man. Oh, I feel so lost and wretched, Mama. You must tell me what to do."

"You must do only one thing," said Eva instantly. "Get that ridiculous story out of your head and go home at once."

Permony looked as if she had been slapped.

"I don't understand, Mama."

"What don't you understand? Ahab is a respectable man without a breath of scandal on his reputation. You're obviously nervous about the baby and your imagination has gone haywire. Listen to me. Be a sensible girl and go home."

Eva stood up. Struck by the finality of the gesture, Permony remained in her seat. The next second Eva was grasping her daughter's wrists and pulling her to her feet. Her strength was all the more astounding given her years and Permony's advanced state of pregnancy.

"You're not listening, Mama," she said weakly.

"I have listened enough!" Eva suddenly roared with anger. "I have done my best to secure your future and make you the most enviable bride in the history of this town. But not only have you neglected to thank me, now you've created some cock-and-bull story to spite me. What kind of mother do you think I am that I would hand you over to a fiend? When your father was alive, you might have had him wrapped around your spoiled little finger, but not me! I swear I'll crush you before you drag me down in a scandal!"

By force she steered Permony to the door. The girl, pale and trembling, could do nothing but yield.

"I'll walk you home before your husband becomes alarmed," said Eva.

"Mama, please! How could you send me back after everything I said?"

Eva pushed her out the door. "You'll hold my hand and we'll walk and you won't speak another word."

Her eyes smudged with tears, Permony turned to get a clear look at her mother. In that second she achieved a final and complete understanding of the woman whose love she had failed to earn despite a lifetime of obedience. There was nothing to do but take back her hand.

"Don't bother, Mama. I can walk on my own."

There was a sharpness in her tone that caught Eva by surprise. Before she could protest, Permony had set out into the night. "Suit

yourself," Eva shouted after her. It was only later, after she shut the
door and climbed the stairs and returned to bed, that it occurred to
Eva that she had never seen her daughter's lavender eyes flash so de-
fiantly before.

Permony started off toward Monarch Street, but her feet soon
followed her tangled thoughts and veered off course. The sky was
primed for the coming of dawn, rich with splashes of saffron, and
the silence grew less thick as more swallows chirped over the rooftops. For a long time, Permony plodded past the endless sleeping
houses before collapsing against a tree trunk. Her feet were blistered
from the thin slippers, yet the pain was nothing compared to the
gash in her heart. A bitter smoke filled her lungs as she cried softly,
and it was then she realized she had taken shelter in the cemetery.

The first trickle of blood did not surprise her; on the contrary,
she was relieved by the unforeseen sense of release. It was only after
she saw a thick, dark pool form between her legs that she panicked.
"Help!" she screamed, but even to her own ear the cry sounded distant. Dew dropped from the sky and beaded her skin. The saffron
light flashed and lit up the town in one blushing coruscation. And
then suddenly Permony saw a legion of demons returning to their
graves. As soon as they scented her, they shrieked aloud and wrung
her belly like a cloth, sucked her lips with rotten teeth, and jumped
up and down on her chest until she lost all air and fell headlong into
darkness.

When Permony opened her eyes, there was nothing to convince
her that she was alive. A bright golden light shone around her like a
halo, and an angry, otherworldly voice was keeping her away from
darkness. She opened her eyes wider and saw a radiant spirit beating the demons with flying fists. "Get to your graves this instant!
Touch her again and I'll get every mutt in town to dig up your
bones!" At this, a warmth seeped into Permony's veins and restored
sensation to her limbs. Something soft and fragile tickled her feet,
and with amazement she saw that the pool of blood had transformed
into brilliant orange blossoms. The baby was alive. The demons

were scattering. Gratefully, Permony looked up at the spirit and recognized her sister, Malin.

Some time later she felt herself being carried on a stretcher. The journey was long and arduous, but Malin's hand never once left hers. The next thing Permony knew was being lowered onto a soft, white bed. An old woman with a delicate touch began kneading her stomach. The pain came and went and came again. Malin was pleading with her to muster every bit of strength. Permony heard herself cry and moan, scream and cry again, her last words slipping, slipping like vapor from between her lips.

THIRTY-NINE

Malin's voice had gone still, but her face was alive with anger, shock, revulsion, and sadness. Sitting next to her on the sofa in the front hall, Meridia mirrored these emotions. Behind them the morning fog pressed heavy against the window. Noah had not stirred from his room upstairs. Malin had not once let go of the baby.

"She told you all this?" asked Meridia. "Then what happened?"

Malin shifted the sleeping child to her right arm and wiped her eyes with her left.

"She'd lost a lot of blood by the time we got to the midwife's. She never knew she gave birth to a son."

"Oh, Permony!" cried Meridia. "What have they done to you?"

Her tearful gaze traveled down to the baby. A beautiful boy he was, thick-lashed and apple-cheeked like his mother, with none of Ahab's paleness or large-boned awkwardness. He was asleep, his face pink and untroubled. Meridia felt her heart tighten as she took his small hand in hers.

"Start again from the beginning," she said. "Try to remember her exact words."

Little by little, the sisters-in-law gave meaning to the horror before them. Meridia brought up her suspicions of Ahab, dating back from the day of Malin's wedding, and Malin admitted she was often beset by the same uneasiness herself.

"I always thought there was something sinister about him. That greedy, predatory leer—as if Permony was some object to be consumed. I should have known he was up to something. Deviants are always looking for respectable wives to shield them."

Overcome with remorse, Meridia hung her head low.

"I tried to warn Permony . . . I failed . . . I should have tried harder . . ."

"There was nothing you could have done. Permony was dead set on marrying him. She wouldn't listen to anything she didn't want to hear. Besides, Mama had only the highest praise for Ahab. Her hold on Permony was much stronger than yours."

"Do you think your mother knew what Permony was getting into?"

Malin's rage instantly broke into a blaze. "Why else would she send her straight back to him? That monster! All she cares about is her name, her comfort, her money. It's no different than if her own hands had murdered her!"

The sisters-in-law traded a long glance. Meridia wanted to ask, Did Daniel know of his mother's scheme and consent? She thought her head would burst until she heard the answer, but at the last second, unsure if she could stomach the truth, she recoiled from raising the question.

Malin, however, had read her mind. "Mama said you refused to let Noah see him when she told you he was sick. I can't say I disagree with you. After what Daniel has done, I myself would find it impossible to forgive him."

Meridia stiffened and stared blankly at her sister-in-law. "Your mother did come to see me to demand Noah back, but she didn't say Daniel was ill. In fact, she said he wanted nothing more to do with me. It was Permony who told me he was unwell."

Malin lifted her brows sharply. "And the letter?"

"What letter?"

"The letter Daniel wrote to Noah—she said you tore it up right in front of the boy!"

A furious comprehension burst upon Meridia like wildfire.

"I never received it," she said. "Are you telling me Daniel tried to contact me?"

She proceeded to inform Malin of her aborted visit to Magnolia Avenue, of the music and laughter and Sylva presiding over the shop. Malin greeted her revelation with a cry.

"It's all lies! The shop has been closed since Daniel fell sick, and he can't stand that slut anywhere near him. Mama must have installed her there just to keep you away. I wanted to come here and talk to you, but she had me convinced you'd made up your mind and didn't want to see him. Please forgive me. I have been so wrapped up in my own grief that I didn't think to question her."

"What else did your mother say?"

"She said he stays in his room all day and doesn't want to see anyone. When I came to visit, she said he was asleep and didn't wish to be disturbed."

"Is he terribly ill?"

"All I know is he's lost his sight for the time being. The doctor says it's exhaustion, I say it's a guilty conscience." Malin watched Meridia intently. "What are we going to do now?"

For a long minute Meridia said nothing. And then she smoothed her skirt and rose calmly from the sofa.

"Your mother doesn't leave us much choice, does she? But first, let me find a bed for that handsome fellow."

She was walking toward the door to hunt for her old bassinet in the attic when the baby cried. Meridia stopped and glanced back. It was unmistakable—the joy, the love, the rapture, consecrating every inch of Malin as she soothed the baby with a whisper. The child who for years had haunted her dreams, forced her to fight demons and endure the bitter cemetery smoke each and every dawn, no longer blue and bloody, but alive. In awe, Meridia turned and slipped into the hallway.

THE CLOCK HAD JUST struck eight when she sent for Leah and asked her to stay with Noah and the baby. A half hour later, she put on her coat and hat and left the house with Malin. The figure they cut as they strode down Monarch Street together was a formidable one. The neighbors, seeing the women's determined faces and armed-for-war postures, were relieved they were not the recipients of their wrath. Meridia turned left at the end of the street, Malin right, their glances crossing briefly to affirm the new bond between them. Both were aware there was little time to waste.

Malin set off briskly across town, past Cinema Garden and the market square and the curious little park that grew winter flowers all the year round. Her destination, a large antiquated house with thick white columns and impenetrable ivy, lay three blocks north of the courthouse. When she got there, she grabbed the lion door knocker and swung it with all the rage in her body. A servant had no sooner answered than she pushed her way in and demanded to see the master of the house. A moment later Ahab appeared in barely hitched trousers—shirtless, hairy, and hulking. It was evident he had just woken up and had not realized his wife was missing. At once Malin tore into him like a panther.

"Your wife is dead. Your baby, too. They died trying to get away from you."

Her dark eyes sharp with anger, she proceeded to tell him everything without omitting a word of Permony's confession. Aware that the servants were listening in the hallway, Ahab moved to shut the door, but Malin only shouted all the louder. She declared that he was a fiend and a criminal, that vileness and abomination were written all over his face, and after what he had done to Permony and to all those hapless girls, she had no wish of ever seeing or hearing from him again.

"I'll give you one hour to disappear from this town," she said, speaking clearly over his protests. "In one hour, I will go to the authorities with my sister's last words on my side. If you should ever come near me or my family in the future, I will broadcast your crime to every man and woman in this town, rally the law and all the spirits against you, and make your name a bane on every young girl's lips. You might think you're invincible, you might have your country's backing to steal from us, but we've got the means to beat you. We will drive you out. We will tear you down. Try us, and we'll ship you back ass first to the windmill hell you came from!"

Malin walked out before Ahab could fully comprehend what had hit him. As she crossed the front door, her feet left the ground, and before she knew it, she was floating high above the street. With the sun warm on her skin and the treetops an arm's reach away, the grief that had shackled her for years sloughed off like snakeskin. People hurried below her, pleasant figures in a dream surely, yet immaterial to the force throbbing inside her. On and on she drifted, all the way past the park with the winter flowers and the market square and Independence Plaza, until Museum Avenue swam into view and she spied her own house perched on a fragrant hill. "Jonathan," she called as she glided into the hall, speaking from the dizzying heights of her ascent. It was only when she saw him looking absently out the window that she came back to earth. He did not rise from his chair or even lift his head, but it did not matter. She had found the words to move him.

"Listen to me," she said, and without sitting down, she proceeded to tell him the events of the last hours: what Permony saw in the cellar, her flight from Ahab, Eva's unthinkable cruelty, Permony's death, and the baby's birth.

"We can raise him as our own," she went on ardently. "You can name him as you wish—didn't you always like the name David? We can be happy again, dearest. Think about it. We can have the family we've always wanted."

Jonathan had shown little expression as she spoke. Now he smiled, thin and strained, as if to indulge a difficult child.

"Are you forgetting something? What about Ahab? It's his son after all."

"I've got him fooled and backed into a corner," said Malin, not without triumph. "He thinks the baby is dead, and he knows that what Permony told me could obliterate him from the face of the town. He won't dare lift a finger against us."

She began to recount in detail her confrontation with Ahab. Jonathan listened without stirring, attentive to a fault, yet something in his eyes was shifting in a way that alarmed her. When she finished, she could hear his answer before he said it.

"It's too late. Nothing can restore what's lost between us."

Malin knelt down and took his hand.

"It's not too late. We can do this together. You loved me once and I believe the feeling still lives inside you. Do not forsake our future now that it's finally here."

Even as she summoned their tender memory together, she could feel him slipping from her. Or had she lost him that day along with the baby, and all that had sustained them since was simply habit and convenience? It was no use. His kind face was an open page she had put off reading for too long. Before she could think of what to say, the awful words had tumbled from his mouth.

"Stop deceiving yourself, Malin. You don't love me anymore, and neither I you."

She had sensed it coming a great distance ago, had imagined how much it would hurt, but now that the words were spoken, they did not cleave her in two. She was still alive. She was still breathing. His gaze fell on her like a caress, gentle yet aloof, and as she met it she felt the weight of the thing that had died between them.

"No, my love, that's not true. That's not true!"

Jonathan withdrew his hand. "There's nothing left for us. We've worn down what we had to the last insignificant bit. I'll see that you won't lack for anything."

Sinking back on her heels, Malin looked at him for a long time without speaking. Color had drained from his handsome face—the

exertion of the last few minutes had clearly tired him beyond measure. Still trembling, still hearing the death knell in her ear, Malin
rose from the floor and stepped back from the chair.

"I'm leaving town to raise the baby on my own," she said. "I
won't risk it with Ahab, and people will talk if I stay."

Malin turned and made for the door before silence became the
final word between them. Then, with her head held high, she passed
the servants in the hall and climbed her way up the stairs. It was not
until she found herself alone in her room that the tears came.

"Stop it, you fool!" she told herself angrily. "Pack quickly and
leave. There's no time to waste. Your child is waiting."

MERIDIA WENT TO THE midwife's first. She had just entered the
little patch of garden in front of the cottage when the woman herself, the same one who had delivered Noah, appeared at the door.
Her wise, good-natured face was filled with wonder.

"Something very strange has happened, madam."

Without elaborating further, she led Meridia to a small windowless room that reeked of disinfectant. Stretched on a metal cot underneath a white sheet was Permony. Her exposed face was
unblemished, her skin radiant, her long black hair lustrous. Meridia
stepped into the room and took her hand. It was warm as fire.

The midwife shook her head in bewilderment. "I've never seen a
dead body keep so well. Not cold or stiff, and nor does it give the
slightest odor. And her face—it was twisted every which way with
pain when her spirit departed, but now she looks as serene as a
saint. Of course I've heard stories about those beings who are so favored by heaven their bodies resist decay long after their death. But
who knows if they're true? One time I heard about a boy who died
from a fall without breaking a single bone . . ."

While the midwife chattered on, a hard knot of guilt settled in
the pit of Meridia's stomach. Permony's tranquil face was that of

the little girl who had suffered her childhood in silence, tormented by sister and mother, and who as a young woman had never found the happiness she deserved. Meridia remembered the fantastical tales they used to weave together—the mermaids and the dragon queens—and how they had laughed and comforted each other while Eva's bees raged against them. They had been inseparable then, closer than blood sisters, and yet in the end she had failed her. She had not fought harder for her, had succumbed to deceiving appearances and allowed her to marry the wrong man. "Save her," Elias had said to her on his deathbed. Now at last she knew his meaning. All these years she had been too slow and stupid to understand it.

"Would you like some water, madam? You look rather pale."

The midwife's voice shattered her reflection. With the greatest difficulty Meridia turned and faced the woman's benevolent eyes.

"I'm all right, thank you." She pressed her lips together, drew a deep breath, and took money from her pocket.

"No, madam, that's too much!" objected the midwife. "I can't possibly take it!"

Meridia pressed the money into her hand. "Please send the body to the funeral home. The father of the baby—he might ask questions. And if he does—"

"I'll tell him the baby died along with his mother," said the midwife. "Last night a beggar woman delivered a stillbirth and the poor dear couldn't afford to have it buried. If I must, I'll throw the dead creature in his face and tell him it's his child. After everything Miss Permony said before she died, I would never condemn that baby to a life of hell."

Despite Meridia's insistence, the midwife refused to take more than her due. Nodding gratefully, Meridia turned back to the cot and stood in silence for a few minutes. When she finally moved to the door, her wet eyes were flashing metal and stone. The midwife stepped back and let her pass.

MERIDIA CUT ACROSS THE square and walked twelve blocks east
to Magnolia Avenue. It was a little past nine when she heard again
the idle strain of laughter and music. This time she headed straight
for the door. In the center of the shop, four women were sitting
around a table, drinking tea and playing a game of tiles. Meridia advanced toward them and flipped the table over.

"Get out," she said in a near whisper, fixing her eyes on the
youngest of them.

One woman shrieked, another gasped. Porcelain cups and ivory
tiles smashed against the floor. The youngest, Sylva, jumped from
her chair and clutched her mouth. With a sweep of the arm, Meridia
sent her crashing to the door.

"Watch where you wrap your thighs," she said as if she were
scolding a child. "Next time, I won't be so gentle."

Eva, finding her tongue, rose with such suddenness that her
chair toppled over.

"What do you think you're doing?"

Meridia ignored her and glared at the other two women; like
mice they scurried to the door. Sylva, having turned deathly white,
was shaking from head to toe. She did not dare look at Meridia, but
quietly sobbed and followed her companions to the street.

"How dare you walk in here and terrorize my guests!" shouted
Eva. "Do you think my son's house is a boarding place that you can
leave and enter whenever you please?"

Meridia did not even glance at her as she darted up the stairs.
Hand gripping the banister for support, Eva followed, neither as
quick nor nimble.

"Have you no shame left? Daniel does not want you or need you
or desire you!"

Meridia did not pause or stoop to insults. She swept down the
hallway to her bedroom and threw the door open.

It was just as she had expected. Ceiling, floor, walls were coated in bees. The infernal insects swarmed the bed, chairs, lamps, blocking all sound and light from the window. As soon as the door opened, they flew at Meridia with their thousand deafening cries. Far from panicking, Meridia did exactly what Ravenna had done during Noah's birth—she seized a chair, ran to the window, smashed the pane to pieces. The bees shrieked as the sun exploded into the room. The fast ones managed to escape, but most caught fire and burned on the spot. Their remains rained down and covered the floor with ashes.

"I knew you would come."

Weak, from the bed, came Daniel's voice. Until then the bees had covered every inch of him.

"Stay where you are," said Meridia sharply. "Be quiet and listen to me."

At this point Eva burst in, huffing and red in the face. "You just can't wait to finish him off, can you!" she exclaimed. "Barging in here and disturbing a sick man after you abandoned him in cold blood!"

Only then did Meridia turn and confront her mother-in-law. A white-hot fury burned in her veins, and she wanted to tear every nerve and fiber that gave the woman's face its perfidious look. How much it cost her, to remain where she stood and say what she must say clearly, she would never know.

"Permony died during labor this morning," she said. "Not long after you threw her out. Malin found her in the cemetery. Before she died, she said that the shock of having her own mother turn her away in her hour of need was too much for her to bear."

Eva blinked, and then opened her eyes wide. "What are you talking about?"

"She died from a broken heart. Permony, your daughter—do you remember her? Drowning in her own blood when Malin found her."

"Permony? Dead? Are you out of your mind? She was well when she went home last night!"

"She never made it, not in her condition. But it didn't matter to you, did it? *You* forced her to return to Ahab, after all the monstrous things she told you about him. How did it feel to toss your pregnant daughter into the night, to reject your own flesh and blood when she needed your help? How could you return to bed and *sleep* after you slammed the door in her face?"

"What's going on, Mama?" demanded Daniel, rising from the bed. He started to fumble blindly forward, but again Meridia stopped him.

"Sit down," she said with a touch of razor. "You'll need all your strength to hear what your mother has done."

Eva's face had become a colorless mask, one hand over her throat and the other sealed over her heart. Without taking her eyes off her, Meridia began recounting to Daniel Permony's discovery of the beast, her flight to Orchard Road, and Eva's subsequent dismissal. She told him about the graveyard encounter between the sisters, how Malin took Permony to the midwife, heard her last words, and watched her die before her child was born. Meridia's voice grew hoarse as she talked, but not once, not even for a fraction of a second, did her stare waver from Eva.

For a long time nobody spoke or moved. And then Daniel said, "Did the baby survive?"

Meridia nodded. "A boy who takes after Permony. Malin has decided to raise him as her own."

"What about Ahab?"

"He won't ask for his son. Malin took care of him."

A hard and severe expression settled on Daniel's face. Narrowing his blind eyes, he turned to Eva and said, "Is it true, Mama? Did you throw Permony out of the house? Mama, answer me!"

A scream escaped from Eva's mouth, followed by a spasm that shook her violently. All at once her right hand sliced at the air, her left still clutching her throat, her eyes wild with the look of a trapped beast.

"I certainly did not! When your sister came to me in distress, I told her straightaway she must leave Ahab. 'Stay here, don't come back. I'm worried for your safety.' We talked for a long time, and it was she who said that she still loved him and wanted to go back. I told her absolutely not, but she was stubborn and determined. 'Then let me walk you home,' I said. 'No, Mama,' she said. 'I want to be alone to clear my head. You go on to bed now. I'm sorry to have woken you.' I kept protesting but she wouldn't hear of it. She seemed strong enough so I never thought, not for once . . . Oh, my dear girl! I'm your mother, son. Do you think I have it in me to turn my back on my daughter? Your wife can say whatever she wants, but you know me better. I'd rather take my own life than put my children in danger!"

She broke into a loud sob and rushed to Daniel with outstretched arms. Swift as lightning, Meridia planted herself between them. The force of her fury pushed Eva back against the door.

"How long will you lie? Your daughter is dead, and yet still you mock her memory. You knew all along that Ahab wasn't the man he pretended to be. Admit it! You dangled Permony in front of him, dressed her up, shoved her right into his lap, knowing exactly what kind of beast he was. Don't deny it, Malin told me everything. Permony would be alive today if it wasn't for your greed!"

"No, I didn't know!" cried Eva. "Ahab deceived me just as he deceived all of you. Had I known, I would never have consented to the marriage. Speak in my defense, son! I consulted you on multiple occasions, and didn't you say that Ahab was the best possible husband for Permony? Didn't you agree with me that he was as upright and blameless as the best of them?"

"I did, Mama," said Daniel gravely. "But it was you who convinced me we had nothing to worry about. When I wanted to look into his background, you said it was unnecessary. Meridia warned me about him, but I refused to listen to her. I believed *you* and so I agreed to let him have Permony. Mama, do you realize what we've done? What you've done?"

Outraged, Eva wept louder. "How could you pin this on me now? We always see eye to eye—why don't you believe me when I say I'm innocent? Don't you see what your wife is doing? She's trying to divide us, make us turn on each other—she's been doing this from the day you married her! I swear, son, I've never kept anything hidden from you!"

This was what Meridia had been waiting for. Without missing a beat, without even noticing the tears running down Eva's cheeks, she sprang on her like a lioness.

"That's a lie. You've been playing us like a fiddle. What did you do with the letter Daniel wrote for Noah? You never delivered it to him."

Eva jerked her head up. The hatred pinching the corners of her mouth was fit to slay a horse.

"My letter? Noah never received my letter? But Mama, you told me—"

"That *I* tore up the letter before Noah could read it?" Meridia was unstoppable now. "That's not all she's done. She never told me you were sick. She came to see me once, but only to say you wanted nothing more to do with me. She threatened to take Noah from me, by crook or by force, and she put that—that *whore*—downstairs in the shop where everyone could see her and made her pretend she was mistress of this house. If you only knew! If you only knew!"

Her voice broke as she dragged the last phrase through her teeth. Jamming her hand into her pocket, she clung to something there as if her life depended on it.

"But Mama—Mama said you refused to see me," stammered Daniel. "She said you only shrugged when she told you I was ill, and you wouldn't allow Noah to come no matter how much she begged you . . . I—I thought you hated me so much you no longer cared for me . . . I never asked her to take Noah from you, and Syl—she—she was nothing—" Suddenly he bit off his words. A nerve on his forehead stood out and trembled angrily. "Why, Mama, why? When I was lying here sick to my soul!"

Eva shook her head with all her vigor. "You got it all wrong, son!

I was only trying to protect you. I thought it was best if you—if you moved on . . . I can explain everything. Please don't turn away from me . . . Please!"

Stumbling toward his wife, Daniel did not heed his mother.

"Don't come any closer," Meridia said, stopping him. "It's finished between us. You've used up all the love I had for you."

She yanked her hand from her pocket and threw something at his feet. It slid with a hiss across the floor and stirred up all the ashes in its path. Without waiting for Daniel's response, she pushed Eva aside and ran out of the room.

"Meridia!" He started after her, but a swarm of fireflies rose from the ashes and surrounded him. Instantly he recognized their furious flapping wings, the bright tiny bullets that had robbed him of sight. Eva screamed in horror. Daniel waved his arms frantically and fell to the floor. The fireflies closed in and plucked at his lids, shooting a terrible pain to the roots of his eyes. "Meridia!" he shouted in agony. "Meridia!"

He groped along the floor and found the object she had thrown at him. No sooner had he touched it than the pain subsided. The furious wings stopped beating, the tiny bright bullets ceased exploding his eyeballs. A thin yellow line danced at the edge of his vision, faint yet undeniable. It was his first ray of light since she left him.

Eva threw herself on the floor and put her arms around him. "What has she done to you? Do you doubt me now? She's a demon! She summoned those creatures straight from hell!"

He struggled to his feet and broke away from her. More light flooded his eyes, and the darkness that for weeks had kept him captive began to crumble like a smashed wall. In wonder, his gaze traveled from the door to the broken window, from the upturned chair to the bed littered with burnt wings. Swaying like a drunk, he looked down on his palm and saw the coil of gold that had restored his vision. It was Gabriel's necklace, once given to Pilar to save Patina's life and redeemed by him as a token of his love.

"Drop it, son! She's put a curse on it! Drop it!"

Daniel ignored this and brought the necklace to his heart. And then he turned to his mother and said, "Get out of my house and don't come back, Mama. You are done talking. Don't let me catch you saying another word."

FORTY

The wake was held three days later. In order to attend to last-minute details, Malin arrived early at the funeral home. With quiet efficiency she put out candles next to the flowers, straightened chairs, paid the funeral director, and confirmed that the caterers would arrive at noon with a hot lunch. At half past nine, two coffins were brought from the inner chambers and placed at the front of the hall. The baby's casket, bearing the beggar woman's child, was sealed. The men carrying Permony's handled it with a reverence befitting a holy object. Malin requested a moment alone and approached the coffin.

Meridia had not exaggerated. Dressed in a royal jade tunic they had picked out the day before, Permony was the very picture of love and loveliness, as empty of pain as she was full of grace. Her veins glowed with the same phosphorescent flame that had kindled Patina's in her last days, illuminating her honey brown skin to the point of transparency. Overcome by the miracle, Malin stood still. She had done her share in tormenting Permony, treating her abominably in order to earn Eva's praise, and every meanness now came back like a knife to her heart. As children, they wasted so much time playing at being pawns, each unwisely falling into their mother's hands, and yet even after they caught on to her tricks, they never became close friends, so powerful was the divisive force Eva had wielded over them. It was now too late for forgiveness—there was only atonement. This, then, would be hers: to raise the child to the best of her ability, to love him as her own, and make him honor his mother to the end of his days. Malin sealed the oath by clasping the warm dead hand, and then for the first and last time, she placed a kiss on her sister's cheek.

Afterward, she could not remember which happened first—the door opening or the wail piercing her eardrums. By the time she spun around on her heels, Eva was already in the room, wild-eyed and crumpled, as if she had not seen a comb or pillow in days.

"What's happened to us, Malin? Your sister—my dear Permony!"

Quick as an arrow, Malin shot down the aisle to the door.

"You have no business being here. Leave before I throw you out."

Eva stopped aghast in her tracks. There was dust and sweat on her face, streaked through by flowing tears.

"Be kind to me," she pleaded, fingering the hem of her heavy crepe dress. "I have no one left in the world. Your brother is furious—he blamed me for everything and wouldn't hear my side of the story. That hateful wife of his told him so many awful things about me, things she had so twisted and blown out of proportion my own son now thinks I'm a perfect monster—"

"Stop it, Mama! I'm not here to listen to your lies. Permony told me everything before she died. Now leave before you embarrass yourself further."

Eva swallowed hard, the deep, dark rings tightening around her eyes. She blinked rapidly in an attempt to understand, yet the effort only increased her air of bewilderment.

"Be kind to me," she repeated weakly. "I'm old and tired and unwell. Can't you see how pale I am? I've walked and walked and I haven't slept in three days. I kept tracing her route from the house to

the cemetery, and from there to Ahab's and back again, and I don't
understand why she didn't make it home. It's such a short distance
and she *was* well when she left me, she assured me so herself . . .
Malin, I've always stood by you from the day you were born . . . Why
won't you believe me?"

Malin answered at once, "You're wasting my time. I'm not interested in your melodrama or your make-believe. You gave Permony
to Ahab knowing full well what he was. I know he asked you to
name her price, and you did! Now Permony is dead. Nothing you say
will bring her back. I shall never forgive you for it. From the very
start you set me against her to satisfy your own vanity. It amused
you, didn't it, to see me going at her? You never loved her, or any of
us—only yourself. I've had enough of you. From this point on, we're
finished being family."

Eva gave a strangled cry. "*She*'s poisoned you, too! I'm your
mother, Malin. Are you going to abandon me like your brother?"

"No, just like *you* abandoned Permony. I mean it. I never want to
see you again. Now go before the mourners come and mistake you
for someone who's capable of grief."

Sobbing and trembling, Eva watched her daughter with horrified
eyes. She had the peculiar sensation of stepping back in time and
looking into her own young face. She recognized that hardness of
will, that defiant and merciless stare, and the denouncing words that
crushed her spirit like a millstone. She had taken part in this scene
before—had in fact carried it off to a triumphant finish—but back
then it was she who had done the disowning, and Patina had been
on the receiving end. Suddenly, as her memory blurred with the
present, Eva felt a slab of gravestone leap out of the past and smash
against her back. The impact buckled her knees and dropped her to
the floor.

"Don't do this to me"—she tugged at Malin's skirt painfully—"I
have every right to mourn my daughter."

"Horseshit!" Malin retorted, jerking her skirt free. "You never
mourn for anybody but yourself. You never consider anybody's feel-

ings but your own. You know what you are? You're a vile, rotten, venomous bitch who's hardly fit to mother a beast!"

Eva sank to her heels, wincing as if a large lump were obstructing her throat. Slowly she lifted her wet lashes and took in her daughter's face.

"You're being cruel," she began again. "I've made my mistakes, and I'm paying for them dearly. But I have always loved you and there's no reason why we can't get on. I'm begging you, Malin, let me see my grandson. I'll go if you say so, but let me hold him just once."

To her surprise, her request was met with a smile. A flame of hope shot through Eva's heart, and she clung to it like a drowning man clutches a drifting log.

"You want to hold him?" asked Malin softly. "Very well. I'll show you where your grandson is."

Eva pulled herself up with difficulty. Her legs were shaking so badly she could hardly stand. When she raised her eyes, Malin's smile had vanished without a trace.

"Do you see that little casket next to Permony's? There's your grandson. Didn't you hear? He didn't make it after all . . . It happened so suddenly yesterday."

Though Malin had not shouted, had in fact lowered her voice significantly, Eva felt she was going deaf from the words. She faltered backward, dividing her glance between Malin and the little casket as if she had no idea what she was looking at. When the cry came, she felt it surge from the depths of her bowels and tear out of her mouth like a primal living thing.

"No! He can't be . . . Meridia told me he was well . . . No!"

Malin smiled more radiantly. "But you never believe what Meridia says, do you? Why should it be different now?"

Even before the questions flung their net about her, Eva knew she had been trapped. For a moment she could only shake her head and stare stupefied at her daughter. Malin's smile was an unbroken taunt, a steel wall constructed from a lifetime of resentments. Eva's head swam. Try as she might, she could not find the laugh or gesture that would dispel the violence of the taunt.

"No," she said. "That woman has never spoken a true word in her life."

With her last strength Eva rallied herself and tottered to the door. A crippling pain from the gravestone slab shot up her back when she tried to straighten her shoulders. Later, Eva would discover that her spine had permanently bent out of shape. From where she stood, Malin watched her mother leave with arms crossed. Not once did she betray her wonder when she saw Eva's feet drag across the floor with Patina's old limp.

THE MAN HAD SPENT three days and three nights outside the house. Noah had first spotted him from the living room window shortly after dinner, leaning against the street lamp with his head bare and his thin frame draped in a heavy overcoat. An hour later, while his aunt Malin was putting the baby to bed, Noah had glanced out the bedroom window and sighted the man again. This time he was standing on the stone steps, staring at him with a beseeching look. Noah went to bed at ten, but twice in the night he woke and stole to the window. The man was there both times, changing his posture and station but not the insistence of his gaze. After each peek, Noah would return to bed and tighten about him the words that fueled his private anger.

Go away. You have no business being here.

On the third night his aunt Malin, who was sharing his room with him, noticed his agitation and asked if there was anything the matter. Not wanting to tell her, he said he was having a bad dream. "But why do you keep looking outside?" she asked, going to the window to check for herself. After a pause, she said that she could not see anything. "You're a little warm," she said, coming up to the bed to feel his head. "Will you get some rest? The baby can't be the only one who sleeps in this house." He nodded, and she pulled the blanket over him before resuming her post by the bassinet. From his mother's room next door came the sound of pacing, which had increased in length and frequency over the past few nights. But he did not want to think about this either, especially with the man lurking outside the house, so he fastened his gaze on his aunt instead. Her rapturous look outshone the lamplight as she bent down and smiled at the baby.

The morning brought glorious sunshine but no respite from the man. He was now standing in the garden, his knees carelessly brushing the geraniums his mother had planted. Noah feared that any minute the man would ring the doorbell. He watched with apprehension when, at a quarter to eight, his aunt Malin excused herself to leave early for the wake. He watched her open the door and climb down the stone steps. He followed her from the window and saw the man wave his hand to catch her attention. Her stare was directly leveled at him, but she walked by without hearing or seeing him. Suddenly his mother darted out, and his heart dropped when he thought she was running toward the man. But she only came out to remind his aunt, from the safety of the porch, to confirm lunch with the caterers. The man, having shouted and gestured in vain, retreated again. It dawned on Noah then that he was the only one who could see him. He alone had the power to make the man visible, or condemn him unseen forever.

All morning long, he observed his mother as she went about her tasks. She seemed fitful and absentminded, paying the grocer's boy without counting the bills, rinsing plates that were already clean, and spilling milk as she poured it into the baby's bottle. He watched her as she sat in the front hall and fed the baby. He knew she had gone to see his father three days before, and she had come home looking immensely drained and dispirited. Now she looked even more tired, faded, as though all the light and bloom had been let out of her. The sound of her pacing echoed in his ear, and with it he noticed her nervous gestures and the pale depressions on her cheeks. He drew up and knelt by her chair. Without lifting his eyes, he asked, "Are you unhappy, Mama?"

She stopped rocking the baby, her fingers tight around the milk bottle. "Don't be silly," she said with a laugh. "How can I be unhappy when you're with me?"

He did not reply but bent his head lower still. He knew that her eyes, no matter what her lips said, would hold the real answer.

After the baby finished feeding, she laid him down to sleep in the bassinet, which she had earlier placed in the front hall. Faintly, she smiled at the little creature, stroked the thick black hair that was so much like Aunt Permony's, and then went to stand at the window. Noah crept over to the bassinet and pretended to play with his cousin. All the while his eyes were studying his mother.

She rested her head against the pane, pensive and aloof as her glance swept across the garden. At her sight, the man came bounding to the window and stopped directly in front of her. Noah held his breath. Only the pane stood between them now; the man pressed his palm against it, imploring her with sorrowful eyes, but her glance passed through him without seeing him. She did not seem to hear when he began rapping on the window, but moved to sit at the desk with her back to the room. The louder the man knocked, the less Noah could hear it. One by one, his mother produced her sketches from a drawer. From where he stood, her back was a pillar of stone. *She doesn't need him,* he told himself in silence. *She's capable of living without him.*

Without a noise he left the baby and approached her. Although the pounding had receded to a patter, Noah did his best to avoid the man's gaze. Going around the desk, he halted a few steps in front of his mother. He was about to speak when the words died on his lips. Her back had deceived him after all. Her face, suspended oddly over the sketches, was a sight he had not wanted or expected to see.

She was panting and frowning, biting her lip with furious devastation. Tears dampened her cheeks, turned her eyes into dark pools of blood. Her neck was bent as if it had been snapped. Noah shuddered in horror. There it was, bared before him, all the hunger that had sustained her pacing, so raw and excruciating it seemed a kind of dying. At once his sharp intuition told him that she had reached the lowest depth of her loneliness, and he had neither the strength nor the means to lift her. Unless he gave her up, cast off the chains that bound them, she would not find her way to the surface.

Noah raised his head and slowly retreated from the desk. Through all this his mother had not noticed him. The pounding on the window became louder. Taking this as a sign, he dashed to the front door and tore it open.

"Papa!" he called to the man, and at last gave him substance.

THE TOUCH ON THE nape came first. A slow, tender burn that spread to her face like a blush. For a second, she relished every drop of it, thought it the most wonderful feeling in the world, before all too quickly her mind leapt into action . . . She stood up in near violence and swung around to face him.

"Don't!" She passed a hand over her face and backed away until she had put half the room between them.

"Please listen," he said, with more calm than his anxious eyes betrayed. "Give me a chance to explain myself."

"Explain?" she challenged, retreating farther still until she reached the shadows. "What is there to explain? I know all the facts, and nothing, no excuses you say will change them. It's done and over with. The only thing left is for you to leave—and leave at once."

She was determined to give her words an irrevocable tone, but a slight break in her voice undermined her intention. He seized this and took a step forward.

"I didn't come to make excuses," he said. "I claim full responsibility for what I've done. I've had a lot of time thinking—"

"You admit it then—everything?" she threw out from among the shadows.

"Everything."

"If you deny nothing, then what more is there to say?"

"Please listen. I've had a lot of time to think since you left, and one thing is clear to me: I must have you back at all costs."

Her laugh came out swift and clean, splintering his argument to pieces.

"Have me back? At all costs? What makes you think you can afford it? I'm not for sale, you see. I never was."

"That's not what I meant."

"Then what *do* you mean?"

Daniel paused. There was no doubt he had aged since she last saw him, but despite his haggard and haunted appearance, he was still so much the green, dreamy-eyed youth who had stood by helplessly while Eva tossed her out of Orchard Road.

"I'm sorry for all the terrible things I've done," he began again. "I was angry and stupid and resentful. When you took your mother in over my objections, it was as if you'd turned me into a stranger in my own house. You grew distant and preoccupied, and you didn't seem to want me or need me anymore. The house was always cold, and everywhere I turned I could only find tension and distress. I know I didn't make it easy on you. You were concerned about your mother—rightfully so—and I should have given you my support. But I was thinking only of myself, of how angry and unhappy I was. Then when I started spending time away, you said nothing. I didn't think you even cared or noticed. And all that time Mama was telling me all the things I wanted to hear. She convinced me I was absolutely in the right, that you had overstepped your bounds and shown me disrespect. One day, when I was feeling especially down, she introduced me to—"

"Go ahead and say it!" she suddenly spat out. "I dare you to speak her name!"

The force of her outburst startled him, but quickly he collected himself.

"I'm ashamed of what I've done. I was like a man under a spell—everything was blurry, nothing was clear, and at times it seemed my thoughts weren't even my own. I didn't realize what I was doing until the damage was done. I was selfish and foolish, but now I'm out of it—free clear out of it because you helped me. Please forgive me. Don't you see that you must, so we can begin again?"

He risked a few more steps and forced her to withdraw into a corner. From the way she lowered her head and clasped her hands nervously behind her back, he saw that his closeness was affecting her. But just when he thought she was softening, her answer sprang from her lips and chilled his blood.

"You don't seem to understand me," she said. "The last thing I want is to start over. You can't wake up something that's dead and buried."

He stared at her, suspended halfway between shock and bewilderment. Then and there he would have given up but for the fact that her eyes had not met his since he entered the room.

"I love you, Meridia. I have never for one moment stopped loving you. Even when I was blind and sick, I could see you and feel you as if you had never left me. My feelings have not weakened. You are my heart, the blood in my veins, and you will always be the only woman—"

"Save it, Daniel! I'm no longer yours to make love to."

"But why should you give me up? Remember our time together, all the joy and happiness we had. We can have it all back, and much more. Think of our son. Do you want him to grow up without his father? If you can't forgive me for yourself, then do it for him. Look at me. I'm still the same man you married. Don't you recognize me? Can't you see that I made a terrible mistake, but now I'm back—back to stay for good?"

She lifted her eyes for the first time, and they blazed on him like drowning stars. Her face was not without tenderness, and when she spoke, he detected a hint of the old warmth in her voice.

"No, I can't see that. You asked me for forgiveness once, and against my father's wish, I gave it to you, because I believed it would be the last time you would ask it from me. But now here we are again, back in the same place. You can make all the promises you want, but there are some things you can't change. Certain ties and dispositions will remain permanent, no matter how honest and good your intentions are. In the end you are bound to follow them . . . I owe it to Noah and myself to stay clear of the same mistake."

He caught her drift instantly. "If it's Mama you're worried about, I swear she's out of my life . . ."

"Just like that? She's out of your life?"

"Yes." He narrowed his eyes and his face went rigid with anger. "I can assure you I've seen the last of her. She's no longer welcome in our house."

Still watching him, Meridia fell silent for a long time before replying, "You make it sound so easy. But it's not her I'm worried about."

"It's not? Then what is it?"

Again, she fell silent and made no move.

"What is it?" he repeated, his voice pared to a whisper. Slowly she turned to the window and unclasped her hands from behind her back.

Bright golden light flooded the room and lit up her stricken face. At the sight his breath caught in his throat, and without pausing to think, he covered the remaining steps between them. "Meridia," he whispered, and engulfed her in his arms. Pressing his cheek against hers, he felt the sting of her tears, and all at once the full enormity of his actions smote him like a blade. He had never seen her cry so openly, bared herself so defenselessly. Urgently he sought her mouth, and as his lips closed over hers, he felt her tremble in his arms.

"Forgive me," he said under his breath. "I will never again hurt you."

She did not resist him, but neither did she return his kiss. Her hands remained stiff at her sides. For a minute she let him have his fill, and then firmly pushed him away. He looked at her with a wounded expression.

"It's you," she said at length. "You've broken every part of me and I can't put the pieces back together. It pains me to see you, to be near you, and the hurt weighs more than my love for you. Now that I know what you're capable of, I can't force it out of my head, no matter how hard I try. When I look at you, I see your mother staring at me, lying, scheming, cutting me down with every chance she's got. Your words sound like her words, your promises like her lies. I used to believe you were the only person in the world who would never hide a thing from me, but now I can't tell anymore. There's too much of her in you . . . I won't risk my heart for the third time. You're always more your mother's son than you were my husband."

"But you can't believe that!" He fumbled for her hands, but she had again locked them behind her back. "I'll prove myself and make it up to you. Please give me a chance—one chance, and you'll see that I'm not the man you think I am!"

He reached into his pocket and brought out Gabriel's necklace. For a moment she stood without moving, mesmerized by the pure, warm glitter of the diamonds. Thinking she was giving him his chance, he stretched out the necklace toward her.

"I redeemed this for you once. Tell me what I must do to redeem it again."

She said nothing for a long time. And then she returned his stare and gently shook her head.

"It's over between us. There's nothing here you can claim."

His jaw dropped. His hand followed a moment later. A hundred arguments rose to his lips, but they withered like flowers before her gaze. If only she would let him hold her again!

"But you don't understand—"

The baby began to cry. All this time they had not been alone. As he watched her hasten to the bassinet, his heart recoiled from the nearness of loss.

She picked up the baby and calmed him. Daniel followed her across the room. He noticed that her tears had dried, her face once again closed unto itself.

"He's a strapping boy." He heard himself speak without recognizing his voice.

"Yes, he is." She nodded. "Permony would have been proud of him."

And then lightly, as if the question had never occurred to her before, she asked him, "Did you know what Ahab was before they married?"

"Of course not," he said at once. "Had I known, I would never have consented."

She nodded again in such a way that he could not tell if she believed him.

The front door opened. A woman's voice could be heard in the hallway. Meridia put the baby down in the bassinet.

"I've asked Rebecca to watch him," she said. "Malin is expecting me at the wake. Will you take Noah?"

"I will," he said. "But give me a moment to play with the little fellow."

Their eyes met for the last time. And then suddenly she reached out her hand and touched his cheek.

"It *was* a great love," she said. "Don't let anyone tell you differently. Take good care of yourself. You'll be happy with someone else."

She turned and moved toward the door. He held on to the bassinet, keeping as still and silent as he could. After the door closed, he became instantly aware of two things: the necklace was still in his hand and the baby's eyes were beaming at him. He tried to smile, but his chin dropped to his chest. He shook and shook while tears fell and blotted the world around him.

The shop on Lotus Blossom Lane closed the following autumn. Despite the fortune-teller's attempt to reverse misfortune, the business continued to lose money, and long before October shed its golden leaves, the bell above the door jingled for the last time. The news soon spread that Elias's widow had lost all her wealth. The baker across the street claimed that the grand remodeling had not paid off—during the shop's final weeks, he could count on two hands the number of customers who walked in through the door. His wife, a dressmaker, disagreed, saying that if anything was to blame, it was Eva's extravagance. "She used to be the thriftiest of women, but shortly before the shop closed, she put in an order for three dresses in one week. All while creditors were pounding at her door!" This theory gained support from Eva's hairdresser, who hinted that her customer had not been "right in the head" since Permony's death. "Malin went away and cut off all contact. Daniel hasn't spoken to her since Meridia divorced him. And we all know how Ahab disappeared so mysteriously . . ."

Eva herself seldom left the house anymore. The butchers and fruit-sellers missed her haggling, and in her absence, they recounted the brazen lengths she would go to in order to get her way. The florists and storekeepers missed her sharp tongue and the vivid way she had for embellishing a story. Some said she was ill, unable to leave her bed. Others said she was succumbing to old age. Whenever they inquired at the house, a surly maid answered the door in a snobby tone, "Madam is resting and doesn't wish to be disturbed."

Meanwhile, a steady stream of customers kept the shop on Magnolia Avenue afloat. A far cry from the days when it had dictated the taste of the town, it became the place where people went if they wanted something "safe" or "traditional," quiet, respectable pieces that would neither lift eyebrows nor excite admiration. Daniel waited on his customers with an almost mechanical courtesy. Many men and women still found him attractive, but he paid them no heed even when they flirted with him openly. Over the past months, he had grown wan and subdued, his hair thinning and his face aging before its time. His boy sometimes kept him company, but never for long. The town had not been mistaken in thinking that Noah was more his mother's son than his father's.

Meridia, for her part, was causing a sensation on two fronts. First, her new shop on 175 Willow Lane was an unqualified success. Yes, she did set up business in her old house (still haunted, still smelling of cooking at all times), and against everyone's caution had the audacity to market her own creations. Once the shop opened, however, the young could not get enough of her rosette rings and woven bangles, and the old valued the intelligence and ingenuity that went into each piece. She did not shy away from using colors, or from putting five different stones in one bracelet. Her designs were marked by bold geometry, by clean lines and dynamic curves that seemed to capture the bright flight of some winged creature. Her business partner, the renegade dealer Samuel, gave her free rein of the shop. He had been heard to say that she was unable to lose money even if she wanted to.

But what pumped the most grist into the town's rumor mill were the brow-raising activities occurring inside 24 Monarch Street. For some time now, even before the divorce became finalized, someone appeared to have been living with mother and son in that command-ing house of glass and steel. No one had directly laid eyes on the person in question, but there had been sightings of two grown-ups huddling in the window (so said a neighbor), three sets of footprints in the garden (this from the milkman), and extra groceries delivered to the door (direct from the grocer). Three evenings a week, a piano was heard tinkling, someone singing, laughter until dawn. Some said it was the kindly ghost from Willow Lane, lured by Meridia to fill the house with the smell of baking. Some said it was Ravenna, returned from her mysterious journey at the end of the world. Others were more practical. "It's simple, you see. Meridia is keeping a lover . . ."

IT WAS HER GOOD friends Leah and Rebecca who suggested she return to 175 Willow Lane to open the shop. "Why not? The ghost has practically been keeping it vacant for you," said Rebecca. Meridia was doubtful at first, pained by the memory of her hard years there, and decided to pay a visit. She signed the lease as soon as she felt Pa-tina's spirit brush her arm. In October, she began turning the entire house into one elegant shop, sparing only the room where Noah was born and where she and Daniel had made love in happier times. This room she kept as an office, furnished with a new skylight, easy chairs, a metal vault, and family pictures crowding the expansive surface of Gabriel's old desk. The shop was not as big or as bright as 70 Magnolia Avenue, yet it offered plenty of warmth and intimacy. As assistants, Meridia hired two girls from the neighborhood, honest and hardworking young women who were grateful for the opportunity. When the shop opened in November, she did not think it would fail, and it did not.

BY THE YEAR'S END Meridia had grown used to her new life. Rising early in the morning. Walking Noah to school. Off to the shop. Lunch with Samuel once a week. Back to the shop. Dinner at home, often with Leah and Rebecca. Sketches, bills, letters while Noah did homework. Bedtime with a book. On weekends the boy went to his father's and she wandered the town alone.

One night, she stood at her window with her pad and pencil, and the fireflies did not come. The next night, she waited again and still she did not see them. On the third night, it began to rain, warm, blood-tasting, splashing her face, pad, and nightgown. When it became clear to her that the fireflies had left for good, she shut the window but did not wipe her face. Just before sadness engulfed her, she saw it. A likeness on the rain-lashed pane, no longer creased or grimaced but smiling. The yellow eyes were spinning still, but bright now like the moon. Meridia laughed as she greeted her old friend, the ghost in the mirror from long ago. In the nights to come, it would appear to her when she felt lonely, the last unlocked and understood message from Ravenna.

THINGS WENT ON IN this fashion until one day in late January. She was on her way back to the shop from Samuel's office when a line of hooded nuns bearing whips and a half-clad man on a cross drew her toward Independence Plaza. The Festival of the Spirits had returned to town.

Twelve years had passed since she first saw those same tents and colorful banners. The booths laden with relics. The pamphlets. The palmists, prophets, exorcists. Once again a giant sheepdog was barking away evil spirits. The same woman in a white turban was selling insurance for the afterlife. A small dove blue tent squatted beyond the cluster of the flagellants. The Cave of Enchantment. Slyly mounted on the roof, Meridia now saw, was a device for transmitting music to gullible maidens.

Feeling nostalgic, she sauntered over to the table that held the Book of Spirits. It had grown as tall as a baby, the pages at the bottom yellowed and mottled with age. Daring the monk's glare, she caressed the spine and was approximating where in the stack her own name might reside when someone jostled her from behind. "I'm so sorry!" a voice exclaimed. What Meridia saw when she turned knocked all the breath out of her lungs.

She had dyed her red hair brown. Traded her outlandish garments for a simple dress. But the face, albeit older and wider, was the same. Grinning at her as if they were two girls cutting school to try on dresses at the bohemian quarters.

"Hannah!" gasped Meridia.

"I've come back," her old friend said, laughing. "For good. My husband died last summer. The doctors said it was his kidney, he said it was my cooking. Now I've grown too old and fat for traveling. Do you know a place where I can stay?"

Meridia sized her up as if she were an apparition. "You're really back?" she said, remembering the letter she had never opened. "In the flesh?"

"Pinch my cheek if you don't believe me."

"For good?"

"For good."

"How do I know you won't leave tomorrow? Or the next day?"

Hannah's grin turned into a smile, tender and wistful at the same time. In that instant all the unspoken things surfaced between them.

"Because I don't think my heart would take it if I leave you again."

Perhaps Meridia started first, perhaps Hannah. Before they knew it, they were laughing and throwing their arms around each other. They were blocking traffic, tempting the dour monk to shove them aside, but they did not care. Boldly they walked arm in arm out of the plaza, hugging, kissing, setting off toward Monarch Street. That same afternoon they moved Hannah's two suitcases from the hotel on Majestic Avenue into the house. This was when the rumor started. As far as the townspeople could see, Meridia was dragging those suitcases all by herself. They saw no other person with her.

⤶

ONE SATURDAY MORNING IN March, Meridia went to the post office to mail a letter. Noah had spent the night with Daniel, and at noon would meet her at the shop to have lunch nearby. At one, Hannah would wait for them at the bookshop café. Noah had said he needed a dictionary for school. That reminded her to stop by the tailor's and order new trousers for him. He was growing so fast and was almost as tall as she was.

Meridia handed the letter to the clerk and paid for the stamp. Though she had not seen Malin since they parted last summer, they wrote to each other almost weekly. Baby Joshua was doing splendidly, and if Malin was to be believed, he was becoming handsomer with each letter. The young mother did not shy away from grilling Meridia about vitamins, the teething process, the efficacy of coconut versus eucalyptus oil, and what methods had worked to get Noah to eat. Malin also spelled out in detail every aspect of the baby's development—his appetite, ailments, sleeping patterns, motions performed, bowel movements. Her incessant fretting aside, there was no denying the joy that filled her letters to the brim. *He is everything I can hope for . . . In all my life I have never been happier . . .* Malin had enclosed a picture of Joshua a few months back, and in it the child was smiling so much like Permony that Meridia thought time was playing a trick on her.

The worst they had feared did not happen. Ahab left town, vanished without a trace, and had not troubled them since. Maybe Malin did scare the living daylights out of him. Maybe he believed his child was dead. No matter the case, Malin decided it was best to stay away another year.

Having mailed her letter with time to spare, Meridia headed to the market square. It was a lovely morning, and the crowd and the noise, never too overwhelming on Saturdays, quickly immersed her in reminiscences. Here was where she had lost Ravenna and grown pale from the butcher's cleaver. There she had eaten her first deep-fried potato cake with Hannah. Daniel had kissed her here, there, and there. For some time, she listened to the voices in her memory, some clear, some muddled, until one, sinewy with confidence, stood out above the rest. Eva's. Before she could help it, Meridia was swept back into the time when she used to follow her on market days, basket swinging like a weapon and arms bared to the sun, bargaining her way with absolute mastery through these very same stalls. She remembered having been amazed by Eva's skill, by how clever the woman was at getting what she wanted. Oh, how young she had been then, how trusting and impressionable! So much had changed that she could no longer recognize her old self.

And then suddenly she saw her—looking the way she had looked a decade ago. Wrapped in a brown coat trimmed with sable, Eva was again arguing with the butcher, her face smooth, her movement brisk, her bosomy figure threateningly planted before him. Before Meridia could make sense of the picture, Eva had dismissed the butcher, hitched up her skirt, and walked away with the best piece of meat in her basket.

Dazed yet unable to resist the spell, Meridia followed. The handsome brown coat billowed smartly while Eva dispersed her greetings. Whether she was human or phantom Meridia could not say, and so refrained from calling her name. At the edge of the square, Eva stopped near one of the benches. Meridia hastened. As she drew near, the shopping basket swung and the brown coat fluttered and Eva turned sharply to the right.

Meridia followed her down a long cedar-lined avenue. The farther she walked, the fewer people she saw, and before long she was completely solitary in her pursuit. Some time passed before she noticed that spring had lapsed into autumn. The sky was gray now, the sunlight cold, and the trees that a moment ago had been lush with leaves stood as bare as lampposts. There was no sound but the rustle of wind, and the houses on both sides of the street looked as if they had never been lived in. Quickening her pace, Meridia clung to the thought that she was merely seeing an illusion. When she reached the end of the long avenue, a thick swirling mist fell from the sky, not the blue or yellow or ivory that had haunted most of her life, but a cold green one. In an instant it blotted out trees and houses, everything but the brown coat billowing in front of her.

She kept up her chase. At times Eva sped up; at others, she slowed down till Meridia lagged no more than a few steps behind. Confined inside the mist, seeing nothing but the brown coat, Meridia did not know where she was, in which direction she was heading, or if she was going in an endless circle. Not once did Eva look back. Now and again, little laughs dropped from her lips, arctic inhuman sounds that added to the confusion in Meridia's brain.

At last the brown coat came to a halt. The mist cleared, and a yellow sea of flowers spread before them. Marigolds. Climbing waist-high and tossing feverishly as though each were dancing. Their scent set Meridia's lungs on fire, so sharp and sweet it nearly brought tears to her eyes. She looked up and found herself standing in front of 27 Orchard Road.

Smothering every inch of lawn, the marigolds made way for the mistress of the house. As Eva approached, the dancing flowers pulled her along like a sliding carpet, and when she reached the terrace where Elias's chair still rocked to and fro, the front door magically opened to admit her. Eva went in without a look back, her arctic laugh piercing the still gray air. The path she cut remained among the flowers, daring Meridia to take it.

Meridia took it. As she walked, she remembered how the marigolds had usurped the land from the roses, gobbling them one by one until there was not a single stem left. She remembered the spot in the center of the lawn where Patina had writhed in pain, the same spot where her daughter's tomb stood before Eva ordered it removed. And there on her wedding night, just beneath the window on the left corner of the house, she had skulked behind the roses and whispered good-bye to Ravenna . . .

When she entered the hallway, an unkempt and insolent maid came out from the kitchen and stopped her. The girl's attitude quickly changed, however, when she learned who her visitor was.

"I'm—I'm so sorry, madam. I didn't recognize you."

"Where is your mistress?" Meridia's tone was far from scolding, yet it seemed to unsettle the maid even more.

"Madam's unwell. She—she told me not to let anyone in."

"Never mind that. I saw her come in just now. Did she go up-stairs to her room?"

The maid gave an uncomprehending look. "Came in? Just—just now? But Madam hasn't left her room since she got sick!"

"What do you mean? I just saw her—"

Meridia bit back her words. Eyes aflame with foreboding, she slipped past the maid and started up the stairs. The girl, looking ter-ribly frightened, made no move to detain her. Meridia had not climbed two steps when a vile odor assaulted her nostrils. She lurched against the banister, gripping it with one hand while the other clutched her nose. Vomit, blood, sweat, excrement. A bell went off in her ear, triggering a thousand gruesome thoughts. Rapidly, she braced herself for the worst.

The stairs stretched without end, an eerie and unwelcome im-personation of Monarch Street. Meridia was halfway up when the house plunged into decay. The varnish on the banister peeled, the wooden steps splintered, the carpet tore, and chunks of plaster dropped from the ceiling like snowflakes. The large window on the landing cracked, broken through by ravenous thorns, and from every pore of the walls oozed slimy brown mold that spread quickly over the floors. There was dirt and grime everywhere, a wintry dark-ness fast descending upon the house. Hand on her nose, Meridia picked her steps carefully, convinced her next would send the stairs tumbling to the ground.

After an interminable time, she reached the landing and swayed down the corridor. Her stomach heaved, and it took all her strength to beat back nausea. A vision of her younger self swam before her. It was her first morning as a bride in this house, and she was walking down this same hallway to obey Eva's summons. That day Eva had taken away her wedding gifts and told her clearly the position she was to occupy in the house. And now, more than a decade later, she had been summoned once again.

What did Eva want?

Meridia entered the bedroom to the sound of moaning. Added to the sweat and excrement was the smell of rotting flesh, of a body unwashed and festering sores. The room was smaller and shabbier than she remembered. The walls were covered in torn wallpaper, the furniture battered, and the rug gaping with holes. Only the grime and mold had yet to enter. Meridia waited until her nausea passed and then stepped toward the bed.

Eva's spine had collapsed onto itself. Under the thin blanket, she curled sideways like a helpless infant. Spit and moan gurgled from her lips, while tears streamed nonstop down her skeletal face. Her two hands, withered like grass, peeked out from the top of the blanket, painfully closing and opening against her chest. She stared with a pleading intensity at the wall and did not realize that she was no longer alone in the room.

Meridia came up from behind and lifted the blanket. Instantly a viler odor struck her—she let the blanket drop again. Eva was lying in her own filth. There was no telling when she had last been bathed or changed.

Retreating in shock, Meridia tried to recall what she had heard of Eva in the past year. Little crossed her mind, for the woman had become a forbidden subject between her and Daniel, and Malin had not been in contact with her mother since she left. Leah once told her in passing that Daniel had been sending Eva a monthly allowance after her shop closed, but refused to see her in person. Clearly he had no idea how ill his mother was. Had he known, Meridia was hard-pressed to imagine him so callous. The maid must be keeping things quiet—holding Eva prisoner while pinching the money.

Meridia was about to call the girl for a reckoning when something stronger than anger checked her: the memory of all the treacherous things Eva had committed over the years. She owed the woman *nothing*. She could walk out of this room and leave that deformed figure to its fate. Surely, after everything Eva had done to her, after everything Eva had done to Noah and Patina and Permony and Elias, she had the right to walk away from this house without telling anyone what she had seen. Her action would be justified, her conscience clear and blameless. No one who had a passing acquaintance with their history would think of holding her responsible.

And yet she could not do it. The sound of Eva's moan clawed into her heart and voided her desire to leave. Shivering on that bed, filthy and broken, was not a tormentor punished for her crime, but a human being in pain. There was nothing to do but help. Meridia walked around the bed and revealed herself.

For a moment Eva received her in stunned silence. And then like an animal bracing for attack, she curled her body tighter and let out an earsplitting cry. Spit flew from her lips, her head jerked from side to side, and her tiny eyes glinted with the sharpness of obsidian. Meridia at first could not understand her, for Eva's tongue, which up till then had served as her most formidable weapon, had knotted up like tangled vine. And then suddenly, clear as a whiplash, the words hit her with all their venom.

"Leave me alone, you devil! Get away from me! Get out! Get out!"

Meridia tried to calm her without success. The horror in Eva's eyes had hardened into hatred. She screamed and screamed with all the strength she had left, her harsh, inarticulate cries bellowing like curses. The stench of vomit, blood, sweat, and excrement thickened like a shield around her. Meridia stepped back. The maid, hearing the commotion, dashed terrified into the room.

"Clean her," ordered Meridia sharply. "Go downstairs when you're done. I have a few words to say to you."

She walked to the door and noticed that with the maid's entrance, the mold and grime had burst into the room, eating away walls and floor and ceiling. Feeling suddenly ill, Meridia ran along the corridor and climbed down the stairs as fast as she could. Eva's screams snapped at her like bloodhounds. The house rolled and wobbled. The moldy steps were so slippery that she had to negotiate her way with caution. The throb of desolation was everywhere. There was no telling when the roof would descend to crush her.

Faint and nauseous, Meridia made it to the terrace. Her lungs were grateful for the gust of air, her heart somewhat lifted at the sight of sky. But even then the scent of the marigolds was no match for the stench of blood and excrement. Eva's curses were still ringing in her ear. For the first time she noticed that her palms were covered in sweat.

She waited for twenty minutes before the maid joined her. By then Meridia knew just what to say.

"I can see you have been neglecting your duties. Stealing from your mistress. Letting her stew here in her own filth. Those days are over. From now on, you will have me to answer to."

The maid, a girl hardly older than twenty, looked at her feet and trembled. Meridia did not relent.

"Abuse and malicious neglect. Premeditated intent to steal and harm. Give me one reason why I shouldn't send you straight to jail! Have you any idea what they would do in there to a young girl like you? Slap balls of iron on your feet. Knock out your teeth. Rape you. And if the living didn't get you, the dead certainly would. Do you know how many people have perished in anger behind those bars?"

And so for the next ten minutes, Meridia drove the fear of the spirits into the sobbing girl.

"Forgive me, madam! I will never do it again! I'll return the money—all of it. I'll do whatever you say, but please don't send me to jail!"

Meridia did not trust her one bit. She resolved to talk to Daniel at once.

"Go up and see to her every need," she said angrily. "Don't think for one second that I'm not watching you."

Limp with fear, the girl went back into the house and scrambled up the stairs. Meridia closed the door and stepped onto the lawn. As she made her way among the marigolds, an unpleasant recollection took hold of her. Scolding the maid, she had felt Eva speaking through her. Her words had seemed to fly straight out of Eva's mouth, her pitiless glare a lesson plucked from Eva's eyes. "There is too much of your mother in you," she had said to Daniel. Now as the marigolds danced and the green mist lifted into the air, she wondered how much of Eva was in her, had been in her all along.

WHEN SHE REACHED THE end of Orchard Road, spring suddenly returned with pink and golden splashes in the sky. The wintry gloom receded, and the trees were once again alive with leaves and blossoming fruit. Walking along the cedar-lined avenue, she took pleasure at the sight of children playing, dogs running, men laughing, women talking. The sounds they made drowned out the last of Eva's curses. From Cinema Garden the wind carried the fragrance of jasmine and gardenia, so strongly aromatic it dispelled the stench of decay from her nose. Crossing the street, Meridia felt life pumping full swing in her blood; she felt alive and alert and vitally sensitive to the marvel of possibilities. She had come this far, she would go further still. She was still young, not yet thirty, there was much yet for her to accomplish. From the thought followed a resolution. Never again would she despair or be lonely. She was Gabriel's child, Ravenna's daughter, and in her hand lay the power to shape life as she wished it.

Meridia swung into Willow Lane and found Noah and Daniel waiting outside the shop. Both in dark blue suits, yellow ties, patent-leather shoes. They turned to her at the same time, one pleased and the other withdrawn, their heads tilted in the same way.

"I'm starving, Mama," said Noah. "Can we eat now?"

"Of course, angel," said Meridia, tucking his shirt collar inside his suit. "But go in first and greet the girls. They'll be angry if you don't."

The boy's clairvoyant look rested on her, and without raising a brow or a question, he seemed to gauge her intention. He smiled mysteriously, almost with detachment, but it was enough to tell her that he approved. She watched him walk into the shop in a manner that made her proud.

Then she turned to Daniel. He had grown thin and stooped, and a lonesome, estranged look had settled on him like a case of grief. His eyes had lost their shine. Yet his face, rugged and unshaven, tugged at her with unexpected tenderness.

"Your mother is ill," she said. "I don't think she can last much longer."

His shock was sincere. Without taking her eyes off him, she acquainted him with everything she had seen, her encounter with the maid, and suggested he replace her as soon as possible.

"This is the first I've heard of her illness," he said. "I'll go over there this minute and take care of the maid. You see, I haven't spoken to Mama since we—we . . ." He floundered and dropped his eyes, suddenly lost in a world he no longer knew or cherished.

She believed him, and it was the steady pull of her gaze that made him lift his head again. For a moment he lingered, uncertain what he should do. And then in a broken voice he asked her, "Is it true you've found someone?"

She did not drop her eyes. Nor did her expression change. In her mind, she was again hearing the sounds of Independence Plaza from those faraway days—the blind violinist and his symphony, the masked monkey jigging to clapping hands, the seer whispering inside the Cave of Enchantment. And then before the bitter memories rose and smote her, she gathered everything that had been saved and told him, "Hannah's a dear friend. I should be so lonely without her."

His face fell. But before her answer could sink any deeper, she suddenly leaned and grasped his hand, the first such gesture since their divorce. Her smile was kind and tender, and as he watched her half in wonder and half in disbelief, she laid down the words that would bring them back to each other.

"Your mother is dying. She's in pain and she has no one but you. Bury her, and come back to me."

ACKNOWLEDGMENTS

I am indebted to my agent, Alex Glass, for his passion and tenacity, and for always providing me with the right answers.

My editor, Kerri Kolen, not only understood the book on all levels but managed to make the editing process a genuine pleasure. I am incredibly fortunate to have her on my side.

Cat Cobain, from across the Atlantic, might have called her notes "pesky," but I call them invaluable. Her enthusiasm is simply infectious.

Special thanks to Lara Lea Allen, the first reader of the manuscript, for loving it enough to pass it along.

To every wise soul who has ever put a book in my hand and encouraged me to read, I thank you always and forevermore.